By Mario Kai Lipinski

Symbols

Published by Dreamspinner Press
www.dreamspinnerpress.com

Symbols

MARIO KAI LIPINSKI

Published by
DREAMSPINNER PRESS

5032 Capital Circle SW, Suite 2, PMB# 279, Tallahassee, FL 32305-7886 USA
www.dreamspinnerpress.com

ISBN: 978-1-63533-692-4
Digital ISBN: 978-1-63533-693-1
Library of Congress Control Number: 2016921402
Published May 2017
v. 1.0

Printed in the United States of America
∞
This paper meets the requirements of
ANSI/NISO Z39.48-1992 (Permanence of Paper).

To all the gentle giants who make this world a better place.

ACKNOWLEDGMENTS

I WOULD like to thank:

Chris McHart and Meg Bawden for their unwavering support.

Harper Jewel for cleaning up a manuscript by a nonnative speaker.

Alexandra Johns, Deb Rhodes, and Jenna Johanis for their invaluable feedback.

My family for just being my family.

CHAPTER ONE

"HE'S A drug lord. The youngest one ever!"

Matt Dermond eavesdropped on Elaine delivering an address to her fan club of Central High junior girls attending her Monday morning audience, the first one after the summer break. She was spreading up-to-date rumors about the new senior student. From what Matt had picked up so far, he had to worry about this one, and knowledge was his only weapon. Over the past few years, he had learned how to listen without being noticed. Keeping the correct distance, the right point to look at, not drawing attention at all. If he was accomplished in one ability, it was the art of inconspicuousness. A skill absolutely required for filling the role of the school's punching bag.

"You've seen that scar on his cheek?" Elaine asked, and her court shook their heads with mouths gaping open. She bowed forward and lowered her voice. "He got it from a knife fight with another drug boss. The other one didn't get away with a scar only."

The girls gasped, and two of them grasped each other's hands. Matt clutched his own lower arms and held them so tight it hurt.

"Every tattoo on his body is for one of his victims, and he's inked all over."

Matt's heart tried to squeeze itself through his ribs. He hadn't seen the new student yet. But even if there were only some truth to these rumors, he would end up as one of those tattoos. He attracted bullies. Like an anglerfish, he had some sort of lightbulb dangling from his forehead, leading every thug his way.

"In his former school, he broke both arms of the quarterback because that poor guy looked at him a moment too long."

The sound of cracking bones wormed into Matt's mind. That crunching noise a neck made when it snapped. Granted, he only knew that sound from movies, but it could well be he would learn about it firsthand when it was the last thing he ever heard.

"O-M-G, there he is…. Shane McAllistair." Elaine grabbed an invisible necklace. "Don't stare!" she added in a whisper.

The girls' heads sank down, and they studied the gray floor tiles. The bolder ones risked a peek or two.

Amateurs!

Matt had perfected the art of watching without looking like it. It was impossible to miss Shane in the crowded hall, for he towered well over most of the other students at six feet seven, perhaps six feet eight. A people-free bubble extended around him. Elaine had done a perfect job in spreading her gossip, and the other students kept their distance in fear for their limbs and more. Matt hadn't seen such a muscular man for real. The white tee Shane wore bulged out at all possible and impossible places, and one of his arms was thicker than both of Matt's legs together. That beast of a man could rip him apart without breaking a sweat. Matt swallowed hard.

Some of the tattoos peeped out from under the shirt, colorful tattoos he couldn't discern from that distance. Was that a fishing pole on his upper left arm? A shiver slithered down Matt's back as his mind came up with some things Shane might do to him with a fishing pole. He raised his head, risking another peek. The scar ran down on the right side of Shane's angular face from his cheekbone to the middle of his jaw. It was just a thin line, but it shone in a bright crimson shade. The brilliance of the scar contrasted with the dark intensity of Shane's eyes. They were deep brown, almost black. His gaze was alert, observing.

Matt took pride in his skills at reading emotions from eyes, honed by years of practice, but he failed at spotting the cruelness in that blackness. Instead a gleam radiated from those eyes, friendly and not sinister at all. So Shane was the worst type of all. Only the most psychopathic people pulled off amiable and cruel at the same time. Matt bit down a sigh. The spikes of Shane's hair pointed upward like reckless spears, and their color matched the dark shade of his eyes. That guy was capable of tearing a heart out and laughing as it still beat in his hand.

Shane stopped before one of the lockers. Such a giant should rip out the door and hurl it across the hall, but he opened it like anyone else. How disappointing! A demonstration of power would have provided more lifesaving knowledge, though Matt could count on finding out about Shane's strength the hard way soon enough. He shook his head, flinging those unsettling thoughts out of it. Nevertheless, even turning the knob of the locker created an ever-changing pattern of flexing and unflexing in Shane's muscles. The sight mesmerized Matt. Those movements inhered a certain grace, a subtle choreography, hinting at the power lying dormant in that mighty body.

The smashing of a locker door thundered, and Matt's mind crash-landed on the reality of the school hall. The two pieces of coal being Shane's gaze rested on him. Shane raised the corners of his mouth for a fraction of an inch only. Droplets of sweat flowed down Matt's back while his skin felt covered with frost. He knew better than to look at anyone in this school for any longer than a blink, and he was staring at the most dangerous guy of all when he forgot about this rule. His legs felt like pudding, but he had to get away. Fast. Before Shane had time to memorize his face.

SHANE DIDN'T intend to smile, but that boy next to the bunch of girls clustering around a cheerleader and pretending not to stare reminded him of Jer. This was crazy because they didn't look remotely alike. The color of that one's hair was a dark blond, sticking out in all directions, and his eyes had the faintest hue of blue, like the sea around a tropical isle. That boy was even tinier than Jer if that were at all possible, and still they shared that gaze. The gaze of someone who knew he was the prey, someone haunted by fear. Shane hadn't thought about Jer like that for what? Three months? First day in the new school and he got all soppy.

Don't get involved! Not this time.

His plan was simple and easy, and Shane would stick to it. He had picked up some of the rumors going around about him and swallowed down a chuckle. It'd be easy to keep a distance in this school. He'd spend only one term here, and college would mean a fresh start. Some hauntings could be left behind.

The small guy had taken to his heels because Shane had scared him off. Good. One more person who told everyone how frightening he was, though his churning stomach begged to differ with that reasoning. It'd take some time getting used to being the badass here. Like a new pair of shoes, he had to break in this unfamiliar role. Who was he kidding? He'd never stand to intimidate anyone, especially if that someone was such a cutie.

Don't get involved!

The plan also included not hitting on anyone, though it didn't make much sense denying that the guy was attractive. Shane had always been a sucker for the small type, and soft features like that boy's crawled under his skin and replaced the churning in his guts with the been-there-done-that butterfly tingling. He stifled a sigh. That wouldn't pose much of a problem anyway, if he judged that guy right. The small one would do everything to stay out of his range. Though it served his purposes, Shane didn't have to like it. Yet a small disappointment now was still better than a huge disappointment later. The Jer lesson had stuck at last.

Shane's cell vibrated in his pocket, his reminder for the appointment with Principal Wagner. If he arrived on time, that might give her impression of him a nudge in the right direction. It'd take more than petty gestures to smooth out the picture his records drew, but he would make do with small steps first, like finding out where Administration was. He couldn't ask his fellow students, not if they kept a minimum safety distance of three yards and avoided eye contact at all costs. Grabbing someone by the collar and scowling the answer out of him might work. Moreover, it'd fire up the rumors, but even that amounted to more violence than Shane intended to use ever again. Causing an all-out panic on his first day would definitely send the wrong message to the principal, yet he liked the overall idea. It just needed a little adjustment.

Shane walked over to the group of girls, who were still busy pretending to be busy. How cheap a cardboard copy of a bad cheerleader cliché could one be? The ringmaster of this menagerie wore her costume in the school colors of maroon and white, complete with a skirt so short it bordered on a Japanese-Manga-schoolgirl spoof. Adding a final touch to the comical impression, blonde pigtails dangled from the sides of her head. Since she was staring at the ground, Shane glimpsed only part of her all-American porcelain face. That was the type—clinging to a half-witted quarterback while giggling like she'd lost it. With a little luck, she acted as the local gossipmonger too.

His audience was assembled, and the show could begin. He tilted his head, squinted his eyes, and just stood there for some seconds. He fixated on the cheerleader, whose gaze was still glued to the floor. "Administration?" Perfect. Shane hit the sweet spot between a rasp and a snarl in his voice.

All color drained from the cheerleader's face until she turned almost as pale as the white of her school uniform. The other girls swallowed, twitched, or moved a step away from Shane, some of them doing all three at once. Slowly, the cheerleader looked up. Shane flexed the muscles in his chest slightly. Her eyes widened, and she let her head sink down again.

"Around that corner. On the left," she said, her voice breaking several times on those few words. Her arm trembled as she pointed in that direction.

Shane almost thanked her, ruining his performance. He grunted instead, turned away, and trotted off.

A moment of perfect silence ensued. The girls even stopped breathing. A collective sigh of relief was the only warning sign for the outburst of squealing and chattering that followed. Mount Chatterbox had erupted.

Mission accomplished.

This would be more than enough fuel for the rumors. Shane bit his tongue to not laugh out loud. That little demonstration already yielded results, for the other students added an extra yard to their safety distance.

SHANE KNOCKED at the door before entering the office, and the smell of coffee and old paper welcomed him. A single desk surrounded by a small fort of file drawers and chairs cluttered up the room. Behind the desk, a woman in her forties hammered away at the keyboard of a computer, a golden sign on the desk identifying her as Mrs. Temple. She knitted her brows in concentration, and the hue of the monitor reflected in her glasses, attached to a cord of an eye-numbing shade of pink.

"Yes?" She didn't even look up from the screen.

"I've got an appointment with Principal Wagner. My name's Shane McAllistair." He used the very opposite of the voice he had given the girls: low volume, sweet, and mellow.

She took her eyes off the screen at last and looked at Shane's midsection, where she would've found the face of most other students. Her gaze wandered up. A little bit of very recent history repeated as her eyes widened and she rolled back her office chair. It was funny with the girls, but it put a damper on his mood when it happened with adults. He was fed up with security people in banks hooking their thumbs into their belts, pointedly close to their weapons, when he entered. He was fed up with salesclerks scurrying away and seeking shelter in the aisles farthest away from him. He was fed up with parents hiding their kids behind them as he passed them on the sidewalk.

Mrs. Temple put on her look of professional disdain again. That look office people gave when being interrupted while performing a task a thousand times more important than the foolish question asked. "McAllistair?"

Her snarl made Shane's toenails roll up. "Yes, ma'am." He smiled so hard that his cheeks hurt.

She mistreated the keyboard, her gaze still boring into him. After a short glimpse at the screen, she snorted and pointed at a chair. "Sit down!"

Overcompensation always followed those first reactions. People acted either overly friendly or overly aggressive once they recovered from their initial shock. Perhaps Mrs. Temple just gave him her standard reception for students.

"Thanks, ma'am."

If Mrs. Temple's demeanor were any indication for the sentiment the administration had for the student body, the talk with Principal Wagner would be a rough ride. Shane sat down. The tingling in his stomach returned, though the butterflies had been exchanged for angry mosquitoes. The new principal terrified Shane at least as much as he had terrified the small one, and he had to appreciate the irony in this reversal. Unfortunately, running away and hiding weren't options for him.

Shane flinched as the door to the principal's office flew open and a woman stormed out.

"Sorry for keeping you waiting. The superintendent and I don't share the same view on next term's budget. Shane McAllistair?"

Principal Wagner was tall for a woman, standing only half a head shorter than he did. Wisps of blonde hair framed her slender face, a curly mane she had tried to tame into a plait, but strands of it stuck out everywhere. Her green eyes shone with a strange mix of friendliness and agitation. Hopefully the superintendent was the target of the latter. She extended her hand.

"Yes, ma'am." Shane got up and shook her hand, careful not to squeeze it too hard.

"It doesn't happen often that a student is taller than me." She chuckled.

It also didn't happen often that he didn't scare the shit out of someone. Or she carried it off very well. In either case, Principal Wagner behaved more maturely than most people he met, and Shane just had to like her.

"Come in and sit down, please." Principal Wagner made an inviting gesture with her arms while her chuckle toned down to a smile.

The interior of her office was spartan, though that description already came close to an exaggeration. Besides her desk—on which everything aligned perfectly—and a file cabinet, there was a small table with hockey trophies, which was the only nonpractical thing. One of the plaques read "National College Masters, 1994." She still was in very good shape, not athletic but wiry.

They both sat down, and she placed a hand on a file on her desk. "I make appointments with every new student, but I have to admit that I was especially interested in meeting the guy described in this record." She paused for a moment. "And I have to admit that I imagined you—differently."

Her smile didn't waver. That was a good sign, wasn't it?

"I know I look…." Shane thought of words that described his outer appearance. Sadly, he only came up with a single one that did him justice. "Dangerous." Was it clever to call himself that in front of his new school's principal? With the sportswoman before him, however, honesty felt like the right approach. "But I'm not." That sounded weak even to his ears. Coming from a scarred and inked muscleman, it verged on ridiculous.

"You seem to prefer honesty, so I hope you won't mind what I say now. If I had the impression you were dangerous, you wouldn't be attending this school." Her other hand joined the one on the file. "I had my fair share of jumping to conclusions just for growing a little more than usual. Please accept my apologies if my remark about your looks came across as judgment."

No one had ever apologized to Shane, not even the people who had later become his friends. They had simply swept that topic under the rug. He may not have been happy with those reactions, but at least he knew how to deal with them. What should he say now? "Thank you." Not witty, perhaps inappropriate, but gratitude couldn't be wrong either.

The corners of Principal Wagner's mouth rose a little more. "You're welcome."

Definitely not wrong.

"Back to that guy from the record." She let her eyebrow shoot up for a moment. "He volunteered for virtually every school activity, from collecting cans to selling cupcakes at the school festival. There isn't a single entry about being late. No detention. He presided over the LGBT alliance club and was repeatedly commended for that job. Heck, compared to this, my school record reads like a felon's." Her fingers clenched into the cover sheet of the file. "And then, without a warning, this model student breaks both arms of a guy who happens to be the school's best hope for winning the football championship."

The record left out that Hayden had also been the best hope for winning the title of "Formidable Asshole in a High School." Breaking Hayden's bones had been an accident, but feeling regret about it? Nope. This lack of remorse still made Shane's blood go cold and frightened him more than actually hurting that pisser. The best reason for not getting involved with anyone in this school.

"You're expecting an explanation, I assume." Shane lowered his gaze to his hands. "But I can't." The accord between Hayden, Jer, and him surprisingly worked. He wouldn't be the one jeopardizing that dearly bought truce. Shane raised his head again.

Principal Wagner stopped smiling and pressed her lips into a thin line. "I hoped for some details, though I didn't expect you to tell me. You didn't even tell the court." She flipped open the record and scanned one of its pages. "Your silence got you a hundred hours of community service." Her smile returned, accompanied by a sigh. "That's a pretty hard sentence for a first-time offender."

Hard maybe, but Shane had deserved punishment. For letting himself go. For forgetting about his strength. For knowing he'd act the same way again in the same situation. He nodded. "Yes, ma'am."

Wrinkles formed on Principal Wagner's forehead as she furrowed her brows. "The court didn't suspend you from school, did it? The… incident… was over a year ago."

"I needed some time off to digest the—" Shane paused for a moment. "—incident." Digest? A strange term for getting over Jer and for convincing himself that he wasn't a thug after all. "That year I worked full-time at the retirement home where I had done my community service."

"You're still a part-time employee there, aren't you?" She flipped through some more pages of the record. "Here is a letter of recommendation from the home. You're working for minimum wage and doing unpaid overtime, a lot actually. There's a quote from one Mrs. Vespucci calling you the best grandchild she never had."

Meeting Estelle had alone been worth the hundred-hour sentence. A grin found its way onto Shane's face, then toned down to a smile. He shrugged. "She's an adorable lady."

Principal Wagner mimicked Shane's half-demented facial expression. "And you're a good guy. You may have strayed from the path a little, but you're a good guy. It's my task to get you back on track and to keep you there. Of course, that can only work if you help me with it."

She didn't ask him a question, but her pause demanded a reply. "I only want to finish high school, get a diploma, and go to college. That's what's most important to me." He needed to forget about Jer at last, survive the hassle that was high school, and prove to himself he could function around people of his age. All these things were at least as important, perhaps even more pressing, but the inner would follow the outer. One of Estelle's lessons. He could try to heed this piece of advice.

Still smiling, Principal Wagner nodded once. "Don't mutilate any of our football players and we'll get along fine." She bent over the desk and placed her hand beside her mouth to whisper, "Ripping out their arms wouldn't do much harm to their game anyway, but this info is confidential."

Principal Wagner and he would get along just fine. With the help of his dad's handpicked list of schools and his mom's annotations, Shane had chosen the best place to help him with getting a grip on his life and reaching his goals. He extended his hand. "Their limbs and your words are safe."

Principal Wagner shook his hand, and his knuckles cracked in her powerful grasp. This tough woman deserved nothing but his admiration. Neither giggling cheerleaders nor scowling secretaries could bring him down. If Shane also succeeded in keeping cute little guys out of his life, there was a real chance that everything would work out at last.

CHAPTER TWO

MATT, SITTING on the floor in one of the far end corners of the school's library, looked up from his book and at his watch. If he waited another quarter of an hour, the lacrosse team would've left the locker room for training. He could safely walk in there and get his sports clothes for the laundry as he had promised his mom. After all, it paid to memorize the schedule of all the teams. Everything paid off that reduced the risk of running into Iain.

A shiver stirred Matt, as it always did when he thought or spoke that name. It started somewhere in his guts and blazed its trail through his body before it ended in his mind. A reaction he could depend on. He could also depend on getting another bruise or leaving a Matt-shaped dent in one of the locker doors when not staying clear of Iain. His hand found the place on his waist where the blackness of the last encounter with him was still fading.

Bruises heal, and high school ends. That is, if he lived to experience the latter. Avoiding Iain and his dim-witted baseball team minions was routine. Matt had learned to melt into the dark corners of the school, and no one knew its layout as well as he did, maybe even including the architect.

With Shane, a new variable had entered this equation, and he tilted it out of equilibrium. Fear had made Matt a kind of conservative, for change could always mean change for the worse. The status quo may not have been perfect, heck, it was the polar opposite of perfect, but Matt had control over it. At least the illusion of control. Shane was wild, and there was nothing in this world that could control him. A cold feeling crept through Matt's body, so that even the library floor felt searing hot.

How long had he gaped at Shane? Half a minute? Even less? Yet Shane lingered in his thoughts, leaning against the wall of his mind with arms crossed over his mighty chest, and glared at him. How much had that short encounter kept him off-balance.

Another shiver ran down Matt's back, accompanied by that strange feeling of being watched. He looked around. No one was here, of course. This was his space, right behind the shelves with the yearbooks of twenty years or more, which even the library guys avoided. In this corner, Matt could exist in perfect invisibility.

"Here you are."

Matt jumped up from the floor while some of his inner organs preferred to stay on the linoleum. The book crashed down before him, making a dull thud much too loud for such a small thing. His vision narrowed down to a tunnel as he entered full flight mode, and his heart set a breakneck rhythm that divided time into neat intervals, each long enough for a single decision.

"Perhaps you should skip some of the coffees." Florenca's voice, a deep alto that put even some guys to shame, always rang with sarcasm. Now it consisted of nothing else. "Even our neurotic beast of a cat is more relaxed than you are."

Matt's heartbeat slowed down, and the discrete tidbits of time reconnected to a continuum. His body knew the procedure of switching between all DEFCON levels at a blink. "I bet your cat is worse at sneaking up on people than you are." So much for perfect invisibility.

Florenca shrugged, and her already short neck disappeared. "Only one of my many Latina superpowers." She bent down and picked up the book, looking at the cover. Her eyebrows met. "Romantic poetry of the eighteenth century?"

Matt snatched the small tome out of her hand. Close to her olive skin, his looked even paler, like a specter's. He smoothed out a page that had suffered some wrinkles from the fall. "Thanks. It's for English homework." It wasn't, but telling her that he read it for fun would start another tirade of taunts and teasing. The other kids already gave him enough of that.

"Speaking of homework, I just didn't get that function stuff in calc."

Florenca was one of the few students who dared to talk to him in public. Being seen with him was detrimental to one's health, something she didn't give a shit about. To be frank, she only approached him when she needed some more "Matt-magic"—his special way of explaining things. But because she had problems with every subject, their meetings had turned into a daily thing. Another constant in Matt's life.

"Okay. Let's find a table, and I'll see what I can do for you."

MATT PUT down his pen. "And that's all you have to know about derivatives."

Florenca scribbled down something on her legal pad. "That wasn't that difficult."

It never was, for she was a clever girl. If she took it upon herself to reread her notes, she wouldn't have any problems at all, though Matt wouldn't tell her that. First, her laziness gave him at least a minimum of a social life, and second, her Latina superpowers included a temperament that made a hydrogen bomb look like fireworks. Last semester she had poured Jell-O over Elaine's shirt because the cheerleader had called her Florence by mistake. "Glad I could help."

She looked up from her notepad and rolled the pencil between her fingers, leaving a gray crisscross pattern on the sheet. "*Mi madre* would like to meet the guy who gets at least some pearls of wisdom into her daughter." The corners of her mouth twitched, and she averted her gaze to the table. "We're having a small fiesta on Saturday. Only close family. She asked whether you'd like to come over. I don't care, but she's rather stubborn about it."

Matt didn't want that. Close family would mean about fifty people minimum, including a dozen of Florenca's cousins. About forty-nine people more than he felt comfortable with. Moreover, he didn't mix well with guys his own age. He tended to annoy them. Spending four hours locked up in a wardrobe at Iain's birthday party some ten years ago and his entire school life served as proof. It was only on weekends that he didn't have to watch his back constantly. That time was holy, not to be sacrificed for anything. Matt's breathing accelerated. "My parents have planned something else this Saturday. Visiting relatives, I think." A good lie should have enough details to be plausible and be vague enough to be bent as needed. This mess didn't live up to any of these standards. "I'm sorry." She would look through that lame excuse for a false smile at a single glance.

She shrugged. Her head still hanging low, Matt couldn't read her face. "As I told you, I don't care," she said.

Florenca shoved her notes into her bag with an abrupt movement, making Matt flinch again. She leaped up from her chair and bolted toward the exit of the library. Without turning back, she uttered, "See you."

Matt looked after her. Yes, he had a knack for annoying people, but she would come back. She always did. She had to.

He wasn't selfish because he needed time for himself, was he? Especially if he spent at least an hour a day casting his Matt-magic for her. That argument, as convincing as it sounded, didn't impress the tiny voice harrumphing inside his head. Matt breathed in with his eyes closed, held the air for some moments, and let it go with a sigh. He opened his eyes again. No matter what, he had to hurry to get his laundry if he wanted to be out of the locker room before the lacrosse team returned.

Avoiding making any noise, Matt closed his locker. He didn't dare to take the time to fold his clothes, for the lacrosse team would be returning any minute now, so he just stuffed them into his backpack. If he took the north exit, there was less chance he'd run into one of the players. Ironically, the guys playing the most brutal game at Central High had mostly left him alone. Beating other guys with a stick and running over them proved how manly they were without having to pick on him. Yet he didn't want to risk provoking them just by being around and breathing.

The sound of steps echoed through the room, perhaps two or three locker aisles away. Time condensed again. Matt's brain switched to full-power mode. Given the noise, it was a single person. Whoever was coming didn't know he was there. If he stayed calm and concentrated, planned his steps, kept his focus, he could get out of this trap without being caught.

This mess was Florenca's fault. He would've been gone in time if it hadn't been for her. Now he had to handle this problem alone. As always.

Matt slid one of the straps of his bag over his shoulder and pressed his body against the lockers. Like a snake, he slithered along the maroon-colored metal doors.

He paused. Listened. Silence. Maybe it was a false alarm?

Matt turned his head to the other side and glanced down the alley of lockers. He tilted his head, raised his ear, and waited for a sound—a sign, anything—but nothing happened. White stars burst before his eyes because he'd been holding his breath. It wouldn't help him if he passed out. If he just let the air flow into him, the other guy wouldn't notice.

He listened again, but the rushing of his blood droned in his ears and drowned out any other sound. Matt had to take the risk. One foot after the other, he tiptoed along the lockers. He had to cross two junctions where he had to leave his cover. He approached the first one and stopped. Still no sign of the other person.

Had paranoia finally fried his brain and he was hallucinating? On the other hand, as long as he could ask himself that question, probably not.

He peeked around the corner—just an empty corridor. As fast as he was able to move without making a noise, he crossed the opening.

His temples throbbed with each step as he closed in toward the next junction. He had already come this far, and he had to hold on just a little more. Matt paused again, craning his neck to look down the aisle—no one. He turned back, took another breath, and slow-dashed across the opening.

Something massive stopped him cold, and the force of the crash knocked him back. Up and down didn't make any sense before the floor stopped Matt's fall. This should have hurt, but the clothes in his bag had dampened the impact.

What had happened?

As if Matt didn't know. The more appropriate questions were "Who had happened?" and "How much had Matt pissed off that who?"

He forced his eyes open, and it took them some seconds to focus. Enough time for his body to release all adrenaline reserves it had left. The awareness of every single blood cell scraping along his veins hit him. His skin glowed, and he shivered at the same time. Could goose bumps form on the inside of one's skin? His brain shifted up another gear.

Would begging for mercy do any good? Could he buy his way out? How much money did he have in his wallet? When would the lacrosse team come back? Would they help him? Or cheer on the other guy?

The blurred mass before Matt's eyes shaped into a person, and all his questions turned moot.

CHAPTER THREE

SHANE HADN'T been mistaken. There was another person in the locker room: the small guy he had noticed this morning, the one with the tropical-lagoon eyes, though now those waters were dark and lifeless. The fear he had seen in them had mutated into something more powerful, and that fright laid its hands around Shane's neck, pressing it close.

As much as he wanted to keep to himself, people shouldn't look at him this way. Damn, especially this guy shouldn't look at him like this. The small one was another Jer, fragile and vulnerable.

What the heck was he doing here?

They hadn't spoken a word, and he was already assuming things, a habit he thought he'd gotten rid of over the last year. And what kind of jerk knocked down a guy and just stared while thinking selfish thoughts?

"Are you all right?" Shane hadn't felt much of the impact, but he had to weigh more than twice as much as the small one. It was no surprise that the boy had been swept off his feet. Conservation of momentum was a mean bitch.

The other guy didn't answer. Still on his back, he tried to scramble away on all fours, but the bag he had landed on held him in place. The boy looked like a turtle that fought frantically to get back on its feet. It was outright tragic to watch this, the curse of his outer appearance striking again.

Shane knelt down. At least sometimes, reducing the height difference defused such situations. "Is everything okay?"

The small guy's eyes turned into massive shapes of black as his pupils widened even more. The paddling movement of his arms intensified, and somehow he actually managed to get away… until he crashed into the metal of the locker door with his head. Shane hissed out through his teeth in empathy, but the other one didn't show any signs of pain. The guy just sat there, stared, and breathed in short, shallow gasps. Shane had never instilled that much fear into a person. This was full-fledged panic, with a generous shot of mortal agony.

Shane swallowed to get the lump out of his throat, but it didn't budge. "I won't hurt you," he croaked around the clot.

The other guy didn't react. With his gaze empty, he kept hyperventilating himself toward a blackout. It was like watching two trains on a collision course, unable to do anything.

"Please listen." He buried the small one's shoulder under his hand, which appeared gigantic in comparison. The guy stiffened up and shivered at the same time.

"I won't hurt you," Shane repeated as softly as possible.

The boy stopped breathing altogether, and Shane yanked back his hand. Touching him had only worsened the problem. A fucking bad idea to begin with, and it hadn't originated in his brain for sure. He fought down the urge to slap himself.

Something happened with the boy. Slowly, he turned his head to look at the shoulder where Shane had touched him moments before. The guy's gaze wandered along his own arm, went on to Shane's hand, and returned to his shoulder. Muscle fiber by muscle fiber, he raised his head and fixated on Shane. With the same excruciating tardiness, he nodded.

Shane had caught the small guy's attention. He had to keep a grip on it before the other one drifted off into catatonia again.

"My name's Shane. What's yours?" His voice came out high-pitched and mellow, as if he were talking to a toddler. Since the panic obviously hampered the other guy's higher brain functions, he shouldn't try anything fancier than small talk.

"Matt."

Had the boy said his name, or had he just exhaled a little too noisily?

"Nice to meet you, Matt." Shane waited some seconds, but the other guy didn't object. So Matt was his name—or he was just too frightened to talk back.

Matt's gaze sank down to Shane's chest, then a little sideways to his arm. His pupils dilated and widened again while he pressed his lips into a thin line, making the corners of his mouth twitch.

The tattoos. The rumors from that cheerleader. Shane was losing Matt again. What if he just told him the truth? On the other hand, Shane didn't have a clue what Matt already knew. Maybe he'd plant some new fears into him just by bringing up those stories, and they might grow into a full-blown panic attack.

"Whatever they say about me is wrong." That was vague and a cliché, something a real thug would say for distraction. Perhaps Shane tackled the problem from the wrong direction. "Tell me what you've heard, and gimme a chance to set it right, please." Letting the other one do the talking was brilliant.

Matt's breathing accelerated, and he pressed himself against the locker door.

So it wasn't too brilliant an idea after all, but Shane wouldn't give up on it yet.

From Matt's perspective, a criminal had just asked him to list the felonies he knew about. That came close to simply begging to get offed. Shane had to change the angle of attack just a tad more. "Beware, so long as you live, of judging men by their outward appearance." Another thing a thug might say, but at least a thug with a minimum of education.

Matt's head shot up, and he stared at Shane's mouth. "Jean de La Fontaine," he said, his voice still a whisper.

It had been a random shot, yet it had worked. Jer wouldn't have known the person who coined that quote, but Matt just proved he had a nerdy side Shane could build on. The butterflies in his stomach put out their wings again, flapping them a little. "So do you let me plead before you judge?"

Matt eyed him, little wrinkles forming between his eyes. Another nod, which would've made any sloth jealous, followed. The seconds stretched out as Matt kept silent. An occasional twitch in his cheek and the unsteady movements of his eyes betrayed that the gears of his mind worked at full power.

"The scar." Matt's voice broke, and he cleared his throat. "The scar. You got it in a knife fight."

Shane had to pay full attention, for even the term *whisper* greatly exaggerated what came out of Matt's mouth.

Matt had chosen the most harmless subject, at least from a criminal point of view. He couldn't know about the grief it caused Shane. Couldn't know that he was saving money for plastic surgery. Heck, even Shane's parents didn't know. They had already done so much for him, he couldn't bother them with that, emotionally nor financially. Getting rid of the scar was just a small step, and it would take away only a little of the terror he put into people, but he'd pay for it himself.

Nonetheless, Shane smiled just because Matt dared to say something at last. "No, not a knife fight. My parents and I had a car accident when I was six years old. We crashed down a bridge into a small river. Mom and Dad got away with a scare only, but the door pillar smashed and cut into my cheek. You'll find some articles about it on the web."

The articles didn't tell about the year of panic or waking up in the night screaming and sweating. They also omitted Nick, who got him out of that dark place with sports and unlimited patience. Shane shook his head, trying to make the thoughts go away.

At least Matt could look up those articles, proof that he wasn't lying. For someone who was set on not getting involved, Shane took quite a lot of interest in Matt's opinion. His old habits were putting up a hell of a fight. Did he even want to win it?

Matt scrutinized his face. His gaze alternated between the scar and Shane's eyes.

Thoughts raced through Matt's mind, if the tics and twitches of his face were any indication. "You're a drug boss. The youngest drug boss ever."

Shane stifled a grin as Matt ramped up the crime level. "In my whole life, I haven't smoked a single cigarette, haven't touched a glass of booze, and definitely haven't done any harder stuff." Whey-protein shakes didn't count, did they? "I'm not any good with money, not a businessman at all. Even if I had ever dealt drugs, I'd have gone under by now." He couldn't offer proof for this statement, but he could appeal to Matt's intelligence. "Do you really think I'd attend a public high school if I were a drug lord? That'd be too easy for the cops to get me, wouldn't it?"

Matt frowned, and the otherwise smooth skin of his forehead lay in deep wrinkles.

He was cute when he was confused, and Shane had to stifle another grin. The butterflies got more daring and flew some loops in his stomach.

"Makes sense." The trenches on Matt's brow disappeared.

Those had been Matt's first words at a normal volume. Shane's plan bore fruit.

"More questions?" The hope for more made his stomach tingle even stronger, and the butterflies were in for some overtime. He would have to thank that cheerleader one day for the sheer amount of bullshit she had come up with.

"Your tattoos. You've got one for each guy you killed." The corners of Matt's mouth rose just a little.

Matt roped in that smile before it could go any further, but it had been there, and it was contagious.

Shane fought to not laugh out loud at the sheer ridiculousness of this story. From assault with a knife over dealing drugs to manslaughter. Quite a career in such a short time. "The tattoos *do* stand for people, but I swear that all of them are alive and well."

Small movements of Matt's eyes gave away that he was taking in all the visible tats.

Shane rolled up the sleeve of his T-shirt, revealing the fishing pole with the trout dangling from it and the quilt made of old pillowcases on his left arm. "I've got one for each person who is important in my life."

"A fishing pole?" Matt's hand moved the tiniest bit, reaching out for the tattoo, but like the smile, he didn't let it go the full way.

Shane would've indulged that touch and would've cherished every single moment, but it hadn't happened and wouldn't happen. It was better that way. For both of them.

No need to be sad, though, for seeing Matt respond like this after going through a panic attack was simply awesome.

"It represents my dad. He actually loves fishing, but he's also one of the most patient men I know. He turned waiting into a form of art." Shane pointed at the quilt. "This one stands for my mom. Name a thing that can be made using a needle, and she can do it." He looked at the colorful picture on his arm, followed its outline with his eyes. "Where she is, everything is just warmer and a tad cozier." And where Shane was, everything was just a little sappier. He couldn't hold back the grin this time. "There are many more. A dumbbell for my trainer and best friend, Nick. Some ballerinas for an adorable old lady named Estelle, who was once a dancer."

He better leave out the single angel's wing for Jer. In hindsight, that tattoo didn't capture Jer's essence at all. What symbol would portray Matt best? Shane would never have to answer that question, but he had to allow his mind to wander, just because it made him happy. And yes, he was entitled to be happy. Sometimes he had to remind himself of this basic fact.

"Any more crimes on my slate?" Another one would give Shane's happiness a boost, if only for the few more moments he could talk with Matt.

Matt's face was glowing. An aftereffect of the tension, presumably, but there was more to it. Shane couldn't put his finger on this additional emotion. Curiosity didn't quite nail it. Elation didn't fit either. A mix of these feelings? Curilation perhaps?

"At your former school, you broke a jock's arms."

The butterflies in Shane's stomach dropped dead. Matt found the only real rock in a box full of fakes and smacked it right at his head.

Shane closed his eyes. He shivered as if cold water trickled down his body. His skin soaked up the icy liquid and froze him in an instant. "That's not a rumor." Now *he* had to whisper because he lacked the strength for speaking the truth out loud.

Even with his eyes closed, Shane knew that Matt, stiff and breathing fast, pressed himself against the locker again. Panic crippled his small body, and that was the only reason he wasn't running away yet. This could only be mended by more truth. To hell with the pact between Hayden, Jer, and him.

Shane opened his eyes. Trembling all over, Matt cowered before him, and his velvety skin glistened with sweat. A sigh crawled up Shane's throat, and he swallowed it down. This was one of the few times reality hit even harder than imagination. He ignored the urge to wrap his arms around Matt, for any further touch might give him a seizure. Shane only had words to work with.

"Yes, I broke the guy's arms, but I did it to defend someone. Someone who couldn't fight for himself." Shane bit back the "like you." "This doesn't make it right, and still, I don't regret it. I regret not regretting, but it'd be worse if I hadn't stopped that... assault." It was tragically funny how the word "assault" could turn into a flowery euphemism. "Abomination" or "atrocity" came closer to the truth, but he shouldn't burden Matt with too many details. And he shouldn't burden himself with telling them.

The locker door moaned at the strain of Matt's body leaning against it. His nostrils flared with every breath, and on his forehead the sweat condensed into small rivulets meandering down his face. Salty drops splashed to the ground, and their noise, how faint it was, rang in Shane's ears.

Had Matt heard anything he had said? The cruel conclusion dawned on Shane that this whole encounter was nothing but torture for Matt, and nothing he could do would change that. He should just back off, should even refrain from apologizing, because every additional second caused Matt more suffering. Shane's chin touched his chest as his head sank down.

"Excessive defense of others."

Shane raised his head so fast that little sparks filled his vision. So Matt had listened, and now he just sat there, his body slack. He had given up on escaping at last.

"Yes." Shane mimicked Matt's whisper. "Not many people know that there was an attack at all and what I did was—" He paused and nodded at Matt. "—excessive defense of others. I'm supposed to be the bad guy in this story." Jer and Hayden saved face because he sacrificed his. All in all, it was an acceptable deal. "There are good reasons to keep it that way, so please don't tell anyone, okay?"

A sigh escaped from Matt's mouth. "Or else?" His face, his eyes, his whole body didn't give away any emotion. The tone of his voice was matter-of-fact and lifeless.

Another cruel insight elbowed its way into Shane's mind. Matt had lived through situations like this before, but usually they ended with the other guy hurting him. His question wasn't rhetorical. He was just trying to gauge how much trouble he was in.

Shane may not have felt the impact of their crash, but now Matt delivered a blow to his guts that took his breath away.

"There is no 'or else.' I'm asking a favor of you. I'm not ordering you to shut up." Shane placed his hands on his thighs to keep those sons of bitches from reaching out for Matt all by themselves. "That info is yours. Do with it as you please. Just because three's a charm, I won't hurt you for no reason."

Matt frowned, and a small fold formed between his eyes.

Obviously Shane didn't follow the usual patterns of such encounters. He created an all-new experience for Matt and overtaxed him with a situation he didn't know how to deal with.

This scene had to look strange from the outside. A small guy cowered before a huge kneeling guy, both of them silent and waiting. Was he supposed to make the next step or was Matt? And how long did it take for "strange" to become "weird"?

The hooting of some guys ended the silence in the locker room. Matt jerked his head around, and his body went rigid again.

Shane didn't need a degree in psychology to see that Matt wanted to get out of there. He must have had a lot of bad experiences to react like this. At least Shane could ensure Matt would leave the locker room without adding another of those experiences.

"I still have to make up for running into you and knocking you over. What about a quieter place with a little less stench of sweat and testosterone? There's a nice café down the street. Maybe a latte and some cake?" Shane had just invented the very opposite of not getting involved. When screwing with his plans, he did it right.

Matt's head jolted back. He flexed his muscles so hard that he was close to breaking his own bones. The offer of coffee and pastry seemed to stress him out even more.

And if Shane had used his brain for thinking instead of his southern parts, he might have come to this conclusion before.

"Okay," Matt said.

Neither the southern parts nor the brain had expected this answer, and they yelled at each other for not seeing it come.

"Can we please leave?" Matt turned his head toward where the voices were coming from and back to Shane.

So he was the lesser evil for Matt. The southern parts cheered, while his brain bubbled out hundreds of reasons how this could only end in a catastrophe.

What did a brain know?

CHAPTER FOUR

FOR MATT, it boiled down to a simple consideration of probabilities. Shane promised not to hurt him. No such promise existed for the lacrosse team. Whatever Shane was up to, and there had to be a plan behind his friendliness, he would strike later. In the end, Matt would suffer, but more time meant more chances for coming up with a plan that minimized pain and damage. The laughing and cussing of the lacrosse players came closer, but Shane didn't move.

"Please, let's go." A whiny tone crept into Matt's voice.

Shane nodded in small, abrupt movements and raised his arm.

The primitive parts of Matt's brain took over, and he covered his face with both hands. He closed his eyes, but the punch he braced for didn't come. He peeked through his fingers. Shane stared at his own hand, which he still held extended before him, and he blinked several times, his mouth opening and closing in a rapid, unsteady rhythm.

Matt's reaction couldn't affect this powerful giant of a man that much. It was ridiculous, unreal, simply impossible. Moreover, his own emotions didn't make sense at all. He felt ashamed. The antelope pitied the lion that was about to have it for dinner.

"You don't need help to get up, then?" Shane closed his hand and caressed his other fingers with the thumb.

Matt got hurt. Always. It was never the other way round. He could deal with being the victim, but being the offender was a novelty. Strangely, it didn't feel any different. It created the same hole where his stomach was supposed to be.

An apology. Matt owed Shane an apology. What came out of his mouth was "No, thank you." He intended to smile at least, but his lips didn't obey.

The moment passed, and Matt had missed the opportunity to set things right. He couldn't bear sitting here any longer and used his arms to push himself up, praying that his shaking legs would support him.

Shane's gaze followed him. Though Shane was still kneeling, he was only slightly shorter than Matt. Without using his hands, he rocked back and rose from the floor in one fluid motion. Another small glimpse of Shane's power. Matt had to swallow. He stood just below Shane's pecs, adding to his feeling of inferiority.

"I have to get my sports bag." Shane pointed behind him.

"Sure." Matt still couldn't manage to smile. On top of the guilt, Shane's locker was where the voices of the lacrosse team came from. He had no reason to smile at all.

Shane nodded, turned around, and walked away, but not before flashing him a grin. Matt's problems weren't Shane's, and nothing kept *him* from grinning.

The situation required another weighing of probabilities. Was it safer to stay here alone or follow Shane? There was a third option of waiting until he was out of sight and then running as fast as he could. But then what? He couldn't dodge Shane forever, and their next meeting would be most unpleasant, to say the least. More voices closed in on him from behind. His feet had decided for him and caught up with Shane, who cracked him another fleeting smile. They walked around the corner, and Matt stopped dead as he saw the six lacrosse players changing in that aisle. Some of them had already gotten out of their shirts.

"Look at these guns. These are muscles," one of the players facing away from Shane and him said.

What was the name of the bare-chested guy flexing his biceps? Whitaker Jones? He was the goalie. There was a goal in lacrosse, wasn't there?

"My six-year-old baby sister got more impressive muscles than those shriveled kiwis, dude."

Matt didn't know the one who answered.

"Then I hope your sister helps you fight when I rearrange your face for being such an asshole, man." Whitaker bumped the other guy in the chest with his fist.

"I can take on two of you any d…." The voice of the other one trailed off as he noticed Shane. The skin around his eyes wrinkled.

"Dude, I'm here. Look at me when I'm talking to you." Whitaker turned around. "Oh fuck!" he added under his breath.

All six of them looked at Shane, who stopped some steps ahead of Matt. Shane gaped back at the guys, letting his gaze wander from player to player. Laughing and fragments of conversations echoed through the room. In this aisle, however, the silence solidified into something Matt could almost grasp. Without taking his eyes off the group, Shane opened his locker and grabbed his sports bag. He took his time shutting the door before he turned his head. "Matt?" Shane's voice sounded harder now, so different and harsh. Matt liked the mellow and soft tone more. Much more.

With small, fast steps, he closed the distance between them. Shane remained between him and the players, who stared at Matt now. Why couldn't he become invisible for real? Shane draped the bag over his shoulder and walked straight toward the group while Matt hurried to keep at his side.

The players backed away from them as if a force field extended around Shane that repelled them. This shield encompassed Matt and formed a domain where he was safe—from everyone but Shane himself. Matt turned around. The faces of the lacrosse team players betrayed the thoughts that haunted their minds. It was like looking into a mirror, for they showed his everyday facial expression at school. Seeing it on someone else felt outlandish. Matt turned back and followed Shane out.

"You're not the only one I frighten, you see." Shane's tender voice returned. Sadness rounded off its edges and rendered it even softer.

Matt looked up at Shane, whose eyes had fixed on a point within some imaginary indoor horizon. So the lion was as forlorn as the antelope.

THEY ARRIVED at the café. Matt's rule of never using the same route too often to go to school had led him here on occasion. He loved the wonderful wood carvings on the window frames, and whoever had made those inlaid works on the door was a real master of their trade.

Inside the school, the two of them had kept silent. However, soon after leaving the redbrick building, Shane had begun some small talk. Listening should have been essential for Matt. Knowledge meant safety, but most of the info just passed through his brain unprocessed. Something about changing school and classes Shane planned to attend, but the details didn't stick. His mind flooded him with an endless stream of plans within feints within ruses to deal with this situation. The things Shane had said and done didn't add up, and the picture Matt had of him was rather blurry and self-contradictory. Only real psychopaths were amiable and cruel at the same time, weren't they? Yet there existed a chance, albeit a very small one, that this friendliness was genuine. Why hadn't Shane just beaten him up? At least this would've made sense and wouldn't have messed with his brain like this.

"Matt?"

He startled. Shane was holding the door for him, and he wouldn't have asked unless he hadn't done so for some time already. Another pang of guilt turned Matt's guts around.

"Thanks." That seemed to be one of the few words he was able to get out around Shane.

Matt stepped inside. The smell of fresh coffee and the sweet aroma of baking contrasted starkly to the dull, cold air outside. This door served as some magical threshold that separated the ordinary world from a peaceful oasis. A dozen guests sat at the small round tables. Some loners, but most of them couples. The barista, a teen not much older than Matt, waved at them as a greeting.

"A really nice place. I love it," Shane said.

Another one of those mismatches. A scarred, muscle-bound, inked giant shouldn't say things like that. Something bothered Matt about this thought, raised his hackles, and he went over it again. He shivered.

When had he turned into such a bigoted prick?

Sorting the world into clean and easy categories served Matt well, for quickly putting people into the right drawers reduced the amount of pain he had to suffer. Blood shot up into his face, though Shane didn't have, and mustn't ever have, a clue what he'd been thinking.

"Yes, it is." At least Matt hadn't thanked him again.

"Lead the way." Shane extended his arm and smiled once more. Or was he still smiling?

They walked over to the counter, maneuvering around the tables. As they passed the first couple, a man and a woman in their thirties, the man stopped midsentence while the woman let her fork sink to the plate. Both of them stared at Shane. The couple didn't even wait until they were out of hearing range or bother to whisper.

"Did you see him?" the woman said with a shriek.

"A gorilla. We should call the zoo and see whether they are missing one," the man said.

The woman giggled.

Matt looked at Shane from the corner of his eye. He must've heard those comments. Still, the smile stuck to his face, and he didn't slow down or miss a step. Being insulted for hugeness was a form of cruelty that Matt hadn't encountered yet. He never would, but cruelty it was. Matt also considered himself an expert in that.

The middle-aged man at the next table "only" stared. The young couple in the corner of the café were polite enough to whisper. Or they were scared enough.

That running through the gauntlet ended at the counter. The young guy behind the counter bared his teeth in an over-the-top grin. Professional training trumped shock, obviously.

"Welcome to the Lazy Bean. What can I do for you?"

"Two latte macchiatos and"—Shane turned to Matt—"do you want some cheesecake?"

Matt nodded.

Shane faced the guy behind the counter again. "And two pieces of cheesecake, please."

"Just a sec." The barista turned around, busying himself with the coffeemaker, which coughed and hissed like an old, moody cat.

Matt reached into his pocket and produced his wallet. He held it out for Shane. "Here."

Wrinkles formed on Shane's forehead. He looked at the wallet, then at Matt. "When I asked you to come here, I invited you." The wrinkles smoothed again, and he whiffed a laugh through his nose. "Why should you have to pay if I…." Shane's face froze. His eyes narrowed. "Do the guys at school soak you?"

Matt's hand began to shiver. The trembling worked its way up his arm, and he grabbed it with his free hand. His heart couldn't decide whether it should sink down into his bowels or jump out of his throat and did a little bit of both. His lungs burned as if he were breathing sand. It wasn't so much the question itself that unsettled him but its bluntness and the concern ringing therein. Matt felt dizzy.

"Do the guys at school soak you?"

Shane's voice pierced his mind, though he was speaking as softly as he had in the locker room. Dizziness turned into nausea. Thoughts hammered against the inside of Matt's skull, looking for a way out. "Sometimes they take the money, but most of the time they make me pay for things. Like coffee. Or cake." The thoughts were gone, and nothing but the beat of his heart sounded in his head. The hand with the wallet sank.

"That's heinous. You reported them, right?"

"No." Matt jerked his head from one side to the other. That would only make things worse.

"Then I'll do it."

"No, please, no." His neck already hurt from the abrupt shaking.

Shane drew in air through his teeth. Just for a moment, he closed his eyes before letting the air go again. "They deserve to be thrown out of school."

"Others would take their place." Matt knew the usual suspects. New players in the game meant new rules, and not necessarily better rules. "It's all right as it is."

"Two lattes and two cheesecakes." The boy behind the counter reactivated his professional grin and pointed at two tall glasses and two plates on a tray.

Grateful wasn't enough of a word to describe how Matt felt about this interruption. It broke the mood of the moment and gave him time to come up with something to deflect the gravity of the topic. He slipped the wallet back into his pocket.

Shane turned away, his head moving last. He mirrored the grin of the barista and paid him with a twenty-dollar bill. "Keep the change."

The guy eyed the bill and looked up at Shane. "Thank you." The professionalism of the grin faded away and real friendliness took over.

"The table over there?" Shane picked up the tray and nodded toward the shop window.

They sat down, and Shane placed a cake and a latte before each of them. He peered at the plate before him. "You cannot let those suckers get away with it."

So much for Shane forgetting about the soaking. That most simple of plans, if it deserved that name at all, had failed, and others hadn't occurred to him yet. Matt picked up the fork and spun it between his fingers. He watched the light reflecting off it. Perhaps he could hypnotize himself and make all the memories go away. He raised his gaze. "It's only money. It could be worse." He sank the fork into the cake.

"It's about more than money." Shane's eyes turned a notch darker, and in them, thoughts chased each other. It bedazzled Matt why he insisted on this discussion and why he cared at all. Shane lifted his head and huffed, his facial expressions stopping altogether. "What was that?" he asked with a hushed voice.

What was what? Matt couldn't follow.

With his index finger, Shane pointed at Matt's plate. Matt looked down. Half of the cake was gone, and the fork rested neatly beside it. Only now he realized the sweet taste and the creamy residue on his tongue.

"You ate it faster than lightning."

A simple statement, yet Shane crammed more emotions into it than those few words should be able to carry. Those emotions washed over Matt and drowned everything he might have felt himself. In his head, the thoughts pounded at their cage again. It'd take another confession to calm them. "The guys at school don't only take my money, they also take my food. Most of the time, half of it is enough to make them go away. If I want to eat at all, I have to eat like this." It was a knee-jerk reaction, an automatism. Only at home did he ever finish a full serving of anything. He was a fucking freak.

Shane's chest and biceps bulged out, his muscles working as he clenched and unclenched his fists, his gaze transfixed on the cake before him.

Matt's thrashing was about to begin. A liberating and comforting thought, for everything would revert to normal, and his confusion would finally end.

Shane grabbed the plate before him and deliberately extended his hand across the table. With almost reverent slowness, he placed his piece of cheesecake beside the half on Matt's plate. As slowly as before, Shane pulled his hand back and put the empty dish before him. "There are two strings attached. You'll take your time eating, and you'll enjoy every single bite."

Nothing. Matt thought nothing. His brain had short-circuited. With it, his emotions had shut down. He looked at the cake before lifting his head to consider Shane. With his feelings gone, Matt saw the real Shane for the first time.

This muscled giant with the colorful tattoos and the scar that ran down his cheek was a boy like him. Perhaps he was a lion that sought Matt's life. Maybe he was a knight in shining armor. But at his core, he was just a boy with problems and issues just like his.

Matt picked up the fork and let it cut through the piece of cake. With nothing to think or feel, he had entered a state of hyperawareness. His hand registered the very amount of resistance required to go through the cake, and every muscle declared to him in full detail the actions it was taking.

Halfway to his mouth, his nose picked up the aroma of the cake and dissected it, from the squeeze of lemon juice to the pinch of cinnamon.

As the creamy mouthful touched his tongue, all his taste buds came alive at once and fired their electric messages up his nerves.

Matt couldn't remember when he had eaten cake for the first time, but this had to be an exact reenactment of that experience. A ball of warm tingles formed in his stomach, then slowly dissolved and spread through his body. He knew this sensation. When his grandma made tea for him, put a single lump of sugar in it, added a dash of milk, and stirred it for him before handing it over with the words "For you, my boy," he felt the same. This feeling wasn't about tea or cake but about kindness.

His brain clicked on again and reconnected him to his emotions. His doubts, his reservations, the panic descended on him. Yet hidden deep within, a place existed that was still warm and tingly. From this place, a smile fought its way through the sticky darkness of fear up to his face. "It's the best cake I ever had. You have to taste it." He shoved the plate over the table.

Shane waved both of his hands. "No, Matt. No." As if handling precious china, he moved the cake back to him. "It's all yours, and no one will take it away from you. Not even a single bite."

This had to be the most convoluted plan ever to jerk Matt around. He couldn't allow himself to accept Shane's kindness as genuine. If he did, he'd only be more disappointed in the end. Nonetheless, the warm place begged to differ and refused to let go of the crazy idea of someone being friendly to him.

"Thank you." He may overuse that word, but he really was grateful for the reminder of how kindness felt, whether it was real or not. "I almost forgot how it is to eat a full meal outside of home." He put another forkful of cake into his mouth, letting the pastry melt on his tongue and savoring the texture of its taste. This was bourbon vanilla, the good stuff.

Shane rubbed his hands over and over again. He bit his lower lip before he flashed another smile and let his fingers finally rest. "Then you should get another chance at it, just to keep your memory fresh. Let's meet for lunch in school tomorrow."

Matt's thoughts came and went faster than he could take them in. Countless voices spoke up inside his head, demanding his attention and shouting one another down. There was no time to wait for the chaotic chatter in his mind to calm down and think everything through. Shane expected an answer. "Sure." That was the meekest voice he could muster.

The smile on Shane's face crumbled apart. "That wasn't an order, only a suggestion." His hands resumed rubbing each other, forming an ever-changing pattern of bulges in his muscles. "You can say no, of course."

Matt couldn't. If someone with the strength to tear him into confetti asked him for something, he'd do it. Playing along guaranteed putting off the evil day as long as possible. "No. Yes. I mean, I'll have lunch with you tomorrow." He bit his tongue to not say "if you want that," because Shane absolutely didn't want to hear that. "I'm looking forward to it." This would've sounded much more convincing if he'd smiled and his body stopped trembling.

Shane studied Matt's face with his gaze of dark brown. His cheek twitched from time to time, making the scar slither like a red snake.

Whatever went on in Shane's mind, Matt's well-being depended upon it, and he squirmed in his chair.

"Wait a moment." Shane's eyes lit up. He rummaged through his bag, produced a pen, and took one of the paper napkins from the metal dispenser on the table. On the side without the café's logo, he began to scribble something. His forehead wrinkled in concentration, and he poked the tip of his tongue out from the corner of his mouth. He finished writing with a curt nod of his head.

"Perhaps having it in blue and white will help you to be more comfortable with the idea of having lunch with me." With both hands and a grin on his lips, Shane presented Matt with the napkin.

The trembling of Matt's body hadn't stopped, and the white piece of tissue shook in his hand as he read the words on the napkin in silence.

> I, Shane McAllistair, being in full command of my mental faculties, solemnly declare not to harm the owner of this napkin, also known as Matt (whose family name I do not know :)). Furthermore, I bestow upon Matt the unalienable right for uninterrupted and full meals whenever he decides to eat with the issuer of this deed. Even if that means I have to fend off every single culprit at Central High School.

Shane's signature followed, a small and curvy but absolutely indecipherable piece of art.

"Dermond. That's my name." Of all the thousand things to say, Matt had chosen this. The voices in his mind had held their breaths and waited for his response, but it didn't even make sense to him. Now the voices, simultaneously and at the top of their lungs, babbled out their suggestions as to what else he could've said.

Shane broke out into laughter, a deep but warm noise that surged over Matt. "Okay, Mr. Dermond. What do you think about this absolutely binding legal contract?"

That was a good question. Some of the voices told Matt to run away. Others suggested playing dead as a viable option. The warm place just repeated "aww" time and again, while the more pragmatic voices advocated reconsidering the opinion about this Shane McAllistair and his enticing offer. The belligerent voices, however, fumed at this obvious farce.

Shane's features became more serious with every second it took Matt to answer. "It's funny, but it isn't a joke. I mean every single word."

Despite the dubiousness of that last statement, Matt nodded. "I'll have lunch with you tomorrow." He smiled, and he didn't even have to force it. However small the chance this offer was sincere, it made the corners of his mouth go up all by themselves.

"Thank you." Shane grinned and folded his arms over his chest.

So Matt wasn't the only one resorting to that phrase. He looked at Shane, a giant who at least pretended to be a gentle one. His tattoos, the fishing pole and the quilt, shone colorfully in the afternoon light. Shane tilted his head slightly to the side, still showing a toothy grin. Yes, this was a boy in a body too powerful. A boy just like him.

CHAPTER FIVE

IT WAS 11:45 a.m., and Shane was a quarter of an hour early. He leaned back against his locker, where Matt and he planned to meet. If Matt showed up at all.

At thoughts like this, the swarm of bees, which had taken over from the late butterflies, droned angrily in his guts. He didn't need a reminder of how much he wanted Matt to come, but the bees brooked no dissent. Objectively, not too many reasons justified that thrill of anticipation. Matt would be afraid of Shane, even if he had asserted on every single napkin in the world that he was harmless.

The napkin. In hindsight, it had been such a childish idea. Still, he didn't regret it. It had helped to break through Matt's armor of panic, and that countered all embarrassment. His interest in a guy who didn't dare to look at him for any extended period of time paved the way for all the old mistakes. One unrequited crush on a small guy obviously didn't suffice to make him any wiser. The Jer lesson hadn't stuck after all. He sighed. The one-sided fling with Jer didn't compare to this situation. Jer hadn't cringed in panic when around him, but what was the difference between running away because of fear or disgust?

Stop it!

This situation was different, and that meant it would work out differently. Perhaps not getting involved at this school had been a futile plan to begin with, but not falling head over heels for a tearful guy wasn't. He could become Matt's friend without history repeating itself. That was, if Matt wanted to become his friend. The bees once more begged to differ on his doubts.

Shane had a free hour, and only a few other students strolled down the hall. With gazes averted, they walked around him in generous arcs. The safety perimeter around him had extended even more since yesterday, and he blamed it on wearing the extra-tight white T-shirt that outlined every single muscle in his upper body. Donning it had been an especially fucked-up idea—the queen of all fucked-up ideas. The shirt would freak Matt out even more. Why had he chosen it in the first place?

To impress Matt.

At times, Shane yearned to gag the voice in his head that sported the annoying habit of blurting out uncomfortable truths. Still, the voice made a valid point. He wanted to show off. Wowing a fearful guy with his body? Not thinking plans through to their end was an old mistake that he should strike off the list already. And in Matt's case, the line between impressing and terrifying was damn thin and skewed.

Shane had enough time to change into something less snug. There had to be a shirt in his sports bag that wasn't a second skin.

"Hey."

He started, and even the bees forgot to buzz for a moment. Matt excelled at sneakiness for sure.

"Hey!"

The shock wore off and the bees droned on, giving their best to compensate for the involuntary break. Matt's timely arrival did away with the option of changing clothes, and maybe Shane fared better without having time to think himself into madness with details like that.

"You're early." What he really wanted to say was "You're actually here," but that would've been a little too honest, even for him. Matt had become even cuter overnight. His hair obviously refused any taming. That was a little unfair, because others spent hours on this perfect disheveled look, and he got it naturally. The tropical sea of his eyes had calmed down, but clouds still hung over their blue brightness.

"Calc course finished early because Mrs. Taylor had to attend a meeting with the school board." Matt lowered his gaze to the ground, and his voice did its best to stay inside of him.

Though Shane hadn't expected much, a feeling of disappointment churned his guts. That cocoon of reservation still engulfed Matt, barely concealing the panic boiling inside. He wanted to grab Matt by his shoulders, shake him, and implore him to relax, but an outbreak like that would probably kill him. Only patience might succeed in the end. Thankfully, his dad had passed on some of those special tranquility genes to him.

"More time for a laid-back lunch, then," Shane said. Honest but not intrusive. Perfect! "The cafeteria is down that hall, isn't it?" He nodded in the direction only because any abrupt movements with his hands would creep Matt out.

"I know some shortcuts." Matt sucked in his upper lip.

That wasn't a statement but a question. Matt waited for his permission. Just giving it would send the wrong signal, and spouting a talk that no chain of command existed between them wouldn't cut it either. Matt's impress-

or-terrify line was even thinner and more skewed than Shane had feared. "It's nice to have a guide who knows his way around this place. I'm eager to learn."

Matt glanced up at him, blinked rapidly, and nodded before he let his head sink down again.

The urge to wrap his arms around Matt grew. He just wanted to pull him tight and tell him that everything was okay. That would be as lethal as the shaking, though.

"Lead the way. I assume they won't have anything as good as yesterday's cheesecake?" Shane's inner hug monster would've preferred the embrace, but bringing up their visit to the café and reminding Matt of the mood of that afternoon had to suffice.

With another nod, Matt turned away and walked off. "Today's mac and cheese Tuesday. It's pretty good." He stuffed his hands into the pockets of his jeans, and his shoulders slumped forward.

At least Matt talked to him. Okay, that was far from a friendly chat, but words *had* come out of his mouth. Even the smallest steps counted.

"It's my cafeteria premiere. Yesterday I ran around school with so many colorful forms that needed signing, stamping, or whatever that I didn't have lunch at all. Glad to hear that it'll be a good first time."

"Uh-huh." Matt shrank even more as he drew in his arms.

That wasn't a word but an answer. Where did hope end and delusion begin?

"Later, I'm planning to have my library premiere as well."

This time Matt only sighed. Shane should just keep his trap shut before he lost him again.

They turned a corner. With eyes wide, the students in the hall whispered to one another and made way for the both of them. Who was he kidding? They didn't even notice Matt. Shane was a man-plow, cutting a clear path into any crowd of people. Matt had just got caught in the wedge. Was Shane doing him a favor by keeping the others away, or was he only torturing him? Even the bees hadn't decided on an answer to this dilemma yet.

Without another word, they arrived at the cafeteria. Matt stopped before the two-winged door and hesitated, hands still buried in his pockets.

Shane opened the door before Matt could second-guess himself out of their lunch. "After you."

"Thanks." Matt entered after one more long second of just standing there and breathing shallowly.

There existed only one type of cafeteria room, meticulously rebuilt in every American high school. If he'd been led here blindfolded and someone had covered the maroon logo and writing on the walls, Shane wouldn't have been able to tell whether he was in his old school or Central High. The same rows of tables and benches. The same glass counters. The same posters. Somehow they even managed to give these rooms the same smell.

"How about you choose a table while I get some food?" Shane asked.

Matt pulled a hand out of his pocket and produced his wallet. He held it out, giving Shane a weird sense of déjà vu.

"You know the rule. I invited you here. I'll pay." Shane smiled, summoning up all the amiability inside of him. This had to come over as inoffensive and casual as possible.

"But you already paid yesterday." Matt's body went rigid.

Shane needed more practice on this inoffensive thing. "Next time, you'll invite me." His face felt tense from the hard smiling.

The color drained from Matt's already pale skin, and he became so stiff his muscles trembled.

Suggesting another lunch before the first one had even begun didn't count as casual either. Especially if your lunch partner was only one wrong movement or word away from suffering a heart attack.

"Don't worry about the money. I've got two jobs. And I can do my only hobby, which is training, for free at Nick's gym. I already mentioned my friend Nick, didn't I?" Of course, the money didn't bother Matt, but he might be able to deal better with this level of the problem. Moreover, Shane was able to deal better with this level.

Matt's gaze wandered over Shane's body, from the left arm to the right across his chest. "The dumbbell. You mentioned a dumbbell tattoo for Nick."

The bees liked that Matt remembered and doubled their efforts to make Shane's stomach a mushy and itchy place. "It's here." He pointed at the upper part of his left pec.

Though the T-shirt hid the ink, Matt looked at the spot indicated.

Shane held his breath. Each time Matt eyed him, another bout of panic followed suit, but nothing happened. Neither good nor bad thoughts zoomed through his blue eyes. No emotions wrinkled his skin, gave him tics, or paralyzed the muscles in his cheeks. That neutrality unnerved Shane even more than Matt's fear. At least fear was a clear-cut thing. The burning in Shane's lungs reminded him to breathe again.

Matt let the wallet sink down in an unsteady rhythm. "Next time, I'll pay."

A definite statement, but his tone sounded as neutral as his face looked.

Shane performed a handstand with his index finger only on that thin and skewed line separating Matt's emotions. Anything could happen, and the smallest change could bring him crashing down on either side of the divide. "We have a deal, then." He fought down offering a high five. Good decisions like this were crucial at this stage. "You go find a table, and I'll go get some food."

"Okay."

Perhaps Shane's imagination ran wild, but the corners of Matt's mouth twitched. That was the closest Matt had come to a smile today. Small steps. He had to keep in mind the importance of these small steps.

Matt turned around and left.

Curiosity commanded Shane's gaze to travel down Matt's back. It was so slender, almost wispy. His gaze didn't stop there and went farther down. Matt's butt was delicate. Shane could comfortably hold it with both hands, but it filled out his jeans with two full bubbles. The bees ventured downward and brought along their tingling to his crotch. He swirled around.

Ten. Nine. Eight….

Donning the T-shirt wasn't the queen of fucked-up ideas anymore. Staring at the rear of the guy he wanted to become friends with and who was cowed enough already without knowing that his butt gave Shane an instant boner, had just claimed the throne. The queen was dead. Long live the queen.

The first step of overcoming a problem was acknowledging it. Matt was cute and sexy. No big deal. Shane had already admitted this yesterday. He just had to remember, had to keep his eyes on the ball. Okay, perhaps he should find a more appropriate image in this case. Food. He'd just concentrate on food for now.

Walking over to the tray dispenser, the same model as in his old school, would be a good start. He took two trays out of it, keeping them stacked together. The cafeteria employee, a woman in her forties with too much makeup and the obligatory hair net, greeted him with a face distorted by shock. One person more or less who petrified before his eyes didn't make much of a difference as long as Matt stopped doing so.

Stop straying thoughts. Focus on food.

He put on his patented shock-melting smile that virtually never worked but he was too stubborn to abandon. "Two servings, please, ma'am."

She could've asked whether he was a student at all or could've cited some regulations about one serving per person only. He had gone through all of this before, but she just grabbed two plates and filled them. Sometimes having the charisma of King Kong helped. She handed the meals over the counter.

"Thanks, ma'am." He placed the plates on the double trays.

Matt had been right. For something coming from the depths of culinary hell known as a school cafeteria, the pasta looked really good. It hadn't been cooked to a mushy pulp, and Shane spotted real herbs in it. He inhaled the steam rising from the plates. It even smelled good. The aroma of most cafeteria dishes reminded him of exhaust gases from a chemical plant.

He walked down the glass fronts of the counters, ignoring the looks of the other serving ladies behind them, and stopped before a display of desserts. Matt was so skinny, and Shane had promised him a full meal, so he put a chocolate and a vanilla pudding on each of the trays. He advanced to the register, tended by a lady in her late fifties or early sixties. She wore no makeup, and laughter lines wrinkled the skin around her eyes, but it was her smile that struck Shane as odd. Any other reaction than shock did.

"So hungry, honey?" she asked as Shane put down the trays.

With Principal Wagner, she was the second school employee to not psych out. This school *was* different. In a good way.

"No, ma'am. It's for a… friend and me." Calling Matt a friend bordered on a lie. Could wishing for something hard enough make it not a lie?

"Ma'am?" She giggled. "That I lived to hear a student calling me that again is a miracle, and it's a little bit of an insult. I'm not that old."

"Sorry, I didn't mean to be rude." Shane waved both of his hands.

"Honey, I'm kidding. I *am* that old." She laughed a little more. "Politeness always counts." With fast fingers, she typed on the register. "Seven dollars and fifty cents."

This couldn't be right. "Ma'am, there are four puddings. I think you only charged me for two."

"Politeness always counts, honey." She winked at Shane. "Sometimes even literally."

"Thanks a lot, ma'am." Shane handed over the money. "And have a nice day."

"You too, honey." She smiled at him again, and he couldn't help but return it.

Shane picked up the trays and left the register. If the day continued like this, it could actually turn out awesome.

He looked around, searching for Matt. Not too many students sat at the tables yet, but Shane didn't see him. Perhaps he had left after all. This thought settled in the middle of his chest and collapsed into a black hole that sucked him in. He swiveled his head from left to right, scanning the entire room. Maybe he had just overlooked Matt, given his preference for lying low. No, he wasn't here. The black hole tore at him with full force.

Wait!

Three guys wearing the maroon-and-white letter jackets of Central High's baseball team blocked Shane's view of some tables at the right far end of the room. There was still a chance that Matt hadn't left.

Fucking hell!

Three jocks gathered around a table in the corner of the cafeteria spelled train wreck.

Shane spun around. "Ma'am, can I please leave my trays here for a moment?" He put them down on the cashier's desk without waiting for her answer.

"Sure, honey, but...."

The rest of her sentence drowned in the chatter of the students as Shane darted across the room.

Staring at Matt's butt had a very short reign as queen of fucked-up ideas. Leaving Matt alone in this place snatched the crown out of her cold, dead fingers before placing it on its own head. If something happened to Matt, it was all Shane's fault.

He sped up his steps, running as fast as he could.

"Matty, Matty, Matty." Iain shook his head and wagged his index finger. "You're such a clever guy." With the same finger, he tapped Matt's temple. "Yet you don't seem to understand the words 'don't eat in the cafeteria when I'm here.'" He bowed forward and brought his mouth next to Matt's ear. "That can only mean that deep down in this bony excuse for a body you harbor a death wish." He lowered his voice to a whisper. "It's your lucky day, because I'll grant you that wish."

Matt's vision narrowed down to a single point. Nothing existed in this room but this spot on the table and Iain's voice. He had known that this lunch with Shane was a bad idea, that it was a milestone on the path to the final catastrophe, though he hadn't foreseen it would also mark the end of his journey. Ironically, Shane wasn't even directly involved in Matt's undoing. Being crushed by a powerful guy like him would've turned his demise into some kind of epic at least. Dying by the freckled hand of Iain lacked any glamour.

"I'm sorry." Matt just said that because Iain expected him to. He'd play his pathetic story up to a right and proper conclusion.

"I'll make sure you are." Iain put his hand on Matt's shoulder, and his fingers bored into the flesh.

"Take your hand off him." Another voice, deep and profound, snarled its way into the place where only Iain and Matt existed.

Iain was still speaking into Matt's ear, so he hadn't even bothered to look up. "Tyler, Eric, can you please tell that guy he has to wait before I can beat the crap out of him? Little Matty here enjoys priority service."

"I said take your hand off him." Shane. It was Shane.

Matt hadn't heard this growl in his voice before. It terrified him, yet it rekindled that warm place inside. The pins-and-needles sensation he had felt yesterday spread throughout his body. This was hope, one of the feelings he only remembered dimly.

The muggy stream of Iain's breath stopped wafting into his ear. "Tyler! Eric! Can't you even deal with a single fucker who…." Iain's hand on Matt's shoulder closed a little more.

Slowly, Matt turned his head to the side.

Tyler and Eric stood a couple of yards away. Their gazes alternated between Iain and Shane, and they took one more step away from the scene as Shane puffed.

Shane stared down at Iain, and the dark shade of his pupils contrasted with the bright crimson tone of his scar.

Iain straightened himself, but he still stood half a head smaller than Shane.

"I'll say it one last time. Take your fucking hand off him." Shane tilted his head to the side. As he breathed in, the volume of his chest almost doubled. "I broke a quarterback's arms, and I don't mind adding the puny limbs of a baseball jerk to that list."

Inside Matt's head, hell broke loose. The voices in there screamed at the top of their lungs, not even using words, just screaming. Shane meant this. He was willing to take on Iain and defend him. Matt had to be dying already, living through some fancy near-death hallucination.

With his free hand, Iain made a placating motion. "Calm down, bro. Matty here and I have a very special relationship. He wants me to treat him like this. He loves it. I love it. It's a win-win situation, dude. I'm a generous guy, so I'm willing to share Matty with you so you can let off a little steam. Just take care that there are no visible wounds, okay?"

"I'm not your bro, and don't you dare call me dude again." The scar pulsated, and Shane narrowed his eyes until only black slits remained. "I hope you're kidding, for if what you say is true, I'll let off a little steam on you and your sidekicks."

Tyler and Eric backed away a little farther, bumping into the wall behind them.

"And I promise there won't be any visible wounds, because there won't be enough of you left to bear them."

Peace came to Matt's head. The voices fell silent. Watching himself from the outside, he noticed that his emotions had left again. No, that wasn't right. The warm place persisted and absorbed the fear, even though Shane had turned into wrath itself. Matt had never seen anything more terrifying, yet it calmed him to the point of perfect tranquility.

Iain took his hand off Matt's shoulder. "Easy, br… man, easy." He moved away, swallowed several times, and wiped some sweat off his forehead.

Never before had Iain been frightened, not even in kindergarten. If Matt's emotions hadn't burned on low flame, this would've been another sight to be afraid of.

"Fuck off, and don't forget your kissasses." Shane breathed fast and in short gasps.

"Watch it, man. No one treats me like this and doesn't regret it." The fear in Iain's eyes made way for another primal emotion—rage. He waved Tyler and Eric over. "I will make you regret this." He took some steps backward. "Ask Matty. I keep my promises."

Iain's minions assumed their positions left and right of their master. All three of them spun around, and Iain pushed open the doors with so much force that they crashed into the wall.

It was over.

Matt looked around the room. No one was eating. No one was talking. No one had missed that scene.

His emotions broke free from their captivity. Like a stampede, they trampled down every sensible thought left in him. The world around him turned black and soundless.

CHAPTER SIX

SHANE WATCHED the doors of the cafeteria fall closed again. That guy was an asshole. Every school had a Hayden, a clone like the cafeteria halls. A searing feeling burned in his guts, and he had to breathe it away. He had felt just like this before breaking Hayden's arms. In and out. It mustn't happen again. In and out. He still felt the urge to take the table before him and smash it against the wall. No one abused Matt to let off steam. In and out.

Matt!

He turned his head. Matt looked smaller than ever, as if his body had crumpled into itself. He just sat there and stared at the table before him. His face was listless, his skin pallid while he breathed slowly in shallow draws.

One of Matt's nightmares must have sprung to life in this incident. The fire in Shane's guts spread throughout his body and transformed. The acid turned into bile. He should have watched out for Matt.

"Everything's okay now." Shane knelt down until they were on eye level. "He won't come back. I won't let him."

Matt didn't move at all. He had even stopped blinking.

"Can you hear me? Matt?" The bile turned everything within Shane bitter. When saving Jer, he had gotten carried away. But when saving Matt, he had let inaction take over. Which failure weighed heavier?

At least he had to help Matt right now. He had to get him out of this state. Shane's head sank down, and he gaped at his hands. In a situation like this, all his strength wasn't worth a dime. He startled. His hands. A defibrillator overloaded the nerves of the heart, made them susceptible to the messages of the brain again. Maybe his touch would overload Matt's mind and it would begin to work all by itself. Perhaps the fear he aroused in him was good for something at last.

Shane raised his hands and let them hover left and right of Matt's shoulders. "I'm sorry for doing this to you." He lowered his fingers on Matt's arms ever so lightly.

Matt inhaled deeply. The inrush of air created an eerie groaning, like the wail of a banshee. His eyes came back to life, wandering around until his gaze locked on Shane. Matt's heart hammered so hard Shane could feel its beat in his hands.

"Are you all right?" Shane asked.

For some more heartbeats, Matt just stared at him while the rattling in his breathing faded away. He jerked his head from left to right, looking with big eyes at Shane's paws resting on his shoulders.

Shane pulled his hands away, palms forward, like a suspect showing that he was unarmed. "Sorry!" He lowered his arms, slowly and steadily. "I'm glad you're okay." A smile sneaked onto Shane's lips.

"Nothing's okay! What have you done? I'm as good as dead!" With each phrase, the volume of Matt's voice cranked up a little more. He clapped his hands over his mouth. "I didn't mean to shout at you." He spoke through his hands, the meekness returning to his voice.

The smile may have come by itself, but now Shane had to force it to stay. Matt had hit the bull's-eye. "You have every right to be mad at me. No need to apologize." Each time he wanted to help, everything turned for the worse. He deserved to be screamed at.

"He'll kill me. Iain will kill me." Matt's fingers still covered his mouth.

Those words weren't intended for Shane. He answered nonetheless. "I won't let him."

Matt's hands dropped down. "What do you want to do? Watch me all day like a bodyguard?" He shook his head.

"That's exactly what I want to do." The sentence didn't capture how serious Shane was about this. "That's exactly what I *will* do."

"No." Matt shook his head again and jumped off the chair, which rocked back and forth some but didn't topple over. "I don't want to spend time with you. Around you, there's only one question on my mind. When will *you* hurt me? Not even Iain ever tortured me like this."

A jagged dagger stuck out of Shane's heart, and each of Matt's words turned it around a little more. "I'm not like Iain." His voice sounded frail and thin. He made a step forward.

Matt backed off, only short of leaping away from him. "Leave me alone!"

He reeled around and ran off. A group of girls, agitatedly chatting with one another and glancing at Shane time and again, blocked his way. Matt barely evaded them, and almost stumbled. He caught himself. Then he was gone.

Shane stood rooted in place. He had gone from not getting involved to just finding a friend to ruining Matt's life. Everyone in the room was staring at him, but he couldn't care less. The opposite of good was good intentions. Shane served as living proof of that. His head drooped, and he didn't have the strength to raise it again.

Matt had left his bag behind, propped against one of the table legs. Shane picked it up. Since Matt would never dare to come near him again, or let him come near, he'd deposit it with the lady at the register. He walked over to the cashier's desk. The bag in his hand wasn't a simple container. It became a relic— a reminder of all the things Shane had botched up.

The checkout lady watched him approach, her eyes gleaming with compassion. She gave him a smile that put lines all over her face.

"Ma'am, could you please give this to my... to Matt Dermond." Calling him a friend wasn't even remotely appropriate anymore.

"Honey, you did the right thing." She took the bag. "That ginger head O'Sullivan is a lout. He's not a good one." She placed the bag under the counter. "Matt will calm down and come back."

She was cordial but mistaken. "Thank you, ma'am. Also for taking care of our... my meals." He looked at the two plates and the four bowls with pudding. What a waste. "I'm sorry, but I'm not hungry anymore."

The cashier reached out for Shane's hand and grabbed it. "Of course, honey." She squeezed it tighter. "I know some students who'd appreciate a free meal."

Shane pressed her hand back. "That's a wonderful idea." Even wonderful enough to lure a fleeting smile onto his lips.

"The Lord never lets down the generous." She let go of Shane. "Never."

"Thanks, ma'am." It'd take nothing short of a miracle to make Matt come back. Even if Shane gave away all his worldly belongings, that wouldn't happen. "Have a nice afternoon."

"You'll have one as well. Trust me." Her smile didn't waver.

Shane turned around.

"You're a good one, honey. Remember that." The smile even permeated her voice.

Nice to know at least one person in this school thought so.

FOR THE third time, Shane went back to the top of the same page of the book lying before him on one of the reading tables in the school library. The tactics of General Custer hadn't worked in the Battle of Little Bighorn, and they didn't work to keep Matt out of Shane's mind. In this regard, he felt for the general. They were both experts at creating plans that sounded good in theory and sucked in practice. Sitting down here and starting to read the material for his history essay belonged to those plans. Repeatedly, the letters on the page blurred, and Matt's face, shortly before he stormed out of the cafeteria, replaced them. For Matt, no difference existed between Iain and him. The saddest cut of all was that he wouldn't have a chance to show Matt he was wrong. That nasty little critter of a thought nagged away at his guts and brain. He stretched his arms, and the sore muscles in his back groaned.

Ouch!

Nick had to change his training plan for good. With Matt on his mind, Shane's concentration wouldn't suffice for any complex exercises anyway. Damn! Not even his aching back shooed the small guy out of his head.

He looked around. No one else studied in the library anymore. He glanced at the clock. A couple of minutes past five. At least he should finish this chapter. Given his current reading speed, that could well take until midnight. He sighed as he lifted the book. Maybe holding it in his hands would help to focus.

"Dear General, you've got one more chance to captivate me."

Talking to dead historical figures wasn't the best sign of Shane's mental health either. He just had to concentrate for four more pages. That was a manageable task.

He had finished half of the second page when something white entered his field of vision. A slender hand pushed the napkin from the Lazy Bean over the table. Shane's head shot up, and the book sank down.

"The things you wrote down on this. You said you meant them." Matt contemplated the white tissue with Shane's handwriting on it.

"Yes, of course I—"

Matt looked up from the napkin and into Shane's eyes. "It took me from noon to now to gather enough courage to come here, so please let me talk first before it's spent, okay?"

His blue gaze bore into him and became a question in itself.

Shane nodded.

"Good." Matt lowered his head to consider the napkin again. "First of all, I want to thank you for what you did, and I'm sorry for having been such a jerk." He stroked the white tissue with both hands and smoothed out the wrinkles. "No one has ever dared to take on Iain."

He hadn't thought of anything else in that moment but to defend Matt. It hadn't mattered that there were three of them against him. It could've been a hundred and he'd have done the same.

A pause ensued as Matt followed the outline of the napkin with his fingers. The movement stopped abruptly.

"What's the price tag for being my bodyguard?" Matt exhaled, making a strange hissing sound. "No one has ever been nice to me without requesting something in return. I have to know what that is before I can decide."

Honest questions required honest answers. "Friendship. That's what I want from you."

Matt jerked his hands away from the napkin but let them sink down to it again. "Why?" he whispered.

"I'm lonely, Matt, and you're lonely." To hell with pussyfooting around. It hadn't served him with Matt so far. "You know that feeling when you come into a room filled with people and there's one person who stands out? Bam! That person makes something click inside of you, and you're friends without having spoken a word." The images of their first meeting surfaced and curved up Shane's lips. "When I saw you yesterday standing in the hall close to that bunch of girls, that was my Bam!" Hell yes, he had tried to talk himself out of it, but that endeavor had been doomed to fail from the start.

Matt grabbed his own hands so tightly that the bones and veins stuck out. "I only felt fear when I saw you."

"I know. Your trust isn't a thing I can take for granted. I have to earn it." Shane tightened his grip around the book because his hands had already decided to reach out for Matt. It was too early for that. "All I ask from you is to give me a chance." He snorted a single laugh. "Perhaps your Bam! happened below your fear radar." Even Jer turning away hadn't killed off Shane's optimism. This day also had some good insights up its sleeves.

A grin grazed Matt's face, but it left immediately. "I *am* lonely. I've always been." More words that weren't intended for Shane. Matt closed his eyes and shook his head. He opened them again. "What if it doesn't work out? If we don't become friends?"

"I'll watch out for you, no matter what. It doesn't take much effort from my side anyway. You've seen how my mere presence keeps people off, even lacrosse players." Shane laughed once more before he straightened his face. "And I can handle Iain."

Matt nodded. "You know that I'll be afraid of you. The fear won't just go away." The volume of his voice dropped a little more. "Maybe it'll never go away."

"I know how fear feels. The real thing, I mean."

"You?" Matt knitted his brows. "Who could intimidate you?"

A cute guy who could make Shane do everything, for example. "Not a who, but a what." How easy it was to tell Matt the things he buried deep inside himself. "Water. Anything deeper than a puddle makes me wet myself." He groaned and chuckled simultaneously. "And yes, pun intended." That confession created a balance of terror between them and brought them to eye level. Funny thing was he didn't lower down to Matt but rose up to him instead. Even funnier was that Matt most probably felt it the other way round.

"The car accident?" Matt dropped his gaze and watched his finger rubbing over the napkin. "You said that you crashed into a river."

Clothes stuck to his skin, a cold wetness that weighed so heavily on him. His mom spoke to him, but his panic sucked away the words, and only the sound of her voice remained. His dad stretched out his arm and caressed Shane's cheek, his hand coloring red.

Shane was the master of his thoughts, and only he allowed them to come. Like a mantra, he recited his therapist's words. He raised his hand to his chest. "The water only reached up to here, but it's the only thing I really remember about the accident."

"I love the sea," Matt said absentmindedly and shook his head. "You're right. The memories are the worst, and the certainty that new memories, just like them, will join the ranks." Matt's finger came to a halt. He looked up into Shane's eyes again.

"I don't want to end up as one of those memories for you." Shane moved his hand over to the napkin, slowly as to not startle Matt, and lowered it on the white cloth, an inch still separating their fingers. "It's about time for better memories. For both of us."

He hadn't noticed it during the whole afternoon, but now the ticktock of the library clock rang in his ears. Time stretched out as he watched Matt come to a decision.

A curt nod, which shook all of his slender body, marked the moment Matt made up his mind. He extended his hand. This time it didn't tremble. "I believe you." The smallest trace of a smile played around his lips. "I believe that your offer and your intentions are genuine. That doesn't sound like much, but it turns around everything I thought to be true until this morning." He extended his hand a little farther, and the smile conquered a little more of his face. "It may not be a Bam!, but some things start small."

Shane grasped Matt's hand before him, closing every single finger around it. It was searing hot, and the skin felt smooth. Like butterfly wings, one wrong movement, a little too much strength could destroy it—could destroy Matt. And Shane was entrusted with this fragility. Maybe as the first person ever. "Small things can be more powerful than they think." Moreover, big things could be sappier than anyone guessed.

They just held each other's hand. If he didn't let go of Matt soon, he never would. He pulled away as slowly as possible, storing up some more moments of touch.

"What are you reading?"

Shane clung to Matt's voice, an anchor that dragged him out of the mood before it could drown him. "Literature about the Civil War for an extra assignment in history." Shane caressed the hand that had held Matt's. He froze and looked at Matt, who scanned the books scattered on the table, so he most likely hadn't noticed. "My plan is to get extra assignments in every subject. The new student is trying to impress the teachers." He sniggered. "I'm a grade grubber."

Matt raised his head. With a straight face, he scrutinized Shane. "It's a good idea." He hesitated. "Who's your history teacher?"

"Mr. Mitchell."

"I never had him." Another moment of hesitation. "Since he doesn't know me, I can give you my essay about the Civil War and you can turn it in. You don't even have to change it." In a whisper, he added, "It got a good grade."

"I won't do that." Shane kept his voice low and the tone smooth, for Matt didn't know any better how to deal with people he feared. "It's a generous offer, but I want it to be my own achievement, even if the grade isn't that stellar. I'm an athlete, and cheating is against everything I've been taught." Moreover, Nick, with his thirtysomething sense of integrity, would kick his butt all the way up to the moon if he accepted.

Matt swallowed. "Not all jocks think like that." He looked around, as if someone had entered the room, and shivered. "I'm sorry."

"You don't have to be." They had only scratched the surface of what Matt had been through, but what Shane had learned so far sufficed to ruin the life of at least two people. Yet Matt was intact, bruised yes, but still whole. "Iain and his dumbos made you do their homework?"

The nod came slow. "It'd buy me a week of peace, perhaps two if it was good enough."

"I told you that I'm not like them." Shane would have to prove this bold statement to Matt one little act at a time. "You don't have to give me anything for keeping you safe, okay?"

Once more, Matt's gaze pierced Shane's eyes. He was looking for something. The skin around his eyes crinkled as he squinted them, and whatever he expected to find didn't show up. Another nod followed, as slow as the one before.

"I could read your essay when it's done and give you a second opinion if you like."

"That'd be nice. Deal!" Shane raised his hand and closed it into a fist.

Matt stiffened up, and his face turned white. He bent backward, though he stood rooted in place.

How fucking stupid could Shane be? "Fist bump. I only want you to give me a fist bump." Too early. Too much. Too close to those painful memories.

Trembling and visibly fighting for every inch, Matt raised his hand. He curled it, finger by finger. Their hands touched.

It wasn't a bump but the lightest of grazes. Matt's hand looked so small close to his.

"Thank you," Shane said. There may not have been much power behind the thump, but it had shattered Shane on the inside. Especially the part for logical answers, which had taken the brunt of it.

After a long moment of silence, Matt broke out into laughter—high and ringing at first, then deeper and barking. He gasped for air. "We always say…." Another fit of laughter followed.

It felt like small fingers tickled Shane all over his body, and he joined in. The to-and-fro of their laughing blended into a two-part round, filling the study room.

Matt wiped away a tear from the corner of his eye. "I'm sorry, but we always say 'thank you' if we don't know what else to say." He swallowed down another cackle. "But I know what you mean." His face straightened. "This situation is so new and unreal. There'll be more misunderstandings like this. Since my comfort zone ends right on my skin, I'll have much to learn. Any progress is something to be grateful for."

Bruised but not broken indeed. This little guy was so much stronger than he thought he was.

"And I have much to learn too." Shane flashed a grin. "Though we don't show any deficits in the gratefulness department."

The room echoed once more with their laughter.

Small steps. And one day, Matt's comfort zone might expand so much that it encompassed Shane. On that day, they would have a real reason to say "thank you."

CHAPTER SEVEN

THE HEAT of the two latte macchiatos seeped through the gray cardboard tray into Matt's hand. Had buying them been a good idea after all? It had sounded like one when he passed by the Lazy Bean on his way to school. Shane made it clear yesterday that he didn't expect anything from him, but being friends included small gifts like this, didn't it? Especially since Shane had already invited him twice.

Being friends. Thinking this felt like confusing the left and the right shoe. Matt had friends. On the Internet. And he had Florenca—whatever she was—but the first person after kindergarten who wanted to become Matt's friend was a two-hundred-fifty-pound hunk who could tear him to bits single-handedly. Shane wouldn't do that. Matt was sure about this. Almost. In case he ever forgot that, though, he carried the folded napkin in his wallet to remind him.

The closer he got to school, the more his stomach churned. That was mostly Iain's fault, but the prospect of seeing Shane again had its part in this feeling. Could a stomach turn around in two different ways? Hopefully, yes, because it'd be so unfair to Shane if he felt the same way about Iain and him. As he had said the day before, he had so much learning to do. At least he excelled at that.

Matt took the last bend, and the school entrance came into sight. His fellow students stood talking to one another and laughing in little clusters on the campus. The cheerleaders, the stoners, the nerds. Little universes surrounded those groups where nothing but them existed. Every single inhabitant of those bubbles watched him. That wasn't true, of course, but paranoia was an inseparable part of his school life. This sensation had even intensified compared to the days before. No one knew about Shane and him, and his fellow students didn't care enough about Matt to be interested at all. Still, he carried a neon sign on his head announcing the news for anyone to notice. Just more moonshine brightening up his head.

He couldn't miss Shane, who leaned against one of the entrance pillars, arms crossed over his chest, one foot propped against the sandstone. Around him, one of those microuniverses extended with only him inside.

I'm lonely, Matt, and you're lonely.

Shane's words made perfect sense. The lion and the antelope dived headfirst into the experiment of keeping each other company. Most fables ended well. Some didn't. Matt's stomach knotted up a little more.

Shane straightened himself and took a step away from the pillar. His face lightened up. This had to be just another figment of Matt's imagination running riot. Why would he affect Shane that much?

"Hey!" Shane's voice managed the feat of sounding profound and soft at the same time. It had rung so differently when he yelled at Iain.

"Hey!" Matt extended the tray with the lattes. "I brought coffee. The left one's with double sugar. That's how you drink it, right?"

"Awesome. You remember how I like my coffee?" Shane took the paper cup.

As he extended his arm, his biceps flattened while his chest bulged out. Every movement he made brimmed with strength. Matt scraped together all of his willpower to not take a step back, ignoring the clutter of voices in his head urging him to get the hell out.

Shane took his first sip and grunted in contentment. "How much?" He reached for the back pocket of his jeans.

"You said that next time would be on me." Matt had talked back to Shane. However trivial the circumstances, it was the first time he opposed anyone.

"Did I say that?" Shane tilted his head and raised one eyebrow.

Matt's heart decided to wait for what happened next and stopped beating altogether.

A grin came over Shane's face. "Yes, I think I did. This time I'm even using it appropriately… thank you!"

Doubling up its beats, Matt's heart compensated for the ones it had missed. "You're welcome." He was smiling, though he had no clue how he pulled that off through all the adrenaline.

Shane took another sip. He paused for a moment. "I'm really sorry about what happened in the cafeteria yesterday." He slightly squeezed the paper cup in his hand. "If you give me your timetable, I'll pick you up from every class. Just promise me not to move around in school alone, okay?"

The reminder of that part of their arrangement wiped Matt's smile away. "You're serious about that bodyguard thing." He intended it as a question, but it came out as a statement.

"Of course I am. Friends watch out for each other, whatever it takes." Shane loosened his grip on the cup, but the paper bore some wrinkles now.

Matt's experiences with friendships may have been limited, but even he knew that such an offer was exceptional on the third day after meeting.

He got out his cell and opened the schedule app. The only currency to offer in return was trust. "I can share my timetable with you." That sounded much too matter-of-fact. Matt would've liked to say something that expressed what he felt, but he didn't have the first idea about his feelings. He just experienced those emotions, unable to stick a label on them.

Shane's face had lit up when he had seen him. Now it was ablaze. "Awesome." He produced his cell.

They connected their phones, exchanging their numbers in the process, and waited for the transfer to be completed.

"That almost works out perfectly," Shane said after studying the plan. "It'll take me a little longer to get to the bio lab, but since it's your last course today, that's not much of a problem, is it?"

All this happened directly before Matt's eyes, but reality had fractured and been pieced back together completely wrong. Like in a dream, everything was too perfect. The colors shone a little too vividly, and what happened was just too illogical. "No, not a problem."

"We can't have lunch together today. Mrs. Temple sent an e-mail yesterday telling me I have to fill out some more forms. I think she made them up just to bug me." The light in Shane's face darkened. "I'm sorry."

"It's okay." Matt would never set a foot in the cafeteria again. Though with Shane at his side, what could possibly happen? "Maybe tomorrow." That gave him one more day to rediscover the courage to eat in school, and it was one more day for reality to revert to logical.

"Cool." The gleam in Shane's face returned with a vengeance. "So, first stop is—" He looked at the screen of his cell. "—English Lit in room A43." He pursed his lips. "Positive side effect of being your bodyguard is that I learn where all the classrooms are." He chuckled. "Lead the way, please." Shane bowed before Matt, accompanied by more chuckling.

Though the situation just got even more perfect, more vivid, and more illogical, Shane's enthusiasm poured into their little universe, filled it up to the rim, and swept Matt away with it. Whatever bond was forming between them could work after all. The lion and the antelope might find a place to graze together.

MATT LOOKED at the empty blotch the penicillium fungus had created in the bacteria culture. Shane did the same with people. The difference was that the fungus actually wanted to clear the space around itself.

"Well done, Matt," Mrs. Cox said. She clapped his shoulder and smiled at him. To the whole class, she said, "We're done for today. Any volunteers for cleanup?"

Matt's fellow students scribbled into their notebooks, moved around the petri dishes, and did anything that made them look busy.

"I'll do it, Mrs. Cox." He had promised to wait for Shane anyway. Inside a classroom, he just felt safer than he did outside.

"Anyone else? Or do you want to let Matt do all the work?" She let her gaze wander from student to student.

Half of the room didn't even know who he was. The other half didn't give a fuck.

"It's okay, Mrs. Cox. I can do it alone."

Matt hadn't even finished that sentence before the other students threw their stuff into their bags and hurried for the exit, minimizing the possibility of being picked to assist. It was all right. He preferred working by himself.

"I'm sorry," Mrs. Cox said. "You volunteer so often, and your friends just take it for granted."

There were so many things wrong with her statement that Matt didn't even bother to correct her.

He shrugged. "No problem."

She touched his shoulder again, still smiling. "I have an appointment with some parents. If there's any problem, you can find me in my office. Just tell me when you're done so I can lock the room later. Okay?"

"Sure." Matt smiled back.

MATT ONLY had to put the bottles with the nutrient fluid back on the shelf and he'd be finished with cleaning up.

As he took the last bottle from Lisa and Jennifer's desk, the lid flew off and some of the clear, thick fluid sloshed onto the floor. Simply wonderful! The two girls had a perfect memory of every single crush they had since elementary school and went over them at full volume in every bio lesson, but they couldn't remember to close the bottle. At least it hadn't been sulfuric acid or such. Matt picked up the lid, screwed it onto the bottle, and put it into the rack. He grabbed some paper towels from the dispenser next to the sink before he crouched down on all fours to mop up the mess.

The door flew open.

"Fuck! He's already gone."

That was Kevin Woiczak.

"I still think it's sick, dude."

Walden Zeddo.

"Twenty bucks for telling Iain where to find Dermond alone. If you don't want 'em, I do, bro."

"Iain'll eighty-six him."

"Dermond's problem, not mine."

"It's fucked-up, dude, fucked-up…." Walden's voice trailed off.

The door clicked shut.

He was dead. This time for real. The scene in the cafeteria had pissed Iain off so much that he now paid his snitches. Cold sweat made his shirt stick to his body. Not even Shane could take on the entire school. Matt's stomach didn't feel weird anymore, because fear had dissolved it into a gooey mass of yuck, and there wasn't anything left that could be turned around.

The door opened once more, and Matt flinched so hard that his head hit the table with a dull thud. He clapped a hand over his mouth to prevent himself from yelping. Kevin and Walden had returned, double-checking for him. Or they had sent Iain over.

"Matt? Are you here?"

That sounded like Shane. It had to be Shane. What if it wasn't him? Matt didn't dare say anything. He pulled his legs in, wrapped his arms around his knees, and rocked back and forth.

Footsteps echoed through the room. Two legs appeared before the table. He closed his eyes.

"What happened?" This voice was deep and mellow.

Matt opened his eyes and looked into Shane's face. Worry furrowed the gentle features as he knelt before him.

"Iain." Matt gasped for air. "He put a bounty on my head." Breathing became more and more difficult as something pressed tightly to his chest. However much Matt fought against it, his lungs didn't fill. He was suffocating!

"Hush, hush." Shane touched Matt's shoulders.

It was only Shane, but Matt's body reacted with the same old patterns that had served it so well all these years. The last air in his lungs escaped with a squeal.

Shane yanked both his hands away, his eyes wide with shock. "Yesterday. Remember yesterday!" He reached for Matt's hand and raised his own fist. Ever so gently, he brought them together. "Just think about yesterday."

The fist bump that had sealed their deal about proofreading Shane's essay. No, that had sealed their deal about trying to become friends. The moment he had made the first step toward Shane. The first time he had trusted Shane.

Matt didn't know how it happened, but the pressure on his chest was gone. If he just concentrated on drawing in the air and letting it go, he could breathe and didn't have to think about Iain or his devious schemes.

Shane put Matt's hand down before he pulled his own away slowly. He avoided touching him, and it was Matt's fault that he thought he had to.

If Shane wrapped his arms around him now, he wouldn't go nuts. Those arms could keep the world away. He'd be safe… and thinking thoughts like these was a sure sign he'd already gone nuts.

"Iain put a bounty on your head?" The wrinkles on Shane's forehead deepened.

"Twenty bucks for anyone who tells him where he can find me alone." Twenty dollars. That was what his life was worth.

Shane's hands closed into fists, and the sinews stood out on their backs. "He won't find you alone. If he wants to get to you, he'll have to pass through me."

The warm place inside Matt sent out waves of heat, for Shane made good on his promise. Shane had said he'd do this, but seeing his words become action turned them so freaking real. In school, their bodyguard plan might work. But what about Matt's way home? Oh damn. Home! The tight feeling around his ribs returned. "My parents won't be home before eight." Even if he made it to his house without being caught, he'd still have to spend hours alone there. A guy like Iain wasn't above breaking a window or smashing a door.

Blood on his bedsheets. Teeth scattered on the floor. His lifeless body lying on the staircase.

Matt fought against the images, shoving them away, but the more he resisted, the more they charged against his mind. "I can't be alone there." A glacier of ice drove back the waves of heat into the warm place and encased it. The worst thing about this wasn't the panic. He knew panic and had countless strategies to cope with it, but Shane seeing him like this made him feel worthless. Twenty bucks was too much money for a pathetic creature like him.

"Come home with me," Shane said.

Emptiness replaced the muddle of Matt's thoughts and feelings. This wasn't the silent darkness of fright but nothingness in its purest form, as if "too much" had turned inside out.

Shane opened his hands and moved them an inch toward Matt, but then he froze. His fingers hovered in midair before he let them sink down ever so slowly. The muscles in his face worked overtime. "I know that you're—" He paused for a second. "—uneasy around me. I'd bring you home and keep watch outside, but I promised my dad I'd take a delivery for him."

He would keep watch outside? Matt's mind got stuck on this detail, but it was most significant, for it revealed how much Shane cared. What did he offer in return? He flinched, trembled, and recoiled at the smallest movement Shane made. Holding on to the status quo wouldn't do anymore. It was time to let it go.

"I'll come home with you." He had done the impossible. "If you really want to." Doubt made him say that, and he pressed his lips closed to stop further words from coming out. The more he talked, the higher the chance of talking himself out of his decision.

Shane blinked, once, twice. He swallowed. "Of course." He swallowed again. "The question is if *you* really want to."

This wasn't about wanting but about friendliness. Every force is countered by a force equal in magnitude and opposite in direction. Newton's third law applied to kindness. "I'll come home with you." Matt extended his hand. "Can you help me up, please?" He didn't need assistance, but it was a first act of good will to pay Shane back.

Shane's face changed to the color of the white tiles that covered the lab tables. Matt didn't know which gaped open more, Shane's mouth or his eyes. He sported the look of a kid who had accidentally learned that Santa Claus didn't exist. "Sure." While Shane reached out for Matt, the color returned to his face, together with a light that brightened everything around him.

Matt's hand vanished completely in Shane's. His grasp was so soft that he would never be able to get him up from the floor. Moments later Matt learned how wrong he was about that. Shane pulled him from under the table and to a stand without Matt doing anything. He opened his powerful fingers, though he didn't draw them away.

"Thanks." Slowly, Matt let his hand sink. "Oh." He looked down. "I have to finish cleaning up and then tell Mrs. Cox I'm done."

Shane knelt down on the floor again. "Let me do this. You can put on your jacket in the meantime. Then we'll go to Mrs. Cox together, okay?"

Matt nodded, for Shane had taken away all his words.

Perhaps kindness didn't behave like an ordinary force after all. Even small amounts of it could cause a tenfold stronger response. This insight was new and so confusing that its impact shattered the shell of ice around the warm place, its heat flooding over Matt.

CHAPTER EIGHT

MATT WATCHED Shane from the corner of his eye. They hadn't talked much on their way to the McAllistair house, and the mood was tense. Not in a bad way, but a feeling that something important loomed ahead accompanied them and they both prepared for it in silence. How much a simple visit threw him off track.

"This is the street we live on. Our house is over there." Shane pointed at a beige home.

The lawn around it was cut short, and not a single weed took away from its perfection. Was Shane the one who mowed it? Small patches with colorful plants formed islands in this sea of green. Perhaps Shane was even responsible for those. He was so full of surprises that Matt didn't have much of a problem imagining him kneeling before one of those patches, a small shovel in his hand, a straw hat on his head, while he tended the flowers with the same patience he showed him. A titter rolled up in Matt's throat, but he swallowed it down.

They walked up the gravel path that led to a small veranda before the entrance. Shane fiddled with his key and missed the lock on the first try. He raised one corner of his mouth and shrugged before he succeeded in opening the door at last.

"Welcome to castle McAllistair." He bowed, resting his arm over his belly. "After you."

Matt forced a smile onto his face. The lion's den or the safest place in the world? Every fiber in him resisted crossing that threshold. Visceral responses like this had protected him. Now he betrayed them. Or did they betray him?

He eyed Shane again. Friendly and terrifying. The first attribute was an improvement; the latter Matt had to work on. Shane deserved that much effort.

"Shane McAllistair from the clan of the McAllistairs, it's my pleasure." Matt bowed as well before he took the last step inside.

Shane rumbled a deep chuckle as he followed Matt and closed the door.

He'd entered and hadn't flipped out. Good. On the downside, the air still crackled with tension.

"I promised my mom I'd throw my jeans into the washing machine and start the cycle." Shane kicked off his shoes. "You can go upstairs to my room. First one on the left. Make yourself comfortable, okay?"

Some time alone to acclimate sounded perfect. "Sure."

"If you need anything, I'll be in the basement trying to remember if it's two cups of laundry detergent or one." Shane grinned.

When he did so, the scar picked up the grin and magnified it.

"Good luck." Matt's smile already required less persuading to come this time.

"I'll need it." Shane opened the door to the basement. The grin toned down and stopped altogether. "Really, if anything is wrong, come to me or call out."

Matt nodded and mentally added one more check mark to the "safest place in the world" side.

A friendly gleam hurried over Shane's face before he headed down.

This house resembled the Dermonds' so much. One could swap half of the furniture and no one would notice the difference. This was soothing and eerie at once. Everything around Shane had two sides that contradicted each other. Matt walked over to the stairs leading up to the second floor.

The walls brimmed with photos in simple wooden frames.

These had to be Shane's parents at a beach and the young boy with the hazelnut eyes him. He was so small, and there was neither a scar nor any tattoos, but the grin was unmistakable. Two teeth were missing. Matt sniggered.

In the next one, a family celebration, Shane was only a little older, but he had the scar and the grin was gone. Matt knew the expression in those eyes. It stared back at him every morning from the mirror.

He turned to another picture, taken years later at a theme park. Shane was already a little taller than his mom and had gained in muscles. A man in his midtwenties stood by Shane's side. He flexed an arm and pressed his eyes closed, faking a dangerous face. Shane looked up at him, laughing. The guy wore a gray sweater with a blue Gym-Nick's-Tics logo on it. So that was Nick.

With every picture, Shane got taller and buffer. In this one, he already had the fishing pole and quilt tattoos. Nick was in many of them.

This one showed Shane beside a guy of about Matt's size with light blond hair. They wore suits, complete with ties and boutonnieres. Shane's arm was around the boy, pressing him tight. The other one laughed and struggled against the hug. Was this the boy he had defended? The one he broke the jock's arms for? Soothing and eerie again, for Matt and that boy looked so alike. Strange Shane hadn't mentioned a tat for him.

In the last picture, Shane wore the blue scrubs of a nurse and sat beside the bed of an old lady. Her bony hand squeezed his. She smiled, but a tear rolled down her lined cheek. Estelle, the ballerinas tattoo, of course.

Matt arrived upstairs. The door to Shane's room was closed, another threshold he had to pass. He took a deep breath before he turned the knob.

What had he expected? Bundles of money lying around because Shane was a drug lord after all? Victims on chains dangling from the ceiling, waiting to have the life punched out of them for another tattoo? Nothing like that.

Shane's room was smaller than what seemed fitting for such a colossus. He didn't have a bed but a sleeper with a bunch of gray cushions crammed onto it. Opposite the couch stood a flat-screen TV. On a small table, fitness and bodybuilding mags lay scattered about. A desk and chair filled the space beneath the window, and books formed a neat pile on the desk. One cupboard and a worn brown beanbag chair completed the furnishings. Posters of muscled men decorated the walls, but Matt didn't know any of them.

Everything about this room was just so ordinary that its normality sucked up the tension until only a vague echo of it remained. Why had he been so uptight about this visit in the first place?

"What do you say about the study of castle McAllistair?"

Matt turned around. Shane had two glasses in one hand and three bottles in the other. Under his arms, he had stuffed a pack of cookies, a family-size bag of chocolate bars, and a huge plastic container filled with small meatballs in a red sauce.

"Comfy." Matt pointed at the food. "How many other guests do you expect?" Not an hour ago, he had cowered under a table and startled at Shane's touch. Now they were kidding around. He had been right from the start. Shane's arrival would change his life. He had just been wrong about the how.

Shane snorted a laugh. "I didn't know what you do or don't like, except for latte macchiato and cheesecake, so I brought a little selection." He chuckled.

The warm place inside Matt answered Shane's efforts with another blaze of coziness.

"It all looks good to me. Let me help you."

He picked the snacks from under Shane's arms before taking the glasses. Shane put the bottles down on the table.

"I don't want to brag, but I made the meatballs myself from Nick's recipe. They're high in protein. Granted, they're high in fat and everything else too, but they taste great." His grin hadn't changed over all those years, though the teeth had grown back.

Despite having skipped lunch, Matt wasn't hungry at all. He never was when he was nervous, and a lot of the adrenaline from the lab incident still circled through his veins. But he couldn't let Shane down either. "So Prince McAllistair is also a chef?"

"My mom called me neither prince nor chef after she saw her kitchen yesterday." Still grinning, Shane gestured for Matt to sit down on the couch. "And modesty forbids me to repeat the words she actually used."

The homicidal drug lord had turned into the friendly boy next door in less than three days. Moreover, this friendly boy had been persistent enough to overcome Matt's defenses. It didn't require wishful thinking anymore to see a real chance for them to become friends.

MATT LET himself slump back on the couch. In a little less than an hour, they had finished all of the meatballs and half of the cookies. On top of that, the wrappings of more chocolate bars than were good for them cluttered up the table. He really hadn't been hungry, but his body had used the chance to stock up. Uninterrupted meals out of home still were a novelty, after all.

"Those were the best meatballs I've ever had." Matt rubbed his belly, which stood out like a small swiss ball. "But now I'm in hog rigor." His eyes had dropped closed time and again in the past few minutes.

"Thanks." Shane beamed at him, but an eyebrow shot up. "Hog what?"

Matt snickered. "That's what my father calls it when you eat too much, can't move any more, and all you wanna do is sleep."

"I have to remember that one." Shane's chuckle sounded so much deeper and manlier than his. "What about watching TV? No movement necessary."

They had talked about teachers and school while eating. Moreover, they had found out that they had to be some of the oldest students at Central High. Matt was eighteen because he had started a year late with kindergarten. As a kid, he had been sick often, and his mom still insisted that his illnesses were the reason for him being so small. Shane was already nineteen. He had skipped a year after the incident with the jock.

What other topics could they discuss? Shane definitely didn't want to hear about his collected strategies for avoiding bullies. That was what his life revolved around, and it was dull. Yet Shane looked at him with his brown eyes, the friendly glow in them Matt had already noticed on the first day. Maybe he actually wanted to hear more about him. At least watching TV gave him time to think about this. "Sure." Matt stifled a yawn.

Shane zapped through the channels. "Oh! I didn't know they'd show live coverage of the bodybuilding state championships." He looked over at Matt and shrugged. "But this will bore you senseless, won't it?" He took aim with the remote.

"No, wait. I wanna see it." Matt's favorite program didn't include muscled men using too much spray tan, but he'd take this chance to learn something about Shane by watching what he liked. "I'll need some explanations, though."

The gleam in Shane's eyes changed—went up a notch from friendly to… more than friendly. "Cool." Shane looked at the screen and pointed at it. "That is Gerard Peterson, a newcomer and secret favorite for the championships."

"I'm not an expert, but you're more muscular than him, aren't you?" Estimating the strength of a guy was one of those strategies Matt had refined over the years. Shane might even be interested in learning about that one.

Shane's head jolted around, and he creased his eyebrows. It looked strange, as the more-than-friendly light in his eyes still lingered there.

The tension Matt had thought gone wasn't. It had rested, but now it opened one eye and glanced at him lazily. "Did I say something wrong?"

"No, no." Shane shook his head in short jerks. "That's quite a compliment. We're close in definition, but he's in better shape than I am."

The scar turned to a darker shade of red.

Matt may not have been an expert in bodybuilding, but he was a keen observer. Shane was playing down what he had accomplished. He was even embarrassed about it. Even as drowsy as he was, Matt couldn't miss that. "Then I'll take your word for it."

Shane nodded and looked at the screen again. He faced Matt once more but spun back to the TV immediately. "I'd love to have his deltoids. Those muscles in the shoulder, I mean." His gaze still on the TV, he tapped on his own deltoid.

Granted, Shane's T-shirt hid his shoulders, but Matt didn't see any difference. The tension was awake enough already, and he shouldn't insist.

He turned to the screen again. After a minute of watching the guy pose, Matt's eyes fell closed and he had to force them open again. Another guy entered the stage.

"That's Trevor Whale, the current champion."

The TV blurred before Matt's eyes. If he just could keep them closed for a minute. Shane said something, but his words didn't come through. Just for a minute.

"I THINK Gerard will make the running. Trevor's not up to his max this year." Shane was talking just to talk.

Matt had brought up the topic of his body, and he didn't seem to be anxious at all. Still, it was dangerous terrain. Over 300 channels to choose from and he'd picked the one showing fucking bodybuilding.

You're more muscular than he is.

How often had this sentence popped up in Shane's head now? Yet what Matt had said became more awesome with each repetition.

Awe was such a strange term, a mix of fear and admiration. Matt shouldn't fear him, but if he admired him, Shane wouldn't object. Musings like this led to muddy places where he shouldn't go. Not after Jer. "The field is extraordinarily strong in this competition." Why did he try this displacement bullshit in the first place? It didn't work anyway.

He startled at a soft thud on his arm. Matt had fallen to the side, and his head rested on Shane's biceps.

"Matt?" More silly stuff came out of Shane's mouth. It was glaringly obvious that he had fallen asleep.

Matt had fallen asleep.

At Shane's side.

On Shane.

He muted the TV, though this wouldn't help much. His heart beat so wildly that its rumble alone would wake Matt up. And there was no way to calm it down. Not if Matt, who had almost died of a stroke in the locker room, was relaxed enough now to take a nap on him.

Matt's cheek rested on the bare skin of Shane's arm. Like ripples on a lake, this touch spread all over and through him. A groan crawled up his throat, and Shane bit his lip to keep it from coming out. He already waded knee-deep in the mud, for no displacement could erase how good Matt's touch felt. It only mattered that he get a grip on these feelings. With a little control, Shane could allow them and still be Matt's friend. He had to master this one thing. For Matt. For himself. Perhaps even for Jer.

Matt stirred and mumbled something. A jolt shook his body. He jumped up from the couch, stumbled backward, and crashed on his backside. On all fours, he scrambled away from Shane until the beanbag chair stopped him.

He grabbed the leather of the bag. Looking like dry desert soil, it crinkled under his fingers.

Shane didn't think at all. Matt needed help, so he lunged off the couch and dashed across the room. With each step he took, Matt sank deeper into the chair. Shane stopped. He had to give Matt more time to recover and extended his arms to show he meant no harm.

"You're safe. It was just a dream." He could only guess at what had happened.

Matt shook his head. "No, no, no. I'm sorry, so sorry."

He had no idea what Matt apologized for, but the painful insight that somehow he was causing this panic attack drilled its way into his head. "Nothing has happened. No need for excuses."

Matt pulled his legs and shoulders in, taking up as little space as possible. "I didn't mean to. Really. I'm sorry, sorry, sorry." His voice dropped to a whisper, and he repeated a litany of sorrys.

"You're apologizing for falling asleep?" The question bubbled out of Shane, and now *he* felt sorry for asking.

A moan drowned Matt's words. "I'm sorry for falling asleep—" He took a deep breath. "—on you."

The touch. Shane shuddered. How could something so wonderful turn into something so wicked? This was punishment for enjoying it in the first place. "It's all right. I don't mind at all." The Shane-doesn't-lie-but-bends-reality version rang so wrong, but more truth would alienate Matt. It had alienated Jer. "Think about it. I wouldn't have waited until you woke if I had a problem with it."

Matt stared at him with big eyes. He looked so pale in contrast to the beige color of the bag, which shivered along with him.

Appealing to Matt's sense of logic during a panic attack wouldn't cut it. Shane could talk all day long, and Matt wouldn't believe him. He didn't have any reason to. Matt needed proof. It was time for action. No, it was time for inaction. "Just listen, Matt. Please listen."

Shane dropped down to his knees, and Matt's gaze followed him.

"I told you that I'm not like Iain, but I'll have to show you." He stretched out his arms a little more. "I want you to hit me, bite me, scratch me, kick me in the balls. It has to be something that'd make Iain go ballistic." He smiled. This had to be the smile that ended all smiles, bearing all the affection for Matt he could muster. "And I won't do anything."

If Matt pressed any more against the beanbag chair, he'd melt into it. The shaking of his head started slow but picked up speed with each turn. His lips formed soundless noes.

"You're afraid that I'm going to hurt you, but you're hurting me right now." Hard words, but Shane wouldn't bend this truth.

The iron grip of Matt's hands slackened. He let go of the leather, straightened himself, and it looked as if he were growing back to normal size. With a slight lurch, he pushed his back off the chair and rose up to a stand. Shane tensed when Matt's knees almost gave way at the first step, but he caught himself. His next step was already more confident.

Standing before him, Matt's breath came in short bursts and wafted into Shane's face.

"Anything you want to do. Don't hold back." Shane braced for the worst but kept smiling. Whatever he had to endure would be less terrible than all the things Matt had been through.

Matt extended his arms and slung them around Shane's neck. He rested his head against Shane's shoulder, leaving no space between their bodies. "If you were Iain, I'd be dead by now," he whispered.

Their first touch had been ripples on a lake. This one was a tsunami. Shane's mind turned brittle and shattered, his thoughts pouring out of his head.

"I don't want to hurt you," Matt said. "In no way." He closed his arms a little more. "I hate snapping like this and running for cover, but it just happens."

"You came here. You hung out with me. Now you're hugging me. There's so much you've already accomplished." Shane let the tidal waves of the touch wash over him. The less he resisted, the faster he'd recover. "I'm patient, like my dad. Be patient with yourself."

"I can't promise you that I'll never flinch or startle again, but I can promise you that it doesn't mean a thing."

Their touch didn't stir up the sea anymore but caused a current that moved over Shane's body. "I said I wouldn't react, but may I return the embrace?"

Shane felt the nodding of Matt's head on his shoulder. He closed his arms around him, the small body radiating heat for two. The rhythm of Matt's breathing rocked Shane's arms.

"Just promise me you'll keep talking to me and you won't run away." He had gone through this once and couldn't bear it again. Yet Matt wasn't Jer. "I can live with you being afraid of me, but tell me what's wrong. Always."

Matt nodded again, and the breath of his whispered yes created a spot of warmth on Shane's shoulder. He tilted his head and rested it on Matt's. The current flowed back and forth between them, gaining strength with each switch.

"You can lean on me. Literally and figuratively. That's my promise." He had to get it right this time.

In a movie, such a scene would've taken place in slow motion to indicate that time didn't mean a thing, but Shane was aware of each second that passed and would never forget a single one of them. Sooner or later they had to let go of each other, but everything in him demurred at opening his arms. How could he miss a touch that was still going on? Matt made no move to end their embrace either. Of course, he could be too frightened to act, but no, not after having that moment together.

The doorbell rang.

"The delivery guy." A good share of annoyance crept into Shane's voice. "Is everything okay with you?" If Matt still needed him, the intruder could rot outside.

"Sure. Answer the door. Your dad is waiting for this, isn't he?" Matt opened his arms.

The moment had passed. Shane let his hands drop and raised his head. He may have lost the touch for now, but it opened up so many possibilities, he didn't have any reason to grieve.

Matt took a step back. His cheeks glowed red, and his eyes blazed with blue light. A smile flashed on his lips. "Go. These guys have even less patience than me."

Shane smiled back. "This won't take long."

It didn't matter how long it'd take to make Matt's fear go away. Good things were worth waiting for.

CHAPTER NINE

MATT PACED up and down in Shane's room, fearing he'd leave trails in the carpet.

He had hugged Shane. The antelope had lain down on the paws of the lion and snuggled up against it. Fucking madness!

The embrace had occurred to him first in order to test Shane. Why, for goodness' sake, had he done it? Maybe he hadn't only been testing Shane, but also himself. What had he been trying to find out, then?

Matt never touched or hugged anyone, not even his mom or dad. Why had he chosen a muscle-bound guy, the type he feared most, to lay his arms around?

He stopped walking, touched his shoulders, and let his hands sweep down his arms. Shane had held him there, much more gently than such a powerful man was supposed to. Matt closed his eyes and for a moment forgot that the hands on his arms were his own. He shuddered. That simple hug had unhinged him, another confusing part of the puzzle. His body vibrated, and he resumed circling Shane's room. He had to rid himself of at least a little of this surplus energy.

Shane had asked Matt to hurt him. That had been out of the question, though he hadn't been afraid of Shane's reaction. This lack of fear still irritated him. Iain, or any other guy, would've killed him for even trying to embrace them. He hadn't exaggerated when whispering that into Shane's ear.

Even stranger were the facts that Shane had hugged him back and that he had asked before doing so. Matt couldn't have done anything to stop him anyway. He hadn't wanted to resist in the first place. Just more madness.

So why did Shane return the embrace? Perhaps being an athlete, he was biased to his physical side, and he might touch people as another way of communication. He had reached out for Matt several times. In the locker room, after the incident with Iain, and in the bio lab. And don't forget about the fist-bumping. Enough evidence existed to call Matt's "touch equals communication" theory valid.

However unusual hugging seemed for Matt, it had also felt... natural, and if someone as manly as Shane didn't object to an embrace, it had to be acceptable. The guys at school never hugged, but they didn't even come close to being normal.

Normal people didn't imitate each other's style of clothing just to fit in. Normal people didn't pick on a weaker guy just to hide their own weakness. Normal people just acted the way they were.

Scarred, inked, and buffed as he was, in the light of those definitions, Shane was the most normal guy Matt had ever met.

The flashlights of photo cameras on the TV screen caught Matt's attention and broke his stride. Shane had left it on, though he had muted the sound. Gerard Peterson had obviously won the championship, for a guy in a suit put a sash over the massive chest of the bodybuilder. His rival, Trevor, came over to shake his hand. Gerard pulled the other man into an embrace, and they patted each other's backs. Two more athletes who didn't mind hugging.

So, when dealing with Shane, Matt had to accept touching. Already being aware of that idea on a subconscious level, maybe that had been what he had tried to find out: whether or not he could stand so much physical contact. He had passed the test, then. He could learn to enjoy hanging out with Shane. Feeling relaxed around him was just a matter of time spent together.

Matt had to go and look for Shane to see whether his reasoning lived up to reality.

It had to.

SHANE SIGNED on the pad the delivery guy gave him. "Here, for you." He handed him a twenty-dollar bill.

The middle-aged man tipped his baseball cap. "Thanks, sport. Sure you don't want my help to get those parcels out of your hall?"

Five boxes of various sizes cluttered up the narrow room.

"That's okay. Thanks anyway," Shane said.

The man shrugged. "You don't look like you need my help. Those are some guns, sport." He whistled through his teeth. "Perhaps I should actually visit the gym I'm paying for." His laughing sounded like barking as he rubbed the bulge of his belly.

What felt more uncomfortable, being feared or being gaped at like some freak? "Thanks, sir." Should he lecture the deliveryman about the importance of sports? Better not. The guy should just go. "Bye, sir."

Once more, the man tipped his cap. "So long, sport." He turned around and trotted down the gravel path.

Shane hurried to close the door before the guy decided that twenty bucks required some more small talk. This had taken long enough already. He'd just put the parcels into the garden shed and then he could take care of Matt again.

"Can I help you?" Matt peeked down over the railing of the stairs.

Shane smiled. "Of course." He wouldn't pass up an offer that meant being close to him.

"I can take a smaller one." Matt pointed at one of the cardboard boxes. "Not much of a help, I know."

"Every additional hand counts." That Matt had come down and asked counted even more.

Shane grabbed two of the almost-square and rather slim parcels, one under each arm.

Matt descended the stairs but stopped as he reached the floor. He eyed the boxes under Shane's arms and then Shane. His forehead wrinkled.

"Something's wrong?" Shane checked the parcels, but everything seemed to be all right. He looked up at Matt. "What is it?" In a softer tone, he added, "Remember, talk to me if there's any problem."

Matt swallowed before he nodded. "The labels on them say they weigh one-hundred-five pounds each." He lowered his head and considered his body. "You're carrying exactly two Matts under your arms." He raised his gaze again. "I knew you were strong, but this is such a tangible figure."

Shane's strength was just there, and he never thought about it. "Yes, I'm strong, but I'm also set on protecting you. This strength works for you, not against you."

Several times, Matt's gaze alternated between the parcels and Shane's face. Each switch broadened the grin on his face. "That makes sense." His grin turned impish. "And if I ever want to be carried around, I know who to ask."

If Matt ever asked, Shane would do it. Matt had no idea he could request anything from him.

"You know I'm kidding?" Still cheerful, Matt raised an eyebrow.

"Of course." Shane returned the grin. Hopefully it hid whatever had given away his thoughts.

"The hundred-five-pound guy takes this twenty-pound parcel"—Matt picked up one of the smaller boxes—"and will crow over the two-hundred-fifty-pound guy with the two-hundred-ten-pound parcels." He studied the tag on his box. "Tom's Fishing Supplies? What kind of fishing equipment is so bulky?"

"First, it's two-hundred-sixty pounds, if you please, and second, it's a flare smoker. Of course, it's the oversized deluxe model. My father wouldn't settle for anything less." They were back to joking around as if Matt never had fallen asleep on him—or perhaps because he had?

"Oversized seems to be the McAllistair family thing." Matt looked at Shane, his face tense.

"And being sassy is the Dermond family thing?" Shane chortled.

Matt's features relaxed, and he laughed along. "No, it's more a Matt thing, though it's kind of a hidden talent."

"Just for the record, I prefer sassy over careful. So let your talent shine."

They chuckled together.

"Though I'm strong, these arms want to get rid of the parcels. Would the hundred-five-pound guy consider following me, please?"

"The oversized prince and chef of this house shall lead the way."

Worlds separated Matt in the locker room and sassy Matt. What else was hiding inside him? A giddy feeling of happiness came over Shane at the prospect of finding out firsthand.

CHAPTER TEN

MATT LOOKED up at Shane, who strolled down Tuscany Street with him. Just like every day since the bio lab incident two weeks ago, Shane insisted on walking him home, and Matt hadn't even tried to turn his generous offer down.

Iain had vanished after the scene in the cafeteria. He could stay wherever he was hiding as far as Matt was concerned. Perhaps he had cooled down and given up, because Shane just never left Matt's side at school.

"Nick finally changed my training plan on Saturday. I hope the sore muscles in my back will shut up for good now." Shane looked down at him. "I told you about every training plan Nick has ever devised for me. You know you can interrupt me anytime? Hasn't the boredom liquefied your brain yet?"

"I didn't know anything about training. It was interesting. Really." Matt let Shane do most of the talking. What could he say anyway?

"We met a good two weeks ago, and I still don't know much more about you than I did on the first day." Shane opened his mouth and closed it again. "Sorry. I didn't mean to sound nosy." He sucked in his lips. "You're not afraid of telling me things, are you?"

"No, for goodness' sake, no." Matt seized Shane's lower arm. According to his touching theory, this was the best way to assure him that everything was all right.

The muscles in Shane's arm flexed, so he apparently got the message. "I just hoped to learn more about you, but if you don't want me to know...."

Matt stopped, grabbed Shane's other arm as well, and turned him around. "That's not it. Everything about me is just so banal. You fear you bore me. I'm absolutely sure I'll bore you."

Shane considered Matt's hands around his arms, and the corners of his mouth curved up a little. "Let me decide what I'll find boring and what not." He raised his gaze and concentrated on Matt's eyes. "You're anything but ordinary."

If friendliness had a color, it was a dark shade of brown, revealed to the world through Shane's eyes.

"I don't know where to start." No one had ever been interested in him. Did Florenca even know his family name?

"You must have hobbies. Tell me about those for a beginning." Shane lowered his head slightly. "But only if you want to."

"It's your day off in the gym *and* the retirement home, isn't it?" Shane hadn't said anything about it, but he must have shifted around his working hours to watch out for Matt. That was reason enough to pay him back with more trust. "I can show you one of them." Matt's parents weren't at home either.

Before Shane had a chance to answer, Matt let go of one of his arms and took a step forward. His hand still holding on to the other stopped him, as the two-hundred-sixty pounds of muscle didn't budge. Matt turned around. With eyes wide, Shane stared at him.

"I can come home with you?"

Returning Shane's invitation was long overdue. Some of the voices in Matt's head still uttered their warnings, but they sounded weak and out of place. They simply reiterated their usual lines, dim echoes that hadn't faded yet. Both of them just had to spend more time together to make those echoes go away. "Only if you want to." Matt grinned as he threw Shane's signature cue back at him.

Shane copied Matt's grin, one facial muscle after another. "I can't wait to see inside castle Dermond." He closed the distance between them, walked past Matt, and pulled him along. "No time to lose."

"I thought so."

Matt still grabbed Shane's arm. One of the voices suggested never letting go of it again. This one was new but powerful.

SHANE HAD to bend over a little more than usual to pass through the door to Matt's room, for the height of the door was below standard. He only noted such things because his size defied any standard.

The room was larger than his own, even large enough for two desks. Piles of books covered one of them, just like his. A white blanket hid the things on the other one, a swivel arm holding a magnifying glass with a ring lamp attached to its side. It looked like an operating table.

Perhaps Matt was a modern Dr. Frankenstein, stitching together creatures from body parts.

"What's so funny?" Matt frowned as he eyed Shane.

Shane tee-heed. "Nothing, just my imagination taking off." He nodded over to the covered desk. "If we ever go to a Halloween party together, what do you think about dressing up as Dr. Frankenstein"—he pointed at Matt—"and his monster?" His finger switched to himself.

A hideous creature that sought the friendship of a beautiful human. That comparison hit the nail on the head, and the laughter got stuck in his throat. Matt was chuckling and hopefully hadn't noticed the shift in Shane's mood before he could glue the smile back onto his face.

"Not a bad idea." Another snigger escaped Matt's lips. "I never attended the school's Halloween party." His face straightened, and his eyes narrowed as if he looked at pictures far away. He shook his head and bent his lips up. "But no, no corpses have ever touched this desk."

Though Matt smiled, something had changed—as if the smile were an afterthought, a mismatched addition to his face. Shane had just been talking nonsense, but he had ruined the cheerful vibe for both of them. What problem did he have with simply being happy?

Matt walked over to the desk and folded back the blanket. Different types of saws, files, and tongs lay beneath it, all orderly and placed side by side. Pieces of wood in many sizes and colors were piled up beside the tools, and an oval disk of oak wood with elaborate carvings, only half-finished, occupied the middle of the desk.

"My grandma gave me my first fretsaw when I was six years old." Matt checked the carvings on the disk with his index finger. "Woodworking. A weird hobby. Even for a weirdo like me."

Shane moved beside him and laid his hand on Matt's shoulder. No reaction. No stiffening up. No trembling. "I lift iron to the point my whole body hurts. And what for? To look even more intimidating to others." He squeezed his shoulder as gently as he could. "You're an artist. You create wonderful things like this. Who's weirder?"

"I don't make them because I want to create something." Matt closed his eyes. "When I saw, file, and paint, at least for some hours, my head's empty. There's only the wood and me. I don't have to think about school or Iain or all the other fucked-up things. This is the only peace I know." He opened his eyes and turned his head to face Shane. "Have known."

The urge to caress Matt's face was overwhelming. He brought peace to Matt, and he wouldn't mess this up with uncalled-for signs of affection. Affection that he shouldn't feel in the first place. "After the car accident, I wanted to do nothing but sit alone in darkness and silence. My parents found Nick, who offered movement therapy, especially for kids. I don't do the training to bulk up but to find the very peace you're talking about." He hesitated for a moment. "In a certain way, we're brothers."

This comparison was beautiful because it hinted at a closeness so much more intimate than friendship. At the same time, the comparison was awful, because in this closeness, it defined a distance they could never bridge. Matt needed a brother, and a brother he'd get.

"Yes, we are." Matt patted Shane's hand that rested on his shoulder and smiled.

Unlike the smile before, this one was genuine, and in it lay all the happiness that Shane needed.

"Look here." Matt took a step away to a cupboard.

Shane's hand hung in the air where moments before Matt's shoulder had been. After taking a deep breath, he let it sink down and followed him.

Matt opened the cupboard and revealed a collection of wooden objects—boxes, woodcuttings, and figurines in all shapes and sizes.

"Wow! Why are you hiding these in there? You should have a showcase for them with spotlights. This one is simply awesome."

He indicated a roughly cube-shaped box, but its sides curved slightly outward. Golden patterns grew around an oval plaque like vines, covering the shiny black surface. Into this plaque, Matt had carved hieroglyphs of the same golden color as the ornaments.

"It's a copy of an Egyptian stele I found in an old archeology book of my grandfather's. I don't even know what the hieroglyphs say. Maybe it's an ancient No Parking sign." Matt tittered.

Shane had to chuckle too. "Then it's the most beautiful traffic sign ever."

Matt took the box with both hands and extended it toward Shane. "If you like it that much, I want you to have it. You can keep your creatine capsules in it, for example." He snickered. "See, I listened when you talked about your training."

"It's not my birthday, and it's not Christmas. It's too big a present, and I don't deserve it." Too many thoughts whirled around in Shane's head, a confused mess not making any sense.

Matt's eyes unfocused. "Every Sunday evening, when I lie down for sleep, I feel this churning here." He stroked his stomach. "Weekend is over, and I have to go back to school the next day." His gaze settled on Shane. "Last Sunday, I lay in bed, and there was a churning, but a different one.

I was looking forward to going to school because I'd see you there." He grabbed Shane's hand and placed the box in it. "Of course you deserve to get something in return."

The wood felt soft to the touch and was still warm from Matt's hold on it. "You don't have to give me anything for spending time with you." Time itself was the gift. "It's like getting paid for… I don't know… breathing." That sounded cheesy, even for Shane, but that's how he felt, and he wouldn't take it back.

Matt pressed his eyes closed for a moment, like a cat did when petted. "Don't think of it as payment, but as a symbol." He reached out for Shane's arm but stopped short before touching his biceps. "Like one of your tattoos. It reminds you that you're important to me." Matt's high, ringing laughter filled the room. "My mom would kill me if I got inked."

He was important to Matt. A shiver ran down Shane's spine, turning all his nerves into white-hot wires. The world was aglow and in danger of drifting apart, but Matt's laughter held it together. The sound infused Shane's mind, tickled every neuron in his brain, and he just had to cackle along. "It took three months and massive help from Nick to persuade my parents to let me get the first ones, the fishing pole and the quilt."

"Does it hurt?" Matt's fingers hovered over the fishing pole.

Shane expected lightning strikes to release from Matt's hand into his arm, for the hair on it already sizzled with electricity, but the relieving burst didn't come.

"A little." Not as much as the things Matt had suffered, or being abandoned by someone you loved. "I keep thinking of the person I'm getting it for. That takes away from the pain."

Sometimes, recalling the tattoo had the same effect.

Or did the reverse.

These thoughts worked like an arrester and channeled the rampant energy away at last, an artificial lightning storm cleansing Shane on the inside until only the awareness of being important to Matt remained. Nothing could ever make him forget this fact.

"Then every time you look at the box, you know that I think of you." Matt closed Shane's hand over the box. "Please keep it."

Maybe it was Matt's touch or it was just the moment, but the empty space the lightning storm had created filled up with happiness. So happiness still hid in there and Matt could lure it out. Shane definitely didn't deserve so many gifts in one day.

"Thank you," Shane whispered. That phrase again, but no other words would have made sense.

Matt's face glinted, and the light rendered him even more handsome.

A monster could befriend a beautiful human. A movie would end now, but in real life, endings didn't exist, only beginnings.

CHAPTER ELEVEN

MATT SAT alone in the library. His and Shane's schedules almost fit together perfectly, but he had to spend two free hours alone every Friday. At least this spare time gave him a chance to hone his skills at being invisible. Shane's protection made his talents rusty.

He chuckled to himself.

Three weeks ago those talents had been his most important assets, and now he only held on to them because they had always accompanied him. His life had depended on them. They even had been his life. Regardless of how much sadness they caused, saying good-bye to such faithful companions was hard. Yet Matt got Invisibility Friday to keep up with those old friends, and he spent it in the one place every student avoided at this time. Moreover, Iain would probably burst into flame, like a vampire setting foot on holy ground, if he entered a place with so much knowledge.

Matt turned the page of the poem, the same book he'd been reading on the day he met Shane, and the little accident with Florenca had created a dog-ear. People used those to remind them of things, didn't they? Matt didn't need any help to recall that day, but it also served as a reminder of not having seen Florenca since then. Okay, the "Shane effect" created a five-yard zone devoid of people, but if there were anyone who didn't give a fuck, it was Florenca. One of her Latina superpowers had to grant her immunity. Matt missed casting his magic for her. Before Shane, she had been the closest thing to a friend he ever had. On the other hand, she had never glowered down Iain in the cafeteria, though she could sow as much terror into the hearts of their fellow students as Shane. Her gaze could cut right through human flesh and perhaps even bones. He shuddered as his imagination provided some vivid pictures of her laser eyes. Shane watching over him was a special thing. Matt couldn't expect others to fight his fights, and Florenca was another old companion he didn't want to give up.

On Fridays, she had often come to him with questions about chemistry. The course on organic chemistry would end in a quarter of an hour. He could pay her a visit and practice moving around in school unseen at the same time.

Matt made it to the lab without incident and undetected. He still had it. From the small gap between the lockers, he watched the students leave the room, but Florenca didn't come out. The stream of people ebbed, and he moved over to the door, risking a peek inside. Mr. Huntington was talking to Florenca. Given the wrinkles on his forehead, they discussed a serious topic.

"Miss Goncalvez, how often have I told you that the laboratory isn't the place to have it out with someone? You're handling chemicals that are potentially dangerous, and the last thing I need is a brawl close to an Erlenmeyer flask with sulfuric acid."

Florenca gave Mr. Huntington the very look Matt had thought about, and he expected the teacher to crumble to pieces any moment.

"That bitch…."

Mr. Huntington sighed. "Lydia, you mean."

Florenca grunted, and her eyes performed the trick of sparkling and being pitch-black at the same time. "Lydia, the bitch…." She paused as if waiting for the explosion, but Mr. Huntington certainly knew better than to buy into her provocation. "She's a racist idiot spreading rumors about me, though she's nothing but a white trash whor—"

"Whoa! Cut it, Miss Goncalvez." Mr. Huntington's face turned a deep shade of red. "First, I don't want to hear that word in my classroom. Second, calling someone white trash is damn racist as well. And third, I don't care in the least about your teenage problems if they endanger my other students." He raised his index finger. "This is your last warning, Miss Goncalvez. If this ever happens again, you'll discuss it with Principal Wagner."

"But—"

"Shut up!"

Matt flinched as Mr. Huntington's shout echoed through the lab. It didn't seem to bother Florenca at all, for she just stood there, glaring back at the teacher.

"I won't listen to you spouting out more insults. You clean the lab. Now!" The muscles around Mr. Huntington's eyes twitched, and he chewed his lips. "I'll be back in half an hour, and the room *will* be spick-and-span then."

Florenca opened her mouth, but Mr. Huntington raised his finger again.

"Don't make me say anything I might regret as a teacher."

Mr. Huntington turned around, stormed out of the lab, and slammed the door to his preparation room closed.

Why did Matt feel so miserable? He hadn't done anything wrong and hadn't gotten a dressing-down. Poor Florenca! She stood up for herself, regardless of how much trouble it caused. That was her kind of magic, something Matt could learn from her. He took a step inside the room.

"Let me help you." Friends helped each other, even if they were only… half friends.

Florenca spun around, and her eyes widened, but the dark light in them persisted. "Did Bigfoot tire of his pet and abandon you at a lamppost?"

"Shane would never abandon me." Three weeks ago Matt wouldn't have talked back to a walking human bomb.

"Then Shane"—Florenca spat out his name—"is a better guy than anyone in this room."

"You didn't show up either." More surprising words coming out of his mouth.

Florenca took a step toward him. His instincts released a potent mix of hormones into his blood, preparing him for flight, but he wouldn't run away. Not from her.

"You spend every single second with Bigfoot." The snideness of her comment was mixed with disappointment, which made her already deep voice sag even more.

"Don't call him that!" Fighting for another person was so much easier than fighting for himself. "And though I don't have much experience with such things, more than two people can talk with each other and hang out together. We're friends, aren't we?"

She stood there and stared at him. Her face froze, looking blank.

What more answer did he need? He had even felt guilty for not attending her family party. She hadn't been joking when she said she didn't care. Matt turned around. He had no reason to stay here any longer.

Florenca grabbed his arm.

When Shane touched him, it always caused something in him, be it fear, like in the beginning, or the warm surge he felt nowadays.

These were only cold and damp fingers clamping around his wrist.

"We are friends," she said.

Usually, everything that came out of Florenca's mouth was a snark. Those words were not.

Matt swiveled his head around. She meant it. That was her truth, but it wasn't his. Like her hand around his arm, her words didn't reach him. The things Shane said always did. "No two friendships are alike." He smiled, for he stumbled over an insight he should have had as a kindergarten kid.

The olive color drained from Florenca's face, and she let his arm drop. Without a further word, she ran past him and out the door.

What had just happened? Matt had only told his truth, and she hadn't covered herself with glory when it came to showing affection. Having friendships complicated his life, but it satisfied him so much more than running away. One more finding he should have made years ago. Florenca was a friend, half friend, or whatever, and he would clean up the lab for her because that was what a friend would do.

SHANE PLACED the single red rose on the tray with Estelle's dinner and picked it up from the trolley. He knocked once and entered her room.

"A nice evening for the most beautiful girl in this establishment." Shane bared his teeth in an excessive grin.

Estelle sat upright in her bed, the white blanket draped over her legs. Shane had never seen her without impeccable makeup or hair. "I may be old, but I'm not demented. You say this every day." She rolled her eyes.

"And you complain about it every day, but do you want me to stop?"

"Of course not." She put on the smile that every haughty British noble envied her for.

He set the tray down on her nightstand. "Now I have to ask you whether you need help with eating, and you'll answer that you're old but not a toddler."

"I never fed a child in my life, so I won't need a child feeding me now." She crossed her arms over her chest, and the golden rings on her slender fingers clicked against each other.

Bringing her dinner wasn't complete without this little ritual of theirs. From the first day on, she had treated him like that, but it had taken him a week to understand that she was playing with him. Anyone who dared to snarl at Shane on meeting him was a special person, and Estelle was one in a million.

Shane sat down on the chair beside her bed. "Bon appétit!"

"*Mon Dieu*. Two words of French and you even mangle those." Estelle looked at the tray and dismissed it with a sneer. "I visited the best Parisian restaurants. The rats in the alleys behind those ate better than this."

She wasn't happy when she couldn't nag, and Shane shouldn't talk back. It had taken him another week to learn this.

Her gaze settled on him, and her already wrinkled face turned into a furrowed mess as she squinted her eyes. "Something's different about you."

She tapped her lips with her index finger before she tilted her head and sighed. "It's so obvious. You're in love."

Shane grabbed the armrests of the chair, which moaned in his grip. "No, I'm not in love." In his body, an argument broke loose. His brain insisted that he was telling the truth, while his heart pouted at this blatant lie. His stomach hadn't decided yet which side to take, but turning inside out was never wrong.

Estelle rolled her eyes again, shaking her head. "Enough men have fallen in love with me, so I recognize that special look. You're a clear case. I can almost see the little pink hearts bubbling out of your eyes. Someone I know? The other cute nurse? What's his name…? Marc!"

"Not Marc. Definitely not Marc." Estelle's standards for cute differed drastically from his. Yes, Marc was good-looking, tall, and quite buff. Even after working in the residence for over a year together, Shane had yet to exchange three complete sentences with him. "I met someone at school. His name's Matt, but once more, I am not in love with him." Shane made a small pause after every word. His brain and heart decided on a standoff and made him add, "I mustn't be."

Estelle smiled again, but this smile wasn't a facade.

"That's how love works for me, Shane, but not for you. On a single evening, I had three dates, got engaged twice, and loved all three of them—at least for an hour." Her hand covered Shane's on the armrest. "Your heart, as big as it is, can only house a single man, a long-term resident, and you don't have much choice in the matter of who moves in." She squeezed his hand. "How long did it take to give Jer up, even after he walked away from you?"

His heart and his brain begged to differ on this question as well. Forgetting about Jer was the only logical thing to do, but a first love defied all rules of logic. There would always be a small part of his heart reserved for Jer, though staying within Estelle's imagery, meeting Matt had finally convinced his heart to post the note of eviction. "I know, but Matt has been bullied and messed around with in such cruel ways. He needs a friend, a brother, and so do I. He's my chance for proving that I can be a friend without becoming an eerie stalker."

Estelle tsked. "Not even Jer would've called you a stalker. You loved him and showed your affection. If that was more than he could take, it wasn't your fault."

If Jer had been gay, it wouldn't have been Shane's fault, but coming on too strong to a straight guy was a fucked-up and egoistical way to ask for trouble. He shrugged. "I don't know whether Matt is gay or not, and I don't have to. We're friends. Period."

Estelle squeezed Shane's hand to the point of pain. "That's not how it works for you." She let go of his hand and patted his knee. "Shane, you already have a scar on the outside. Watch out so you don't get too many of those on the inside."

Jer had drawn blood, but his wound could still heal without leaving a mark. Matt's presence alone helped with the healing. "I will."

She primmed her lips. "Then tell me at least about the guy who can turn this mountain of a man into a pile of rubble."

"Wait." Shane got his cell out from his pocket and opened the photo album. "This is him." He handed the phone to Estelle.

Her gaze alternated between the screen and Shane's face. "Small and boyish." The haughty, noble smile returned. "At least you're consistent."

Was that a good or bad thing? "I know." He grinned. "They may be the same type, but Matt's so different. He's warmer than Jer had ever been. Look at the next picture."

Estelle wiped over the screen.

"He gave the box to me as a reminder of being important to him. Isn't it beautiful?"

"Yes, it is." Estelle looked at him from the corner of her eye, and her smile became lopsided with a touch of impishness. "He seems to be a really good friend." She exhaled the last word.

Shane laughed out loud. "As I said." He'd never change Estelle's mind once she made it up, so he wouldn't waste energy trying. Especially if he needed all of it not to fall in love with Matt for real.

"May I forward the picture of the box to my cell? I'd like to show it to someone who's interested in knickknacks like this."

"Sure."

Her fingers wandered over the touch screen.

"My mom is even challenged when using the remote for our garage, and you can handle a smartphone."

She kept her gaze on the screen. "Once she's trapped inside a jail with crones and dodderers as her only company, she'll learn how to operate the one thing that allows her to have a conversation not dealing with her bladder, intestines, or the other inmates' grandchildren."

Shane smirked, but Estelle was too busy with the cell to notice.

"Hey, you have me to talk to."

She looked up at Shane. "And you could be my grandchild. At least you've got tattoos and a criminal past. That aces Mrs. Kellerman's preschool stories and Mr. Tottenham's college boasts anytime."

When Shane grew old, he wanted to be like Estelle. Perhaps a tad less bitter and a whiff heartier, but as cool and as open to new things. The ballerinas on his arm would remind him of that.

And the angel's wing on his pec would remind him of not falling in unrequited love again.

CHAPTER TWELVE

MATT WALKED circles in his room. Shane had sounded so crestfallen on the phone. Of course he had agreed at once when Shane had asked to come over. Had he done something to make him feel miserable? It just had to be something else. Nonetheless, he looked forward to seeing Shane on a Saturday. Was it uncomradely to be happy about the visit of a friend who felt sad?

The doorbell rang, and Matt almost stumbled as he raced down the stairs, barely catching himself on the rail. He took a deep breath before opening the door.

Even the broken sound of Shane's voice hadn't prepared Matt for the picture of misery before him. Shane's head hung low, and his shoulders slumped forward. Deep, dark rings around his eyes hinted at a sleepless night. Despite being pale, his cheeks were glowing through a thin film of sweat. Some locks of his dark hair peeked out from under a gray beanie.

"Hey." A light flashed up in Shane's eyes, but it went out as fast as it had come.

Matt swallowed. "Hey!" Whatever made Shane feel like this had to end. "Come in. My parents are shopping."

"I jogged over because I just couldn't walk. I'm wet and smelly. You don't want me inside."

"You're damp, and it's cold. Those are two good reasons not to stay outside. Come in!" For the first time ever, Matt gave an order. Worry worked as one hell of a motivator.

A smile touched Shane's lips. "You've been warned." The step over the threshold wiped his smile away. He knelt down, took off his backpack, and opened it. "I'm here because of this." Shane produced a package wrapped up in a white cloth.

This shape was unmistakable. "The box?" Matt refused to think about why his gift grieved Shane. For him, it was a symbol of their friendship, and it mustn't cause feelings like that.

Shane closed his eyes and nodded. "When I said that it was too big a present, I didn't know how true that was."

This explanation didn't help in the slightest to ease Matt's confusion. "What do you mean?"

"Estelle... I told you about her?"

Matt pointed at Shane's right arm. "The ballerinas."

Shane opened his eyes and looked at him, another short flash of joy hurrying over his face. "You remember." He shook his head. "Estelle sent a picture of the box to a friend of hers who deals with antiquities and art." Shane's chest expanded as he inhaled deeply. "He says that such a piece of work is worth at least five hundred dollars." The air streamed out of him in a long sigh. "Five hundred bucks! I cannot accept something from you that's so valuable!" Shane held out the white package with both hands.

Matt floated above the ground, for the way Shane worried unmade all of his own worries. He didn't return the box to end their friendship. He did it to preserve it.

"I get the wood for free from a friend of the family. The paint and the glue cost me ten dollars at most. I'd never sell it, so for me, it's worthless." Matt curved up his lips and shoved Shane's hands away. Shane didn't resist. "But knowing that you have it, that it reminds you of me, that's something no money in the world can buy."

"Estelle's friend said that it takes some hundred hours of work to create something as elaborate as this." Shane let his head sink down.

"A hundred hours of peace." Matt never accounted for the time he spent on one of his projects. They took as long as they took. "I like the idea that something that already brought me peace now belongs to someone who volunteered for this job."

Shane looked up and extended his hands again but stopped as Matt shook his head.

"I insist that you keep it." Attachment served as an even better motivator than worry.

Light suffused Shane's eyes, and this time it kept shining. "I'll never sell it either. I'd rather starve than part with it."

A minute ago, Matt had feared that Shane had given up on them. Now those few words expressed better than any oath that this would never happen. Peace existed beyond his working desk. "Speaking of starving, you look like you need breakfast and, even more so, a coffee."

Shane chuckled. "That bad? I haven't eaten since the e-mail arrived yesterday late evening, and I didn't sleep at all last night."

Matt could chide Shane for this—or feel touched. Or simply both. "Up to my room, sit down on my bed, and wait for breakfast." He could get used to giving orders.

The box pressed to his chest, Shane saluted. "Yes, sir, Matt, sir." He placed the wrapped package into his backpack, much more carefully than necessary, and got up from the floor.

The spectacle of Shane moving and the flow of his muscles beguiled Matt. Shane probably wasn't even aware of his power, but Matt saw it in every motion he made. This raw energy had frightened him in the beginning, but now it made him feel… what? Once again, he didn't have a name for this emotion. Whatever it was, it intensified as Shane walked by and left a trail of his scent behind. Matt closed his eyes and soaked it in.

Kitchen. Breakfast. Coffee.

The message of his dutiful self almost got lost in the chattering of the other voices. That mess always happened when Shane was around, and he had given up on finding out what the voices were discussing.

USING BOTH hands to hold the tray with Shane's breakfast, Matt pushed open the door to his room with his foot. As he had been ordered, Shane sat on the bed. He had taken off the beanie and his jacket, revealing another one of those snug white tees, which seemed to be the only kind of shirt he owned. This special one showed even more of Shane's biceps than the others. Matt put on a friendly expression and mentally kept his fingers crossed that it covered up the unnamed emotion crawling onto his face.

"I hope you like pancakes when they are cold. Or cereal, toast, bananas… or anything else I found in the kitchen." Obviously, they both had problems estimating how much a person ate. Shane had instigated the meatball massacre, and Matt had just set in motion the breakfast bedlam.

"You took that starving thing a little too seriously." Shane's smirk extended up to his scar. The same thing happened when he grinned, which was intriguing and spooky at the same time. "But I am hungry. Thank you." He relieved Matt of the tray and placed it on his thighs.

Matt rolled the office chair over from his woodworking desk.

Shane smiled at him while chewing on a pancake, which he had stuffed whole into his mouth. "Good," he mumbled around it.

"Did you go over my remarks on your Civil War essay?" Talking about school on a Saturday ranked low on the weekend quality scale, even on Matt's. But if he didn't say something, he'd just sit there and watch Shane eat. Funny enough, gaping at him munching away held an exceptional fascination, and that made Matt even more of a weirdo.

Shane nodded and swallowed down a large chunk of toast he had dipped in Grandma's strawberry jam. "Your comments were so helpful. My grade will go up one notch just because of you." He grabbed the coffee mug from the tray.

Matt's cheeks pulsed in sync with the beat of his heart. "It was already excellent as it was." He lowered his gaze and rubbed his thumb over the back of his other hand.

"You don't have to spare me. I know that I'm more brawn than brain." Shane snickered before taking a generous sip of coffee.

"That's not true. Likening the Lost Cause to the German stab-in-the-back myth is really brilliant." Not many of their fellow students even knew one of those terms, to say nothing of connecting them. Shane was too modest.

As no answer came, Matt raised his head. Shane just peered at him. Though every muscle in his face stood still, thoughts entered and left his eyes in quick succession, like actors on a stage in a lively play.

"Ouch!" Seemingly not paying attention to his hand, Shane had spilled some coffee onto his shirt. He winced, and more of the hot beverage sloshed out of the cup. He looked down. "Fuck!" His head shot up. "Sorry!" He put the mug onto the tray.

The brown liquid spread through the fabric into a large stain.

"Gimme your tee. I can rub the coffee out." Matt extended his hand. "Quick!"

Shane's gaze wandered from the stain to Matt and back, his mouth opening and closing.

"The faster we get it out the better." Matt had caused this mishap. He shouldn't have brought up the essay and distracted Shane. "Gimme your shirt. Please!"

Ever so slowly, Shane put the tray down on Matt's bed. He grabbed the edge of his tee, pulled it over his head, and handed it over.

"I'll be back in a minute." Matt jumped up from the chair and hurried toward the door.

Again, the voices in his head tried to tell him something. However, since they were impolite enough to scream at him all at once, he had the right to ignore them.

"YOUR SHIRT'S clean, and I put it into the dryer. In half an hour, it'll be good as new." Matt entered his room again and stopped dead. He knew what the voices kept telling him. Shane was sitting on his bed—shirtless. Yet Matt hadn't realized it until now, which opened up a new—and frightening—dimension of displacement.

Shane crossed his arms over his abs. A little too late, for the sight had already burned into Matt's mind. Those muscles were an eight-pack. He didn't even know that such a thing existed. Moreover, he didn't know where to look. Shane's face would've been a good place to keep his gaze, but it was also the least interesting one. By sheer power of will, he brought his head up and experienced déjà vu. Once more, Shane's facial expression had frozen altogether, and his eyes whirled with thoughts.

"You're afraid of me." Shane's voice came out thin and frail, somewhere between a whisper and a moan.

"No!" This answer bubbled out of Matt before he had satisfied himself that it was true. Yet something as spontaneous as this had to be the truth. "It was a shock, but not a bad one, more like a surprise. A sho-prise?" He was talking bullshit and took a deep breath before continuing. "I know it sounds strange, but I didn't expect that many muscles."

With each of Matt's words, Shane's shoulders sagged a little more, and he pressed his arms against his stomach. Ironically, doing so made his biceps bulge out more. Instead of hiding his body, he turned it even more impressive.

Matt talked big about friendship, trust, and peace, but then he betrayed Shane and himself by reeling off the same old patterns. Something was fundamentally wrong with him, his psyche twisted beyond repair. No. Nothing could be that broken. If it were, it had to be replaced. "I swear I'm not afraid of you. Of course I know that you're muscled, it's fricking obvious, but I just chose to ignore it. Before I met you, more muscles meant more pain, and more pain meant being more careful. I'm sorry for letting a knee-jerk reaction get the best of me."

Shane's facial muscles resumed their work. A twitch in his cheek. A quirk in the corners of his mouth. A frown on his forehead. He relaxed, and the thoughts in his eyes came to a rest before the subtlest trace of a smile settled on his lips. "Come here, please." He beckoned Matt over.

Not even a split second of doubt occurred to Matt before he crossed the distance between them, reflecting Shane's smile back at him. Perhaps his mind wasn't in such bad shape after all. It just needed a little polishing.

"Gimme your hand, please." Shane held out his, palm facing down.

If Shane asked for something, he'd get it. Matt extended his arm.

"Muscles don't mean pain. Actually, they are made of quite a lot of water, proteins, amino acids, and in this case"—Shane closed his fingers around Matt's wrist in a gentle grip—"at least 10 percent sappiness." Sniggering, he lowered Matt's hand to his pec.

Matt breathed in sharply, and a tremble shook his body as their skin touched. That was his litmus test for really being able to stand physical contact. The pre-Shane and the post-Shane parts of Matt's mind wrestled with each other, fighting an unequal fight. Though it was younger, even a newborn, the post-Shane mind brimmed over with strength.

"Shh, it's okay. Relax."

So the fight raged on Matt's outside as well, but the low vibrations of Shane's voice flowed through him, ending the skirmish for good. His trembling stopped.

Matt nodded. Then with the slightest movement of his hand, he explored this unknown territory. Short brown hair curled into tiny locks on Shane's chest and tickled his palm. He giggled. "Your pec feels so firm." He increased the pressure, probing the muscles.

Now Shane chuckled. "If you say so."

With a broad grin on his face, Matt nodded once more. He eyed Shane's arm. "May I touch your biceps?" He felt like a kid who had overcome his fear of a steep slide. Now he just wanted to use it over and over again.

"You don't have to ask. Indulge yourself!" Shane stretched out his arm.

Matt lifted his hand off the pec and let his fingers glide over a protruding vein on Shane's biceps. There were so many details to take in. His own arm was one smooth shape, but numerous bumps, dents, and skeins littered Shane's. A landscape of mountains and valleys extended before him, just waiting to be mapped. Like his chest, the biceps felt firm, yet the skin was smooth and silky to the touch. Matt looked up, and they beamed at each other.

"Can you flex it, please?" Matt wanted it all. Shane had been right; these muscles meant no danger. They were artworks. Different from the trinkets he made himself, but definitely art that required as much dedication and effort.

Shane's smile faded, and he furrowed his brows. "Of course, but are you sure that you…." He swallowed. "Perhaps that's a little too much for you." He shrugged with one shoulder only. "I'm sorry. I didn't mean to patronize you."

"You worry for me. I understand that." Understanding didn't quite nail it, for Matt's brain wasn't involved at all. The warm place inside let him feel how much Shane cared, and this insight rang truer than anything he had ever grasped by logic. "Show me, please."

Shane nodded, and glee dimpled his cheeks. He looked at Matt but seemed to see right through him, as if he concentrated on images before his inner eye. His hand closed into a fist before he brought his lower and upper arm into a right angle. The size of the biceps under Matt's hand more than doubled.

"Wow," Matt whispered. "It's larger than my head… and not frightening at all," he hurried to add. Still, this sight stirred him. Gooseflesh covered every square inch of his skin. He felt delight, a little awe, and this unnamed emotion that seemed to originate from the warm place.

"It's really okay for you?" Shane turned those words into a mix of question and statement. His eyes focused again, and his face went ablaze with a shimmer that Matt could only call bliss.

He had to feel more of Shane.

Indulge yourself!

He had permission to touch Shane everywhere, so he didn't have to hold back. Slowly Matt raised his other hand and placed it on Shane's scar, tracing it with his index and middle finger. Shane's stubble scratched along his skin. The scar itself was soft, and the stitches formed a regular pattern like markings on a road.

Shane closed his eyes. "I've allowed no one to touch it, with the exception of the doctors and my parents."

Matt had gone too far, and a cold feeling like dew freezing on a winter window crawled over his back. "I'm sorry!" he whispered and jerked his hand away, but Shane gently pushed it back onto his cheek.

"And you." Shane opened his eyes again.

One touch and two words sufficed to burst everything inside him. Shane's eyes shone with friendliness, yet his gaze bored directly into Matt's mind. It cut right through every thought, and nothing that had ever occurred to him could hide from it. Matt lowered his head. He had nothing to conceal, but what if Shane found the warm place or realized that he was the one who kept it burning? He had to say something to break the silence and to distract

Shane from the traitorous chaos running inside him. Still, Shane's body before him—its muscles, the tats—kept him from thinking.

In this messy stream of consciousness, a single detail caught his attention. This was the anchor he needed to drag himself out of the current. "Who does the angel wing tattoo stand for?"

CHAPTER THIRTEEN

SHANE'S EARS rang like they did after a loud bang, but the soft sound of Matt's voice asking the wrong question had caused it. Or had he asked the right question? Telling Matt about Jer meant telling him everything. Shane couldn't come out to him, not after literally making Matt feel him up. He was punished again for gorging himself on his touch.

Matt gaped at him, and he couldn't know that his question wasn't nearly as innocent as his gaze. He screwed his eyes up as the seconds ticked away without anything happening. "Did I say something wrong?" He took a step backward, drawing his hands away from Shane's arm and face.

The fear had returned. Not full-out panic as before but a discomfort that tensed Matt's body. For Shane, this was the worst punishment possible.

He bowed forward and grabbed Matt's shoulders. Matt went rigid.

"Don't move away from me! Please!" Pleading for Matt to stay was contradicted by clutching him. If Shane didn't give him a choice, there was no point in asking. He couldn't hold on to Matt's mind anyway. He let his arms drop and his head with them.

"I won't go away." Matt placed his hands around the back of Shane's head and pressed him close to his chest.

The beat of Matt's heart, though accelerated and excited, patted Shane's mind and soothed him. He couldn't ask Matt to stay close if he didn't let him in. "His name's Jer, Jeremiah, but he hates his full name." Did he hate it as much as he hated Shane? "He's the one I broke Hayden's—the jock's—arms for."

"The blond guy in the photo over the stairway?" Listening to Matt's voice through his body sounded strange, like hearing it from far away.

Matt was so observant. He had noticed the picture, yet he hadn't asked about it. The sad conclusion was that fear had prevented him from doing so. Just another reason to tell him more but not all. "Yes, that's him." In that photo, everything was still all right. His mom had taken it before the prom. Before he had confessed that he loved Jer. Before Hayden's attack.

"You became friends after you saved him?"

That would've made a nice plot for a romantic movie. The dreadful giant pining after Prince Charming of the Misfits but stays unnoticed. Then the fateful evening on which the giant saves the prince. Love ensues. The end. Reality just loved to be a bad sport, though. "No. We were friends before, but I told Jer things he couldn't deal with. Things about me." Those *things* had made Jer back off and scream at Shane to not touch him ever again. "I cannot tell you. Not yet, but I will tell you."

Matt caressed his head, and Shane nestled up against his chest.

"It's okay. You don't have to."

"I will. I promise." The question was whether it got easier or harder to tell as more time passed. The right moment for a coming-out just didn't exist. Shane wasn't a coward, but the thought of not spending any more time with Matt felt like the marrow was being scratched out of his bones.

"What happened?" Matt let Shane's hair curl through his fingers.

"He cut our friendship and ran away, directly into Hayden's arms." In reality's plot, the giant defeats the evil jock, but the prince never speaks a word to the giant again after forming a pact not to reveal what happened that evening. Perhaps reality was the better screenwriter after all.

"I won't go away, because a guy who fights for someone who gave up on him deserves better."

Matt's words trickled through Shane's skin and spread through his body, making him feel hot and cold at the same time. The angel's wing didn't convey Jer's true nature. Shane had wasted that symbol on the wrong person. Still, it would always remind him of looking more closely before passing a judgment and that the cliché of love rendering men blind wasn't one.

"Matt, honey, did you put that shirt into the dryer?"

With a jolt, Shane sat upright on the bed. Matt's hand still hovered in the air where his head had been. On his face, another sho-prise showed, but this one tended more toward shock. They both turned to look at the door.

A middle-aged female version of Matt entered the room, the only difference being her burgundy-colored pageboy hairstyle. She stopped dead in her tracks, and her eyes widened. It was eerie, for an almost one-to-one reenactment of Matt returning to his room only minutes ago played out before them.

Matt took a step toward her, almost like shielding Shane from his mother.

"Mom, this is Shane. I told you about my friend from school."

Shane's gaze darted to Matt. For the first time, he had called him a friend. Shane smiled and couldn't help it. *Oh fuck!* He was sitting half-naked in front of Matt's mother. Miss Manners certainly didn't have a rule for a situation like this. He jumped up from the bed and regretted it immediately, for Mrs. Dermond's eyes grew even wider as she saw him at full height.

"Nice to meet you, Mrs. Dermond." Shane extended his hand and cursed the size of his paws. If pure will alone had been enough to make limbs shrink, his hand would've vanished by now.

For some seconds, nothing happened except Mrs. Dermond's gaze switching between Matt, Shane's hand, and the shirt. In her face, every muscle kept working. She wouldn't return the handshake, so why was he still holding out his hand? For a situation like this, there had to be a Miss Manners rule, but he didn't know it anyway.

"It's still wet." Mrs. Dermond draped the shirt over Shane's arm without touching him.

"Mom! You—"

"Thanks, Mrs. Dermond." Shane interrupted him, because however his sentence continued, it wouldn't make the situation any better. He pulled the shirt over his head, but getting his arms through the sleeves had never taken this long. The two people staring at him didn't speed up the dressing either. He finally succeeded, and the wet fabric sticking to his skin wasn't the most uncomfortable sensation here.

Meeting Matt's mother couldn't have gone worse. But the encounter hadn't ended yet, so there were plenty of possibilities to make it even more unpleasant. At least she hadn't walked in on them while Matt explored his body. That would've been hard to explain, and Matt definitely didn't need any more trouble. Life was complicated enough for him without his parents breathing down his neck with suspicions about being gay.

"Honey, could you help us bring the groceries inside?" Mrs. Dermond only looked at her son. Though Shane didn't know her, he had an idea what she was trying to tell Matt with her eyes.

"Shane can help. You'll help us, won't you?" Matt's voice had that distinct sound of a kid invoking pester power.

He meant well, but the more he pushed, the more his mom would resist. That was Shane's law of repulsion, gleaned from years of experience with panicky people. Still, he couldn't blame Matt for his heroic desire to fight for him. Was Matt aware of the reversal of roles and the irony therein?

"You can't ask one of your guests to do your work." Mrs. Dermond's gaze shifted from pleading to commanding.

"I'm afraid I have to go anyway." A situation was really fucked-up when it could only be mended by a lie, even if this excuse helped to calm the tense moment between a son and his mom. Moreover, a liar was really fucked-up if he justified the untruth with a greater good.

"Can you please see your schoolmate out, honey? I'll go help your dad." Mrs. Dermond faced Shane, but her gaze rested on Matt. She nodded curtly, turned around, and scurried out of the room.

"I'm sorry for this." The corners of Matt's mouth drooped. He looked at Shane.

The term *having the blues* had to be inspired by eyes like those. Shane couldn't leave with this picture being the last memory of Matt until Monday.

"Don't worry. This was one of the more pleasant first meetings I've had." Strangely enough, he wasn't even lying. "You know I have to grow on people. And yes, pun intended this time."

"You're a big chunk to chew on." Matt flashed a grin. "That's right."

A smiling Matt was a much better memento for this morning than gloomy Matt, though Shane would have a hard time forgetting about this day at all. If he concentrated enough, the memory of Matt's fingers grazing his skin almost felt like the real thing.

Shane made a fist and stretched out his arm. "That's worth another fist bump."

A sly way to rake in another touch, but the corners of Matt's mouth rose a little more as their fists connected. So Shane didn't have much reason for feeling remorse. He had felt guilty for such a long time that a little break was overdue. When he looked at Matt's face, glowing with happiness, the idea of the guilt gone forever one day didn't seem that absurd at all.

MATT CLOSED the door behind Shane. His mom had asked him to help with the groceries, but if he saw her now, he'd tell her right to her face what a hypocritical liar she was.

It's not what's on the outside that counts.

It was her mantra. A false mantra.

She had used it to calm him when the kids in kindergarten kept laughing at him for being so small. She had repeated it when Aunt Monica lost her hair due to chemo. She had prayed it when his dad had been unemployed and they could only afford secondhand clothes.

The mantra was only applicable to others, because if it worked against her, she just forgot about it.

Matt's heart hammered up into his throat, and his fists closed by themselves. He couldn't stand being in the same room with her or even looking at her now.

Worst of all, Matt was guilty of the same unfair behavior she was. He had suspected Shane of being a more vicious version of Iain, a dumb jock two-point-oh. Like his mom, he had stared at him, had avoided touching him, and had simply been afraid for all the wrong reasons. A glowing white hole formed in Matt's guts, a burning sensation of restlessness. What if he just ran after Shane, hugged him as tight as he could, and apologized once more for her ridiculous shenanigans?

He reached out for the doorknob.

"Honey, your dad and I want to talk to you about… this guy." The fingernails-on-blackboard tone that she usually reserved for moments of being righteously enraged about nothing rang in her voice.

The knob felt cold in Matt's hand, and the throbbing of his heart made his fingers twitch up and down. He just had to turn it around and leave the house, but he only ran away in the outside world, not at home or from home. In any case, he couldn't evade this confrontation.

"His name's Shane." Matt let his hand glide off the knob. He closed his eyes and took a deep breath before turning around. After breathing once more, he opened his eyes again.

His parents stood side by side, both making faces, as if telling him someone had died. Apparently she had succeeded in setting his dad against Shane. At least his mom had met him face-to-face, but it made a fool out of his dad that he passed judgment on someone he didn't know. As if wearing a suit and tie for the weekly Saturday shopping didn't suffice for that.

Matt and his parents remained silent. Did they expect him to justify inviting Shane here? He wouldn't grant them that satisfaction.

"You didn't tell us that he's that type of guy." She rolled statement, accusation, and conviction all into one.

The burning sensation from his guts crawled up his throat. "What type of guy? I told you he's muscular, that he's got tattoos and a scar. I even told you he had to do community service for coming to the defense of someone. Someone like me. What did I leave out?"

His mom shook her head. "He isn't muscular; he got slabs of muscles. He hasn't got tattoos; he is a walking picture book. Moreover, the scar covers half of his face. No normal guy looks like this, only brutes and criminals. No one is sentenced to community service for nothing, and that defense of others nonsense is only his side of the story."

Matt's hands closed to fists again, and his fingernails sank into his flesh. Focusing on the pain helped him to not scream at her. "And you learned he's a brute because you took your time to talk to him? Oh wait, you only told him that his shirt was still wet. Or are all people who smile at you and offer you a handshake criminals? Of course, all inked people are notorious liars, though I have to admit that lying is something you really know about."

"Watch your tone, young man." His dad raised his index finger. "You're talking to your mother."

"My mother"—Matt sneered out those words—"wouldn't snub my best friend." Best friend. Only friend. All the same for him, but how would his parents know about his social life or lack thereof? And why their sudden interest? They hadn't cared before, and there was no need to do so now. Matt had watched out for himself, and he'd fared well without their meddling.

"You can have better company than him. What about that Hispanic girl?" His mom tilted her head and smiled.

So Florenca being a Latina was the only thing she remembered about her? She wasn't only a hypocrite, but also a racist in disguise. "I'm a walking library and a free tutor for her. In the weeks we have known each other, Shane has done more for me than she has in years."

His mom advanced a step forward and spread her arms. "But he's already having a bad influence on you, honey. You never talked back before you knew him."

"Because before him, there was nothing worth talking back for." During dinner, the Dermonds discussed Matt's accomplishments at school, his dad's new contracts at work, and his mom's latest acquisitions for her garden. Even the parish newsletter brimmed with more potential for controversy than their family matters. He never told them about the bruises that Iain had given him or why he ate three servings of chili and was still skinny as a rail. Don't ask, don't tell had been invented by their family.

"We're only worried." His dad laid his hands on her shoulders. "Your mom thinks it'd be a good idea if you stopped seeing him."

She nodded.

The blood drawn by his nails felt warm running down his fingers. Matt shook his head. "No," he whispered. Giving up Shane was not an option. He'd rather cut open his veins with a chisel. "I'm turning nineteen next month. A little late for picking my friends, isn't it?" His voice came out even and calm, as if his throat had detached from the rest of his body and mind. It formed the eye of the storm that was his insides. "I will not and I cannot dump Shane." Matt's life had centered around adaptation and fluidity. Following the flow and hiding in it had kept him well and sane. Yet he had deformed so much, he didn't recognize himself at times. Only around Shane did his self become solid and he was Matt, simply Matt. Sure, woodworking gave him peace, but he paid for it with emptiness.

His mom pressed her eyes into slits and knitted her brows. "You're right. You're old enough to make your own mistakes. We cannot keep you from seeing him, but he won't come here again. I don't want rabble like him in my house."

Her last sentence was a slap to Matt's face. No, it stung worse than a blow. How embarrassing to share half his genes with this woman! From her he had adopted the mind-set of judging people without knowing them. Iain might have had his share in developing this habit, yet his mom had lived it right before his eyes. It may have saved him a bruise or two, but how many opportunities had he let pass by because of fear? What if that narrow-mindedness had prevented him from getting to know Shane? An icy sensation crawled up his spine and made him shiver.

His dad looked down at his mom. He opened his mouth but closed it without saying anything. So Matt wasn't the only coward in this family who followed the path of least resistance. *No.* From this day on, he'd never follow that path again.

"But I want you to know"—her face relaxed, and she smiled, tilting her head again—"you can always come to us if anything is wrong."

That was the end of this discussion. They would never talk about Shane again. When they ate mashed potatoes and sausages this evening, they'd chat about Matt's geometry course, his dad's negotiations with that big law firm, and his mom's new gardenias as if this scene had never happened. Don't ask, don't tell. It didn't matter. He had Shane to talk to about the important stuff. Shane might have secrets, but so did Matt. Feeling that nameless emotion, for example.

Chapter Fourteen

THE ONLY good thing about this Monday morning was that Shane would see Matt anytime now. Over the weekend, his mood had taken so many swings that he felt tired and exhausted. He had been down when he brought back the box, then up when Matt urged him to keep it, and even more up when Matt's fingers had wandered over his body. The touching of his scar had caused the sensation of a thousand little embers right beneath his skin, warming him on the inside and making him shine on the outside. In hindsight, even confessing about Jer had liberated him, though his coming-out was now looming over him as his personal sword of Damocles. Meeting Matt's mother had been another damper for sure, but people just took time to get used to him. Matt was the best example of this.

It had been the night from Saturday to Sunday that had really fucked with him. Every time he closed his eyes, the memory of Matt's touch resurfaced and eliminated everything else from his mind. Each nerve remembered the skin-on-skin contact and was overzealous to boast about this experience, telling its neural friends over and over again how absolutely fricking awesome it had felt. Shane's southern regions, normally not impressed that easily, had given standing ovations, but jacking off to Matt was so off-limits that it didn't fit on any map—one of those ancient maps with the warnings about dragons and monsters written on the edges. Those beasts lurked beyond the Sea of Kinkiness. Shane had gotten up and trained instead with way too many arm curls and what felt like hours of skipping rope. Ultimately, he dropped to his bed and fell asleep before his head hit the pillow. Yet Matt had hijacked his dreams. Though Shane couldn't even remember what they had been about, one of them had turned wet. The last accident of this kind had happened when he was fourteen. He was more than glad that he knew how to operate the washing machine and that his parents loved to sleep late on Sunday mornings.

Shane's arms still hurt from the curls, and the nagging thought of getting off on a fantasy about Matt just wouldn't leave him alone. Technically he hadn't done anything wrong, though. So much for the guilt gone for good.

He definitely wouldn't tell Estelle about wetting his sheets, because she'd smile her haughty smile, and then she'd flaunt her infallible insights about the nature of love. Matt was a friend only, and Shane wasn't one of those sex-crazed bonobo apes that couldn't control themselves. If he channeled the surplus energy into even more training, he'd reach his goals for this year by the end of October and the ones for next year by the end of November.

Matt turned the corner leading to the main entrance of the schoolyard. It didn't matter how deep Shane was lost in thought or how many other people crowded the street, Matt's small frame worked as a beacon, attracting his attention and making him smile. His brain released the cocktail of hormones that he had nicknamed "liquid happiness," powerful enough to melt the pain, the tiredness, and the guilt away. Shane was a Matt-aholic, and proving Estelle wrong required confessions like these. The more he admitted how much Matt affected him, the easier it was to keep a grip on those feelings. Shane startled. He had been wiggling from side to side on his feet without noticing. No, he couldn't deny the Matt effect.

Something bothered Matt. He dragged his feet, and his head hung low, almost touching the cups on the cardboard tray he carried.

"Hey." Matt looked up for a second, he even smiled, but his chin went down to his chest right away.

"What's up?" This pitiful sight urged Shane to wrap his arms around Matt and keep away whatever was getting him down. Unfortunately he was most likely a part of the problem.

Matt shrugged and sniffed air through his nose. "It's nothing." He placed the tray on the low wall around the schoolyard.

Shane knelt down, tilted his head, and looked up at Matt. "It's not nothing. As your friend, you can, no, you have to tell me." He put his hand on Matt's shoulder. Perhaps that wasn't too good an idea, because Shane's crotch remembered that weekend as well. For once his brain and heart teamed up against the down low, chiding it for drooling over an upset friend like an asshole.

Another smile flashed over Matt's face, and he placed his hand on Shane's. Fine lines, like spider silk, spread from his eyes and shooed away the smile. "Even if you know that what you have to tell will make your friend sad?"

Shane curled his fingers on Matt's shoulder, squeezing it as carefully as he could. The muscles in his shoulder were tied up in knots, and Shane continued to massage it with gentle rubs. "Seeing you like this already makes me sad. If speaking your heart helps you, then yes, tell me."

Matt laid his head to the side and rested it on his own hand. Shane's brain and heart sighed in relief. If Matt's hand hadn't acted as a buffer, that touch would've caused an uproar below Shane's belly button that the allied organs couldn't have controlled anymore.

"My parents"—Matt raised his head—"banned you from their house." He whispered those words but stressed every single one with sad gravity.

Not "home," not "our house," but "their house." However devastating the message was, those two words removed any doubt about how Matt felt about the situation. What he thought about him was the only thing that mattered. Shane squeezed Matt's shoulder once more. "That's okay. At least they didn't order you to not see me again."

Matt heaved a sigh. "They tried."

The tidal forces of opposing feelings threatened to rip Shane apart. Matt had decided for him, making Shane's brain release a little more liquid happiness. On the other hand, he didn't want to drive a wedge between Matt and his parents, and bitterness mixed into his mood. "Your parents are only protecting you. They don't know me, and I'm scary as hell." He put his other hand on Matt's shoulder, holding him tight. "You don't have to fight my fights."

"Like you do for me?" Matt looked at him. The innocent blueness of his eyes turned dull as it filled up with grief.

Shane couldn't contradict what Matt had said, though he became aware of this double standard only now. It was a matter of course that he protected Matt from Iain, but now that his little friend had his own battlefield, Shane didn't want him there. "Actually, I haven't fought for you." Telling Iain to fuck off in the cafeteria didn't count as a fight. "You—" He shook Matt once for emphasis. "—struggled down your tear, and you're battling with the memories of your past each day. You're the fighter. I'm only here for backup." As the strange novelty of Matt acting on Shane's behalf wore off, a sensation of lightness took its place. If Matt cared enough about him to confront his parents, what else might he be able to do?

Matt blinked in rapid succession. "You're more than a backup. You keep me going in the first place." A radiant light drove the sadness out of his eyes, tinting the space between them in the lightest of blue.

"Ditto." Shane's cheeks hurt from grinning. "A prime example of symbiosis."

"You're such a nerd." Matt guffawed. "A brawny nerd." His laughing made his body shake.

"I can't refute that." This was how Shane wanted to see Matt, sassy and happy, but Matt's life had to be good as a whole. "Regarding your parents, is there anything I can do to help the situation? I could ask Nick to talk to them or, even better, Estelle." Sending his own parents would only convey a fishy impression. "If another adult tells them about me, they might be more willing to listen."

The amusement faded from Matt's face, but a hint of it remained—just enough to brighten his features. He shook his head. "That's not how my mom ticks. She only listens to herself. Even Dad doesn't stand a chance once she has made up her mind." He shrugged, making Shane's hand dance up and down with Matt's shoulders. "Then again, she's so in need of harmony that you won't be a topic anytime soon."

Shane's parents never stopped talking about anything that irritated them. Two families, two ways of dealing with things. "I just don't want to cause you any more trouble."

"You won't"—Matt laid his hands on the sleeves of Shane's shirt—"but I might be late for the first time in my school life if we don't get in soon." He let his hands drop.

Fortunately the fabric of the sleeves had kept their skins from touching. This would've caused another crotch riot for sure. "I definitely don't want to be responsible for spoiling your perfect record." Shane took his hands off Matt's shoulders. Not an easy feat because it felt as if someone had glued them in place. Having something to busy his all-too-sticky fingers with, Shane reached for the cups and passed over the one with Matt's name on it.

"Thanks." Matt took the coffee. "And not only for this." He raised the cup and smiled the warmest, most affectionate smile Shane had ever been gifted with.

So it didn't require touching to draw the interest down south. Shane turned around and stepped behind Matt, hoping his... predicament went unnoticed. "You're welcome." He ignored his sleazy part's suggestion of putting his hand on Matt's back and pretending to shove him on. "Let's go."

This was all about self-control, but given the rate Matt's presence used up Shane's determination, it was also about time to worry. Yet all those feelings in Shane took up so much space already that they didn't leave any room for worries.

SHANE WALKED through empty school halls while all the other students cheered on their basketball team in a scrimmage. He was on his way to pick up Matt, who waited at his locker. Shane's crotch had kept its peace since this morning, and he had had enough time to prepare mentally before seeing him again. Hopefully. The weird idea that spending even more time with Matt might help had occurred to him, like getting an overdose. But Matt could as well be the living equivalent of chocolate. It didn't matter how much Shane had already eaten, he could always stuff in another bar.

He sighed.

If he had to give up Matt, it'd feel like cutting off his own foot. As a last resort, he had to let Matt decide by telling him that he was gay and how attracted he was to him. Hoping history didn't repeat itself verged on wishful thinking, regardless of how much Jer and Matt differed. And resisting the temptation would ultimately mean that he and Matt would stay close and become even closer. He cringed at the crudeness of this logic, but it helped him to not scream out loud and to not punch holes in the metal doors of the lockers he passed by.

Shane had to free his mind of those dark musings, so he headed for one of the restrooms. He turned on the cold water and splashed some of it onto his face. His reflection looked back at him from the mirror, and he watched the water drops running down his scar. It had never looked more hideous than it did right now. Still, Matt had touched it and hadn't shown any signs of disgust. Shane traced the crimson flesh with his index finger and closed his eyes. It was still so easy to pretend that it was Matt's hand on his face. He opened his eyes, pooled another handful of water, and cast it onto his skin. The cold liquid stung his cheeks, but the pain ousted the thoughts that threatened to overrun his mind. He had no reason to despair. Matt was his friend, even a good enough friend to oppose his parents. What else did he need? He wouldn't allow his horniness to ruin something as precious as this friendship.

A clanking noise echoed through the blue-tiled room. It came from the door, and Shane turned his head, but no one entered. Another person scared off by him? Shane preferred no one see him in this state anyway. He turned the faucet off, took a disposable towel from the dispenser, and dried his face and hands. Matt was waiting for him, and he couldn't get any more prepared than he was now. He took one last look in the mirror to test his smile. Convincing enough. Shane turned around and pressed the door handle down, but it didn't budge. If the janitor had locked the room, the handle should still work, shouldn't it? He pressed it again, using more force. The wood of the door groaned, but nothing happened.

"Fuck!" Shane bellowed.

The one door he was behind broke and jammed itself. How fricking likely was that?

A freezing feeling crawled away from Shane's spine like icy tentacles clutching his back.

"No!" The severity of his conclusion sucked up the sound of his voice.

If he called the janitor to get him out of here, it'd take too long. The small room didn't allow for a running start, so breaking open the door wouldn't work either. He wasn't *that* strong. Though he felt cold, droplets of sweat rolled down his back. He jerked his head from left to right. There had to be something he could use to bust the door open, but the sparse fixtures of the room wouldn't help him at all.

The window!

He was on the second floor, but given his height, it wasn't too far of a drop. He dashed over to the window and yanked it open. Shane skipped checking the ground for lack of time, grabbed the sill, and hauled himself over it. This wasn't any different from chin-ups, only the other way round. He extended his arms as long as he could before he let go of the sill. Crouching down, he absorbed most of the impact as he landed in a flowerbed of red dahlias, but a burning pang jolted through his kneecaps. Shane clenched his teeth, jumped up, and ran off. He just had to ignore the pain. Hopefully Matt was still somewhere close to his locker.

CHAPTER FIFTEEN

MATT CLOSED his locker and looked at his watch. Shane should arrive anytime now. He was never late, and he was never angry or upset about anything. If Shane had told him that his parents wouldn't allow him into their house anymore, that would've devastated him, but not Shane. He worried more about Matt and the relationship between him and his parents. Shane's reaction rendered his mom's behavior even more ridiculous.

Enough about this.

He had turned that problem over in his mind for the whole day, without new results. His mom wouldn't budge, and whether he wanted it to be true or not, he was as stubborn as she was. Since the Dermond house had been declared a DSZ, a de-Shane-erized zone, he would make it a DMZ, a de-Matt-erized zone. It wasn't the safe haven it used to be if his parents wouldn't allow in the only person who really cared about him.

Somehow he had to make up for how his mom had treated Shane. They could do something together next weekend, but what? He didn't do much of the stuff people of their age were supposed to do. What was the last movie he had seen in a cinema? He had never visited a club and didn't even know which one was hot and which one was not. Perhaps Shane knew?

Shane smelled so good this morning.

The voices inside Matt never stopped talking as long as Shane was on his mind. Or reminded Matt of him if he wasn't.

Would Shane let me touch him again?

At least they spoke up one after another most of the time now, though they talked nonsense or raised silly questions. He didn't need that.

How would it feel to be touched in return?

Thoughts like these had never occurred to him before, and he defiled the friendship with Shane by having them.

If he was honest with himself, spending the weekend with Shane wasn't about apologizing for his mom's behavior but about being close to him. Each time he made a confession like this, the voices shut up for a while, as their only reason for existence seemed to be annoying him with inconvenient truths. Their silence served as a self-rewarding system for honesty. His mind was indeed a very strange place and worked in even stranger ways.

Then there was Shane's secret. What was terrible enough that it had driven Jer away? Matt had assured Shane he didn't have to tell him, but he was a nerd. Secrets and nerds just didn't go well together.

One of the voices in his head spoke up again, but it wasn't talking about Shane for a change. It didn't actually use words and sounded more like someone breathing into his ear. His hackles rose. Run. He should run.

A hand grabbed him by his shoulder. Without turning around, he knew it wasn't Shane, because those fingers held him too hard, and the touch felt all wrong.

"My dear Matty, what a coincidence."

Matt had recognized Iain even before he had spoken up. Yet the fear didn't come. The stream of his consciousness continued, even heightened as it focused into a single strand of perfect awareness.

"It's so difficult lately to have a nice little talk just between the two of us." Iain spun Matt around. The slyness of his smirk left the scale, looked unreal like a comic book villain's evil grin, and Matt almost cracked up.

"Shane will be here anytime now." His voice became the audible extension of his composure. Matt's fear had prevented him from realizing it during any of the many incidents before, but the childishness of Iain's games stuck out now. No one outside of this school would respect such a dork. Matt could only pity him.

"I fear you're mistaken." Iain wagged the index finger of his other hand. "Your watch bulldog won't be joining us today."

"You're lying." That sounded much surer than Matt was, but Iain was just trying to get under his skin. Only his old self would've fallen for a trap like this.

"The bad company of Mr. McAllistair is already ruining your manners, Matty." Iain pouted and tilted his head like a snake sizing up its prey. "It kinda hurts my feelings when you call me a liar. As if I ever lied to you."

In fact, Iain had done about everything to Matt, but he had never lied. It hadn't been necessary, and it wasn't necessary now. A blitz of coldness jolted through Matt's body. "If you've hurt him…."

Iain's grip on his shoulder tightened, and the pain made Matt suck in air through his clenched teeth.

The smirk on Iain's face vanished, and he narrowed his eyes to slits. "In your place, I'd be more worried about myself."

Now Iain was mistaken. Only Shane mattered. Matt's blood had turned into icy shards, and his stomach had become molten sulfur. Yet the single thread of awareness and the tranquility remained, and he clung tightly to both of them. He had to remain strong, not for himself, but for Shane.

Tyler and Eric weren't here and were probably keeping Shane away. This coward left the dirty work to his henchmen. Just more reasons to pity him. Still, not having backup constituted a weakness. The time had come for Matt to play some childish games himself.

"Touch me and Principal Wagner will learn about everything. Every slap, every bruise, every bite of food you ever took from me." More. He needed more. Something that'd hit really hard. "I have copies of every essay I wrote for you and your gang of dumbasses."

Iain dug his fingers deeper into Matt's sweater and pulled him close. The warm air of his breath wafted into Matt's face. "You wouldn't dare."

Bingo! "With your academic record and without a full baseball grant, colleges won't even touch you with tweezers." Matt brought himself closer to Iain until their faces almost touched. "Principal Wagner is notorious for dealing with cheaters... like you." He hissed out the last words.

Iain's fist connected with Matt's cheek. A scrunching noise rumbled through his skull, and a twinge ran down the overstretched muscles of his neck. The iron taste of blood in his mouth turned his stomach around. Static filled his ears while white stars went nova in the darkness behind his closed lids.

No punch had ever hit harder, yet it hurt less than all of them.

Matt controlled this situation, had wrested it away from Iain, and tricked him into making a mistake. The foul stench of Iain's breath kept blowing into his face as he forced his eyes open. He felt the bloody saliva running down his chin and croaked out a single laugh. "No visible wounds. Forgot that?"

Iain opened his hand, and Matt's legs gave way under him. He dropped to his knees.

"I'll kill you!"

He looked up at Iain. These weren't empty words, but Matt had won, no matter what. Iain had run out of moves, and every action he took would only make things worse for him. "Checkmate." A grin, surely crimson from the blood, came about on Matt's lips. This was how victory felt.

Iain just stood there, breathing shallowly. Tremors shook him, and shiny beads of sweat rolled down his pale face.

A blurred shape shot past Matt and smashed Iain into the row of lockers. Shane, using all of his body, pinned him against the maroon metal. Iain's face contorted in pain.

"I'll rip you apart, you fucking son of a bitch." Shane was panting and forced each syllable out on a single gasp of air.

"No," Matt whispered. He had to stop this. With both hands, he reached out for the locker and pulled himself to a stand. Halfway up, his knees gave out again, though he never reached the floor.

Still pressing Iain to the locker, Shane held Matt by his armpits. He stared at him with eyes wide. His lips shivered, but no words came out.

"Please, don't," Matt said.

The punch, nothing that Iain had ever done, had hurt as much as the sorrow in Shane's eyes cutting through Matt's heart. It was the look of a wounded animal, broken and despairing.

"You're better than him." Shane was, but Matt couldn't say the same about himself anymore. He had acted as cruelly as Iain, perhaps even more so. Words hit harder than fists and left venom in the wounds they cut, slowly consuming their victim from the inside. Matt turned his head to look at Iain. Fear showed in his eyes, and it wasn't Shane he was afraid of. "We're even."

He and Iain held their gazes. They had come to an agreement without needing a single word and sealed it with a nod.

"Let him go, please." Matt faced Shane again and smiled, putting the weight back on his feet and relieving Shane from the burden of holding him.

Ever so slowly, Shane released Iain. His arms sank down. Iain wheeled around and staggered for a few steps before he darted away as fast as his wiry baseballer legs could carry him.

Matt kept looking at the intersection of halls where Iain had vanished. It didn't feel like a victory anymore.

"I would've killed him for you."

The second death threat within minutes. Once more, those weren't empty words.

"I know." Yet this time Matt cared. "Jer might be able to live with letting you take the blame." He switched his gaze to Shane. "I am not."

The sadness held Shane's face in a firm grip, rendering his usually friendly features hard and lifeless. "But unlike Jer, I failed to protect you. Twice." Shane sobbed out the last word, and tears coursed down his cheeks. One of them followed the outline of his scar, leaving behind a red trail of wetness. He reached out for Matt's face and caressed the spot where Iain's fist had connected, a bruise already forming on the throbbing skin for sure. "I am sorry." Shane went down to his knees and slung his arms around Matt, pulling him tight. "So sorry."

Shane's warmth soaked into Matt. His smell, that mix of laundry detergent, shower gel, and musk, drove out all other sensations. The firmness of Shane's muscles against his body was tangible safety. "Shhh. You didn't fail me." Shane had unlocked Matt's strength. Only for him, Matt had led the battle against Iain. He had never cared for himself enough to fight back, but for Shane, he hadn't hesitated for a split second to do what was necessary. *Necessary?* Shane couldn't know that he had also saved Matt from his dark side. The part of him that had enjoyed torturing Iain, the part that had grinned its bloody grin and hadn't given a damn whether Matt lived or died. Shane's mere presence tamed that darkness and drove it back into the cave where it had come from. "You never will."

"I'm failing you right now!" The warm breeze of Shane's breath swept over Matt's ear as he whispered those words. "The things I told Jer, which sent him running...." His voice was frail and broke on every word. "I had feelings for him, much deeper than friendship." The volume of his voice dropped to one notch above silence. "I have the same feelings for you." Shane opened his arms.

Matt's heart pounded so fast that its beats flowed together and mingled into a buzzing drone. His head swam from the voices talking over one another. The warm place. The unnamed emotion.

Desire.

This had to be its name, had to be the truth, for this word hushed the voices.

Matt leaned back. More tears gushed out of Shane's closed eyes, though the sadness in his face had left and a detached emptiness had replaced it.

It had taken so long to solve the puzzle of the unnamed emotion, but the solution dazzled Matt even more. He didn't know what to make of it, for nothing in his life had prepared him for this. Was this uncertainty part of the answer? In the poems and plays he craved so much, the lovers didn't know either. They just loved.

Matt let his hands glide through the dark mass of Shane's hair until his fingertips met at the back of his head. He bent forward and placed his lips on Shane's, the salt of the tears burning his sore flesh.

This was the answer. This was the truth. This was desire.

SHANE HAD snapped. It was the only reasonable explanation for what was going on. He couldn't cope with another guy running away from him. His mind had collapsed, making things up to soothe the pain.

If this were nothing but totally fabricated bullshit in his head, why did Matt's mouth taste like blood? Why did his knees still burn from crashing down into the flowerbed and running through the school? Why was he still crying?

It was fucking real, happening right now. This realization rushed through Shane's cells, every single one of them, turning them into goo as it passed. He was melting, and gravity threatened to dissolve him, but Matt's hands on the back of his head held him together. From the tips of his fingers flowed a magnetism that gave Shane form.

Though Matt pressed his lips onto his, they weren't kissing yet, as if Matt waited for a sign, seeking permission to proceed.

Shane opened his mouth slightly and let the tip of his tongue skim along the outline of Matt's lips. Nothing that his tongue ever touched had felt so soft. This was cream and honey molded into flesh and blood.

Matt flinched, retreated for a fraction of an inch, but in the next moment, he pulled Shane in with his hands. He parted his lips and let his tongue imitate what Shane's had done. A moan escaped from him, a warm stream of pleasure trickling into Shane.

His arms acted all by themselves as they slung around Matt and enclosed him in a tight embrace. Matt's small frame fit into them, as if holding him were their only purpose. Shane slipped in a little more of his tongue, eliciting another moan from Matt. The electrical current, the one he had felt when Matt had been in the McAllistair house for the first time, returned with a vengeance, creeping all over and through him. Shane's hair sizzled and stood upright from the high voltage of their touch.

Their tongues met. In small jabs and gentle circles, they explored each other, satisfying the curiosity the intriguing trespasser had piqued. Though it was their first kiss, it inhered a rhythm and harmony that came about without cumbersome words. Following their unwritten score, they drew back at the same time and looked at each other.

Matt's eyes moved restlessly, zooming over Shane's features. Though the bruise already cast a black shadow over his face, his cheeks were alight with a glow. This light was beautiful, intriguing, and expelled the last remnants of darkness from Shane's mind. A golden shine filled it up instead.

Every single muscle in Shane's face curved up his lips. A single laugh bubbled out of him. He pulled Matt close again, snuggling up against his good cheek. Matt let his hands sink down and laid them on Shane's flanks, but his arms were too short to fully return the embrace. Still, he pressed them tightly against him.

Matt felt searing hot, a glowing furnace of white heat. His smell, sweet like cotton candy and as spicy as nutmeg, sneaked into Shane's mind, almost driving him crazy with craving. It *was* crazy because nothing warranted such despair. Matt rested here, in his arms, hugging him, kissing him back—and he would stay.

Both of them had remained silent since Shane's confession, though this silence wasn't bothersome. Yet this moment called for some profound words that wrapped rationality around this entangled jumble of emotions.

"You're gay," Shane said.

Okay, those weren't the grand words this moment deserved, but he couldn't blame himself. Despite being confused as hell, the sentence hadn't come out as complete gibberish. Nothing to be proud of, but also nothing to be ashamed of.

"I think so."

Shane's words hadn't cut it, but Matt's answer didn't either. This moment convoluted into an even greater mess. Shane let go of Matt and sat back on his feet.

"What do you mean, you think so?" The second he asked that question, he didn't want to know its answer anymore.

Matt caressed his own cheek where they had cuddled up. "I've never felt like this about another boy. No, I've never felt like this about anyone." His face looked angelic with that trace of a smile on his lips.

"You must've had a crush on someone." When Shane had hit puberty, he had fallen in love with someone about every week. Things had slowed down until he ended up with Estelle's one-person heart, and then Jer entered his life. Shane may have been extreme, but even Matt, however controlled and stoic he was, couldn't escape from the power of hormonal chaos that was adolescence.

Matt's smile wavered, and the shadow of the bruise darkened his face. "Every guy was just another potential bully. If you're the school's punching bag, the girls aren't interested either. I switched—" He hesitated. "—it off." He closed his eyes.

It. Matt didn't even dare label these feelings with their only proper name.

"How can a person live without love?" Shane shook his head. Matt brimmed over with so many emotions that they bubbled out of him and made the air around him crackle with energy. He could never keep those inside.

"Do you have any idea how hard it is to know that no one will ever return your love?" Matt pressed his eyes shut. "There's fear and despair, and then one day you realize you can't bear it anymore." He opened his eyes. "It's much easier to shove those feelings into the deepest corner of your mind, to lock them up and throw away the key." A little of the smile returned. "But then you came, became my first real friend... and more." His voice pitched up, turning his words into a question.

Matt didn't just discover that he was gay. He rediscovered love, and Shane was supposed to be the one who brought it back. But he didn't possess this magical ability, so it couldn't be true. If it were, it was too much of a responsibility. Each of his puberty crushes had felt like the one and only love. Matt didn't know what he was talking about.

"That's the point. You have no idea how true friendship feels. How can you be sure that you're not confusing it with *more?*"

The color drained from Matt's face, making the bruise stand out like a dark island on a sea of white, and his mouth dropped open. "I'm not a kid anymore. I know what I feel." He furrowed his brows, and anger creased the skin around his eyes. "You claim to have these feelings for me, but all you're doing now is coming up with reasons—fake reasons—to back out. Why are you messing with me like that?

Shane had brought up those things *because* he had these feelings for Matt. Why didn't he see this? "I've promised to protect you. That's what I'm doing here. I cannot let you make a mistake you'll regret later." He reached out for Matt's arm, for a touch would convey what his words didn't, but Matt pulled away.

"Don't touch me!" Matt held his hands before him like a shield.

"Ask yourself, 'Are those feelings for real?' Friendships can run deep, and no two friendships are alike." Shane had to appeal to Matt's logic. Only this way, he would understand.

A shudder rocked Matt, and he pressed out a breathy groan. "The only mistake was ever letting you into my life. You should've ripped off my head when I crashed into you. That would've been less hurtful than playing with me." He reached into the pocket of his jeans, got his wallet out, and produced the napkin from it. "All these words are lies. Filthy lies!" Matt threw the white cloth at Shane, but it corkscrewed onto the floor without even coming close to him.

"Matt!" Ignoring his protesting knees, Shane got up from the floor.

"Keep away from me!" Matt took a stumbling step back. "Keep away from me!" He whirled around and pelted away, almost crashing into the wall as he turned right into the main hall.

That was what Jer had said. Word for word. He'd sent another person he loved running. With Jer, Shane had been too reckless. With Matt, he was too fearful. No matter what he did, the result was the same.

Matt had asked him whether he had an idea how hard it was to know that his love would never be returned. Yes, he had, and it was Shane who denied himself that love. This insight hurt even more.

Shane was kneeling on the floor again. He hadn't even noticed going down. With both hands, he reached out for the napkin and brought it to his nose, inhaling Matt's smell. His tears soaked into the white paper and smeared the ink of the lines written on it. It didn't matter. Matt was right. These were all lies, and they were not worth preserving.

CHAPTER SIXTEEN

MATT LEANED against the wall of a house a block away from school. He was panting, and the beat of his heart played a staccato on his ribs.

How dare Shane doubt the sincerity of his feelings? Matt wasn't an imbecile who couldn't tell friendship from love. Of course, calling those emotions "love" was over the top, but what he felt for Shane definitely lay on the same side of the spectrum as love. A younger sibling of love, still growing up, but he had no doubts about its true nature.

His hands clenched into fists, and his nails bore into the sores they had left on Saturday when talking to his mom. The pain soothed Matt, for it reminded him of the outside world. He just had to get out of his mind because it had turned into an inhospitable place. The voices were shouting and spewing out insults, and they targeted him, not Shane.

He was running away again… just like Jer. He had run away after the confrontation with Iain in the cafeteria. He had almost run away after his mom snubbed Shane. Running away was his answer for everything, and had it ever made things better?

Another Matt dwelled inside of him. This Matt was strong enough to confront his mom and brave enough to take on Iain. That was the Matt he wanted to be, and he had become him for Shane.

Shane enabled him to do things he thought impossible.

Shane set him free and released the things that fear and panic had held prisoner inside of him.

Shane made him a better version of himself.

Matt needed Shane, and Shane wasn't a liar. He had feelings for Matt, so perhaps he needed him as well.

No two friendships are alike.

Those were the same words Matt had used to explain to Florenca that their friendship wasn't on par with the one between Shane and him. They had made Matt go nuts. The idea of Shane dismissing their connection as trivial had grabbed a large chunk of his mind and torn it out. It must have been the part that knew that Shane had tried to tell him something else. Shane cared too much for him to hurt him like that.

Matt had overreacted. He had to talk to Shane, set things right and apologize, but running away had complicated this to the point of hopelessness. Old Matt wasn't fit to handle this situation. New Matt had to do the exact opposite of what his former ego would've done.

Old Matt would've run away. He would've dealt with this all by himself.

So first, new Matt should stay, *and* he should seek out help. He should talk to someone.

But who?

Definitely not his parents.

Oh, by the way. I'm into boys, and not only into boys, but also into the one boy you don't want me to be with. We're having some starters trouble. Opinions?

That was the worst way of coming out to them, let alone it was the last thing he wanted to do right now. He didn't understand his feelings for Shane himself. They just filled him up to the brim, not leaving any space for rational considerations. How was he supposed to explain them to someone else?

Florenca?

She went to Mass every weekend and had the temper of a belligerent bull, so a gay Matt would only serve as her *muleta*. Righteous Catholic wrath would rain down on him, and she'd probably punch his other cheek— if she cared at all.

He should talk to someone who knew Shane. However, in school, no one did. Heck, most of the students didn't even know Matt. What about Shane's friends? Not too good an idea, because they would side with their buddy. Still, they could explain his reluctance and help Matt prepare a sincere apology.

So, Nick or Estelle?

Estelle was a resident of a home for elderly people, but which one? What was her family name?

That left Nick. He owned a gym. In one of the photos over the staircase, he'd worn a shirt with a logo on it. What did it say? Matt still recalled the very first comic book he had ever read, even remembered the page numbers of every picture in it, so it shouldn't be that difficult to come up with a logo he had seen mere weeks ago.

It was blue writing on a gray sweater.

A pun.

It was funny.

Gym-Nick's-Tics.

In Matt's stomach, a ticklish feeling replaced the rage and despair. He pulled out his cell, opened the browser, and searched for the name.

Nicolaides Sports. 1443 Bellington Street.

The search had also brought up a small map. That address wasn't even five minutes away, right at the beginning of the shopping promenade.

It definitely wasn't too good an idea, maybe it was even a fucking bad one, but he couldn't come up with anything better. Matt pushed away from the wall and walked down the street. After a few steps, the rhythm of his feet sped up. He was running again, but for a change, he wasn't running away.

THE GYM looked so… normal, not like the run-down place with shifty people hanging around that his imagination had cooked up. Its entire front was made of glass, giving view to a tidy interior dominated by a semicircular counter crafted from beechwood. The lighting tinted the room in warm and pleasant shades of yellow, unlike that cold neon light that turned most shops into such miserable places. Aluminum letters formed the "Gym-Nick's-Tics" logo on one of the walls, and spotlights tinged them blue, making it look exactly as it did on the shirts.

Matt's heart was racing again, or still racing. He had lost track. Old Matt wouldn't have come close to a place where people went to build their muscles. New Matt didn't feel good about being here either, but he had to go through with his plan. He took one last breath before he reached out for the handle of the glass door and pulled it open.

The reception area was deserted. Good. Some more seconds to get used to the gym.

One of the walls was plastered with pictures and postcards. Most of them showed Nick hugging people and smiling. In one, Shane and Nick stood to either side of a woman who held up a pair of giant pants much too large for such a small-framed person. She grinned as if she'd lost it. Matt reached out for the photo and touched Shane. His lips bent up.

Among the pictures hung a framed university diploma.

"…confers the title of Doctor of Philosophy upon Agathangelos Nicolaides…."

So, Nicolaides was a family name. Why did Nick use a shortened version of his surname?

"Sorry for keeping you waiting. A little cookie crisis in the nutrition group."

The chuckle that followed resembled Shane's. It wasn't as deep or resonating as his, but they sounded alike, as if they were chuckle cousins. Matt turned around.

Nick was taller than he expected. He'd seen him next to Shane in photos, so he should have known better. Laughter lines spread from the corners of Nick's mouth and got lost halfway across his angular face. They didn't show up in the pictures but made him even more amiable in person. His eyes were a much lighter shade of brown than Shane's, almost amber. He wore his graying-at-the-temples brown hair in a crew cut.

The smile on Nick's face died, and his mouth dropped open. "Oh my God, who did this to you? Wait a moment!" He spun around and opened a freezer that stood at the wall behind the counter. He took out a blue gel pack, wrapped it in a gray towel with the gym's logo on it, and hurried over to Matt. "Press it against the bruise."

Before Matt could do or say anything, Nick was already holding the cool cloth against his cheek. "This should help to ease the pain."

Matt raised his hand to hold the ice pack himself. "Thanks, Dr. Nicolaides." At least he had a clue now where Shane had learned about friendliness.

Nick chortled, letting his arm hover in midair. "For the second time, oh my God. My father is Dr. Nicolaides. My name's Nick." He extended his hand.

Matt shook it. "I'm Matt and—"

Lines formed on Nick's forehead, and he squinted his eyes. "Matt? Shane's Matt?"

Again, he should have been prepared for that. Nick was Shane's best friend. Unlike Matt, Shane was used to talking about important things in his life. However, referring to himself as an "important thing" bordered on delusions of grandeur. He nodded nonetheless.

"That Liam gave you this?" Nick eyed his cheek.

"Iain. His name's Iain." Nick was a complete stranger, and he knew more than his parents did about his life. Though it was sad, it was also soothing that someone else cared that much about him.

"I know how insensitive it is to ask because you're the victim here, but Shane's not with you, so did he do anything… rash?" The wrinkles on Nick's forehead deepened.

"No, he didn't." The question wasn't insensitive at all. Nick worried about Shane, and Matt could relate to this. "I didn't let him."

The smile returned to Nick's face, and the lines disappeared. He put a hand on Matt's shoulder. "Sometimes the big boy needs someone to watch over him. He should be glad to have found a friend like you."

Matt just wasn't sure whether Shane saw it the same way after what had happened. He nodded once more.

"Still, something brought you here. I don't know how much Shane told you about me, but I can't be that interesting that you'd come here for me alone." A small burst of laughter followed.

Coming here hadn't been a bad idea after all. He met Nick only minutes ago, yet he understood why Nick and Shane had become best friends. His openness was disarming and contagious, and when a recluse like Matt said this, it counted doubly.

"Shane told me how he feels for me." Hopefully, Nick knew about Shane's feelings and this allusion would suffice. Matt couldn't put his own emotions into words, let alone explain what Shane felt. What if Nick didn't even know that Shane was gay? It was a little late for second thoughts, though.

"And that douche—" Nick snickered under his breath. "—came on too strong and scared you off? As I said, he needs someone to stand behind him and give him a good slap from time to time. At least that much he should've learned from the Jer debacle." His eyebrows soared. "You know about Jer?"

Surprisingly, Nick didn't side with Shane, but he hadn't heard the whole story yet. On the positive side, Matt hadn't blurted out one of Shane's secrets. "Yes, I know about Jer. And no, he didn't come on too strong. Actually, it was me who kissed him."

Nick's face crinkled, and he shook his head. "Just to get this straight…. Shane, let's say, likes you very much. And if a kiss is any indication, you also like Shane very much. Still, you show up here alone. I fear I'm missing some of the finer details."

Matt could also relate to Nick's confusion. "Shane's the first person I've ever had feelings for." Nick needed more details, and Matt wanted to share them, but this kind of talk felt as if he wore a shirt that was two sizes too small, even despite Nick's encouraging personality.

"You mean the first boy?" Nick raised both eyebrows again.

"No, the first person."

Nick laid his other hand on Matt's shoulder, and his smile expressed nothing but sympathy. "Shane flipped out when you told him, didn't he?"

A rush surged through Matt's body. Hope had brought him to the gym, and Nick's words poked that ember into a small flame. "Yes." He smiled back.

"This talk calls for Nick's herbal tea mix number three, also known as tranquility and serenity." Nick let go of Matt's shoulders. "Take a seat while I go to the kitchen, okay?" He pointed at the barstools around the counter.

"Sure."

"It'll only take a minute." Still smiling, Nick left through one of the doors.

Matt put the cooling pack down on the counter and heaved himself up onto one of the high barstools. Hopefully, Nick would return soon. When working with wood, it didn't matter how long a single project took, but that kind of patience didn't transfer well to situations like this. The real world was just a notch more complicated than his cuckoo land in the clouds.

Nick came back with a tray in his hands. On it, he carried a steaming glass pot, two glass cups, and a plate with chocolate cookies. A tea ball, secured with a tiny chain, swam in the pot, and a brownish-green cloud was forming around it. The aroma reminded Matt of opening the cupboard to Grandma's spice rack, a memory strong enough to kindle the warm place.

"It has to steep for some more minutes." Nick placed the tray on the counter. "Meanwhile, take an emergency cookie." He shoved over the plate before cupping his mouth with his hand to whisper. "Eat them fast, before the people in the nutrition group get scent of them." He winked.

Matt wasn't hungry at all, but he had to see the cookies as some kind of medicine. After all, a doctor had prescribed them. He took a bite, and the chocolatiest taste ever spread on his tongue.

"If I read the look in your eyes correctly, I'll send my grandaunt Eudora your compliments for her recipe." Nick's smile turned roguish.

His mouth full with another bite, Matt nodded, returning a chocolate-colored grin.

The features of Nick's face straightened. "Regarding Shane's reaction. I don't say that I understand everything that crosses the big boy's mind, but this is about fear." He picked up one of the cookies and flipped it through his fingers like a coin. "Shane had quite a crush on Jer. With you, the situation is, excuse my choice of words, even more messy."

"Shane said that he feels for me the same way he did for Jer." What about Matt complicated the situation? That their feelings were mutual? But this made it simpler, didn't it?

"He said so? Then he's even more of a douche than I thought. Comparing his feelings for Jer with the ones for you is like comparing that dirt mound of a hill in City Park with Mount McKinley." Nick dropped the cookie, and it shattered on the counter. "Sorry, I should leave telling you things like this to Shane."

If Shane had told Matt about those feelings in such plain words, it would've caused a meltdown. Having a messenger in between took at least some of the impact out of this dropping bombshell. Nonetheless, his stomach did its best to rid itself of the cookies while his brain turned into sticky guck. "Please, go on!" He reached out for Nick's hand and squeezed it.

Matt had just felt up a stranger. He had never done things like this before Shane, but Nick only resumed his smile and patted his hand in return.

"The big boy is afraid of living through another Jer tragedy. Shane's the first person and the first boy you ever liked. Just for the sake of argument, who says you won't change your mind? When the enthusiasm settles, you might find he's a friend only. Or that you aren't really into other men." Nick paused and tilted his head, obviously expecting an acknowledgment.

Just for the sake of argument, Matt nodded, though his resistance against those insinuations had a physical quality and felt like something tugging at him. Even the voices in his head took offense at Nick's assumptions, cussing out words that he would never speak in public.

"Jer dumped Shane the very moment he made a move on him. Hard, yes, but clear-cut. Can you imagine the effect on Shane if he let himself fully into a relationship with you and then you changed your mind?"

This discussion was all hypothetical, yet a pang of commiseration shot through Matt. He had seen Shane almost break down when returning the box or when he had confessed about the angel-wing tattoo, but Matt's mind excelled at blocking out such things. Shane was strong and powerful. Period. Still, he possessed this softer side, even more attractive than his strength.

Contradictions seemed to be an indispensable part of love.

Matt learned all these things about relationships in fast-forward. Ironically, the bullying and humiliations had taught him to adapt, and that was what he would do. On the other hand, they had also taught him the power of fear. Of all people, he should know best where Shane was coming from. "It would destroy him."

"Exactly." Nick used the tea ball to stir the infusion and poured two cups. "Drink! As effective as a double scotch. Almost." He chuckled. "My contribution against underage drinking."

Matt took a sip. The taste kept the promise made by the spicy aroma. Strong but not unpleasant, though it was a far shot to call his state tranquil and serene. Too many thoughts mixed up in his head and created a mental white noise that felt like the opposite of calmness. He had come here to talk. If too many thoughts beleaguered him, he had to let them out. Matt looked at the brown liquid in the cup. Like the steam rising from it, he had to let go.

"Fear keeps you safe, but safety isn't everything. I missed so many wonderful things because I was afraid." Shane had made Matt come out of his cocoon, and now it was up to him to return this favor. "Just because something happens for the first time, it isn't less real. One moment a star is only a cloud of gas. The next moment it ignites, and no one doubts that it will keep burning. Nothing stops a chain reaction." Maybe it was the tea or the talking, but the static in Matt's mind ebbed. The thoughts came out of his head and turned into spoken words. They transitioned from vague ideas to solid reality—his reality—and that was the only one that mattered. He had to let Shane into this reality. It was as simple as that. "A friend and a boyfriend are two different things. Even I know this. I want Shane to be both."

"You heard that, douche?" Nick chuckled.

Matt raised his gaze from the cup. Nick looked past him at a point above his head, so Matt turned around.

"Every single word." Shane looked down at him, the slightest smile playing around his lips.

CHAPTER SEVENTEEN

SHANE *HAD* felt exhausted again. Not because of the sprint from school to the gym but from experiencing a week's worth of emotions crammed into an hour. Seeing Matt, being in the same room with him, and hearing him say those words recharged him within seconds. In Matt's presence, he just couldn't suffer. Matt was right. Nothing could take back the initial spark, the Bam!

Matt's eyes widened, and he turned pale, just to blush and glow in the next moment as he went through all stages of a sho-prise in less than a blink. "I'm sorry for running away. You're here. Don't be angry with me. You're actually here. You don't have to be afraid."

Shane put his finger on Matt's lips. "Shhh." The sensation of softness flooded over him, and he had to hurry to get his thoughts out before another wave of emotions drowned them. "First, I'm sorry for not believing you when you told me how you feel. Second, I'm not angry with you. What for? And third, I know. Now."

Slipping off the barstool, Matt slung his arms around Shane's waist and laid his head on Shane's chest. The warmth of Matt's breath permeated his skin, seeping everywhere. Shane placed one hand on the back of his head and closed the other tightly around him. If any fear had remained, the intensity of this embrace burned it away for good.

Nick cleared his throat. "Matt, I hope you don't feel betrayed because I texted Shane, but sometimes you just have to nudge two people together for their own sakes." He snickered. "Especially with stubborn specimens like you two."

Matt laughed into Shane's chest, causing more huffs of coziness to stroke him. He moved away slightly. "Everything the doctor says."

"At least one of you pays due respect to me." Nick chimed in, laughing. "I have one more prescription for you." He raised his hand, holding the key to one of the treatment rooms. "Thirty minutes of privacy. You both have a lot of things to talk about."

Shane took his hand away from Matt's head and grabbed the key from Nick. "Thank you." It didn't take more words to tell his friend how grateful he was for everything that he'd done. For listening, for giving advice, for just being there when needed.

Nick nodded. As always, he was smiling.

SHANE HELD the door open for Matt and followed him into treatment room three. It was normally used for massage sessions, and the table in its middle had a hole in which to place one's face. Knowing Nick, Shane figured this room had also overheard its fair share of on-the-fly psychotherapy.

Like everywhere in the gym, Nick had paid special attention to the lighting, selecting warm and soft shades. The various oils used for the massages made this room smell like a Far East bazaar, foreign and exotic. Right now, the place also felt a little kinky, because Shane's imagination concocted some other applications for those oils. The situation between Matt and him had changed, but it still wasn't okay to have thoughts like those. Or was it?

"So, here we are." Matt looked around the room. His gaze settled on Shane, and a lopsided grin grew on his lips. "Do you have any idea how to start such a talk?"

"I don't even know whether it's okay to touch you." One moment ago, Shane had fantasized about Matt being slick with oil, and now his second thoughts fought back with a vengeance. It didn't help that they had kissed earlier and then shared the most intense of embraces just minutes ago.

Matt chortled and lifted himself up onto the massage table. "Then I'll start this talk by granting you an unlimited touching license." He patted the place beside him. "I already got one from you on Saturday, didn't I?"

The bluntness of Matt's approach made Shane laugh. He should found a sassy Matt fan club, even if he were the only member. "Yes, you got one on Saturday, and you don't have a clue how unlimited it is." Perhaps it was too much innuendo, but this was supposed to be an open talk. For once, he would simply skip overthinking everything Shane-style.

He sat down beside Matt, who managed to put a perfect mix of roguishness and insecurity onto his face.

"We've settled the touching question, then." Matt took Shane's hand into his own. With his thumb, he followed the lines on it. Almost whispering, he continued, "I want you as my boyfriend, I really do, but I have no conception of what that actually means, except that it's more than just being friends."

The gentle touch of Matt's fingers and his sincerity liquefied Shane again. Carefully, he leaned up to Matt just for the feeling of support. "I haven't been in a committed relationship either." He placed his chin on top of Matt's head. "But I don't think that there's a book of rules we have to follow. We have to find them ourselves." He inhaled the aroma of Matt's hair, and this time he didn't fight down the gush of pleasure it caused.

Matt nestled closer to him. "We have to be honest with each other. That's most important, I think. Not being open about our feelings almost ruined everything."

That was one of those self-evident pieces of advice from a four-color-print, high-gloss brochure for teenagers, but their own experiences turned this eye-rolling bromide into a pearl of wisdom. Shane didn't have to spare Matt, because he was a tough one. "Agreed." He closed his hand over Matt's thumb and felt the beat of his heart in its pulsing.

Slowly Matt brought their entangled hands to his mouth and kissed Shane's knuckles, the lush silkiness of Matt's lips stealing his breath. "You didn't have a relationship, but you did have sex, didn't you?"

"Yes, I had sex." This openness thing worked. "But I don't expect you to have sex with me anytime soon." Shane's mouth worked faster than his mind, and what it said sounded just like another attempt at sparing Matt. Yet no uproar of heart, brain, or other body parts followed, so it had to be the truth.

"I want to have sex with you, though I don't have a clue what that means either." The high-pitched sound of Matt's cackling echoed through the room. "I'm an eighteen-year-old virgin, so there's a lot to catch up on." Some more snorts of his laughter shook both of them before they faded away. "Being honest, it's also a little scary, but you're so patient and cautious— and just you—that I want no one else as my first."

This was too generous an offer, like the box. On the other hand, it was a heartfelt wish they both shared. Shane just had to avoid taking advantage of Matt at all costs.

He would begin with wiping his slate clean. "I don't want to scare you anymore, but you have to know how sexy you are for me. After the touching on Saturday, there was… an outrage below the belt that ended in a wet… surprise." Flowery descriptions? He had to keep in mind that Matt could take the truth. "Just being close to you gives me a boner." Letting the guilt out transformed it and took away its power. Another one of those self-evident wisdoms that only made sense when experienced firsthand.

"Do you have one right now?" Matt's voice came out hushed.

"You bet." Shane held his breath, for this talk crossed every boundary he had set up for himself.

A moment of silence ensued, and Matt rested his chin on their entwined hands. "No, it's not scary. It's even kind of flattering, however unfamiliar it is. No one has ever thought of me like this."

Shane let go of the air in his lungs. "Or just didn't tell you." Matt was too cute not to be noticed at all.

Matt chuckled. "If you say so."

"I suggest another rule. No self-belittling," Shane said.

"Agreed, but it applies to you as well, Mr. I've-got-an-A-plus-for-my-history-essay-but-would-grouch-about-it-until-I-saw-it-with-my-own-eyes."

They both guffawed, rocking each other.

"Of course."

Shane had to get one more topic off his chest. "Please don't think of this as patronizing, but I want you to take your time with your coming-out. I had the most sympathetic parents... and Nick, of course. Still, it was a major step with many sleepless nights and brooding days. The decision is all yours, and you don't have to be considerate of my feelings." It was their relationship. It only needed the two of them. Shane didn't require anyone else's acknowledgment to be happy.

"I wouldn't know what to tell right now anyway." Matt moved away and turned his head to look up at Shane. His gaze of light blue fixated onto Shane's. "But I owe *you* a real coming-out. I am into you as a boy, and I'm not confusing anything. I can't give you a logical explanation, but I know that these feelings are true. You may have been the catalyst, but this is me. Just me."

He brushed the smooth skin of Matt's forehead with his lips. "I believe you." And just as important, Shane believed in those three words himself when he spoke them.

"We're boyfriends, then," Matt said.

This statement sounded plain and simple, though uncounted implications resonated therein. Yet it rang absolutely true and was the most natural thing.

Shane didn't feel giddy or excited, only calm and safe. "I think we already were when we entered this room."

"Perhaps we've always been." A leer came about on Matt's face. "Just with a little more angst and panic, and less of this." Matt pursed his lips and placed them on his.

Shane was home at last.

Two kisses had been enough to turn Matt into an addict. The idea of having another person's tongue—and saliva—in his mouth had always felt gross in theory, but boy had he been wrong. It was like a caress, only a thousand times more intimate. Their tongues brushed along each other. For the umpteenth time, a wave of goose bumps traveled down his body. He hadn't known that he could also get them on his back, legs, or... balls.

Shane broke their kiss and panted. "Our half hour is almost up." He flashed a grin. "It'd be absolutely Nick to tear open the door, poke his head in, and check on us."

"We talked as he wanted us to, and making out is just part of our negotiations." Matt grinned back and traced along Shane's scar, making him close his eyes. "Nick is simply awesome. He doesn't know me, yet still talks to me like an old friend."

"Yeah, that's absolutely him too." Shane sighed and squinted his closed eyes. Matt waited for him to purr, but he didn't. "You have to meet Estelle. She's... different, but you'll love her, and she'll love you."

Should he introduce Shane to Florenca? Better not. They were talking about real friends, and she had made it clear that they weren't. "If she's only half as cool as Nick, I'm looking forward to getting to know her." The new Matt really did, much to the surprise of the old one.

"And you have to meet my folks, of course. I've told them so much about you." Shane yanked open his eyes and a jolt of his body almost swept them off the table. "They don't know how I feel about you." His nostrils flared as he breathed out. "I'm sorry. Talking about parents is dumb and thoughtless." He let his head sink down to his chest.

"No, it isn't." Matt lifted Shane's chin up again with one hand. "It's not your fault that my parents are pricks."

Mom and Dad!

Matt was already late, and he had the bruise. He had completely forgotten about it, but with the memory, the throbbing returned. His mom would blame Shane for it. That was a given. Even from far away his parents could ruin this wonderful moment.

"If meeting my parents freaks you out, you don't have to." Shane swallowed so hard that Matt's fingers, still resting on Shane's chin, bobbed along.

His face must have betrayed his thoughts, though Shane had read them wrong. Matt's other hand joined the one on Shane's chin, supporting his drooping head. "No, that's about my own folks and this." He turned his sore cheek. "Granted, meeting your parents isn't one of my heart's desires, but meeting my own anytime soon and having to explain the bruise really creeps me out." Their truth agreement required him to be honest about Shane's parents.

Shane followed the outline of Matt's bruise with his index finger. "Why don't you simply tell them what happened?"

"I haven't told them about any bullying in the last five years. They'd raise hell in school, and I just want to forget about this whole thing with Iain." His silence came close to running away again, but it was also an act of diplomacy. "There's a good chance for a lasting truce between Iain and me, and my parents would only stir things up again."

"*We* have a truce with Iain. You're not alone in this." Shane grabbed Matt's head so that they were holding each other now. "Let them think I did it. I don't mind." His lips curved up a wee bit.

"I won't let you take the blame for this." His parents might keep him from seeing Shane if Matt didn't challenge their wrong suspicions. When had his body stiffened up and his muscles begun to tremble? "I'd rather come up with another story about dodgeball or running into a door. Those have always worked before." His mom's prejudices could still pose a problem, and he might be grounded no matter what. The trembling became a shaking, and a feeling of cold settled in his guts.

Shane let go of Matt's head and closed his arms around him. The heat of Shane's body and the cold of his clashed, and both refused to yield to the other.

"Perhaps I can help." Nick's subdued voice came from the door. "Let me take the blame."

Matt and Shane both turned their heads. Nick made a serious face. Though Matt hadn't known him for long, this had to be a rare occurrence.

"I shouldn't endorse lying to your parents—" Nick shrugged, and a trace of a grin sneaked back onto his lips. "—but if you do it anyway, it has to be as perfect as possible." He crooked his fingers, and impishness crept into his grin. "Follow me!" Nick disappeared into the hall.

They looked at each other.

"He's usually good with sly things," Shane said. "The way he talked my parents into allowing me to get the tattoos would've turned every car salesman green with envy."

Why did Nick care so much about him? This question made a beeline for a new dilemma. He shouldn't drag Nick into his problems, at least not any more than he had already. Matt's ideals about friendship may have stemmed from century-old books, but their age didn't render them obsolete. "I can't expect him to do this."

Shane chuckled with his mouth closed. "He won't leave you much of a choice, I fear." He pecked Matt on the forehead, making a smacking noise. "We can hear his plan out at least."

"Yeah, we can do that." Listening to a friend belonged to those ancient ideals, and Nick had already shown that he valued this one as well.

WHEN MATT and Shane arrived in the lobby, Nick was hacking away at the keyboard of a computer behind the counter. He looked up, grabbed a webcam, and pointed it at Matt. "Say cheese!"

A red light flashed on the cam before Matt had a chance to comply.

"Don't worry. We'll take another one when the bruise is gone." Nick put down the cam, looked at the screen, and his fingers flew over the keys again. "Your family name and your address?"

"Dermond. Number 132 Lombardy Street," Matt said without giving a second thought. The doubts followed promptly. "What do you need them for?"

"Just a sec." Nick's eyebrows wobbled up and down as he concentrated on his task.

Matt faced Shane and nodded over to Nick. Shrugging, Shane grinned back. So he'd be the last one to learn what was going on here.

"Done." Holding a blue plastic card, Nick raised his hand and grinned like a madman. "Congrats on your free lifetime premium membership to the exclusive Gym-Nick's-Tics Sports and Spa Club."

Matt's mouth dropped open, and he couldn't close it again.

"Part of your premium package is special care by one of our most talented personal coaches, Shane McAllistair." Nick shifted his gaze to Shane. "*If* Mr. McAllistair is willing to fill this role, that is."

"Of course, you nutjob." Shane placed his hand on Matt's shoulder. "Nothing in the world could make me refuse that offer."

Matt looked up at Shane, who fake-scowled at Nick. Many words whizzed around in his mind, but none of those took the right exit to his mouth.

"A little more respect for your superior, Mr. McAllistair." Nick made the same evil face he had in the picture of their theme park visit, succeeding even less to make it convincing this time because his eyes were shining with almost childish glee.

"I cannot accept this." Matt hated being the buzzkill, but this was just too much. Accepting advice was one thing. Accepting something worth thousands of dollars was something completely different.

Nick's lips settled back into a smile, finally reconciling his eyes with the rest of his face. "Of course you can." He wagged the card in his hand. "Shane is family, and by extension, so are you. My *manoula* will chase me through town armed with her rolling pin if she learns that I charged a family member." He laughed before his expression became serious again. "I can still remember being a high school kid in love. It's just so difficult finding a place to share thirty minutes all by yourself if you're still living with your parents. Shane knows where the keys to the treatment rooms are. There's your place. And moreover, your membership here is part of my plan." A smile tiptoed back onto Nick's lips.

"Your plan being?" Matt would decide later about accepting the membership, however convincing Nick's argument was. When confronted with multiple problems, he preferred to solve them one at a time. Another strategy that had proven itself in what already seemed to be another life.

Nick's smile transformed into a sly grin. "My ancestors came up with the Trojan horse, and that was one hell of a ruse. So just have a little faith."

Shane rubbed Matt's shoulder and pulled him a little closer. That was Shane's way of reassuring him, and Matt gave in to it. He had a boyfriend and a new friend now, both of them willing to risk their necks for him. The waves coming from the warm place inside carried away what remained of his doubts.

CHAPTER EIGHTEEN

DUSK WAS already fading into night when Nick and Matt trotted up the paved path that led to the entrance of the Dermond house. Matt still refused to call it home after the talk with his parents on Saturday. Everything in his life had changed for the better, but this house hadn't. It had meant safety for the old Matt… and had become a jail for the new one.

The flashing lights of the TV illuminated the window of the living room while the rest of the house lay in darkness. All of the Dermonds' lives consisted of staying at home, watching TV, pursuing their hobbies, and only leaving the safety of the four walls for job or school. It was a prison indeed.

"Let me do the talking," Nick said. "If your parents ask you anything, just give short, concise answers. Try to look shaken." Nick glanced down at Matt. He had been his usual cheery self during the car drive, but the moment they arrived here, a switch had been flicked and Nick had fallen silent. Ironically, seeing an outgoing person like him also suffering from stage fright took away from Matt's.

"I don't have to try to look shaken."

Today he had been bullied and had stood up to Iain at last.

Shane had confessed his feelings for him, and Matt had poured his heart out in return.

They had been together, almost split up, then reunited within an hour.

For fuck's sake, he and Shane were boyfriends now!

Every single item on that list sufficed for a serious bout of feeling shaken. As the frosting on that emotional cake, all of these truths were about to be bent like a pretzel for his parents. He wouldn't have any difficulties in portraying a convincingly shaken Matt.

Nick made a chuckling noise, his nervousness tinting it hysterical. "Definitely true." He clapped Matt's back, something that Shane might have done.

They had left the gym twenty minutes ago, more than enough time to miss Shane already. Matt's body yearned for the firmness of his muscles pressed against him, the warmth and comfort they brought, and his mind longed for Shane's mere presence. The faster he lulled—no other term fit—his parents with the upcoming parade of lies, the faster he could reward himself with the phone call they had promised each other. At least he could listen to the deep hum of Shane's voice then.

"Use your full title and name, preferably in every other sentence. Keep a straight face, and don't smile too much." The last part might get a little tricky. "Nick" and "smiling" referenced each other in a dictionary, and Matt's parents were as cheerful as bricks. If he hadn't been the spitting image of his mom, Matt wouldn't have doubted for a second if someone told him he had been adopted. Thinking about it, he even would've preferred being adopted right now.

They stopped in front of the door, where the small bulb above the entrance cast a dim light over the two of them. Matt had never knocked at this door before, which added to the overall strangeness of the situation.

"Enough stage directions." Nick adjusted the tie he wore. Perhaps donning it was a little over the top, but Matt's parents weren't supposed to know what a typical manager of a gym looked like. Besides, a tie suggested trustworthiness. To emphasize this impression, Nick had even shaved before coming here. "Break a leg!" With a smile on his lips, he offered Matt a fist.

Bumping it gave Matt another flash of remini-Shane-ce. "Break a leg."

After huffing and literally wiping the smile off his face with his hands, Nick knocked at the door.

The seconds between the executioner raising the axe and sensing the cold breeze on one's neck had to feel the same. Matt startled as the knob turned. Thank heavens his dad answered the door. A little more time before his mom entered the stage and turned this play into a drama.

"Yes?" His dad's gaze wandered from Nick down to Matt. "For goodness' sake, what has happened?" His head snapped back to Nick. "And who are you?"

"Good evening, Mr. Dermond. My name is Dr. Agathangelos Nicolaides. I am the owner and manager of a physical rehabilitation facility." Nick extended his hand.

His dad stared at it, confusion warping his brows. After too many seconds for Matt's taste, the two finally shook hands.

"I am devastated to have to tell you that Matt suffered an unfortunate accident while attending a trial session at my studio. Another member made a mistake while using one of our training machines, and a side arm hit Matt's face." Nick placed his hand on Matt's shoulder. "I thoroughly examined your son. Thanks to the Lord, he escaped with nothing more than a scratch." He tilted his head slightly. "Please accept my sincere apologies, and let me assure you that our equipment fulfills the strictest safety regulations, even German ones."

Matt fought down the urge to turn his head and look at Nick. He'd simply gape at him and run the risk of ruining the credibility of the performance. Nick's impersonation of a serious businessman was so convincing, he had to suffer from a mild case of multiple personality disorder—or he was just one hell of a talented actor.

His dad eyed Nick, then Matt. He gnashed his teeth, his brows still furrowed. "A trial session?"

A father shouldn't ask this first when he learned that his son had met with an accident. He wasn't to blame, though, because the very fact that it happened during a trial session in a gym constituted the weirdest part of the story. Maybe his dad knew him after all.

Matt stared at the ground, avoiding eye contact with his father, and shuffled his feet against each other. "Phys ed is my weakest subject in school, and I read in a career brochure that colleges prefer students with a rounded profile. So I made an appointment with Dr. Nicolaides. His studio has excellent ratings on the web." It really did, and his parents could check this for themselves. Nick had come up with the idea of linking Matt's gym visit to his academic career. This was Nick's take on the Trojan horse, and his parents would fall for it because they just loved bragging about Matt's academic prowess.

"Who is it, darling?" The door opened a little more and gave view to his mom.

Enter the Diva!

"Jesus wept!" His mom clapped a hand over her mouth, but her fingers never touched her lips. She reached out for Matt's head with both hands, yanked it to the side, and inspected the bruise. "This was that Shane guy. I knew he'd do something like that."

Matt whipped his head away from her grasp and backed off. "It wasn't him!" He flinched at the vigor of his own voice. His emotions flared up at the only thing that wasn't a lie, making it sound like one. Nick's cleverly conceived plan was going down the drain because Matt couldn't keep a grip on himself. His mom just had to pull the right strings, and he danced to her liking. He was a pathetic puppet.

"No, Petal, it wasn't Shane. Dr. Nicolaides… right?" His dad waited until Nick nodded his acknowledgment. "Dr. Nicolaides already told me that Matt had an accident in a fitness studio that he visits for bringing up his phys ed mark." For a moment, his gray gaze rested on Matt. A hint of mischief flashed up in his eyes before he turned to his wife. "Something he obviously forgot to tell us." He put the lightest of emphasis on "forgot."

They had an accomplice in Matt's dad. Knowingly or unknowingly? That was a good question. Nonetheless, he had managed to mention Nick's title twice, had casually dropped the reason for Matt's unusual venture, and had shifted the focus away from the bruise to the defiance. Heck, his father did better in this charade than him.

His mom's gaze switched from Matt to Nick, continued to his dad, and returned to Matt. "Is this true?"

"Yes, Mom, it's true." How easily this lie rolled off his tongue, but she had brought this on herself. Not that she deserved to be lied to. But if she wasn't able to handle the truth, it was the right thing to spare her the need to cope with it. Matt didn't even buy into this rationalization himself, but at least it was a tad more mature than thumbing his nose at her.

"In order to express how much I regret this incident, I offered Matt a free one-year membership at my studio." Nick tapped his fingers against each other. "I hope this adequately compensates for the inconvenience."

Matt had contributed the idea of mentioning the free membership. His mother meticulously collected every coupon she could find anywhere, filling two folders with them at any given time. Her inability to pass up anything that came for free was her Achilles' heel, to stay in the metaphors of Greek mythology. Matt had also suggested toning it down from lifetime to a single year, because anything too good to be true could raise suspicion even in a scrimper like her.

"Oh." His mom's face lit up, but then she harrumphed. "We'll consider your offer, Dr. Nicolaides."

For someone fluent in Dermondese, that translated to "Of course we will accept this offer, but in order not to appear greedy, I'll pretend to have to ponder it."

"I would be glad if you accepted." Nick gave her a curt nod and faced Matt. "I will uphold our appointment on Friday to devise your training plan unless you decline to attend my studio. Apart from the positive effect on your marks, there are so many health benefits garnered from regular exercise that I hope you decide in favor of a membership."

They hadn't planned that last part, but Nick's improvisation was a well-thought addition. In her own twisted way, his mom cared for him, and she definitely wanted him to be healthy.

"Mrs. Dermond." Nick bowed slightly. "Mr. Dermond. It was a pleasure to meet you, even if the circumstances were not too delightful."

His parents nodded back.

"See you on Friday, then, Matt. Good-bye!"

"Good-bye, Dr. Nicolaides." Perfect. Matt had remembered to sneak in Nick's title one more time. He watched him disappear into the darkness.

It had worked. Sure, a roasting awaited him, but the anticipation over Shane's call would carry him through that. He made sure he still looked shaken, reining in the smile that Shane's name brought to his lips, and turned around.

CHAPTER NINETEEN

SHANE SPRAWLED out on his sleeper and grabbed one of the gray cushions. He squeezed it in his hands till it was a tiny ball, threw it down to the floor, and jumped back to a stand. Matt and he hadn't set a time for their call. They had only decided it'd be better if Matt called him as soon as he got his parents off his back.

What was taking him so long?

Nick had arrived back at the gym over an hour ago and related the whole meeting with the Dermonds, probably verbatim, impersonating the participants with different voices. He was good at imitating Mrs. Dermond's inflections, but Nick's Matt didn't even come close to the original.

If the original would just call….

Though Matt's parents had fallen for the ruse, Mrs. Dermond had suspected Shane of giving Matt the bruise. Her assumption was so ridiculous. He would rather hurt himself than hurt Matt, enduring anything to guarantee his safety. The waiting-for-Matt's-call adrenaline mingled with the how-can-she-even-think-that adrenaline, and he felt like his skin was peeling off from the itching.

He eyed the dumbbells beside the beanbag chair. His muscles still felt sore from overtraining them on Saturday, but he needed to do something. Otherwise the jitters would crumble his body to pieces, and his parents would find a small heap of Shane dust where he now stood. Okay, perhaps not exactly a small heap.

His cell slithered across the table, propelled by its own vibrations. Before the first note of the ringtone sounded, he had snatched up the phone.

Incoming call: Matt.

Shane swept across the display, but his fingers hit way off the Accept animation. He took a deep breath. What made the cell shake more, his tremors or the phone's vibrations? He tried again. This time his index finger eventually obeyed.

"Hey there, boyfriend." Shane let the last word dance on his tongue. A slight bow on the "boy," a little rolling of the "fr," and a tiny bounce to the "iend." Not bad, especially since all he had expected to get out was a high-pitched squeal.

For a moment there was silence. "With giving me goose bumps in my ear, you've finally caused them in all places of my body." The cutest of chuckles warbled through the phone, giving Shane his own share of all-body gooseflesh. "Congratulations, boyfriend." Matt's own little jig for the word "boyfriend" caused Shane's blood to rush southward again, though he desperately needed it in the upper regions.

"We're even, for you keep giving me one very special bump." What more evidence did Shane need that his brain was starved of oxygen? He had switched from avoiding mentioning sex at all costs to bubbling out innuendo almost every time he opened his mouth. He wouldn't blame Matt if he hung up right now.

Instead of a silent line, another mind-bending chuckle filled the ether. "You wheedler. I can't be that much of a turn-on."

"Dollars to donuts, you are." At least no one could accuse him of not going the full way, even when scaring off Matt with horniness.

Another moment of silence followed, but the unsteady sound of Matt's breathing came over the phone. Was Matt suffocating from shame or holding back a good and proper fit of laughter?

"It'll take some time getting used to your… courtesy."

That was a very "Mattish" way to refer to Shane making moves.

"So keep it coming."

Shane let himself slump down to his sleeper again, for Matt's cuteness swept him off his feet. Getting it into his pighead that Matt could bear quite a brunt would also take some time. That was how he had survived all these years. He suffered a blow, went down to the floor, and got up again. His boyfriend didn't only turn him on, he also made him feel proud. "You ask for it. You'll get it." They had all time in the world to test each other's boundaries, but they also had some pressing matters to discuss. "Nick already told me about the meeting, but how did the talk with your parents go?"

Matt whiffed. "Was okay. Not too bad. I didn't count, but they assured me many, many times that I could talk to them, even if we have different opinions on certain topics." Audible quotation marks hovered around the last words. He breathed out again, something between a sigh and a groan. "Just for the record, the certain topics are you. They didn't drop your name, but that wasn't necessary."

At least they had swallowed the story Nick had cooked up. "Don't get upset because of me. I can take it." His demons were different ones, and like

Matt, Shane knew how to deal with them. Most of the time, that was. "Did they decide on the gym membership yet?"

"Nope, but you can see the dollar signs in Mom's eyes, and I'm not worried about getting their permission. Regardless of their decision, nothing could keep me away from there."

A fighter indeed. "Would be nice, though, if you could officially visit the gym." Including some unofficial visits to the treatment rooms.

"Yeah. I really like my personal coach. Would be a pity if I had to skip… training with him." So great minds *did* think alike.

Shane flinched as his hand touched his boner, and he bit his tongue to not moan into the cell. Those little fuckers of his fingers had crept up on the bulge all by themselves. Just to keep the suckers busy, he fondled one of the cushions instead. Jacking off while talking to Matt was a no-go, but if he just asked him nicely…. He pinched his thigh with his fingers that were already sneaking back to his crotch, and he sucked in air through his clenched teeth.

"Everything okay with you?" Worry rang in Matt's voice, turning it mellow and rounded.

The truth. Shane had to tell Matt the truth because he could take it. "My hand seems to be quite interested in the special bump, and I had to teach it some manners." He lowered his voice. "I'm sorry."

This pause lasted longer than the ones before. Shane had finally overstepped the mark and deserved a little more than some pinching.

"What for?" Matt's surprise sounded genuine. "I want to add another rule to our book. Full self-service rights if the other one isn't there." He hummed. "I'd like to amend this by a right of first touch if the other one *is* there." The soft bellows of Matt's laughter pulverized the last bits of Shane's ability to think. "That's what you get if you give a nerdy virgin a try at talking sexy."

Shane's boner twitched and threatened to shred his boxers to pieces. "According to little Shane, it was a very good try." He allowed his hand to settle on his crotch and grabbed his cock through the fabric of his training pants, making him hiss again. It had been a hopeless fight to begin with, and now that he even had permission…. "Oh, before I forget, agreed and agreed."

Matt's cackling made little Shane squirm in big Shane's hand.

The laughing faded away. "Tonight will be the first time that I actually think about a person when jerking off."

This sentence, as simple and blunt as it was, became a dozen spears impaling Shane, piercing through him and into his very core.

It told about the pain Matt had suffered, the pain Shane seemed to be the remedy for, however hard it was to believe.

It revealed that Matt was a sexual being, a fact Shane couldn't accept yet despite all the things that had happened.

It proved beyond any doubt that Matt desired him just as much as he desired Matt.

"Come over and spend the night with me," Shane blurted out.

MATT HAD heard Shane's words, loud and clear. Yet he had to swallow down the question "What did you say?" It was a movie cliché, a really bad one, but he felt sympathy for every scriptwriter who had ever used it, because it happened just like that in real life. Luckily he had already been lying on his bed. It would have been an unpleasant meeting with the floor otherwise. And the second one caused by Shane.

"It's Monday. We have school tomorrow, and I don't think my parents will let me go tonight. Especially not after coming home with a bruised cheek." None of those reasons sounded convincing, even to his own ears. How was he supposed to dissuade Shane from an idea he himself wanted to become reality more than anything else?

"We could at least ask our parents. Worst-case scenario, they'll say no."

Or chain Matt up in the basement to protect him from himself, for he had obviously lost his mind. The Matt they knew didn't go to gyms, and he didn't have sleepovers with friends. Dammit, he didn't even have friends, at least not ones he should spend time with. They'd know at once where he planned to go.

Still, it was just a simple question, and hadn't he sworn to stop running away? "I'll ask them, though I don't think they'll let me go out on a weekday without a good reason." A sigh slipped out of his mouth. "And I won't add another lie to the list." At least the cliché of one lie leading to the next he'd prove wrong.

"No lies. I like that." Shane's smile reverberated in his voice. "Are twenty minutes enough to talk to your folks?"

"Plenty." Matt wouldn't get into another discussion this evening. If his parents declined, he'd accept it. Question was, whether his parents would leave it at that or insist on another talk. However, the potential reward offset all trouble. "Until this matter is settled, I invoke the right of first touch. So hands off little Shane!"

"That's only fair." The deep drone of Shane's snigger reminded little Matt that he also participated in this game. "I'll call you, okay? I don't think I could stand waiting to hear from you again tonight."

Matt wouldn't do much better than Shane in this regard, but this was tit-for-tat. "Twenty minutes from now. Go!"

MATT TIPTOED out of his room. Why exactly did he avoid making any sound? Perhaps some primal instinct told him that sneaking up on his prey was a sound strategy. His field of expertise covered evading the predator, not being it.

Light shone through the gap of the door to his dad's home office, and divide and conquer appealed to Matt as an even sounder strategy. At least if he asked his father alone, he had a good chance for only getting a simple no as an answer without additional drama.

He knocked on the door. His dad liked those little signs of politeness, even in the family, and he would make use of everything that tipped the scale in his favor.

"Come in." His dad's voice sounded friendly, so he wasn't too pissed anymore.

His father sat at the desk and jabbed at the keys of his notebook, using his signature two-finger system of typing. He looked up from the screen and raised the corners of his mouth. Definitely not pissed.

"Am I disturbing something important?" Matt nodded at the computer.

Gesturing for him to close the door, his dad shook his head. "Don't blab to your mom that I told you, but she asked me to check out Dr. Nicolaides and his studio on the web."

The money she could save hadn't fully convinced her. This reaction didn't fit his mom, and Matt's heart sank. The chance for getting a positive answer to go out plunged if the situation was that tense. "And?"

His dad's smile became heartier. "No reason to make such a sour face." He lowered his gaze to the notebook and swept over the touch pad. "Dr. Nicolaides turns out to be a highly acclaimed sports scientist and is considered the state's leading expert in training psychology." He scrolled farther down. "As you said, the ratings for his studio are excellent." He looked up again, and a tad of impishness invaded his features. "When your mom learns this, she'll claim it was her idea to send you there in the first place."

"She will." Matt couldn't help but smile back at him.

"You didn't come here to hear about the gym, did you?"

Matt shook his head. It was just a simple question. Nothing more. "I'd like to go out tonight, and I won't be home before tomorrow." His question became a third person in the room, lingering in silence, waiting and anticipating.

"Haven't you got school tomorrow?" His dad pursed his lips.

He hadn't said no yet, and Matt almost forgot to answer. "Yes, but I've got some free hours. Classes won't start before ten o'clock."

"You won't be alone, I assume." With his lips still pressed together, his dad twisted his mouth.

"No, I'll be with a friend." Matt didn't want to lie, but Shane's name didn't come out either. Speaking it wasn't necessary anyway.

His father closed his eyes and massaged the bridge of his nose. He let his hand sink before he opened his eyes again. His gray gaze rested on him, no emotions showing in it. "Please look at me, Matt, and assure me that you trust this... friend. Assure me that he treats you well and that everything is all right."

His dad gave him "the eye," his alleged ability to look straight into the minds of prospective employees and customers at work and know their every thought and motive.

Matt's head contained many secrets his father shouldn't learn, but that didn't matter. The sincerity of his relationship with Shane stood out from those. It flared bright like a lighthouse, and his dad should see it.

"I trust him more than I do myself. We watch out for each other, and he'd rather have his hands hacked off before raising them against me. Having met him changed my life. No, having met him gave me a life to begin with."

Matt held his dad's gaze. The color of Matt's eyes was all his mom's, but the Dermond men shared the same lightness of shade, as if a single drop of ink had been dripped into too much water. The subtle grayness went ablaze with the softest of emotions, the kind Matt had never seen on his father before. "If you have one true friend, you have more than your share."

It was a quote by Thomas Fuller that Matt had read in a biography once. His dad had never shown much interest in literature or philosophy. Hard facts and numbers, those made up his world. Matt had known him all of his life, yet his father still had some surprises up his sleeve.

"Matt, I'm glad you've found your share of true friendship. That's what a father wants for his kid." His dad blinked, and the emotions in his eyes abated but didn't leave. "So obviously I don't have a choice but to let you go out tonight."

Somehow Matt managed to bite back the question "What did you say?" a second time, but it was nip and tuck. He nodded. His blood had been completely exchanged for concentrated wooziness now that nothing stood between him and spending the night with Shane. *Wait!* "What about Mom?"

A roguish grin appeared on his dad's lips. "Mom treated herself to a double administration of EST."

Elder schnapps therapy. That meant two things. She was *really* upset about the whole situation with Shane and the gym, and she would snore happily on the couch in the living room until midmorning next day. Then wake up with a head the size of a medicine ball.

Matt grinned back at his dad. Perhaps sassiness was a Dermond family thing after all, though they apparently preferred to keep it under the bushel.

"The story for your mom goes like this. You spent the whole night in your room and left early because you had a project to work on in the school library."

So much for not bringing up any more lies. At least his dad had suggested it. After a double treatment of EST, his mom might not even realize that anything unusual had happened. He could postpone having a guilty conscience till he knew for sure. It was difficult enough to keep the multitude of other emotions under control. If he let any of those register with him, he'd be running around the house, alternating between screaming and babbling. Once more, he only nodded.

"If you've still got half an hour, I can drive you there."

That would work out perfectly. He could begin packing some things, even before getting the call from Shane. He'd simply go crazy if he just sat around. "Thank you, Dad." Matt smiled the friendliest smile he could find inside himself. At last he had one ally in this house.

"You're welcome." Creases formed on his dad's forehead, but he shook his head and his face relaxed. "See you in half an hour, then."

Matt turned around and already held the doorknob in his hand when his dad asked, "You didn't get the bruise in the gym, did you?"

An ally deserved to know the truth. "No, I didn't," he said, still facing the door.

"You'll have your reasons for not telling us who did it."

Matt jerked his head around and looked into the stern face of his father. "It wasn't... my friend."

"I know, Matt, I know." The smile on his father's face reappeared. "But perhaps it's still better not to tell your mom that one of the trainers at Dr. Nicolaides's studio is a certain Shane McAllistair."

His dad had known, yet had heard him out. Matt could call this house "home" after all.

CHAPTER TWENTY

MATT AND his dad turned the last corner onto Normandy Street, where the McAllistair house lay. They remained silent, but this was the comfortable silence between a father and a son. An understanding father and a basket case of a son.

The forces of fate obviously gave their best to make up for all the stuff they had fucked up in Matt's life so far. At least it explained all the good things that had happened today, including Shane's parents agreeing to the sleepover as well. How many good things meant an overdose?

The cone of their headlights illuminated a figure, hunched down and sitting on the curbside. This shape was unmistakable, the silhouette giving away Shane at a glance. Matt's heart beat double-time, and the warm place went out of its way to provide an appropriate level of heat for that sight. He and Shane had already spent so much time with each other, yet the coming hours would all be new and filled with firsts.

Shane's dark shape jumped to a stand and took a step to the side into the light of a streetlamp.

More heart stuttering? Check!

More heat? Check!

"That's him?" his dad asked.

"Yes." Matt only aspirated the word, for the warmth burned his breath away.

"He's huge. I can see where your mom is coming from."

Matt's head snapped to the side, and he stared at the dimly lit figure of his father.

His dad took one hand off the steering wheel and waved it in a placating wigwag. "Not my opinion."

He had already envisioned his dad putting the hammer down and speeding past Shane, intent on saving his son from the thug waiting on the sidewalk. "Just give him a fair chance, and he'll prove how wrong Mom is."

"He has already convinced you." His dad lowered his hand to Matt's knee. "That's all I have to know."

Matt had never considered sharing his thoughts with his dad. Why should his father be interested and value them at all? He was just a boy who didn't have a clue about the world or how it worked. Maybe the adults didn't have one either. They just had more experience that helped them guess at what the world might come up with next.

The car came to a halt. Shane didn't move, and his insecurity stole the color from his face, making the scar stand out, even in the twilight.

"Thank you once more." Matt placed his hand on his dad's and looked at him. The darkness swallowed most of the details, but his father's face radiated happiness.

"See you tomorrow." A held-back chuckle gurgled through the car. "It's impolite to let your host wait."

Matt turned his head. Shane had his hands in his pockets, head tilted to the side while he shuffled his feet. He had to leave the car as fast as possible to end both their miseries. He tore open the door and leaped out.

Crossing the distance between them, slinging his arms around Shane, and kissing the living daylights out of him—that was what Matt yearned to do, but with his father watching them, this part of their reunion had to wait. "Hey." A grin pussyfooted onto his lips.

"Hey!" Shane breathed in deeply, his chest threatening to burst through his shirt. Nonetheless, the softness of his features made him look so gentle.

They obviously shared the same qualms about having to restrain themselves, and Matt stifled a sigh.

"I'll just get my things out of the trunk." He pointed to the rear of the car, already walking toward it.

Shane approached the passenger side, inhaled one more time, and bent down. He extended his hand. "Nice to meet you, Mr. Dermond, and thank you for bringing Matt here safely."

Matt watched the scene through the rear window. He held his breath, for the resemblance to what had happened on Saturday with his mom was just too striking.

"Nice to meet you, Shane." His father reached out for the giant paw. "Though I'm not a sportsman myself, even quite the contrary—" He snorted a laugh. "—I admire the dedication of an athlete, and obviously you are one." They both shook hands.

So that was how a sho-prise looked from the outside. It suited Shane and made him even cuter. Matt bit his lower lip to not snigger.

"Thank you, Mr. Dermond." Shane's sho-prise toned down to a friendly face.

"Maybe we could get a family discount at the gym?" his dad asked.

Shane jerked his head around and stared at Matt, his wide eyes reflecting the light of the streetlamp. Matt hadn't told him on the phone how much his dad really knew, and he gave him a single nod. Shane answered with a toothy grin.

"I'm sure you can talk about it with Nick, umm, Dr. Nicolaides, I mean." Shane faced Matt's dad again.

His father was kidding. Hopefully. They had to keep his mom away from the gym at all costs.

"I will." Matt's dad let go of Shane's hand. "I want to apologize for how my wife treated you. She tends to be... overprotective when it comes to our only son."

Matt opened the trunk, as if not watching them talk or not being seen would take away from the embarrassment.

"She wants him to be safe," Shane said. "I understand that."

"I'll work on changing her mind, but even the most stubborn donkey is docile compared to Matt and his mom." More snorting came from his dad.

The trunk lid definitely didn't shield him from the parental powers of awkwardness. Matt closed it with a *whoomph*.

"See my point?" His dad whispered loud enough for him to hear.

Shane shrugged, and Matt wanted to rip the grin off his lips. Or kiss them.

"Bye, Dad," he proclaimed in a firm voice.

"Bye, you two."

Shane closed the door, silencing the chuckling from inside the car. Together they watched Matt's father drive away.

"You didn't tell me how cool your dad is." There was no accusation in Shane's voice, only a slightly annoying trace of amusement.

"I learned just an hour before you did." As a matter of fact only Matt's interpretation of his father's behavior had changed. His dad hadn't ignored him but had let him make his own decisions. He treated him like an adult, yet Matt had been too much of a kid to notice.

"Do you think he's got a... hunch about us?" Shane asked.

He *still* was a kid, for this thought hadn't even occurred to him. "He didn't say anything, but I think so. I've never slept anywhere else, and begging to spend the night with you on the very day I got bruised has to raise some suspicions." The warm place expanded, for it also had to accommodate his admiration for his father. He looked up at Shane, whose eyes flickered, searching Matt's face for some hints they didn't seem to find.

"That's okay for you?"

Matt stretched out his arm and let the back of his hand slide down Shane's cheek. "Of course it is." He couldn't talk to his dad about being gay yet. On the day he could, he simply knew his father would smile and say something like "It's about time you told me." Matt was looking forward to that day… and he dreaded the day he had to tell his mom.

Shane grasped Matt's wrist with tender fingers and rested his head on Matt's hand. He closed his eyes like a happy puppy—a two-hundred-sixty-pound, purely muscled puppy. "My parents surely have more than a hunch, but they won't say anything either." Shane turned his head slightly and nibbled on Matt's knuckles. "Remember, you don't have to tell them anything."

That Shane's parents knew they were boyfriends belonged to Matt's lesser worries. Meeting them in the first place ranked much higher on this list, closely followed by… "What if they don't like me?"

What if they saw him as just another Jer, someone who would hurt their son and discard him at the smallest sign of trouble?

Shane opened his eyes. "Knowing my parents for more than nineteen years, I can safely say they'll adore you." He flashed one of his slyer grins. "They'll love you more than they love me."

Tonight had shown how much parents could surprise their kids, and unfortunately, that door could swing both ways. "I'd already be glad if they don't usher me out like my mom did with you." If Shane's parents were watching them, seeing how they fondled each other on the street, this might very well happen. Matt let his hand sink down.

Shane laid his arm around him and turned him toward the house. "In her defense, I ushered myself out."

Only because Shane had beat her to it.

"Gimme your bag, and let's go in."

Before he could answer, Shane snatched the bag out of his hand. Matt had planned to hide behind it when meeting Shane's folks, but each time he allowed Shane to do something for him, his face lit up, including the scar. Matt didn't have the heart to ask for it back. "Yeah, let's go."

His arm still around him, Shane led him up the path and opened the door. Once again, the threshold changed into a solid wall, and Matt struggled to break through it. The presence of Lord and Lady McAllistair rendered the castle a completely different place, and his not-so-good friend Insecurity still lurked around.

Shane closed the door. He kicked off his shoes, and Matt followed his example.

"My mom's already hovering an inch above the couch, I guess." He simpered. "Let's wait a few more seconds, okay?"

A few more seconds sounded good, but for a Band-Aid, the supposedly painless method of removal was ripping it off as fast as possible. The same was probably true for meeting Shane's parents. "Can we just get it over with?" Matt was hyperventilating and just couldn't stop.

Shane pressed him close. "Hey, you survived crashing into a terrifying six-foot-eight guy in the locker room. You will survive meeting his parents."

Matt's breathing calmed down, only because of the closeness of Shane's warm body. He nodded. "I might also need some cake afterward."

"That's the spirit." Shane snickered before raising his voice. "Mom, Dad, Matt's here."

It took exactly three seconds until a woman's head, covered with dark brown hair like Shane's, appeared in the doorway to the living room. She smiled so hard that Matt feared her face might split into two. Though Shane and she shared the same hair color, the color of her eyes was different—a dark shade of green. As Matt had already estimated from the photos, she was only half a head taller than he was, so she presumably hadn't contributed any of Shane's giant genes.

"Welcome, Matt. I'm so glad to finally meet the guy Shane can't stop talking about."

Before he could answer, she stormed right at him and had him in a bear hug, pressing the air out of him. Maybe she was part giantess after all.

"For goodness' sake, Heather, let the poor fella breathe." A low voice came from the door, followed by a humming chuckle.

Mrs. McAllistair let go of him and smoothed the fabric of his tee around his shoulders. "Sorry, Matt." She giggled like a teenage girl.

Mr. McAllistair walked up to the spot beside his wife. Confirming what Matt had gleaned from the pictures, he stood a head taller than her. His thick hair was a dark blond, almost the same color as Matt's. Looking into his eyes was like looking into Shane's.

Nature had taken the most striking features of his parents, united them in Shane, and added some ten inches in height to round out the mix.

"Please indulge my wife's exuberance, but as she said, Shane doesn't talk about anyone else lately, so we're quite curious, to say the least."

Mrs. McAllistair poked Mr. McAllistair in his ribs. "Indulge this!"

He rubbed his side, glowering at his wife, but held such affection in his gaze that she couldn't take offense.

The sheer number of things going on at once had fried Matt's brain. Though he wasn't looking at Shane, he virtually felt him rolling his eyes at his parents.

Shane huffed. "Mom! Dad!" A good portion of despair resounded in his voice.

The McAllistairs straightened themselves, a grin sneaking back on their faces time and again. However much Shane's parents may have differed from his, they shared that mischievous pleasure in embarrassing their kids. Their grin jumped over to Matt.

Mr. McAllistair extended his hand. "All this said, it's really nice to meet you, Matt."

They shook hands.

"Nice to meet you, Mr. McAllistair."

"Please, call me Gordon." One last shake of hands underlined this request before he let go of Matt.

"And I'm Heather." She extended her hand but let it drop in the same moment she pulled him into another embrace. It was absolutely clear now from whom Shane had inherited his predilection for hugs and touches.

"Nice to meet you, Heather," Matt croaked out with the little air she had left him.

She opened her arms and backed off, her face beaming all over. "You both have better things to do than spend time with two geezers like us. What are you up to? Games? TV?"

"Perhaps they want to study," Gordon chimed in, scratching his chin and looking up at the ceiling.

"Perhaps we'll do just that." Shane grasped Matt by his arm and gently pulled him toward the stairs.

"It was really a pleasure meeting the both of you," Matt said as Shane shoved him up the stairs.

They were two stairs up when Gordon said, "Whatever you study, I hope you'll study safely. Ouch!"

Heather moved her elbow away from where she'd nudged her husband's side. "You didn't say that!" She grabbed him by his ear and dragged him into the living room, out of Matt's sight.

They kept talking, their agitated voices echoing through the house. Not understanding what they were saying was most likely the best for him.

"More than a hunch, definitely." Matt tittered. He should have been stirred and devastated, but the McAllistairs had put on such a hilarious show that he couldn't hold anything against them.

"First thing tomorrow morning, I'll put myself up for adoption." Shane spun Matt around and placed both hands on his shoulders. "I sincerely apologize for those two maniacs downstairs who used to be relaxed and down-to-earth parents until this very evening." His features sagged, and he let his head hang low.

Matt laid his hands on Shane's waist, and the sensation of firmness and warmth washed over him. He shook his head, both to clear his mind and to disagree with Shane. "Don't apologize for your parents. I wondered whether they might not like me, and what I got was the heartiest welcome of my life. Everything's all right." He ran his thumb up and down Shane's waistline as far as he could with his hands still in place. In this small patch alone, his muscled body offered more details than Matt could possibly explore in one evening. "Even the last thing your dad said didn't bother me at all. My geeky mind appreciates clear-cut situations more than uncertainty." His geeky mind also urged him to further explore the shape of Shane's body. All for the sake of science, of course. "Knowing that they know helps me somehow. I hid all my life, and here, I don't have to. Does this make sense at all?"

Shane's features came to life again. He kneaded Matt's shoulders but used only a fraction of his strength. "Even a lot of sense." He turned his head around, checking the staircase, bowed down, and placed a kiss on the tip of Matt's nose. "They might think that they know, but we'll decide when we tell them." The same impishness that had shown on the faces of his parents lodged itself onto Shane's. "Oh, wait." He let go of Matt and hurried over to the door of his room. "Ta-da!" He pushed open the door and waved him over.

The room lay in near darkness, only illuminated by some fairy lights draped around the sleeper and tea lights burning on the table. Shane had folded out the sleeper, its mattress lying directly on the floor. The cushions were arranged the way a kid would do it to build a fortress.

"I only had a quarter of an hour. On second thought, it's rather corny and unimaginative and quite blunt—"

Matt slung his hands around Shane's neck and pulled his head down before locking their lips. Their height difference complicated silencing Shane with a kiss, but it worked nonetheless. Matt moved back, their foreheads still touching. "It's beautiful." A chortle bubbled out of his mouth. "The advantage of having a virgin boyfriend is that all the cheesy stuff still impresses him."

His stomach filled up with butterflies, bees, dragonflies, and every other fluttering animal on earth.

When he entered that room, he wouldn't leave it as a virgin.

He backed away from Shane to see all of his face. This was the guy who took the fright out of this thought and turned it into the most wonderful idea. This was the guy Matt wanted.

Chapter Twenty-One

Shane swallowed hard.

Virgin boyfriend.

Matt gave himself over to Shane and looked at him without reservation and full of trust. It was frightening, empowering, and every other emotion that had ever arisen in a human being. To hell with his doubts. This wasn't the moment for rational thought. This was the moment for feelings alone.

He grabbed Matt by his armpits and deliberately lifted him up. He took in every detail of Matt's face—the smoothness of skin, the fine blueness of his eyes, the fullness of his lips—and he had to smile. The love and desire showing in his beautiful features didn't allow for any second thoughts. Shane pressed Matt close, who slung his legs around him in return. Their lips slid along their cheeks until they found each other, and their mouths connected. The warm streams of their breaths mingled as Matt moaned.

Their kiss unbroken, Shane carried Matt over to the sleeper, where he lowered him down as gently as possible. Matt opened his legs and slumped onto the bedsheets.

"Just a sec." Shane got up, hurried over to the door, closed and locked it. "We don't want my parents to find out with their own eyes, do we?"

Matt snorted. "That'd be too much, even for my geeky mind."

"I thought so." Shane grinned, stepped over to the bed, and knelt down beside it. He swept a strand of Matt's tousled hair out of his face. "Speaking of too much." His grin faded. "If anything we do is more than you can take, tell me. Punch me in the gnads if necessary, but don't let me do anything you don't want." If they just lay close to each other, did nothing more than kiss and cuddle, it'd be enough for Shane to lead the happiest of lives.

Matt's facial expression turned serious, almost solemn. "You won't do anything I can't handle. I simply know."

The totality of his trust caused a jolt to run through Shane that began in his mind, branched out, and followed every nerve down to its end. "Promise me anyway." Matt's body and soul were so delicate, even the thought of chipping them ever so slightly cramped Shane's guts.

"I do promise," Matt said in a whisper and clasped Shane's lower arm, giving it a squeeze.

At this touch, air rushed into Shane's lungs, and another bolt of energy darted through him. "I think we should take off where we finished last." He put Matt's hand down and grasped the hem of his own shirt. In one smooth movement, he pulled off the tee and discarded it on the floor.

With cheeks blushing, Matt let his gaze wander over Shane's torso. One corner of his mouth soared. "Oh, that was already foreplay we did on Saturday?"

"I confess! I really, *really* intended to take away your fear of muscles, nothing more. But I enjoyed it a little too much for that." Looking up at Matt, he lowered his head to the sleeper. "Please forgive me for my sins."

Matt reached out for Shane's cheek and traced the scar with his fingers, the other corner of his mouth joining the smile. "We're both guilty, so there's nothing to forgive."

In their wake, Matt's fingers left a path of tingling intensity on his skin.

"Then this isn't a sin either." Shane let his hand crawl over the sheets and up Matt's waist. He closed his fingers around the edge of his shirt, but Matt seized his wrist.

Shane lifted his head off the bed. "Too much?" A bitchy voice in his head kvetched about the untimely interruption, but his admiration for Matt's courage to actually stop him slapped it into silence.

"No, for goodness' sake, no. I... I only...." Matt puffed. "My body isn't as perfect as yours. I don't want you to be... disappointed."

"Just because I'm muscled doesn't mean that I expect you to be." Shane let his head sink down to the bed again and brushed through Matt's hair with the fingers of his free hand. "Do you expect me to be as clever as you are? By this logic, I should just shut up, because everything that comes out of my mouth only painfully illustrates that I am not."

Matt parted his lips, but Shane placed his index finger on them.

"You've got enough brain and I've got enough muscle for the two of us." The grin returned to Shane's face as he followed the outline of Matt's lips with his fingers. "My perfect boyfriend is small and slender. His untamed hair sticks out in the cutest way possible. With his blue eyes, he drives me mad and can make me do anything for him. Sound familiar?"

"You really know you're cheesy, don't you?" His mouth said that, but the rest of his face sided with Shane and indulged in the sappy sweetness of those words.

"You don't believe me?" Shane raised his head again and opened his mouth in mock exasperation. "Then I have no other choice but to show you how perfect you are."

Once more he had to persuade Matt with deeds, not with words. He sat up on the bed, tugged at the hem of Matt's shirt, and waited. After a small moment of indecision, Matt let go of his wrist at last. Shane lifted Matt up with his other hand and got him out of his tee while he was still lying down.

Matt's body was absolutely smooth. Not a single hair showed on his chest or stomach. Only a hint of fluff, some shades lighter than the hair on his head, covered his armpits. Two halos of light brown, not much larger than a nickel, surrounded his nipples. His waist was so slim that if Shane wrapped his hands around it, there would only be a couple of inches left between his fingertips.

Shane skidded over to Matt on his knees. His lithe chest rose and fell in a steady rhythm, but his cheeks were on fire, their glow visible even in the twilight of the room. How could so much human be stuffed into such a small body?

"These two shoulders—" Shane bent forward and lowered his lips to each of them. "—perfect."

Matt inhaled deeply, and the pace of his breathing sped up.

Shane wandered down. "These two nipples—" He circled around the small buds with his tongue. "—perfect."

The lean shape of Matt arched up, as if electrified by the slick caress.

Never lifting his tongue off the soft skin, Shane ventured down and placed a kiss on Matt's belly button—a small swirl that moved clockwise on the otherwise smooth sea of his stomach. "This navel. Perfect." The little maelstrom would suck up Shane's soul if he stayed there for too long, but it was damn worth the risk.

Matt groaned and curled Shane's hair with his fingers.

Shane let his hands slide up on both sides of Matt's body while smothering his belly with kisses. The floating of skin on skin caused a prickling sensation of static, raising the hair on Shane's arms. He lifted his head up. "As far as I can see, everything's perfect up front. Where should I check next? Your back?" Shane grabbed Matt's shoulders softly and began to roll him around, but Matt clutched his hands.

"No, here." Matt guided him down to the elastic waistband of his track pants.

Shane's gaze flicked back and forth between his hands on the gray fabric of Matt's pants and his face. Was Matt ready to take this step? Shane's breathing quickened with every turn of his head.

"Please!" Matt's voice turned into a haunting appeal. "Please!" A whisper only, but so urgent.

That plea wiped Shane's mind blank. Matt wished for it, and Shane would grant him anything he asked for. He pulled down the waistband.

Matt lifted his legs so that Shane could remove the pants. Those legs were so small. His hands could easily reach around each of Matt's thighs, but they fit in with the rest of his body, forming a harmonious overall picture without looking diminutive on him. Even here, he couldn't find a trace of hair. Matt wore black briefs, and a lovely bulge stretched them out to the max, painfully reminding him of the tightness around his own crotch.

Shane's temples pulsated, and small drops of sweat ran down his nape. He needed to cool it down or he'd shoot straight into his boxers without him, or Matt, touching anything down there.

He moved a little, aligning his knees with Matt's hips, and bent down over the legs. One after another, Shane stripped Matt's socks off his feet, and his breath caught. He had never been into feet. He didn't hate them, but he didn't love them either. Yet now he looked at the little wriggling shapes of Matt's toes. Even the large one was a tad smaller than Shane's thumb, and he wanted nothing more than to suck on them. His cock bobbed up and down in its cotton cage. This had nothing to do with slowing down, and going all foot fetish on Matt was a sure way to send him running. Shane filled his lungs with air. He just couldn't let this chance pass. A little toning down might do the trick.

"These two feet—" He placed two short pecks on the insteps. "—perfect."

Shane glanced at Matt from the corner of his eye. Not even a wrinkle formed on Matt's nose, but a choked moan gushed from his mouth. Matt was a savorer, and a subtle smile crept onto Shane's lips.

He kissed his way up Matt's ankles, calves, and knees, each and every one another piece of perfection. With fleeting smacks of his lips, Shane worked his way up Matt's thighs and closed in on the bulge. All he felt was the smoothness under his lips and the burning sensation these touches brought to his loins. Shane had given up on thinking. There wasn't enough blood in his body to operate both the north and the south, and the logical part of his brain couldn't comprehend or endure the intensity of this moment anyway.

"Gimme your hands." Matt breathed those words, yet they filled up the room and jarred Shane down to his bones.

He obeyed, for he had no choice in the matter.

Matt placed Shane's hands on the waistband of the briefs and made sure to hook his thumbs into it.

Their gazes locked. The redness of Matt's cheeks deepened, even covering up the black shape of the bruise. Matt smiled, and with a single nod, he wiped away all qualms remaining in Shane's mind.

He moved his hands down, his thumbs following the line of Matt's legs before dropping the black piece of cloth to the floor.

Matt's cock jumped up and down. Maybe it felt embarrassed by the gaping stranger? It had no reason for being anxious, though, because that stranger had only fallen in love with it. The slight upward bend was adorable and ended in a consummate pink head with no foreskin hiding its beauty. Its size perfected the harmony of proportion that was Matt's body, and finally—hair! The same fluff covering his armpits adorned Matt's crotch, bringing a velvety shimmer to his balls.

Shane didn't dare to move. The awareness of being the first one allowed to see, being the first one allowed that close, paralyzed him. This was a first for him as much as it was for Matt. Shane had had sex before— hot sex—and he had had feelings for men—deep feelings—but never both at the same time. Here with Matt, lust and horniness clashed with humbleness and bliss. All at once rawly physical and subtly spiritual. This powerful collision of forces lifted Shane up and kept him grounded at the same time.

Matt lay still, his chest heaving with quick draws of breath, watching, waiting.

Shane had to make good on his promise to show Matt his perfection. He closed in on his cock and let it glide along the scarred cheek. Every muscle in Matt's body flexed, arching him off the sheet again. His cock head smoldered with heat and felt even softer than the rest of his skin. The one part of Matt that hadn't been touched met the one part of Shane that he hadn't allowed to be touched. That realization sent another wave of electricity surging through him. He gasped, and the rush of air created goose bumps that roamed over Matt's skin.

Matt's arousal mangled the wee bit of restraint left in Shane. This evening was all about Matt, and he should be the one who was in control. He kissed his way up Matt's stomach, over his chest, up his neck, and ended beside his ear, doing nothing but breathing against it for some moments. Matt shivered in the rhythm of Shane's breath.

"It's your turn," he whispered.

SHANE'S WORDS echoed through Matt's mind, but it took a moment until they broke through the haze of excitement. His eyes snapped open, and Shane was already sitting on his heels. The muscles in Shane's chest bulged out while his stomach flattened, tensing up for the rise to a stand. When they had first met, Shane's power had mortified Matt. Now it caused a flare of heat to travel through his body, originating in the warm place. Matt's cock twitched again. Thankfully his face was already burning so hot that Shane wouldn't see him blush because of the loss of control over his member. All the walls that Matt had erected to keep his feelings inside were gone. Shane's kisses had made those walls crack, and his touches had torn them down.

Shane rose up to full height. "It's an obscenity that I'm still dressed while you're not."

He was grinning, but he was dead serious. It showed in his eyes. He bowed down, offering him a hand. Matt grasped it, and Shane pulled him up. Not letting go of the one he was already holding, Shane reached for Matt's other hand and shepherded both of them to his waistband.

"You know the drill." Shane's grin still lingered, but it had lost most of its slyness and had transformed into a smile.

Matt smiled back, but he didn't have a clue how that smile had found its way through the mess that was his insides. He felt horny and insecure, safe and everything else. At the same time. With equal intensity. He concentrated on his fingertips resting on Shane's flanks and used this sensation to gain the upper hand over that chaos. Matt filled his mind with the warmth and hardness of Shane's body and let them oust everything else.

"Ready when you are." Shane chuckled.

The deep rumbling noise threatened to tilt Matt out of balance again, so he got down on his knees and pulled Shane's pants with him before his brain could get too mushy for even that simple task. It turned out to be a bad idea, though, because the card house of his sanity finally collapsed at the sight of Shane's legs. Matt looked down at himself. All those muscles, veins, and sinews had to be there too. It was an anatomical fact, but they were hiding very well. His gaze switched back to Shane. Like on his chest, dark hair covered the front of Shane's legs, thinning out on his shins.

He took one of Shane's feet into his hand and peeled off the white ankle sock. The other sock followed suit. Matt had never touched the feet of another person, let alone another guy, but with Shane, there was nothing weird about it. He brought his own foot forward for comparison. Shane just made everything around him look dwarfish. Granted, Matt wasn't actually much taller than a dwarf. He eyed Shane's boxers. They were bulging out, barely holding little Shane prisoner, though that name certainly didn't do the inmate justice.

Matt looked farther up at Shane's face, where the last remnants of his smile died away.

"Get up." Shane bent down and grabbed him by his armpits. "Please, get up." He pulled Matt to a stand again. "I… I don't want you to cower before me… with that look on your face."

Shane's breathing accelerated, and his nostrils flared. He was working himself into a panic attack. Matt had gone through enough of those himself, but seeing Shane have one squeezed his heart tight. He had to make it stop and put his hands on both of Shane's cheeks.

"Shhh. I'm not cowering before you, and that look… I'm marveling at my boyfriend." Shane liked sassy Matt, so sassy Matt should have a try at calming him. "Are you telling me I'm not allowed to marvel at my boyfriend while on my knees? The insolence!" He pursed his lips and crossed his arms over his chest.

Shane stared at him. His eyes darted around, and his facial muscles twitched time and again. The tics slowed down and finally stopped. A little bit of Shane's smile dared to return. "I'm repeating myself, but you're perfect."

"And I'm still not sure whether I share this assessment." Matt let his arms drop and raised the corners of his mouth. "To make that clear, you cause a whole bunch of feelings in here"—he tapped his chest—"but not fright anymore." It was only weeks ago that he *had* cowered before Shane, but Matt couldn't even remember how it felt to fear him.

Though Shane's lips trembled, he continued to smile. He closed his eyes and inhaled. "You won't marvel at… *it*." He nodded down. "Perhaps it'll even frighten you again." His voice became subdued and thin.

If Shane intended these mysterious insinuations to keep Matt from fully undressing him, he hadn't grasped the concept of curiosity and the power it held over a geek. Only a minute ago, Shane had begged Matt to get him out of his clothes, and now his insecurity had won out again. Matt had to say something, something that assured Shane his fear had left for good, but the words lurked in his head and evaded his mind, staying just out of reach. Perhaps words weren't the right tool for this job anyway. He should borrow a page from Shane's book and show him instead of tell him. He clasped Shane's boxers and counted the beats of his own heart. Shane had five of those beats to stop him if he preferred to not let… *it* out, but he stood poised, waiting for the judgment to be passed. Five heartbeats later, the boxers dropped to the ground.

After Shane's cock stopped bobbing, finally freed from its sartorial jail, it stood straight out at a right angle from his body. His dick looked good-sized on him, but everything that looked good-sized relative to Shane was huge in reality. It would take two and a half of Matt's hands to cover the entire length of the shaft and the uncut tip would still poke out. The diameter of Shane's cock only slightly fell short of Matt's wrists. Two big veins ran along its top and bottom, circling around in a slow twist. Shane was shaved, but a slight shadow of his dark hair had already grown back. His balls were enormous. Both of Matt's boys would easily fit into one of his, and the left one of those behemoths hung a little lower than the right one.

His head turned dizzy, partly due to the stunning view and partly due to the fact that he had stopped breathing. Shane's cock was awesome. No, it was epic to the power of awesome.

"It's a monster, I know." Shane's voice dropped another notch, an equal mix of sadness and despair weaving into it.

Matt put his head back to look at his boyfriend's face.

"I'm sorry." Shane opened his eyes. The same mixture of sadness and despair that tinged his voice darkened them.

Slowly at first, Matt shook his head, but the shaking quickened into a frenzy. "No." Only a croak escaped from his mouth. He swallowed. "No," he repeated firmly. "Take it back. Take that apology back!" A grin settled on his lips. "This cock and these balls… perfect." The first nude man Matt saw close up was of stunning beauty. So far everything in his life had gone wrong, but everything that had to do with Shane went just right. The forces of fate stumbled over each other, trying to make their amends. Who was he to stop them?

Shane's features froze altogether. The sadness and despair left his eyes, but the shock and bewilderment that replaced them weren't any better. Shane needed physical proof again, so Matt reached around the base of the fat shaft and let his hand glide up its length. The heat of Shane's cock seeped into his fingers, and he had difficulty holding on to it as it squirmed in his grasp like a ferocious beast.

Halfway up, Shane's hand clamped his. Shane panted, and his whole body trembled. "If you finish that stroke, I'll finish." He drew in more air, his forehead glistening with sweat. "Not yet. Please, not yet."

Matt had been so absorbed by Shane's awesomeness that he had forgotten about himself and his own horniness. Just because he didn't pay it any notice, didn't mean his body gave him a break, though. His dick shone red and pulsated, and he was only a flick and a whiff away from shooting, himself.

No more words. No more sorries. No more worries.

Matt's hands shot up and tugged on Shane's shoulders. Shane understood the not-so-subtle hint and went down on his knees, bringing their faces level. With full force, Matt flung himself at Shane, grabbed his head, and their tongues met in a fierce kiss. No space should remain between them. The soft shape of his body snuggled up against Shane's firmness, and their skin, damp from sweat, stuck to each other. Matt's cock was trapped between them and wouldn't hang on for much longer. The friction made its nerves scream out with ecstasy, his brain already teetering on the verge of a breakdown. Shane closed his fingers around Matt's hips, pressed him close, and lifted him up some inches off the sleeper. Matt slung his legs around Shane's waist, and the hold on his hips slackened. He slid onto Shane's thighs, the massive cock skidding up his butt crack. The sensation of hot flesh gliding over his hole turned the last remnants of his mind to gunk, and he groaned into Shane's mouth. It felt as if his crotch were imploding and exploding at the same time. He couldn't hold back anymore and gave in to the current pulling him under. The sheer amount of his first shot gushed out from everywhere between their bellies. Beneath Matt, Shane's thighs tensed up, a feral roar rolling up his throat. Warm wetness hit Matt's lower back, and the next wad of his own cum erupted from him. Thrill and exhaustion shook Matt before another of Shane's loads sloshed onto his skin, a crisscross pattern of heat on his already searing body. His groin contracted a last time. The convulsion sent ripples through him that interfered with themselves and echoed off his insides. The full length of Shane's dick slapped against his ass, and a final splash of jizz trickled down the small of Matt's back. They broke their kiss and rested their heads on each other's shoulders. Their breaths came and went in perfect synchronicity, and their movements flowed into each other, following a tacit accord.

Matt sent a silent prayer of thanks to the forces of fate. By giving him Shane and granting him this evening, they had paid back their debts in full.

CHAPTER TWENTY-TWO

IT WAS well past 3:00 a.m., and the tea lights had burned down a while ago. Shane was tired, but he couldn't go to sleep without losing precious minutes with Matt. Their foreheads rested against each other, and their fingers twirled lazily through each other's hair. Aligned in a casual touch, they lay side by side. Not twenty-four hours ago, he had been ashamed of having a wet dream about Matt. The wet reality surpassed this dream in every way possible, and a chortle gurgled out of his mouth. Matt didn't even stir at the sound, because in the last half hour they had taken turns having such odd outbreaks of glee.

"Can I ask you something and you won't get mad if the question is fucked-up?" Matt's whisper, strangely magnified by the contact, resonated through their entangled bodies.

"That's two questions already, and am I mad yet?" Shane stole a quick peck from Matt's lips.

Matt giggled, contributing the next joyous sound to their game. After some moments of silence, he asked, "Was that sex already? All we did was rub against each other and jerk off." He tugged slightly at Shane's hair. "Sorry. The nerdy part of me needs to know."

Shane moved his hand down to Matt's nape, circling it with his fingers. "My definition of sex is: making each other cum." Sex wasn't all about penetration. What more proof did they need than this night? "So tonight, we did it five times. Okay, five and a half times if you count my little 'brushing over your nipples with my half-limp cock can make it spurt' accident." It had been as awesome as it had been hilarious, and they laughed out loud at the memory. "And we really should stop apologizing to each other for no reason. What do you think about not saying sorry for the rest of the year?" This would be harder for him than for Matt.

"Agreed." Another cackle sputtered out of Matt's mouth.

"Oh, I almost forgot." Shane rolled to his side of the sleeper and reached behind its sidewall, producing the golden cardboard box he had hidden there. He went up to his knees and held the box out with both hands. "Here, for you."

Matt knitted his brows. "You have a gift for me?"

Shane grinned. "Actually, it's a regift." He hesitated. "Does that word even exist?" Whether it did or not, the term fit perfectly. He looked down at the box and pressed his lips tight. "Gold is a little tacky, I know. Usually my mom hoards dozens of these boxes, but I had to choose between this or an eyeball-melting shade of orange."

"Was that an apology?" Matt glowered at him, but it was as real as a pink baby unicorn.

"Of course not." Shane bared his teeth in another goofy grin. "So without any further ado." He extended his hands a little more. For a change, there wasn't a tirade of doubts and second thoughts clamoring in his head. He didn't feel guilty at all. This long waited-for silence was Matt's gift to him.

Matt accepted the box and eyed it. His gaze went up to Shane and down to the present in his hand again. With excruciating slowness, he untied the bow and lifted off the lid. He blinked several times, and a smile came about on his face as he removed the napkin from the box.

"I had to rewrite most of the text. By a sudden inspiration of genius, I used a tear-proof pen this time." The words on the napkin were true, even truer than ever, and they were worth being preserved after all. "You might not need it anymore, but I want you to have it anyway."

Matt stroked the napkin, drawing his fingertips slowly over the white cloth. "That poor little fella almost suffered as much as we did, and it's a good thing to have a reminder of that." With utmost care, he folded the napkin and placed it in the box again. "I never thanked you for giving it to me in the first place." He put the box down beside the sleeper, caressing it a last time.

Shane's grin picked up a few notches of slyness. "You thanked me five and a half times this evening."

A chuckle eruption shook Matt. "As much as I would like to thank you a sixth and a half time, my body isn't quite up to this… umm, challenge."

"I couldn't get off another time either. My balls are dry as dust." The heap of tissues by the side of the sleeper contained about every ounce of cum that had been in both their bodies. So much for not accepting Matt as a sexual being. "We may not shoot again tonight, but we can do this."

Shane lunged forward and seized Matt by his waist. He threw himself onto the sheets, pulling Matt with him. With a slight twist of his hands, he spun Matt around, slung his arms around him, and held him tight. They ended up in a spooning position, which Shane got down pat by wrapping one of his legs around Matt's. "Gotcha!" He nuzzled the top of Matt's head and planted a kiss on it. "And I won't let go of you until morning." A faint voice spoke up in Shane's head, wondering whether he still had to ask for permission. No! Matt had promised to stop him if he went too far. This was a matter of trusting Matt, not of trusting himself.

"Resistance is futile. I see." What came out of Matt's mouth was something between a snigger and a satisfied burble. He snuggled up closer to Shane.

No more sex tonight, but just lying close to Matt and listening to his breathing, feeling the beat of his heart was even better than getting it on. Steaming hot repetitions of this evening lay ahead of them. Many, many repetitions.

When Matt's body became limp, Shane buried his nose in his hair. If Matt woke up now, he would nestle up closer instead of leaping away in panic. Shane smiled. With this wonderful thought filling his mind, he drifted off to sleep.

WARM BREATH on Matt's ear woke him from sleep, but drowsiness kept his eyes shut. The firmness of Shane's presence surrounded him. This had to be the most awesome way to start a day.

"Good morning, boyfriend." Shane taught the word another dance, and this time, goose bumps formed on the outside of Matt's brain.

Now they had definitely occurred everywhere on his body.

"You can doze a little longer while I go shower, okay?"

Matt turned his head, and his nose grazed Shane's. He finally opened his eyes, and it took them a moment to focus on Shane's face hovering above him. The smile that greeted him illustrated the word *angelic* perfectly, however archaic that term was.

"Good morning, boyfriend, and sure." Matt's voice sounded raspy and still full of sleep, but the blissful mood was so contagious he had already contracted it.

"Have a nice little snooze, then." Shane's hand swept over Matt's cheek. "A quarter of an hour. That's about fifteen minutes more than I want to waste on not being with you."

Shane excelled at dishing out schmaltz. Yet being honest with himself and silencing the voices in his head with his confession, Matt reveled in those mushy tidbits. That was how Juliet must have felt when Romeo compared her to the sun.

Still smiling, Shane rolled to the side, breaking the touch of their entwined bodies, and a feeling of loss billowed through Matt.

"Wait!" He bent over to Shane, grabbed his cheeks, and placed his lips on Shane's. Only the tips of their tongues brushing along each other, this kiss wasn't nearly as wild as the ones last night. But that didn't take away from the passion and affection in it. Matt moved back a little. "I hope that this will help you with those hard minutes."

Drawing in a deep breath, Shane closed his eyes. "The kiss made it worse, I fear." He giggled, and seeing a two-hundred-sixty-pound guy giggle was a noteworthy sight. The cutest thing Matt had ever seen. "I'll hurry." Shane opened his eyes, pecked Matt once more on the forehead, and got up on his feet. He opened the door and peeked outside.

The sight of Shane's naked ass, bubbly with hot inward dents accentuated by his muscles, was noteworthy too. Cute wasn't the word that came to Matt's mind, though, and the bulge of his cock spoke a clear language. Sporting massive morning wood passed as a sign of admiration, didn't it? Especially if the guy parading it could count the monthly instances he got an early boner on the fingers of one hand only.

"Looks clear." Shane turned his head around and grinned, but his grin toned down to another perfect rendition of an angelic smile. "Miss you already." He blew Matt one more kiss and slipped out of the room, closing the door behind him.

Huh, Juliet, in your face!

Matt let himself slump onto the sheets again. A little touching, a kiss, and the sight of Shane's butt had cranked him up enough to bury the idea of snoozing for good. Should he take care of his hard-on himself? Nah! First, Shane's parents were in the house, and the door wasn't locked anymore. Not the best circumstances for a second meeting with Shane's parents. Second, Shane might invoke the right of first touch after his shower. Matt sighed, and his cock bounced in anticipation, slapping against his belly. So all he could do was wait and keep his fingers crossed for a sixth and a half time to happen this morning.

Most certainly, patience wasn't one of his strengths. And he had to pee. Not too badly, but waiting for Shane to return before taking a leak might ruin his seduction plans. Enough reason to handle this problem right now. There had to be another bathroom in the house. He could just sneak downstairs and be back before Shane. Matt put on his pants and shirt, for running into Shane's parents while butt naked was only a tad better than being caught jerking off.

He opened the door a tiny crack, listened, but could only hear the splashing of the shower. His mind promptly spewed out some images to go with the sound. The stream of water cascading down Shane's powerful chest, foam trickling down his strong legs, and Shane's hands soaping his awesome crotch with slow circling motions. A flare shot through Matt's groin, and his dick jumped once more, indignant at still being ignored by his owner.

Easy, boy!

Bumping into Shane's parents with bulging pants ranked somewhere between being naked and being caught wanking on the unpleasantness scale. Matt's problems always revolved around staying away from people. Some things never changed, obviously. He had just switched from avoiding Iain to avoiding Shane's parents. Another thing that hadn't changed, simply thinking Iain's name twisted Matt's guts around. At least the nausea shooed his boner away—something Matt had to thank Iain for one day, but only with Shane around to protect him from any repercussions.

He tiptoed down the stairs and waited for one of the steps to squeak, just to add to the list of clichés getting a bang from becoming true for him. But the clichés still seemed to be fast asleep, for he reached the first floor without further incident.

The aroma of fresh coffee and bacon filled the hall. Matt soaked them in, eliciting a growl from his stomach, which had obviously forgotten that Iain had turned it around only a minute ago. Light shone through the kitchen door standing ajar while hushed voices and clanking noises came from inside.

"And? Made up your mind about Matt yet?" Gordon asked.

Oh fuck!

The only decent thing was to wheel around, hurry up the stairs, and pretend to not have heard a thing, but curiosity trumped decency anytime.

"He seems to be so nice, but…." Heather's voice trailed off.

"But what?"

"You know very well about the 'but.'" Her words rang hard, yet concern softened her tone.

"Of course I do." Gordon sighed. "He looks exactly like Jer. They could be brothers, even twins."

"I'm not so much worried about his looks but about Shane having to go through all that shit again."

A vast barren stretched out where Matt's mind used to be, and his blood became a black, viscous liquid, turning each pulse into a pang as his heart tried to pump the muck through his veins. He pushed open the door.

"I'm not like Jer, not the slightest." Matt's hands curled into fists, and his body trembled all over. "I won't allow anything to happen to Shane. He's the most important person in my life!" His voice grew shriller with every word.

Heather sat at the table with both hands around a coffee mug while Gordon tended to bacon and eggs at the stove. Both of them froze, holding their breaths and not even blinking.

Matt, however, was panting. What had he done? And even more importantly, why had he done it?

Gordon recovered first, the seriousness of the moment tautening his usually friendly features. "First of all, I'm sorry that you had to hear that." He pushed the pan to the back of the stove and turned around to face Matt. "I believe you, but the more important a person is, the simpler it is to hurt that person."

This couldn't be true. Matt didn't want it to be true. He shook his head frantically. "No. I will never hurt him. I love Shane!" Matt slapped his mouth shut with both hands.

It was too early to say those words, even he knew this, but he hadn't said them in vain. He had saved up emotions for one and a half decades. All of them burst out of him now, compressing the usual time for realizing the depth of his feelings for Shane. What was usual for a relationship anyway?

He loved Shane. However true this sentence was, Matt couldn't share it with Shane. Not if he wanted him to stay his boyfriend. In any case something overhasty like this would scare him away. The question remained whether telling Shane's parents was any better.

Heather gave her answer by flying off the chair and seizing Matt in a bear hug that put any grizzly to shame.

"I'm sorry too," Heather whispered, the warmness of her words rippling over Matt.

Shane was so lucky to have a mom that actually cared for him. "You don't have to be." The world had to stop being sorry for him, and he had to stop being sorry for the world. His no-apologies pact with Shane applied to everyone else from now on.

Heather opened her arms and took a step back. "We're not saying that you will hurt Shane, but after Jer, we're just... warier." Her lips bent up a tiny bit.

"Of course you are." Matt had to convince them how seriously he took this relationship, no matter how long this would take. "I love Shane. That's the truth."

"I really think he's in good hands now." Heather grabbed Matt again, even tighter than before, and he snuggled up against her.

He hadn't thought about this before, but she was right. Shane rested in his hands as much as he rested in Shane's. Matt sometimes forgot about their relationship being mutual because Shane was so attentive. "You already knew we were a couple before, didn't you?"

Gordon placed a hand on Matt's shoulder. "We suspected so, yes, but we didn't know for sure."

Despite their reservations, they had welcomed him with so much friendliness. Matt wouldn't disappoint them. He'd take care of Shane in all ways possible.

"Heather darling, I assume Matt's too polite to say so, but you're smothering him again." Gordon was smiling, for Matt could hear the amusement in his voice.

She let go of him, just to give her husband a not-so-friendly punch on his arm. Heather glowered at Gordon for a moment, but when her gaze switched back to Matt, she reverted to her cheerful self. "Do your parents also know?"

Matt's throat constricted, and he couldn't speak, so he shook his head. This was the second time he had told strangers about his feelings for Shane and, consequently, the second time he had come out as gay. Still, he would rather count the freckles on Iain's face than tell his mom either thing.

Heather caressed his cheek. "Despite what you might think, parents do understand, and they want to know. If their kid is happy, they're happy."

His dad had said the same thing, but Heather and Gordon didn't have all the information. He lowered his head. "My mom banned Shane from our house." Matt heaved a sigh. "She didn't even try to get to know him."

Gordon lifted Matt's chin up. Though there wasn't any logical reason for it, a trace of a smile still lingered on his lips. "That's the cross our Little Thumbling has to bear. As Heather said, we want him to be happy above all else, but it also makes me proud to see how well he deals with people and their prejudices." He squeezed Matt's shoulder. "Trust Shane to handle the situation with your mom, and give her time to get used to him. Time doesn't heal all wounds, but it helps with a good deal of them."

Shane had chosen well when he had decided on a fishing pole to represent his dad.

All the McAllistairs' smiles were highly infectious. Matt caught this one, even though the tension between his mom and Shane might be one of the sores that time couldn't cure. He'd probably find the courage to confront her at last, especially if Heather and Gordon joined the ranks of his allies. Maybe they already had.

"For a change, it's nice not to be the last ones to learn about someone important in Shane's life." Heather snickered, stopped suddenly, and raised her eyebrows. "Could it even be that we're the first?"

Matt pulled up one corner of his mouth. "Nick knew before you."

"Of course he did." Heather rolled her eyes. "But tell me that we beat Estelle this time. Please!"

A moment of silence ensued before all three of them burst into laughter.

"What's going on here?"

Matt whirled around. Shane, wearing a towel draped around his waist and hair still wet, stood on the last step of the stairs. Confusion furrowed his brows, and the muscles around his mouth twitched.

"Nothing." Matt walked over to Shane and looked up at him. "Only a guy kidding around with the parents of his boyfriend."

One Mississippi. Two Mississippi. Three Mississippi.

Shane's mouth fell open, and his eyes threatened to drop out. He pointed at Matt. "You?" His finger switched to his parents. "Them?" He shook his head. "How?"

"It kinda slipped out." Matt shrugged and grinned. "And in light of our no-apologies pact, there's nothing I can do about it." Sassy Matt was the best man for breaking news like this.

Shane stared at him for some more Mississippis before his features relaxed and his lips mimicked Matt's grin. He took the last step downstairs, placed his hands on Matt's shoulders, and turned him around so that he faced Heather and Gordon again. Shane pulled him close. "Just to make it official, Mom, Dad, may I introduce to you Matt Dermond, my boyfriend?"

Another breakout of laughter resounded through the kitchen, but Heather's and Gordon's eyes showed more than mere amusement. Maybe this was the look of parents who knew that their kid was happy.

Chapter Twenty-Three

IT WAS Thursday afternoon, and the long Monday night was still taking its toll on Shane. Yet the idea of visiting the new mall at the outskirts of the city with Matt to shop their grand-opening sales was too alluring to let pass. It meant a twenty-minute train ride there and back, but the four shopping bags in his hands brimming over with new clothes had been worth it.

They had just boarded the train back and already checked three coaches for an empty compartment but hadn't found one yet.

"Here's a free one," Matt called from the end of the aisle and beckoned him over.

Shane walked along the corridor, careful not to hit any of the passengers with the bags. The gaze of a little girl who sat on the lap of her mother followed him. Her large brown eyes widened even more, but she wore a huge smile. She gave Shane a short wave. Returning her smile, he nodded back at her. The girl whispered something into her mom's ear and sniggered. Kids often reacted like this, exhibiting more openness and maturity than any adult. One of the reasons Shane hadn't despaired yet.

Matt already sat by the window as Shane put the bags down, almost blocking the whole seat opposite them. He sank down beside Matt.

"I could've carried at least one bag." Matt primmed his lips.

So Matt hadn't given up yet, even after their fifteen-minute debate on the way from the mall to the station, which Shane had been sure he won.

"Of course you could have." Shane poked Matt's ribs with his index finger.

Matt gave a jump, and a single snort of laughter slipped out of his mouth. Shane had discovered his ticklish spot.

"Hey, that's not fair." His lips still pursed, Matt crossed his arms over his chest.

Shane grinned, for Matt did so firstly to show how pissed he was and secondly to protect his sensitive parts.

"I know, but I'm not allowed to apologize." Shane laid his arm around Matt and pulled him close. "Just indulge your brawny friend with letting him do what he can do best—carry heavy things."

Matt let his arms sink down from his chest and cuddled up against him. "Brawny *boy*friend, you mean."

Shane startled and looked around. The other passengers either hadn't noticed or didn't care as they read their newspapers or talked to one another. He huffed. Granted, this was a train full of strangers, but Matt was too careless when it came to trumpeting his coming-out. Best example was telling Shane's parents on the day after they'd met him. If only one person they knew got wind of Matt being gay, a whole bunch of new problems would knock at their door. Yet Matt was so happy right now, beaming from ear to ear, that maybe Shane was just frightened of his own shadow. A train full of strangers might actually be a safe place and a good training ground for Matt.

"Take this away! I cannot sit." A lady, roughly the same age as Estelle, stood before them and wagged her walking cane before Shane's nose.

The woman's face looked as if a ferret had been transformed into a human, but the process had failed somewhere in between. She got that expression in her eyes Shane had seen on other elderly people in the retirement home. They shouldn't mess with this one. Even though there were enough free single seats in the coach, he took down one of the bags and squeezed it behind his legs.

"Sorry, ma'am." Shane gave her a curt nod and a smile.

She answered him with a grunt that raised his hackles before she slumped onto the seat. With both hands, she grabbed her purse tightly and glowered over at them.

Best strategy to deal with these kinds of people was to ignore them. Estelle had taught Shane that during his first week at the home as a strict rule for survival. According to her, those peeps were jerks and suffered from what she called the "dried-prune syndrome."

Matt opened the shopping bag beneath Shane with two fingers and ogled the contents. "I also could've paid for these myself."

That had been the other debate, and Shane thought he had won that one too.

"I conned you into buying those, so it's only fair that I paid for them." Shane bumped Matt softly with his shoulder. "And before you ask again, yes, I really do think that you can wear bright blue pants. And yes, they look absolutely gorgeous on you."

All of Matt's clothes were black, gray, or another dark color, probably as some kind of camouflage against potential bullies. Matt still had to realize that he didn't have to hide anymore. However, buying those pants for him didn't qualify as a selfless act, because Shane enjoyed too much the way they flowed around Matt's ass.

"I'm not a gold digger." Matt gave Shane a shoulder bump in return, and his features darkened.

"Good gracious!" At the last moment, Shane replaced "Oh fuck!" with this ancient crap. He shouldn't give the dried prune sitting across from them any reason to have a bitch. "I may have two jobs and not many expenses, but if you chose me for the dough, you're in for a disappointment." He paid for this insolence with one more shoulder bump. "Seriously. In addition to heavy load transportation, indulge your brawny boyfriend with allowing him to buy you a gift for no reason sometimes."

Matt looked up at Shane, and the expression in his eyes went from sulky to mischievous. "I didn't choose you for the dough but for the beef." Even the mischievousness didn't stand a chance against the next feeling making its appearance. "And I chose you for just being you." He placed a small peck on Shane's cheek.

"That's right-out disgusting." The old lady spat out onto the floor. "Not enough that you buggers flaunt your abnormality on TV and harass us normal people with your perversions. Now you have to romp in public for everyone to see. There are kids here, you filthy pigs."

Coldness crept up Shane's back and trickled into the last corner of his body. He didn't give a crap what she said to him, but she couldn't talk like that to Matt.

Shane opened his mouth, but Matt beat him to the punch.

"In my humble opinion, speaking the very cusswords you just spouted is much more detrimental to the well-being of kids than seeing two boys kissing—" Matt tapped his lips with his index finger, pretending to think. "—and using the word 'kissing' for what we did requires a rather liberal interpretation of that… procedure."

Sassy Matt was in full mocking mode. That absolutely fucked with the idea of not stirring the dried prune, but the warm ball of satisfaction that formed in Shane's stomach returned good value for that. How far Matt had come. This crone was a bully, nothing more, but Matt stood up to her as if it were the only reaction he knew.

The woman opened and closed her mouth several times, and her face changed color from a sickly white to a not-much-healthier shade somewhere between violet and red. She clutched the handle of her cane, making her bony knuckles stick out. "You may think of the Nazis however you want, but they knew how to deal with scum like you." A sneer came about on her lips, lopsided and skewed, as if her mouth didn't recall how to smile for real.

In Shane's guts, the warm ball of satisfaction died away, and the cold feeling reclaimed his intestines. He had endured a lot of slander, mostly for his looks but also for being queer, yet no one had ever wished him to a concentration camp. That cut deeper than any door pillar ever could, and this wound would leave another scar.

Matt's body tensed, tremors shaking it. His eyes narrowed to slits, and their innocent blue darkened with unspoken threats. He was ready to pound and tear off the bitch's face with his bare hands.

Shane bent to the side, pressing against Matt ever so slightly.

Dear universe, please let him get this hint!

Where their bodies touched, he could feel Matt's pulse racing even through the fabric of their shirts, but with each second of closeness, the choppy beat slowed down. Matt pushed back against him, intensifying the contact between them. A bubble, powered by reassuring each other, formed around them, and nothing could penetrate there.

Matt's chest expanded. "That was the most ignorant thing I've ever heard, and I know a lot of really dumb people."

Fiery pain flashed through Shane's palm, but he didn't even flinch. His reflexes had taken over, and he had intercepted the cane without thinking. This hag had actually dared to lash out at Matt. The coldness in him ignited, and heat flared up in his face, his scar throbbing.

The old lady tore at the cane, trying to wrench it out of his grasp, but he closed his fingers around it even more. She wouldn't get another shot at attacking Matt.

"Help! Help!" the crone yelled with a voice that could shatter glass.

What the fuck?

The door of the coach opened, and the conductor stormed in, accompanied by a bulky bald man in a dark blue uniform.

Shane let go of the cane, and the old lady crashed into the backrest of the seat with a yelp.

"What's going on here?" The conductor looked at Shane, then at the woman. He arched his brows.

Glaring down at Shane, the security guy moved his hand over to the baton dangling from his belt.

Whatever story this shrew would cook up, they would believe her. Two young hooligans, one of them a model thug presumably just out of juvie, molesting an old, friendly lady made so much more sense than the truth.

"Those two boys said the most unpleasant things to me." Whoever this woman was, she had nothing to do with the one who had sat there mere seconds ago. Her features had softened, and her voice sounded warm, yet a little weepy. "The small one wanted to steal my purse. When I tried to make him stop, the big one struck at me." A tear coursed down her cheek. "All my money for this month is in that purse."

She was pulling off the show of her life. Who was the filthy pig here?

The conductor eyed him and Matt. He shook his head, and his mouth distorted into a frown.

Silence had fallen over the coach. Without even looking, Shane knew that everyone stared. He turned to Matt, whose face paled and all the anger in it vaporized. Matt was still trembling, but it was a different kind of shaking—he was in panic mode. However this situation turned out and whatever consequences arose, seeing Matt afraid again meant the worst punishment for him. The urge to bury Matt in his arms burned so powerfully, but an embrace would only whip up more feelings against them. More importantly, it might be too much for Matt right now. Once more, he had failed his boyfriend.

"Mommy, why is the granny lying?"

Shane jerked his head around. It was the little girl who had waved at him and still sat kitty-corner from them.

The girl, her forehead in wrinkles too deep for such a small face, looked up at her mom. "The boys kissed like Uncle Henry and Uncle Barney, and then the granny hit the small boy with her stick, but the giant saved him." She pressed her tiny lips tight. "And what's a Nuhzee?"

At a wheezing sound, Shane swirled back toward the old lady. Her facade crumbled for a second, and the sternness she had forced away for the conductor warped her features, terror written across them. She shot daggers at the little girl with her eyes, and only after some moments, she remembered that the whole coach was watching her. Her lips molded into another eerie attempt at a smile. "Oh, honey, what a lively imagination you've got."

"The little sunshine actually may have a lively imagination," an elderly man sitting in the compartment directly across said, "but every word from her is true." The man addressed the conductor. "Fortunately, she didn't repeat the horrible things that this—my good education prevents me from using another word—'lady' has said."

A young woman sitting across from that man nodded. The middle-aged couple that sat with the little girl and her mom murmured with each other, giving dirty looks to the old lady. Fragments of whispered conversations whirred through the coach and crescendoed into an agitated hubbub that was only just short of turning into a riot.

Shane gasped, for he had never experienced anything like this. People feared and sometimes simply hated him, but never had anyone stood up to take his side. A wave of gratitude—neither cold nor hot, only wonderful and electrifying—shot through him. Matt's fingers closed around his. They were still quivering, but this was a third type of tremor—the overwhelmed one.

The crone lost control of her face entirely. All the mass of her wrinkled skin sagged down, wobbling around as her cheeks twitched. Her mouth stood open, and her eyes flitted around.

"Quiet, please, quiet!" The conductor raised his voice and made a placating motion with his hands. He waited for the people to calm down and faced the old lady. "Ma'am. In a case like this, I'm not authorized to remove you from the train. But for your own security, I strongly suggest you… get lost."

Applause thundered through the coach, and the conductor beckoned the passengers to become quiet again.

The hardness latched back on to the crone's face, her features aflame with rage. She jumped up from her seat and waved her cane around as if it were a medieval pike. "You will all rot in hell with those—"

"Shut up!" the mother of the girl interrupted her. "I don't want my daughter to hear any more of your obscenities!"

Another wave of applause followed. The old hag grunted once more before she wheeled around, ripped open the door, and flounced out of the coach.

The conductor exhaled and faced Shane and Matt. "I'm sorry, guys. I hope that you'll enjoy the rest of your trip." He lifted his cap.

"Nice definition, by the way." The security guy nodded at Shane in approval.

The wave of gratitude still cascaded through Shane and broke on his insides, its little siblings reaching every place within. "Thanks," he whispered. "Thanks to all of you," he said with more force and let his gaze wander through the coach. So many friendly faces looked back at him.

He turned around. Matt's trembling had stopped at last, and now he sported the most amiable smile in the whole place. They squeezed their still entwined hands.

Matt's eyes flashed up. "We have to thank one person in particular." He rummaged through one of the shopping bags and produced the box of chocolate they had bought for Shane's parents. "They won't mind us giving this to someone else, will they?"

Shane shook his head. "Definitely not." It was safe to say they would even insist on handing it over to this special person.

They got up together and walked over to the little girl sitting diagonally across the aisle. Shane knelt down as Matt pulled on his hand.

The little girl watched him with friendly curiosity in her eyes and lowered her head to consider his biceps. "I love the pics on your arms, giant. This is my favorite color." She beamed at him and nudged a soft pink part of the quilt with her tiny finger.

He had seen many reactions to his tattoos, but how adorable was this? "Thank you, little lady. That's my favorite color too, and call me Shane, please."

The girl tittered. "Sure, giant Shane."

Okay, she would insist on calling him a giant, but dainty little girls like her were allowed to.

Matt's smile deepened even more, and he held out the sweets for the girl. "It was very brave of you to tell the truth, and giant Shane and I want you to have this as a reward." He faced her mother. "If that's okay?"

Cute boyfriends were allowed to call him a giant too.

The mother nodded and tousled her daughter's hair. "What do you say if you get a gift, Natalie?"

"Thank you!" A bright light radiated from Natalie's eyes, and her small hand closed around the box, which looked huge in comparison. She pressed it against her chest like the most precious thing in the world.

Shane fought down his tears. Why was he holding them back anyway? He was a sappy wimp who didn't look like one. No need to be ashamed of that. He put his arm around Matt's waist and glanced at his face. Who was happier, Natalie or Matt? Shane chuckled inside, but the fading pain in his palm summoned back the images of the crone whipping out at Matt and killed off his silent snickering. Matt was the very opposite of a wimp and perhaps even a little too brave, overcompensating for his life so far. They had been lucky this time, getting so much support from everyone, but Matt had experienced firsthand what could happen if he became careless about coming out. Hopefully he would be more cautious in the future.

CHAPTER TWENTY-FOUR

MATT HELD on to the yellow grips of the black ribbons with all the power that was left in him. His shirt was drenched with sweat, and every part of his body trembled. Suspension training had sounded like so much fun when Nick and Shane had explained it earlier that Friday afternoon.

Nick had called it "a little dangling from ropes and some easy, classic exercises on those ties." Nothing to it! It was a modern form of torture, and the Spanish Inquisition would've loved these devices.

"One more push-up, Matt, gimme one more." Shane's voice roared in Matt's ears.

His considerate, loving boyfriend and this relentless drill sergeant were one and the same person, however hard this was to believe. Not even Iain had ever ordered him around like Shane did during training. Thinking Iain's name never failed at riling him up, though. With the last reserves of strength, he pulled himself into an upright position. Matt was panting, and the rest of the gym looked blurry, for his eyes refused to focus.

"Well done, champ." Shane clapped him on his shoulder, and Matt swayed back and forth from the impact.

"If I survive this, I'll tell you what I think about you calling me champ." Matt had to press out every word during the short pauses his body left him before gasping for air again. He shook his drooping head, and at last, crisp vision returned.

"As long as the customer is sassy, he can train on."

Though Matt wasn't looking at Shane, he couldn't miss the barely muffled chuckle in his voice. Yet there lay some truth in those words. "Have mercy on me, and give me a short break at least."

"There's only one exercise left"—Shane clasped Matt's shoulder—"but as an elite life member, you earned yourself an isotonic drink on the house before we resume. Wait here for a sec."

Matt felt so bushed he wouldn't go far anyway, even if he tried to escape. He better bite back that comment, because it would earn him one more set of repetitions just for being defiant. "That'd be nice."

Shane squeezed Matt's shoulder again and let go of it. What a pity that he hadn't kissed him instead, but not here, and not yet. Shane wanted

Matt to be more secretive. He hadn't said it in so many words, though he kept reminding him about every five minutes after the incident with the old woman to take his time with coming out.

"Can't wait to be back." Shane's voice died as he walked away.

Matt had a minute or two to recuperate. This afternoon proved beyond any doubt that he and sports just didn't go together. Like cousins who've only seen each other once in their lives, their meeting was awkward at best. Still, training in the gym meant more time with Shane. He had yet to decide whether spending time with this slave driver who only looked like Shane was a good thing. Hell yes, it was.

"Hey you!" a young man's voice said behind his back.

Those exact words had started so many instances of bullying that Matt shuddered. Time disconnected as his body switched to high alert, and adrenaline surged through him. All exhaustion dropped off. He was ready for flight.

Don't be a douche!

He was safe here. Nick tended the counter just around the corner. Shane would return any moment. Many other people trained here right now. Unlike the students at Central High, they wouldn't look away… most probably not. Matt closed his eyes and took his time to breathe once more. He was safe here. That should become his credo. He turned around.

Two guys, sixteen or seventeen maybe, stood behind him. One of them was a head and a half taller than he was and blond. The other boy was only a tad smaller than his buddy, his hair a dark brown. Both of them were buff, showing off their muscled arms with sleeveless shirts. How much damage could they do before anyone came to his rescue? The voices in Matt's head screamed at him to at least take a fricking step away from them, but never again would he listen to those yells.

"Hey," Matt cawed and cleared his throat.

"You're here for the first time, aren't you?" the blond one asked. He was the one who had spoken first.

Matt nodded. "Yes." Everything was all right. They only wanted to talk. His heart refused to beat slower, though, for it claimed to know better than its owner did on what to do. The voices, still making a din in his head, endorsed the heart's assessment.

"You did awesome on the suspension ropes," the brown-haired boy said. "I've trained regularly for three years with the other machines, and I just look fucking ridiculous hanging down from them."

"You *are* fucking ridiculous, dude." For this, the blond guy had to take a punch on the shoulder that looked rather painful, but he only grinned.

The brown-haired one faced Matt again. "You're training with the Beast, right? You just have to give your best, then. No one pulls shit with him." The grins of these two looked like identical twins, and Matt wondered if they were actually related.

"The Beast?" A befitting name for that slaver lord who had replaced Shane. The corners of Matt's mouth curved up, and his heart grudgingly accepted that it didn't have to burst through his chest. Best of all, the voices shut their traps and pretended to never have piped up in the first place.

"Yeah. Shane went into beast mode as a kid, and then the switch broke." The blond boy gave his friend a smacking high five.

"Dillon. Jared." Shane walked up from behind, holding a small plastic bottle in his hand. "Aren't you supposed to bench press until your puny arms fall off?"

The two guys flinched, but it obviously took more to wipe the slyness off their faces.

"How much did you hear, Shane, dude?" the dark-haired boy asked.

"Enough that you'll fucking love your next training plans, Jared, dude." Shane's grin bested theirs with one arm bound to its back.

"Okay, okay. We're off to bench press again," Dillon said. "Nice to meet you, umm...."

"Matt. Nice to meet you too."

Dillon raised his hand. What did he want? But of course! Their high five hit hard, and Matt's fingers cracked alarmingly. This was the first guy his age who respected him. Well, the second one counting Shane, and he would bear some pain for a feeling as epic as this.

"Knock yourself out, Matt." Jared offered him a fist, and Matt bumped it back.

The two boys strolled to the other side of the gym, whispering to each other and laughing.

Shane moved closer to him and bowed down slightly. With lowered voice, he asked, "Did they frighten you?"

Matt's fingers closed into fists, and the muscles in his face tensed up. Shane knew him too well not to notice what was going on. On one hand, it was awesome that he could read him with ease, but on the other hand, Shane had caught him in the act of something that he should've gotten over by now. "In the beginning, a little bit." His confession turned into a meek whisper. He wouldn't lie to Shane, however embarrassing the truth was.

"They're nice guys and harmless." Another muffled chuckle got stuck in Shane's throat. "Mostly." He laid his arm around Matt's shoulder. "You fought down your fear, and you were even smiling at them when I returned. What more can you expect of yourself?"

Matt leaned on Shane. "I don't want to be afraid ever again. That's ridiculous, I know." Only to Shane could he say such things. No one else would understand.

"You suffered enough terror for two lives. Needless to say, you're sick of it." Shane curled his fingers on Matt's arm. "Yesterday, you didn't show any fear when you owned that bitch."

"That was different. She attacked you, blaring her bullshit, and I had to make her stop." For Shane, it was still so easy to be strong. "Your mom said that you're in good hands with me. I would've let her down if I didn't fight for you."

Shane's body convulsed, and he cringed before a single snort of laughter exploded from his mouth.

So, he found the idea of Matt caring for him funny? "Why are you laughing at me?" Matt pushed away, but Shane held him in place, tightening his grip.

"For goodness' sake, I'm not laughing at you!" Shane stepped before him and went down on his knees, fixating onto Matt's eyes. "You don't really think I'd do that, do you?" Worry strained the muscles in his face.

Shane wouldn't laugh at him. He never would. The residual adrenaline from meeting Dillon and Jared had turned Matt itchy and fretful. Usually his body spent all its energy on running, hiding, and trembling. Now it used that power to flail around instead. He had struck out at the person who least deserved it. Unfortunately he wasn't allowed to apologize for his bitching. He simply shook his head.

"I laughed because I thought the very thing about fighting for *you* yesterday. You only beat me to cut her down to size." Still holding the bottle with one hand, Shane let the back of the other slide down Matt's cheek. "I shouldn't have laughed. It was insens—"

Matt put his index finger on Shane's lips. A kiss would've worked better, though. Still not the place and still not the time. "No apologies, remember? Especially if it's not your fault." That also came close to an excuse. At least it eased a little of Matt's bad conscience. He let his finger drop.

Shane nodded. He licked his lips as if savoring the taste Matt's finger had left behind. "What do you say about skipping the last exercise and visiting the treatment room instead?"

The drill sergeant was gone, and Matt's boyfriend had returned. He definitely liked his boyfriend better. He leered. "What a splendid idea... Beast."

SHANE GUFFAWED. "I'd hoped you never found out about *that* nickname." He could live with being called "the Beast" in the gym, accepting it as a weird compliment, but Matt thinking about him like that made his stomach grumble.

"Too late." Matt showed his perfectly white teeth in a not so perfectly nice grin. "But don't worry. I like the beast on... oh, my mistake... in you very much."

The beast below Shane's waist reared its head as Matt called out its name. Shane extended his hand with the bottle, grinning back at Matt. "Drink this. You'll need the extra hydration and minerals." The beast down low would have to wait a little longer. If it woke up on the training floor, he would have to deal with a lot of other nicknames worse than "the Beast." Of course Dillon and Jared would happily provide them.

Matt took the bottle, downed it in one gulp, and wiped his mouth with the back of his hand. "What are we waiting for?" He knitted his brows. "Oh, I should take a shower first, shouldn't I?"

"Not necessary." The sweat only intensified Matt's smell, and it would be such a waste to get rid of it. Shane got up. Hopefully his bulge wasn't too noticeable yet. "You'll have to shower later anyway," he added under his breath.

Matt's cheeks were flushed from exhaustion, but they turned a notch more crimson as the redness crawled up from his throat.

"This might become handy too." Matt picked up his towel and draped it over his shoulder.

If they didn't leave soon, someone would notice Shane's growing boner. "How farseeing of you." He shoved Matt forward with his hand. Not that good an idea, for the touch drained even more blood from his brain to the beast. "No questions please, but walk right in front of me, okay?"

Matt nodded, and the muscles in his neck tensed as he obviously struggled to keep a laugh in.

The ten steps it took them to leave the training area felt like more— many more—but they managed to get to the corridor leading to the spa area without running into anyone. Here they could risk walking side by side, and Shane caught up to Matt, who discarded the empty bottle into a waste bin.

"I did some research." Matt lowered his gaze, the muscles in his cheeks working. He even looked cute when he was embarrassed.

"What kind of research?"

Matt's head sank farther down until his chin touched his chest. "I watched—instructional videos on the web."

This time Shane wouldn't laugh. Mentally punching himself in the balls helped him to not crack up, but a sly little smirk was allowed, wasn't it? "You watched porn?"

Matt yanked his head up and opened his mouth. "There are tutorials for real." The shock on his face mixed with a lopsided grin. "Okay, okay, most of those are thinly veiled porn, but they're instructional nonetheless." The grin won out.

"And did you learn anything?"

Matt had pulled off the feat to amuse and move Shane in equal parts. Only Matt would come up with the idea of theoretically studying sex. He used the scientific method with geeky consequence, which was even cuter than his embarrassment and gave rise to another southward rush of blood.

"Take that look off your face!"

Since Matt couldn't get rid of his own grin, Shane didn't take that request too seriously.

"Have you ever entered the words 'gay sex' into a search engine?" Matt asked. "You get way over 300 million hits. It was hard work to look through all of those."

"*Hard* work. I understand." The images of Matt sitting in his room and jerking off while taking notes on arousal and efficiency of stimulation should have been funny. They were fucking hot instead. The beast bobbed again in his boxers.

Matt's elbow bore into Shane's ribs so softly that it resembled a caress more than anything else. Another attack of the beast followed, and Shane's underwear only barely survived it.

"Feel free to mock me." Matt chuckled. "But you'll appreciate my *hard work* when I actually know how to get fucked by you."

Shane's cock dropped down cold. Matt talking about fucking should have made the beast go off, but it came out so abruptly and unexpectedly that his blood froze instead.

"You…." Matt swallowed. "You don't want to fuck me?" He sucked in his lips, and the blush faded from his cheeks.

Shane stopped dead in his tracks. "It's not about what I want, but do you really want"—he gestured at his crotch—"this up your ass?" Shane could never enjoy fucking Matt knowing he was in agony.

"I don't want *this* up my ass, but I want *you* inside of me. There's a difference." Matt grabbed both of Shane's wrists. "I watched enough porn to know that you're huge, and I know that it'll take patience to get you in there, but that's what I really want."

"They all say that, but...." Shane bit his tongue. "You don't want to hear about the men before you." He felt like shit. What he had said topped the list of the absolutely worst things he could break to Matt. It was bad enough to breach their no-apologies pact. "I'm sor—"

"Don't!" Matt's hands tightened around Shane's wrists. "Whatever happened with those men, it weighs down on you." He raised Shane's hands and placed short kisses on each of their backs. "Tell me, please! I will listen."

Shane still forgot how strong and sturdy a mind lived in this small and fragile body. His mom was right when she said that he was in good hands. He nodded. "Each and every guy who sees the monster—"

"Your perfect cock, you mean." Matt gave Shane's wrist a squeeze.

"Okay, my cock." That was a good compromise, wasn't it? "When guys see my cock, they implore me on their knees to fuck them because they never had such a big one, because it must feel awesome to have it inside, because it's a dream come true... just fill in some whacky reason." Guys never were sexy when they begged, but Shane couldn't snub them. He was too kindhearted—or dim-witted—for that. Until... no, he mustn't think about that. "Half of the head gets in at most, then the begging starts again. They cry and weep, and I pull out. Then that's it, end of date." Too late. The memory sneaked back, and the gruesome images floated through Shane's mind, bringing with them the helplessness of that night. He couldn't tell Matt about the one and only time he actually had fucked a guy, could he?

Matt wiggled Shane's arms. "You can tell me everything." He didn't insist but simply invited him to go on.

However Matt got inside Shane's head, he was glad to have him there. No one knew about that incident, not even Nick. It was about time to share it with someone, to share it with Matt. "One guy didn't want me to pull out. I had just turned eighteen. He was in his late twenties. We met in a club but ended up in his place. That man didn't beg. He offered me his ass, bit into the sheets, and didn't moan once. You can't imagine how happy I was that finally someone was able to bear me. I came, collapsed onto his back, and kissed his nape, thanking him over and over again." Shane gaped into

Matt's eyes. He was flooding him with all those details about a fling, and Matt looked back at him without the slightest sign of disgust, only worry and apprehension. He turned his arms around and grabbed Matt's because he needed to touch him back.

"And then?" The smile on Matt's face was so subtle that no one except Shane would notice.

"He asked me what the heck I was doing, said I wasn't supposed to cuddle with him but fuck him raw. I was shocked and pulled out to find blood all over the rubber." It had been one of the most haunting and terrible things that he'd seen in his life, only surpassed by what Hayden had done to Jer. "I panicked, but he just laughed. He said next time we should forget about the lube, and I shouldn't pound him like a pansy but destroy him for real." Shane closed his eyes and inhaled before the memory could choke him. "He even offered me a hundred bucks if I forgot about the condom too. I ran from his place." Only half-dressed and even leaving his jacket behind, Shane had just wanted to get out. Fortunately, he had had the presence of mind to take his wallet and phone with him, yet he had never returned to get the jacket.

With a jolt of his hands, Matt freed his arms and slung them around Shane's waist, pressing his small body against him with all the strength he had. Shane closed his arms around Matt in return, watching out not to hurt him.

"That's so terrible," Matt whispered, the warm air of his breath wafting through the fabric of Shane's shirt.

Matt's head left his stomach, and Shane opened his eyes, looking into friendly blueness.

"I don't want you to fuck me because it's some kind of freaky trophy, and I definitely don't want you to destroy me. I want you to fuck me because I yearn to be with you in any way possible. I know you'll be so careful and patient with me that we'll make it the most wonderful moment ever."

Matt's candor became a physical thing, a flow that surged over Shane. Those memories had churned up darkness in him, but it couldn't exist in the presence of that kindness. He would fuck Matt someday. It would happen. And it would be wonderful.

"Just be patient with me too." Shane bent down to peck Matt on his lips. He couldn't care less whether anyone saw them. The sweet taste bypassed his brain and shot directly into his cock.

Matt pressed closer. "Oh, the little beast isn't patient at all." The grin returned to his lips. "There are many more things from the instructional videos that piqued my scientific curiosity. It'll take some time to gather enough data on those before we should consider the fucking experiment." Matt turned around in Shane's arms and faced away from him. "To the lab!"

The feeling of Matt's back rubbing against his cock made a visit to the treatment room more urgent than ever. Shane raised his arms, seized Matt by his armpits, and lifted him off the ground a few inches. "My legs are longer. We'll get there faster if I carry you. All for the sake of science!"

"For science!" Matt chuckled, and his body fidgeted.

Shane sprinted off, carrying the most understanding and compassionate boyfriend in the world. His arms had never held more precious freight.

Chapter Twenty-Five

MATT DRANK in the air. The aroma in the treatment rooms was breathtaking, in the most literal sense. A sweet yet spicy odor surrounded him and tickled his nose. It was how a harem had to smell. Not the worst comparison, considering what they were up to.

Shane turned around after locking the door. The bulge in his training pants had grown even larger compared to a minute ago. He grinned. "So, Dr. Dermond, what kind of experiment did you have in mind for today?"

"Good that you ask, Dr. McAllistair." Matt pointed at the massage table. "First, can we bring this cot to a forty-five-degree angle?"

"Of course, Dr. Dermond!" Shane knelt down and twisted some knobs below the head of the table.

Even a mundane task like adjusting a table created a symphony of muscle that rippled all over Shane's body. Bulges rose out of his back and flowed into his skin again, just to reemerge at another place. On his biceps, veins popped out while skeins created pathways on the vast plains of his lower arms. Matt's own beast—okay, baby beast—smacked against the inside of his briefs.

Still kneeling on the floor, Shane raised his head. "Is this to your liking, Dr. Dermond?" The muscles in his face tightened as he fought to keep a serious expression and to not grin, but the result was a sweet grimace somewhere in between.

"Very good, Dr. McAllistair. Would you please sit down with your back against the elevated part of the table?" Matt liked this role-playing stuff. It had seemed weird in the porn videos, but in reality, it worked. Role-playing on their second date with sex. That had to set a new record for kinky coolness.

Shane lowered himself onto the table. The bulky trunks of his legs only barely fit onto the black leather cot, hanging slightly over the edge on one side or the other.

"You can put your feet down to the ground. This works even better for the experiment, I think."

Shane's face relaxed when he didn't have to balance himself on the narrow table anymore. "I'm curious about this *experiment*." His eyes shone with the gleam of a kid waiting to unwrap the first present on Christmas morning.

Matt stepped beside the cot and skimmed along Shane's leg with his body. Shane gasped. The results of the experiment were promising so far. He put his hand down on Shane's thigh, and once more, the complexity of shape and the firmness under his fingertips crept up his nerves and fueled a lightning storm in his brain. The results in both subjects were indeed very promising. He slid his fingers up the leg, slowly moving to its inside. Shane's bulge twitched more fiercely with each inch traveled, while the moan coming from his mouth swelled with the dwindling distance.

"If you do that a little longer, that alone will make me shoot." Shane wheezed, and his hand found the small of Matt's back, caressing it by curling and uncurling his fingers.

"I hoped for some more empirical studies before concluding this experiment." Matt's voice turned breathy and thin, the air stolen by the current that flowed from Shane's hand on his back, through his crotch, and to his hand on Shane's thigh.

"I'll do my best, but I can't promise anything." Shane's body arched up from the table, and one more of his groans boomed through the room.

Seeing Shane, powerful and strong, coming apart under his fingers was an aphrodisiac in itself. More arousing than anything he had seen on the web. Matt's cock pulsated in his briefs, and each throb caused a pleasant sting to reverberate through his body. This might actually be over sooner than he wanted. Time to speed things up.

Matt grabbed the waistband of Shane's training pants and boxers and pulled them down, Shane assisting him by lifting his ass off the cot. The clothes landed in one corner of the room.

Shane's cock was neither a monster nor a beast. None of the dicks on the web had even come close to this perfect piece of manhood. Matt may have been slightly biased in this assessment, but as an artist he recognized true beauty when he saw it. The desire to touch the huge length of Shane's cock welled up in him, but his hands were not supposed to make Shane cum today.

He turned his head to look into Shane's face. The angelic expression was back, strangely mixed with blushed cheeks and small beads of sweat on his forehead.

A horny angel.

Matt took the chuckle that cropped up in his belly, and by sheer power of will, transformed it into a smile.

"Ready for the real experiment, Dr. McAllistair?"

Shane nodded his head, breathing in an unsteady rhythm and whistling through his teeth.

Now it'd show whether watching the instructional videos had any merit. Matt faced Shane's cock again, bowed down, and closed in on the base. If any smell in this world deserved to be called male, then it was the aroma of this crotch. It was Shane's usual odor, only a hundredfold stronger and richer. A whiff of this scent sufficed to intoxicate Matt, but the intensity of the sensation felt like salt had been sprinkled on the raw ends of his nerves. He inhaled deeply, and everything around him faded. For this moment, the world was made up of nothing but Shane's aroma and Matt himself. He moved forward slightly, and as his nose grazed along Shane's balls, a roar shook the room. Matt peeked up, and the angelic part of Shane's expression had been overrun by the horniness. Shane was panting, his scar standing out crimson on his flushed cheeks, and the beads of sweat united into small streams that flowed down his face. Still eyeing Shane, Matt gave the sac a small lick. The smell of Shane's crotch condensed into a taste on his tongue, and his legs almost gave way under him. Shane roared out once more, that sound shaking the building to its foundations. Anyone getting a spa treatment in one of the neighboring rooms would be running for their lives right now. Matt returned his full attention to Shane's cock and placed his lips on its base again. Prepared for the explosion of taste in his mouth, he managed to keep standing upright—if only barely.

Shane's body reared up off the cot, his hand sinking into Matt's hair. "Oh, fucking grace!" His already deep voice dropped another octave, and the table resonated with its power.

What Matt was doing wasn't completely wrong, and a contented smirk settled on his lips. Phase two of the experiment would show whether more self-praise would be justified. He sought out one of the veins running up Shane's cock with his tongue, and the blood vessel felt so much larger on his lips than it really was. Another thing he had learned from the web, the tongue acted like some crazy magnifying glass—a fact that gave Matt's confidence a few cracks. If a vein already felt like it was totally filling his mouth up, he would simply choke on Shane's meat. He had to find out for himself. Matt let his lips follow the pulsing vein, and the crazy comparison of his tongue licking over velvet emerged from an even crazier place in his mind. The texture of Shane's skin was as soft as that fabric, just less fuzzy. He should have cracked up at this thought, but he didn't. His brain was so busy with sorting the torrent of impressions flooding in from all over his body that the idea of laughing about some lame joke he came up with himself only made it roll its nonexistent eyes.

Matt's nose slid over the ridge of Shane's cock head, still sheathed by foreskin. Shane growled. The roars before had sounded primal and wild, but this noise could only come from the Beast itself. Matt's overburdened brain redirected that bellow directly to his loins, and he shuddered. For some heartbeats, he had to concentrate on breathing or he wouldn't have breathed at all. Yet inhaling close to the head of Shane's cock proved fatal, for the scent it exuded was at least a factor of ten times stronger than the smell around his balls. His brain simply gave up, and the intensity of sensations washed over him, raw and unfiltered. The room around him turned dark. He grasped the last straw, totally focusing on Shane's aroma and turning the problem into the solution. The odor would act as his lifeline to this side of consciousness.

Shane's hand on the back of his head clamped, tugging on his hair ever so slightly. Matt drew back, for the pulling was gentle but still painful. Shane's fingers opened up with a jolt.

"I'm sorry. Sorry! But please don't stop...." The rest of Shane's sentence drowned in a gurgle. Instead of speaking, he caressed the back of Matt's head in slow circles.

His brain registered the breach of their no-apologies pact, shrugged its neural shoulders, and directed his hand to Shane's cock.

First problem first.

The tips of Matt's fingers made contact with the searing flesh of Shane's member, causing a tremor to rip through the powerful body. Matt retracted the foreskin and exposed the flawless acorn shape of the cock head, the gorgeous form glowing red with arousal. *What a sight!* He inhaled once more, opened his mouth slightly, and lowered it down on the tip of the head.

Shane only whimpered. Was Matt doing something wrong after all? Yet the stroking of Shane's hands picked up speed, and the pressure on the back of his head increased. Maybe Shane was just going through his very own episode of brain shutdown. Matt let his tongue circle around the slit. Shane's moaning pitched up before his other hand soared to his mouth, and he sank his teeth into it. The sudden silence irritated Matt, even more so than the wailing. He spread his lips a little more.

Careful with the teeth. Don't take too much at a time. Don't forget about your tongue.

Reciting the tips he'd learned on the web kept him from losing his mind entirely. His brain had resumed working, but only in some kind of emergency mode. His body was on fire. The parts that weren't smoldering yet resonated with his quickening pulse. Shane's whole cock head rested inside him now. Though its enormous shape filled his mouth to the max, he longed to take more. Matt bobbed his head back and forth, allowing more of Shane's length to slide in with each stroke. He ran his tongue over the lower rim of the bell-like form and found a landscape as complex as the rest of Shane's body. It'd take years to chart it all, and wasn't that just one wonderful outlook? The tip of Shane's cock head poking at the entrance of his gullet wrenched Matt back into reality. *Shit!* His throat would tighten and he would gag… but nothing happened. Obviously, his body agreed with him on keeping as much of Shane's cock inside for as long as possible. Slightly less than half of its length had vanished inside his mouth already. For his first blowjob ever, that was a remarkable achievement.

"Easy, Matt, easy… I… fuck…." Shane tugged on his hair again, prying him away. Though pain shot through Matt's scalp, he fought back and stayed put.

Shane's dick contracted between his lips, and the first wad of cum splashed into his throat.

HOLY FUCKING shit!

Shane's cum shot into Matt's mouth, and he couldn't help groaning.

This couldn't have happened. This shouldn't have happened!

He had to pull out; he had to…. The next shot of jizz erupted from him, sending a wave of pleasure up his body. Shane was in ecstasy while Matt suffered. He couldn't do anything more disgusting and despicable, but a third load followed while he thought these idle thoughts.

Shock seemed to paralyze Matt as well, for he didn't even try to get away from the spurting cock. His lips remained glued to the shaft. Matt's mouth constricted around Shane's member—he was swallowing!

A hot flash of panic rippled through Shane, and his stomach spasmed, making him retch. He scrambled back, but the cot at his back stopped him cold. The air in his lungs escaped with a squeal. He bowed forward, reached out for Matt's head with both hands, and pushed him away from his erection. The fourth shot hit Matt square on his cheek. Matt wouldn't forgive, no, he mustn't forgive him for this hideous failure. Shane had fucked up for real this time, and he may have just lost his boyfriend.

Matt blinked rapidly, and his lips shivered. His face melted into the white of the tiles on the wall, and the yellowish streak of cum stuck out from the fading bruise. "Have I done something wrong?" Matt's voice quivered along with his lips, and it sounded almost transparent.

All thoughts gushed out of Shane's brain, leaving behind a shapeless void in his head. The heat of panic cooled down and crystallized into shards of ice that pierced his insides. Matt's question didn't make sense at all. Shane understood the words, but their meaning remained a square peg to the round hole of his mind.

"I didn't mean to gross you out." Matt closed his eyes. He sank onto the table and clung to it with both hands. His legs were twisted in a strange angle, so they didn't support him at all.

What was he talking about? He didn't blame himself for this, did he?

Shane had to say something. Anything. "Huh?"

Matt opened his eyes, and furrows formed on his forehead. "You freaked out when I swallowed." He hesitated. "You didn't want me to, did you?"

"You let me cum in your mouth *on purpose?*" That's what Matt had just implied, but Shane couldn't trust his brain anymore if it came up with such bullshit.

The furrows on Matt's forehead became trenches. "The porn scenes where a guy shot into the mouth of another were so freaking hot." He extended his hand and let it hover over Shane's thigh but made no move to lower it down. "I thought you'd like that too." He averted his eyes to the ground and snuffled, wiping his nose with the back of his hand.

Once more, Matt stole all words from Shane's mind. The agitated beat of his heart hammered in his head, echoing through his empty skull.

Matt let me cum in his mouth.

Repeating that phrase didn't help to understand it in the slightest.

Matt swallowed my jizz.

Even if the words refused to obey Shane, Matt had to know that he hadn't done anything wrong. He grasped Matt's hand, letting every single finger close around the slender shape. It felt warm, and Matt's pulse raced as fast as his.

Matt looked up into Shane's face before his gaze sank down to their hands. A flash of a smile hurried over his lips but didn't dare stay. "You're not mad at me?"

He had to release the words, simply allowing them to do their own bidding. "You just took me by surprise. I wasn't prepared for that much… devotion." Not perfect, possibly even awkward, but it was the closest to the truth as words could ever come.

"That much devotion?" Matt sucked in his lower lip and chewed on it. "Yes, I feel that much devotion toward you." He released his lip from its toothy prison. "To be honest, swallowing your cum was something I wanted for myself. I did it for you too, of course, but my motives were selfish. I used you." A dimple formed on his right cheek only.

Shane let his thumb glide over the back of Matt's hand. "Gulping down your boyfriend's cum when sucking him for the first time is anything but selfish. I don't feel used at all. I *cannot* feel used." Cozy warmth seeped through Shane's guts, but this was more than postorgasmic bliss. "You blew my mind." He chuckled. "Pun intended."

Matt snorted, and his laughter made the cot rumble.

Shane crooked the fingers of his free hand while pulling on Matt's with the other one. Matt pushed himself up the massage table, crawling over Shane's legs. When Matt's belly brushed along his cock, the beast already began to stir again.

They were face-to-face now. Shane reached out for Matt's cheek and wiped off the cum with his index finger. He turned around to get rid of the spunk with one of the paper tissues on the tray beside the table, but Matt grabbed his wrist before shaking his head and bowing forward. Matt's gaze locked on him. He opened his mouth slightly and licked up the jizz. The warm and wet touch of Matt's tongue on Shane's skin unleashed a shudder that darted along his body. A sigh slithered up his throat. The realization that Matt just ate his cum again sent another jolt of bliss down his spine. Shane clutched Matt's head to pull him in for a kiss. The taste of his cum blended with the sweetness of Matt's mouth into an exhilarating mix. Their tongues wound around each other, and the swelling intensity of their kiss jarred Shane. The beast reawakened for real.

Matt moved back slightly, and the hot breeze of his breath warmed Shane's face. "Ready for round two?" he whispered.

"What about you? I just got the best blowjob ever, and you got the shaft."

Matt let out a guffaw that rang right down into Shane's marrow, just to head farther south straight into his cock.

He slapped his forehead. Letting out the words as they came didn't make for such a clever plan after all. "Pun not intended this time, I swear."

Matt held his stomach, the last convulsions of his laughter ebbing away. "You've got enough shaft for sure, and I got a lot of it already." He bit his cheek as another bout of tittering announced itself by shaking his belly. "Seriously, I enjoyed every second of the first time. Your definition of sex is making each other cum, I know, but sucking you is so damn hot that

I can pass on shooting for now." He smirked. "You can pay me back later. With interest."

Matt's comment was lighthearted and sassy, but to Shane's ears, it sounded like the sweetest declaration of love. Though he would never admit it to Estelle, she had been right from the start. He was in love. Head over heels. And in Shane's case, that was quite a distance. He loved Matt, but the time hadn't come to tell him yet. Not in a dimly lit borrowed-from-Nick-for-some-privacy room. Not with the both of them horny as hell. Not without pants. A grin slipped out onto Shane's face.

Matt raised one eyebrow. "What's the matter?"

"Nothing." Shane folded his hands under his nape and lay back. "Just the thrill of anticipation."

"No time to waste, then." The impishness of Matt's smirk beat the hell out of Shane's grin.

He loved Matt, and he would wait for the perfect sappy moment to tell him. This moment would need candles, another golden box, perhaps with a ring in it, and cheesy classical music.

Matt's mouth closing over the head of his cock ended Shane's planning all of a sudden, for Matt sucked his mind right out of him.

CHAPTER TWENTY-SIX

Thursday, Three Weeks Later

MATT CLOSED the door of the bio lab, strode down the hall, and headed for the staircase. He was still the only one volunteering to clean the lab, but it felt different now. This chore had once been a pretense to stay away from the school halls where danger lurked behind every corner. These days Shane would protect him from anyone and anything, even if a pride of lions raided the school hunting for tiny antelopes. Matt swallowed down a chuckle that prickled in his stomach. Snickering in public without reason would look weird, even for him.

A group of three guys passed by, discussing something with expansive movements of their arms.

Not a single extra beat of his heart. No rush of adrenaline pushing him to flight. He didn't even flinch. Bolstered by the safety Shane offered, Matt had dared to look at his fellow students for real. Just like him, most of them only wanted to finish high school with the least hassle possible.

Matt sped up his steps and hurried down the stairs, for Shane had to be waiting already, given his Germanic sense of punctuality. Sadly, it'd only be a short meeting before Matt had to attend one of his beloved phys ed lessons. Those had become bearable at last after he'd begun training with Shane. He turned the corner and froze. Iain, Tyler, and Eric hung out before the row of lockers. They talked noisily, but their words got lost in the busy hall. Those three, however, made Matt's pulse go up, and a generous dose of adrenaline shot into his veins. He had to stay calm. They mustn't notice how much they still affected him. No incident with Iain had occurred in the last four weeks, but their truce was volatile. Even porcelain constituted a sturdy material in comparison to this arrangement. Matt sucked in a good draw of air, gave the oxygen some seconds to suffuse into his blood, and let it go again. He commanded his feet to move. Surprisingly, they obeyed, blinded by the out-of-character audacity of their owner.

Head high. No trembling. Neutral face.

He walked by Iain and his subordinates, and the maroon color of their jackets alone triggered Matt's next DEFCON level. His heart wandered up, throbbing at breakneck speed in his throat. Three heads swiveled around, and three gazes landed on him.

Don't look away.

Matt was new to the staring game, but it couldn't be that difficult if those three could pull it off. Maybe he should defend himself by attacking. Not quite Sun Tzu, but with those opponents it was more than enough of a strategy. He gave Iain a nod, and Iain stiffened for the fraction of a second but long enough to notice. Had his freckled face also become a little paler? Matt shouldn't get too cocky, though. He passed by them. Unfortunately, he didn't have the one-hundred-eighty-degree neck of an owl, but in the moment before he turned his head away, Iain nodded back. That was weird to say the least. The fear that he'd ruin Iain's baseball career seemingly still made him wet his pants and served as the glue holding their truce together. Matt was new to this kind of balance of terror too. But he could live with it. Live very well with it.

Each step farther away from the three lowered Matt's pulse, and the tension made way for a tingling sensation that coursed through his body. He had only experienced this feeling once, and Iain had also been part of that. Matt was high on victory. His thoughts whirled. He was free. After all these years, he could close this fucking chapter of his life.

Shane doesn't have to protect me anymore.

This insight clashed with the other thoughts circling in Matt's mind and caused a chain-reaction collision. When his clogged-up brain churned to life again, it took some moments for his gray cells to run smoothly. Yet they spewed out an interesting interpretation of that insight. He wouldn't be Shane's burden any longer, and if Shane didn't have to be Matt's bodyguard, they could be boyfriends only. A perfectly normal couple.

The tingling feeling in Matt soared, and his skin crawled, but in an absolutely awesome way. Infinite possibilities opened up before them. Something like… this. Matt eyed the banner that the school party committee, ruled by Elaine, had put up over the main hall. "A ball night in October." A cliché. A corny, tacky, tasteless cliché. Shane would love it. And the party would be more like an extra prom in autumn that Queen Elaine bestowed upon her subjects. The perfect debut for Shane and him as a couple.

Matt picked up speed. He had to get over to the stadium soon, but he had to ask Shane first. The party was a week from Saturday, one day after his birthday. That was the gift he wanted.

He almost crashed into a girl, but he circled around her in a playful dance. "Sorry." He grinned at her, and she gawked back at him, bedazzlement on her face. His fellow students would also need time to get used to the brand-new, shiny Matt.

When Matt arrived, Shane was rummaging through his locker, head buried inside as if trying to crawl into it.

"I don't have to turn around to know it's you, Matt. I'd recognize those steps among hundreds."

"Since you're psychic, you probably already know what I want to ask you." Matt's face stung from his wide grin, but he couldn't stop.

A chuckle, strangely distorted with a metallic echo, came out of the locker. "The spirits aren't that willing today, so I'm afraid you have to ask me anyway." Shane snickered once more. "At least the spirits could tell me where I put my Chem 101 book. Ah, here it is." His grin rivaling Matt's, he emerged from the locker and waved the book with a triumphant swing before he stuffed it into his backpack.

Seeing Shane still took Matt's breath away every single time. Why in the world had this handsome giant of a man picked him as his boyfriend? Shane would probably insist that Matt had been the one who had picked him. Whoever had done the choosing, it was time for the world to learn about their perfect choices. "Do you have any plans for Saturday after next?"

Shane pursed his lips sideways. "That's a trick question, isn't it? Your birthday is the day before that on Friday."

"It wasn't a trick question, but you passed anyway." Matt enjoyed delaying the moment of asking Shane to the party, but at the same time, he hated every second he had to wait for the answer. "Let me elaborate. Do you have any plans for Saturday after next, one day after my birthday, and do you think it's outrageous to ask for a certain gift in particular?"

Shane knitted his brows, and his grin died away. "You're not talking about—" He looked left and right and continued with a lower voice. "—fucking you?"

Matt had suggested this as a present before—half tongue in cheek, half hoping. "I'd still love *that* gift, but I also accept that you're not ready for it yet." As the bottom, Matt should be the one who worried, shouldn't he? Especially with a top whose package required extra handling, but Shane's gruesome experiences required Matt to show patience. He heaved a sigh.

A wisp of a smile appeared on Shane's lips, and he swept over Matt's upper arm with his hand. Matt closed his eyes and let the shiver pass through him, waiting for its tide to ebb. Shane's touch was such a nice gesture, but it was too fleeting, too restrained, too vague. A gesture toned down for the public. Matt needed more, and he was ready for more. He opened his eyes. "Do you want to go to the school party with me?"

Shane's hand glided down Matt's arm, and his eyes narrowed. "You mean as friends?"

"No, as boyfriends. It'll be really formal, with waltzing and…." An electric jolt raced up Matt's spine and jarred his brain. He hadn't even considered that Shane might decline.

"It's too early." Shane's hand slipped off Matt's arm. "It's too early for you." He inhaled deeply, and the volume of his chest almost doubled.

"Or is it too early for *you*?" Matt whispered, though he wanted to scream. "Are you ashamed of me?" He almost choked on his words. Did Shane already regret his choice? But he didn't know about the new Matt, didn't know that he could stop playing watchdog. Matt had to tell him and had to set things right….

Shane clutched him by his shoulders, but Matt's brain refused to register the pain, for it was already doubling over in its own agony.

"That's fucking crap, Matt. How can you say something like that? You know that's not true." Shane kept his voice low, but its deep sound droned in Matt's ears. "I'm so proud to have you as my boyfriend that I want to run out onto the street, grab every person there, and yell into their faces that you're mine."

The ground beneath Matt opened up. He was in free fall, and the world rushed past him in a blur. "Then go to the party with me. Yell it into their faces!" He encompassed the hall with a sweep of his hand.

"If they know, the teachers will know, and if the teachers know, your parents will learn that you're…." Shane's words died away, and the muscles in his face strained.

"Gay. They'll learn that I'm gay." The pain from his shoulders trickled into his brain at last.

"Have you thought about the consequences? Do you really know what this can do to your life?"

His dad probably knew already, and his mom would only take offense at Shane being his boyfriend. The consequence would be that he could stop lying to his parents. His life would become almost perfect. "You trusted your parents, and you had to tell them. I feel the same about mine." It was only four weeks, but Matt felt so sick of hiding from his mom. She may still not deserve to be told, but he deserved to tell her, and Shane deserved not to be tucked away anymore like some embarrassing piece of tchotchke.

The grip on his shoulders slackened, and Shane kneaded them. The gentleness returned to Shane's hands, easing the pain they had caused in the first place.

"Even if your parents are fine with us, what about everyone else? Think about what happened on the train." The gentleness returned to Shane's voice as well.

"You mean a train full of strangers supporting us against a single hypocrite?" Someone would always object to their love, but the number of people who didn't, who even endorsed it, grew every day. Shane had it wrong.

"I don't want you to get hurt ever again." Shane nodded to himself. "Coming out here in school is like painting a target on your back. As the former LGBT alliance president of my old school, I hate myself for saying this, but staying in the closet is so much safer for you." A short-lived smile flashed on Shane's lips.

"But in this closet, no one sees how much I love you."

Matt shouldn't have said those three words. Not in a fight. Not as casually as he had.

Shane's hands dropped down from his shoulders, and the coldness of reality crept in to replace their warmness. His mouth quivered, his scar squiggling on his cheek. All color flowed from his face, and his breath came and went quickly. From this pallid whiteness, the two pieces of charcoal that were his eyes stuck out and scrutinized Matt.

"What I said is true. I love you, Shane." The truth had to be clad in dignity or it didn't have any merit at all. This much the poems and plays had taught him about love.

A light sparked up in Shane's eyes and turned them into embers, tinting his face with their blaze. "I—"

"No!" Matt screamed. "Don't say it." He leaped back. "Don't say it, just because I did." His lungs couldn't fill as fast as they should. "If you say it, I have to be sure that those are your words, that you mean them." He had thrown away this precious moment, and Shane mustn't repeat his mistake.

"I really—" Shane stepped forward and reached out for him with both hands.

"Please don't!" he shouted, louder than before, then backed up. "Please don't!" he repeated in a whisper.

Shane froze, his hands hovering in midair.

"Not here. Not now." Matt shook his head in short, quick jerks. "Tell me later. Just tell me later." He closed his eyes, forcing himself to breathe slower. Shane's presence, his warmth and his scent, approached Matt and surrounded him. He yanked his eyes open.

Matt put his head back as far as he could, for Shane stood so close that he filled up his entire field of vision. The angelic smile floated above him, and the affection from Shane's eyes poured onto him.

"Later, then." Shane's voice was mellow, and its softness caressed Matt.

"I love you," Matt said, fainter than a whisper. "I have to go. Phys ed." He yearned to fling his arms around Shane, smother him with kisses, and never let go again. He had spoiled his own moment, but he wouldn't spoil Shane's. All these things were to happen later, and this later would be perfect. He took a step back. "Later, then." A grin flashed on his lips. Matt spun around and dashed forward a few steps, only to stop again. He faced Shane, waved at him, and without waiting for his answer, darted down the school hall.

Later would be perfect indeed, and for once, Matt didn't hate waiting.

CHAPTER TWENTY-SEVEN

SHANE HADN'T moved for a minute. He still stood where Matt had left him in the now-deserted school hall. The bell had rung, and he was late for chemistry, but Mr. Huntington couldn't teach him anything about the reactions going on inside him at this moment. These were the only reactions he was interested in right now.

I love you, Shane.

The fascination of those words didn't diminish. It got even more intense every time he repeated them.

I love you, Shane.

A shudder ambled down his spine, roamed around in his guts, and strolled back to his head, taking all the time in the world to finish its casual walk. Definitely more fascinating than before.

He wouldn't moan about how different the moment had been to what he had imagined. That this moment had taken place at all was the only thing that counted. Moreover, he would have the chance to create his own sappy version of it, and Matt wouldn't refuse to hear the words then.

If Shane cut chemistry today and asked one of his colleagues to switch shifts at the retirement home, he'd have barely enough time to organize all the things he needed. Flowers? Chocolate? Candles? Time was too limited to buy a ring, though, and he didn't know what size anyway. Asking for a ring that would fit the cutest fingers in the world would only result in confused faces at the jeweler's.

What about sex? Was it appropriate to have sex on the evening they declared love to each other? Miss Manners couldn't have a rule for this either.

Shane laughed out loud. Two sophomore girls, sauntering down the hall and chatting with each other, stopped cold, turned pale, and made a U-turn. Any Olympic runner would've nodded in praise for the time it took them to go from standing to full dash. Shane bit his lip. By now his fellow students should've learned that he was harmless. Yet today, even frightened schoolgirls couldn't bring him down.

So what about sex now? Matt and Shane loved each other, and sex had become an important part of their relationship. In the light of their mutual love, even fucking didn't seem as frightening as before. He would buy condoms, normal-sized and extra large, and some lube. Just in case. Shane looked around to make sure he wouldn't scare anyone before he chuckled this time.

He could find some classical music in his dad's collection. Check that item off the list. He was still missing a gift, something to sweep Matt off his feet, something that showed him how seriously Shane took their relationship.

The party!

They hadn't decided on the party. Shane's stomach still turned at the idea of Matt coming out to the whole school, but he had promised to leave this decision to him. Four weeks wasn't nearly enough for such a far-reaching move. It had taken much longer for Shane to come to terms with being gay, and even longer to tell Nick as the first person. On the other hand, Matt had made leaps of progress in regard to gayness. Not much longer and he would be a better queer than Shane himself. Another chuckle erupted from him. Fortunately there still wasn't anyone around to be afraid. Even if he didn't agree with Matt about the pace of coming out, he should support him. He *had* to support him. What would change anyway? Their fellow students avoided them, and they avoided their fellow students. No one would dare to challenge Shane the Gay Drug Lord by laying a finger on Matt. Elaine's rumors were yesterday's gossip, but something always stuck. Finally they could make out and cuddle everywhere. What more reason did Shane need to decide for the party?

The committee sold the tickets from nine to five, so he could get them right away. He shouldered his backpack and headed for the student representation office, which was just around the corner. The door stood open, and he entered. Like Shane, the universe was in a lighthearted mood, for it had arranged for Elaine herself to be the one tending the ticket sales counter. He reined in another snicker that gathered in his throat. After his first day, he hadn't seen the blonde cheerleader again. Most likely because she moved heaven and hell to stay clear of him. Performing The Evil Shane Show for her had been a blast, but now a stab of regret hit him. Hopefully she'd sell him the tickets and wouldn't leave an Elaine-shaped hole in the wall instead.

Elaine, dressed in her school uniform of course, sprawled over the counter. She scribbled onto a yellow legal pad with a pen that had pink feathers dangling from its end.

"Hey. I'd like to buy two tickets for the party." Shane used his milk-and-honey voice, though it had yet to show whether the effort made any difference.

"For a couple? We've got that great discount for—" She looked up, and her gaze sank back down to the counter at once, her pigtails swishing wildly. Her face turned white, blending into the uniform, exactly as it had on their first meeting. "—couples," she breathed out. Her hands were shaking, and the pen left erratic patterns of zigzags and circles on the paper.

Wow! The Evil Shane Show had impressed her for real. At least she wasn't fleeing or yelling for help yet. Her question was a good one, though. Shane might as well commission a full-page ad in the newspaper to announce that Matt and he were boyfriends if he told Elaine. Just admitting that he was in a relationship would send the gossip avalanche rolling. Matt alone set the pace for his coming-out, and he should decide when it happened.

Moreover, Matt might actually be pissed if Shane ruined his grand entrance at the party. He pinched his thigh to not laugh out loud. Sending two girls running with the maniacal laugh of a supposed thug sufficed for one day.

"The tickets are for a friend and me. No couple discount." If he spoke a little more high-pitched, all dogs within a mile would go crazy. "How much?"

Elaine kept staring down at the counter, doing nothing but trembling, breathing, and remaining pale. What could he do to break through to a frightened cheerleader?

"My last dance lesson took place over two years ago, and I hope I can still do the waltz." Miss Channing from Miss Channing's Dance Academy probably still treated her sore feet and would insist that Shane never learned the waltz in the first place. She hadn't charged him anything, on the condition that he never mention he had attended one of her classes.

"The waltz is so easy." Elaine lifted her head up. "It's only one, two, three, and…." Her voice trailed off, but at least her head stayed up this time.

"For the sake of the school's foot health, I'd better skip the waltz." Shane smiled his killer smile. Elaine probably thought of it as just that, only with a more literal interpretation of the words. "How much for the tickets?"

"Hundred dollars for both." Some of the color returned to her face.

A hundred bucks for a party? Yet seeing Matt happy was worth it. Luckily, Nick had paid him only yesterday, and Shane still carried the money in his wallet.

"The waltz is optional, and since you're not a couple…." Her voice died off again, and her features stiffened up. She produced two tickets from below the counter and put them down without a further word. With a brisk jolt, she hid her jittering hands behind her back.

This situation could only go downhill from here, so he hurried to place a hundred-dollar bill on the counter, avoiding any abrupt movements, and picked up the tickets. "Thank you so much!" Shane meant it, neither irony nor sarcasm involved. He didn't express his gratitude for the awkward experience Elaine created, but for coming up with the hilarious rumors about him. They had sparked the first conversation between him and Matt, and who knew how things would have developed if they hadn't had her bullshit to talk about. "See ya at the party."

Elaine's eyes widened, and she only nodded. It would definitely be interesting to watch her reaction when he and Matt showed up as a couple next week.

Shane left the student representation office with long, quick strides, letting Elaine off the hook as fast as possible. That scene had been strange, but he had the tickets. He still had so much to do and decide. What should he wear? What about food? Should he buy something extravagant to eat? Caviar? Oysters? What about drinks? They both didn't do booze, but this moment cried for champagne. And he had to prepare a speech to wrap up the most important words in his life so far.

I love you, Matt.

SHANE PLACED the golden cardboard box with the party tickets in the white wicker basket he had borrowed from his mom. The gift for Matt completed his collection of gimmicks he needed for their special moment. A declaration of love to go. For the umpteenth time, a giggle burst out of him. This day warranted all the giggling and chuckling that wanted to come out. He had acted like a kindergarten kid on a sugar rush all day, and he was allowed to.

His cell, lying on the table, showed 5:00 p.m. He only had to dress up, though that posed a tough decision. Matt loved the tee-and-sweatpants combos like the one Shane was wearing right now. On the other hand, this moment deserved a little more glamor, but a suit looked so formal. Maybe a compromise? Tee and suit? Or shirtless and suit, like a stripper? He giggled again. Shane would leave Matt the pleasure of stripping him. Being honest, he'd have as much pleasure as Matt, perhaps even more so. Tee and suit sounded perfect for this. With the dress question answered, it was time to pick up the phone and invite Matt over. He closed his eyes and inhaled, filling his lungs to the max. Shane wanted nothing more in the world than to have Matt here in his room. Still, the jitterbugs ran rampant in his stomach. Finally he understood why people got cold feet on the day of their wedding, but he wouldn't back out. He was too sure about his love for Matt. Shane let the air stream out of his lungs and opened his eyes. Ready or not, here he came. His hands were remarkably steady as he reached out for his phone.

The doorbell rang, and he leaped several inches off the ground. His heart defied the laws of physics somehow and didn't jump with the rest of his body. It met the jitterbugs in his stomach and greeted them by tripling its beat. Obviously the rest of him wasn't as steady as his hands. He wasn't expecting anyone except… Matt. Shane twirled around, tore open the door, and stormed out.

Ouch!

He rammed the doorframe, but even his shoulder falling off wouldn't keep him from welcoming his boyfriend. Matt's surprise visit was the cherry on the cake that was today. Taking four steps at a time, Shane hopped down the stairs. He leaned into the curve around the railing and by a whisker missed the wardrobe that stood in the hall. The doorbell rang again, and he smiled. Even when Matt was impatient, he was adorable. Shane turned the knob and yanked open the door.

"I've been expecting—" His voice faltered. It wasn't Matt. "—you."

Two police officers in dark blue uniforms waited before the door. One of them had his hand on his holster, the handle of the gun peeking through his fingers. The other one had been talking into a radio attached to his shoulder, but he released the button, and his arms sank down. They looked up at Shane, and every negative reaction to seeing him for the first time crowded their faces—fear, disgust, shock, and one emotion new to these ranks, discontent with the fact that of all people they had been sent here.

"Shane McAllistair?" the one with the radio asked with a gruff voice.

"Yeah, that's me." Shane felt dizzy, his mind buzzing with scraps of thoughts. Why were the cops at his door? He hadn't broken any jock's arms lately, hadn't even been close to it.

"Mr. McAllistair, you're provisionally arrested for aggravated assault on Mr. Matt Dermond. You have the right to remain silent…."

The rest of his words drowned in the boom roaring through Shane's head. The world around him didn't reach him anymore. It was as if he were encased in cotton, and there was only blackness.

Matt had been attacked.

Someone must have eavesdropped on them earlier today, had heard that they were boyfriends, and that cowardly bastard had struck out at the weaker one. Acid circled through his veins, corroding them and spilling out everywhere. His body was on fire. The jitterbugs died, and a swarm of flesh-eating scarabs replaced them. He'd kill the asshole. He'd rip out each of his limbs before crushing his skull with his bare hands. Iain! It must have been Iain! Whatever this sack of shit had done to…. Matt!

"How is Matt? How badly is he injured? Is he…?" Shane banished that last question from his mind. He mustn't finish it.

The officer who had been talking squinted his eyes. "We're not authorized to discuss any details of the crime with you, Mr. McAllistair." He shifted his jaw left and right. "Do you understand the rights I just explained to you?"

Why wouldn't they tell him about Matt? They had to tell him. "How is he?" Shane's legs buckled, and he plunked onto his knees. "Please." A breathy stream came out of his mouth that only vaguely resembled a word.

The policemen looked at each other, and the gunner shrugged, raising one corner of his mouth as well.

The radio guy faced him again and laid his hand on Shane's shoulder. "Mr. McAllistair, we're not permitted to reveal the condition of Mr. Dermond to a suspect." His grip on Shane's shoulder tightened. "But listen closely. We're arresting you for aggravated assault. That's something different from murder."

The officer's sentence trickled into the empty space of Shane's head and bounced off the walls of his skull. Letter for letter, he grasped its meaning. Matt was alive! "Thank you!" He still could only breathe those words. Shane had to know the full details of Matt's condition, but the cop had already said more than he should have.

The gunner produced handcuffs from his belt, yet his colleague waved his hand. "I don't think those are necessary." He fixed Shane with his gaze. "They aren't, right?"

Once more, Shane's brain needed all its capacity to unravel the meaning of the officer's words. He nodded. The more he cooperated, the faster this misunderstanding would clear up and the sooner he could see Matt. "Can I leave a note for my parents?" He was allowed to make one call only, and he'd call the Dermonds. His parents could take care of the rest, like contacting their lawyer.

The gunner crossed his eyes and opened his mouth, but the radio guy beat him to it. "Of course, Mr. McAllistair."

Shane put one foot on the ground and rose up from his knees slowly, so as not to give the gunner any wrong ideas. "Thank you so much. This will only take a minute." He made way for the officers. "Come in, please."

The nice people in this world turned it into a bearable place. On the other hand, it wasn't worth living in a world with scum like Iain in it who harmed a wonderful person like Matt. His life was entangled with Matt's. Whatever happened to Matt, Shane would share his fate. No matter what fate that was.

CHAPTER TWENTY-EIGHT

SHANE HAD lost track of how long he'd been sitting in the interrogation room alone. Fifteen minutes? An hour? It'd been at least enough time to come up with too many gruesome pictures of Matt's injuries—crusted blood, torn flesh, and bones poking out. He shuddered. Just staring at the walls helped. His brain needed something to occupy it, even if it was only the gray concrete around him.

This room could have been a soundstage straight from a crime series on TV. One table screwed to the ground and two chairs made up its furniture. A lamp hung from the ceiling, its bulb much too bright, yet half of the room lay in twilight. Opposite him, a mirror covered most of the wall, for every interrogation room was required to have one by cliché. Shane looked at his own reflection. Was someone watching him through the half-transparent glass right now while wondering what cat had dragged that miserable piece of shit in?

The detective kept the piece of shit waiting. Matt certainly had to be asking himself why Shane hadn't shown up at the hospital already. The Dermonds hadn't answered their landline, and he should have known better than to call them. They were with their son, taking care of him, of course. That was what he was supposed to be doing, but the people at the precinct had taken their time with unnecessary paperwork. Telling them that he had done some shopping and had been home around two o'clock obviously didn't suffice as an alibi. No one had listened when he told them about Iain either. So much effort and wasted tax money for a mere misunderstanding while the son of a bitch who had hurt Matt was still free. Shane eyed his hand, cuffed to a metal hook on the table and blackened from the fingerprinting. The officers here at the station didn't take any risks. He had been lucky with the ones arresting him.

Had his parents already found the note? A pang of remorse stung Shane's chest and squeezed his heart. His parents would have to visit their son in a police station for the second time. Two times more than they should have had to, though tonight he definitely didn't deserve being here. They didn't deserve this either.

The door opened at last, and a thirtysomething-year-old man slogged into the room. Deep black rings extended beneath his eyes while way too many wrinkles spread away from their corners. His features were hard, and he primmed his lips, making them almost disappear. He slumped down on the chair opposite Shane, rested his head on his arms, and gazed down at the table. Brown stains covered his fingers, and the smell of old cigarette smoke and pizza wafted into Shane's face. This had been a handsome man once. Traces of this beauty still lingered, but his job, his life, or whatever had drained most of his charisma away.

"We can do it the easy way or the hard way, Shane. You don't mind if I call you Shane, do you?" The cop still burrowed his head in his hands.

"Of course not, Detective…?"

"Just call me Detective Shit End, because that's the end I got tonight." He raised his head, and his gray eyes looked as dull and lifeless as his face. "So, easy or hard way?"

His charm had died along with his attractiveness. He wouldn't like Shane's answer, even if it were the truth.

"I didn't attack Matt. The very thought is ridiculous." Shane twisted his mouth. "That's the hard way, I fear?"

Detective Shit End groaned through his clenched teeth and nodded. "Can't you punks admit for once what you've done? Just for variety?"

"I can't admit what I haven't done." It'd be the *very* hard way.

"Oh, this is the first time I've heard that one." The sarcasm wiped away the last remnants of likability from the detective's features. "But perhaps I can give you some hints, and we'll see if we don't find something you can admit after all." He produced a rumpled sheet of paper from his shirt pocket and unfolded it onto the table, then smoothed it with his stained hands. "I have about twenty witnesses telling me about a fight between Matt and you in the school this afternoon."

Fight? Even overthinking and hypercareful Shane wouldn't call that a fight. Something couldn't be a fight if it ended in a declaration of love, could it? "Matt and I had different opinions on attending the school party. Nothing serious."

The detective managed to grin and look annoyed at the same time. "Nothing serious? All of the witnesses agree that Matt yelled 'No!' and 'Please don't!' at some point during this nonserious exchange."

"He wanted us to go to the party as… friends, and I didn't." Only Matt decided when to come out. Telling this asshole of a policeman about their relationship wouldn't change anything. Perhaps it would even make things worse.

Detective Shit End scratched his chin. "So, you didn't want to go to the party?"

"No, I didn't." They were wasting too much time on this. Matt was waiting for him.

"According to one of my witnesses, you purchased two tickets for the party about fifteen minutes after the fight—pardon me—the nonserious exchange." The policeman followed some lines on the sheet with his finger. "Let me quote. 'The youngest drug lord ever bought two tickets, but not for a couple.'" He let his gaze wander over Shane's arms. "Nice tats, by the way, Mr. Drug Lord."

Shane ignored that last part. "I didn't want to go the party but then changed my mind." This discussion was heading to a dark and awful place. "Matt and I are b… best friends." Still Matt's decision. "So I changed my mind and wanted to give him a treat with the tickets."

"Fifty bucks is quite a generous treat for a friend, isn't it? Especially for a high school student like you." The detective shrugged. "My friends don't even buy me a beer at the bar."

"I've got two jobs, and perhaps you need better friends." Shane sucked in air through his teeth. He shouldn't goad the guy who was pissed already simply because he had to be here.

"Maybe you're right about my friends." The policeman jerked his head sideways. "So let's summarize. The two of you didn't have a fight about the party. You didn't want to go while Matt did. And then you bought the tickets to indulge Matt. That's your version, right?"

"Right." That wasn't his version. That was the truth, minus one or two details.

"You don't mind if I give you my version?" The detective paused, head down but still peering up at Shane.

Shane nodded. This could get interesting.

"Here we go. *You* asked Matt to accompany you to the party, but he said 'No!' and 'Please don't!' Those weren't the answers you wanted to hear, and you bought the tickets nonetheless." Detective Shit End eyed his notes again. "The witnesses also agree that you approached Matt and stared him down before he ran away."

"I didn't stare him down, and he was late for phys ed. That's why he scurried off." Why did he bother to put things right in the first place? The detective had made up his mind, and nothing Shane said would change that. And why didn't the police simply ask Matt? He'd tell them that this theory was bullshit. A feeling of cold dripped down from Shane's brain, trickling along his spine and freezing his intestines. He wouldn't leave here tonight. They wouldn't let him go see Matt, and he still didn't know what had happened, didn't know how badly hurt Matt was. The handcuffs cut into his wrists as his body took things into its own hands, and he jumped up from the chair.

"Sit down!" the detective screamed, only half sitting himself and propping himself up on the table with both hands. "Hit a nerve then, did I?"

"No." Shane's voice got caught in his throat. "It's not true." He slid onto the chair again. "It's not true," he whispered. The coldness reached his hands, turning them white, and they began to shiver.

The detective dropped back onto his chair with a thud. "Fortunately that's not up to you to decide, punk." He perked up his lips and snarled. "I'm also more than curious about the relationship between you two. The witnesses said that the both of you are inseparable. Tell me, Shane, are you a closet homo hitting on small and helpless guys? Does it turn your crank to make them suck you? Or do you like to suck them, perhaps?"

"Shut up!" All Shane wanted to do was jump up again and punch that grin right off that face. Breathe! He had to breathe the anger away. In and out.

Fuck it!

That breathing crap wouldn't work. Not this time.

The detective's sneer wrinkled his face, giving him the looks of an ancient oil portrait with cracked varnish. "Hit another nerve, obviously."

Shane stared down at the table. Streaks of heat floated through his body, burning everything they touched, but the coldness remained. "I'm not a closet homo," he pressed out through his teeth. He raised his gaze. "I'm an openly gay man. Check my school file if you have to." Detective Shit End had probably already done so. The cop was only teasing Shane. Naive as he was, he had fallen for the trap. "Or do you think that every gay man is a rapist?"

The sneer crumbled away. "I am asking the questions here."

Who hit a nerve now?

"So, you're a gay *man*." Detective Shit End drew quotation marks in the air. "What about Matt? Is he a gay *man* too?" Another set of quotation marks.

"That's something you should ask him about." It had become a question of honor not to out Matt before this homophobic jerk.

"He just can't answer me right now." For the first time, the detective's eyes lit up with an emotion other than disgust, but cruel satisfaction became him even less.

"How is he?" The coldness stiffened Shane's body, and his mind shattered as its biting grasp closed around his brain. Matt wasn't waiting for him. He wasn't sitting in a hospital bed and pouting because Shane hadn't shown up. He was suffering, maybe even fighting for his life. Shane had to get out of here. Now! He sprang to his feet and yanked at the chain of his cuffs. The metal cut into his wrist, and the wood of the table bent, creaking and moaning.

The click of a gun being cocked echoed through the room. Shane froze.

"I said, sit down!" The detective stood before the table, held his weapon with both hands, and aimed it at Shane's head.

Inch by inch, Shane sank onto the chair. It wouldn't help Matt if Shane's brain caught a bullet.

The detective flumped down, still pointing his weapon at him. "One more time and that's it. Got me?" His flushed cheeks glistened with sweat.

Shane nodded.

The cop lowered the gun to the table but kept it clutched with both hands so hard that his veins popped out.

"How is Matt?" Shane was pleading, and he didn't care what the other guy might think of him as long as he just got an answer.

"You haven't killed him… yet." The detective pulled up one corner of his mouth, and cruelty consumed the rest of his face. "Disappointed?"

Shane rested his forehead on his hands. Hot wetness ran down his cheeks, dropped onto the table, and mingled with the blood dripping from his wrist. Red clouds in salty waters.

"You haven't heard the rest of my version yet."

The detective paused again, but Shane was beyond talking to this mofo. Matt. Only Matt was important.

"After buying the tickets, you skipped your lessons and went to find Matt to tell him that he would go with you to the party. Matt refused, you snapped, and you beat him to a pulp. Sound familiar?"

Shane stared at his blood. How much more was Matt bleeding? How much more pain did he have to endure?

"Unfortunately we have to let you talk to your lawyer. He'll be here in an hour or so. Since you abandoned our cozy little chat, we're finished here. You'll wait in your cell, punk, where you can rot forever as far as I'm concerned."

Shane should've let the detective kill him. One short twitch and his suffering would have been over.

No!

As long Matt was alive, Shane had to fight, but Matt was the strong one, not him.

CHAPTER TWENTY-NINE

THE COPS had taken Shane back to the interrogation room. Once more, they shackled him to the table and left him waiting without saying a word.

He had calmed down, as much as a person whose boyfriend had been beaten and sent to the hospital could calm down. No one bothered to tell him any more details. Not knowing was the worst of all. They could point all the weapons they had at him, could cuff him, could treat him like shit, but not knowing about Matt's condition would still win out.

Agitated voices came from just outside. Shane strained his ears, but only dull snatches of yelled words made it through the thick wood of the door. Someone pressed down the handle and opened the door a crack.

"My client has the right to meet me with every person I deem necessary to participate in this briefing. If you don't want this precinct sued from here to the dark side of the moon and back, you'll grant me access to this room now. Do I make myself clear?"

The answer came as a grumble that Shane didn't understand. The door opened, and Mr. Sanderson rushed in. He hadn't changed a bit since he defended Shane in the trial last year. His black hair seemed to be glued in place, though he didn't use gel, wax, or any such thing. The light green of his eyes blazed when he was enraged, and damn, he was cross right now. He flared the nostrils of his hawkish nose as he huffed in derision.

Before addressing him, Mr. Sanderson spun around to face the door again. "It's always the same with Precinct Four." He waved at someone outside. "Follow me, please, as soon as you've undergone the body search." Mr. Sanderson reeled back, smiling now. "Good evening, Shane. I'm sorry for taking so long, but you encountered the hospitality of Precinct Four already, I presume?"

This police station was one of the circles of hell Dante had forgotten to mention, and Detective Shit End ruled it as its arch demon. "The officers who arrested me were nice, but the rest...." Shane shrugged.

Mr. Sanderson's gaze wandered down to the handcuffs. "They haven't chained you to the table, have they? I'll order them—"

"It's okay, Mr. Sanderson. I don't mind." The longer the cops stayed out of here, the better.

"Sheesh. You're a nineteen-year-old kid, not Al Capone himself." Another green lightning bolt of rage flashed in his eyes. "What happened to your wrist? Did they abuse you? Most people at Precinct Four are capable of that." He raised his voice and stretched his head slightly, so that the cops outside surely heard the latter part.

"That was my own fault. I made—an awkward move." Shane wouldn't tell Mr. Sanderson or anyone else, but the pain soothed him. The shared ache brought him closer to Matt, connected them.

Mr. Sanderson snorted once more. "If anything like this happens again, tell me. They deserve to be dragged to a court and convicted out of existence." He twisted his head toward the door. "Ah, here they come."

Shane's mom charged into the room. Her eyes were red and swollen, and her otherwise impeccable hair had turned into a tangled mess. "My Little Thumbling!" She had Shane in one of her bear hugs before he got halfway up from his chair, and he dropped back to it with a bang. Her arms crushed his shoulder blades, but for goodness' sake, Shane didn't want her to let go of him.

He pressed his cheek against the side of her head. "You're here." It came out as half question and half prayer of thanks.

"Of course." His mom opened her arms. "We're all here." She let the back of her hand slide down his scarred cheek.

Shane looked up, and his heart launched itself against his ribs. "Dad! Nick!" With only two exceptions, everyone who mattered to Shane and lived in this town was here.

"Estelle insisted on coming too. But we talked her out of it." A subtle smile brightened his dad's face.

This accounted for one of the exceptions. It would've been too exhausting for Estelle to make that trip. Her mind was still sharp as a razor, but her body had lost its edge. Shane didn't have to add grieving an old lady to the growing heap of bad karma he was piling up. "How did you achieve that?" Finding the theory of everything had to be ridiculously easy in comparison to swaying Estelle.

Nick's lips curved up into a sly smirk. "She couldn't resist my Greek charm."

It must have been a clash of titans. Shane would've loved to see the confrontation between those two. It bordered on a miracle that the city hadn't perished in an epic cataclysm put in motion by that encounter. Matt would've…. Shane closed his eyes and forced back the ripples of misery rising up inside him, but they kept flooding him and washed over his defenses.

"Everything will be all right. I know it will." Nick's voice sagged from the worries that burdened it.

Shane opened his eyes and wanted to smile, but his lips didn't budge. "I don't even know what happened to Matt and how he…." The rest of his words got wedged in his throat.

Nick stepped up beside him and placed his hand on Shane's. "Mr. Dermond called me at the gym."

A jolt went through Shane's body. He turned his hand around and grabbed Nick's, squashing it with all his strength. "What did he say?" He pressed the words around the lump in his throat.

"Matt's condition is stable, but he's in a coma. Mr. Dermond promised to call me again when they know more." Nick gritted his teeth. "Matt was beaten inside a storeroom for baseball bats, so the police assume that the fucking scumbag of an attacker used one of those." He whistled through his teeth. "Buddy, my hand…."

Shane let go of Nick. "Sorry." A coma! This was even worse than dying. Matt was trapped somewhere between death and life, imprisoned in his own mind, maybe living through the assault over and over again. This precinct wasn't hell, but what Matt was going through was. Shane's emotions merged into a single feeling—love, hate, sadness, all the same, but many times as strong as each of them alone.

His mom placed her hand on his cheek again, rubbing it gently while his dad grasped both of Shane's shoulders and squeezed them.

"You told us Matt's a fighter. Believe in your own words," his dad said.

His mind resisted the tranquility of his father's voice, but he couldn't parry something as powerful as this calmness. This force of nature untangled his feelings. They were still intense by themselves but tolerable now. Shane leaned into his mom's touch and pulled up his shoulder to feel his father's hand with his other cheek.

"I know this is hard and the most inconvenient time," Mr. Sanderson said, "but we have to prepare for the hearing tomorrow."

"Hearing tomorrow?" Shane's brain had switched to autopilot and merely repeated the last words it had heard.

"Did they tell you anything at all?" Nick roared. He never raised his voice, which made his outburst even more intimidating.

"Dr. Nicolaides is right," Mr. Sanderson said. "We could probably get you out of here on the procedural errors alone, but I strongly recommend attending that hearing." He sat down on the other chair and focused on Shane's eyes. "It's not a real trial, but if we can persuade the judge tomorrow, chances are good that all charges will be dropped and the investigations surrounding you will be abandoned."

The sooner the cops stopped suspecting him, the earlier they could concentrate on finding the real culprit. If he got out of here as a free man, he could take care of Matt. Maybe he would even try tracking down that bastard who had laid hands on Matt himself. He'd start with Iain, making him wish that the cops had found him first. "I agree."

Mr. Sanderson nodded. "Please excuse my brutal candor, but this is important for my defense strategy. You didn't harm Matt?"

Both his parents' hands cramped, and Nick opened his mouth, but Shane beat him to the answer. "I understand that you have to ask this. No, I didn't hurt Matt."

Mr. Sanderson's gaze rested on Shane. After some seconds of scrutinizing, he nodded again, and his eyes lit up. "I believe you." A single snort of chuckling sputtered out of him. "That's a good sign for tomorrow. I have to ask another inappropriate question. This time, you actually want to be defended?"

Another understandable request, for Shane had driven him close to despair when refusing to cooperate in the case of Hayden's broken arms. "I will fight this time." He had to. For Matt.

A lopsided smile came about on Mr. Sanderson's face. "Very good. I still have to prove to you that I'm a capable attorney-at-law." He straightened his features. "I've read Detective Webb's preliminary report, and he came up with quite a fanciful story, to say the least. What exactly is the relationship between you and Matt?"

Of course Mr. Sanderson had to ask this too. Shane would fight, but was dragging Matt out of the closet in a public hearing fighting or cowardice?

"They're boyfriends. The cutest and most loving couple I've ever seen," Nick said.

"Don't!" Shane jerked his head around to face Nick. "I know you mean well, but I can't out Matt. Not before his parents. I won't speak about Matt and me just to save my own skin."

A fold formed on Nick's nose bridge, and he squinted his eyes. "If you won't say it, I will." He puffed. "Do you think Matt wants you to go to jail for something you haven't done just to keep a secret that doesn't have to be one?"

Using Matt for his argument was a foul move. Shane was already lying on the floor, and Nick kept kicking him. A best friend shouldn't do this.

"You hate me for this, I see." Nick's face smoothed out, and a trace of a smile sneaked up on his lips. "You're my best friend, and friendship isn't always about doing what your buddy wants, but doing what is best for him."

"Nick's right," his mom said, and Shane turned his head around. She knelt down, and the same worried smile that was on Nick's face settled on hers. "I know you, my Little Thumbling. You want to protect Matt at all costs, but I'm absolutely sure that Matt feels the same about you. He wouldn't hesitate for a second to step forward and tell the world about your love."

Their love. Was it that obvious? Okay, for his mom it was. She looked through him as if he were made of glass. She always had, and she was right about Matt. He had even told Shane that the world should see their love, so Shane should put back his own wishes. He nodded once at his mom and pecked her forehead. He faced Nick again. "I'm sorry, man. Will you tell the court about Matt and me tomorrow? I'd be honored if you did it."

"The honor will be all mine." The smile shifted up a gear and changed into Nick's trademark grin.

"You're not betraying Matt." His dad massaged Shane's shoulders. "Don't think that for a minute. Promise me you won't think that."

Shane was as transparent to his father as he was to his mother. "I promise." He wasn't alone in this. Whatever happened and however hard these times would be, he wouldn't be alone. Matt needed a strong Shane, and Shane could borrow strength from his family—Nick and Estelle included.

He turned his head to look at Mr. Sanderson. "What else do you have to know to get me out of this place by tomorrow?"

The lopsided smile returned to Mr. Sanderson's face. "That's the attitude I want from my clients."

Shane would fight, and he'd win or go down trying.

Tomorrow everyone will know about us. I wish you could be there to see it, Matt.

CHAPTER THIRTY

SHANE SAT in a chair on a small podium beside the judge's table, the padded seat a comfortable change from the hard cot in his cell. Mr. Sanderson, his parents, and Nick hadn't arrived yet. Last year, he had followed the trial while sitting with his lawyer and his family. Nick had had to take a seat with the audience. Those were some differences already, and Mr. Sanderson kept reminding him that a hearing wasn't a trial. Shane's guts didn't mind the finer judicial distinctions between those types of litigation and had turned to mush like last year. A room brimming with strangers didn't help him get a grip on his nervousness either. Why on earth were so many people interested in him? More than likely, they had come to hear the gruesome details of the attack on Matt. Seeing the suspected brute just gave them an extra thrill. Shane let his gaze wander over the crowd of probably fifty people. Some of them balanced laptops on their knees while hitting away at the keys and talking into their cells. For the trial last year, Hayden had held his part of the bargain and convinced his parents to keep the media out of the affair. They had had to call in some chips, but the journalists had stayed away. Making it to the front page with this hearing was definitely Shane's least favorite way of having his fifteen minutes of fame, and the presence of the reporters cramped his chest a little more.

Yesterday he had refused to tell a single person about Matt being gay. Now it would become a headline on the news. This couldn't be in Matt's best interest. Could he still talk Nick out of making his statement as planned? Before making that decision, Shane had to apply the WWMW test. What would Matt want? He closed his eyes and waited for an answer.

Are you completely insane? I'd parade down Main Street dressed in a rainbow sash only if it helped you to get out of there and come to me at the hospital as soon as possible. Go and tell them!

Even the imaginary version of Matt in Shane's head was cute when it got rebellious. Shane reined in his smile and opened his eyes again. So the plan still stood.

He scanned the rest of the audience. It was a diverse mix of people, ranging from high school students like him to folks Estelle's age. Some of the bolder ones unabashedly stared back at him, shaking their heads and whispering with their neighbors. The more timid specimens averted their eyes when his gaze swept over them. One slender guy in a gray hoodie even ducked behind the man in front of him. As the suspect of a violent crime, Shane's dangerous vibes had gained an additional dimension, and he couldn't blame the people for being wary. Hopefully the judge was more open-minded than the spectators were.

The wait for this morning hadn't been a piece of cake either. The assholes of Precinct Four had put a homeless kiddo in his cell just to frighten the poor boy. It took over an hour to get through to Adrian and convince him that he wouldn't hurt him. Giving up his generous jail meal for a hungry Adrian helped with the persuasion. Shane hadn't felt like eating anyway. At least Adrian's company had kept him from brooding. When Adrian fell asleep, though, Matt returned to Shane's mind and haunted him all night long. He hadn't even tried to think of anything else. What else could he think of? Despite the lack of sleep, Shane was wide-awake. His squishy intestines worked way better than caffeine.

Mr. Sanderson, his parents, and Nick entered the room, taking their places at a table to his left. Nick, dressed in a black suit and light blue tie, gave Shane a thumbs-up and a grin that was over the top, even by Nick's standards. His dad settled for a calm nod with a smile, and his mom blew him a kiss. Team Justice had assembled.

To Shane's right, a blond guy in his midtwenties sat down at another table: the prosecutor, obviously. His facial muscles flexed and unflexed as he read over a file. Detective Shit End… Webb… joined the man and considered Shane with a scornful look. This was Team Evil.

Mr. and Mrs. Dermond appeared in the main entrance, and Shane's breath caught in his lungs. A police officer guided them to empty seats in the front row, both of them dragging their feet down the aisle as they followed him. Their faces were pale, their eyes sunken, most likely because they had spent the whole night with Matt in the hospital. Still, a smile did flash across Mr. Dermond's lips as he looked at Shane. They greeted each other with curt nods. The tight feeling in Shane's chest slackened, and his heart expanded into the additional space to beat more freely. That was the first sign of good news within the last twelve hours. Not even Mr. Dermond believed that he had laid hands on Matt. When Mrs. Dermond raised her gaze, however, she contorted her lips sideways, and her eyes filled up with anger that turned them dark. She had no doubt that Shane was guilty. He couldn't blame her for this and even pitied her. She not only had to deal with Matt's coma, but she would soon learn, together with a bunch of strangers in a court, that her son was gay and that he had kept his relationship with Shane from her.

"Please rise for the Honorable Judge Ruth Bilodeaux," the bailiff called out.

The tingling of Shane's sludgy guts shot through his body, making him want to scratch his insides. He got up from the chair that, at least this time, the cops hadn't chained him to. He turned his head. Judge Bilodeaux was a woman in that age range that was difficult to guess—anything from the midforties to the midfifties. Her full face of dark brown skin showed just the slightest trace of wrinkles. She stood at the same height as Matt, perhaps slightly taller, but she occupied three times as much space. The glasses dancing on her stubby nose almost covered the upper half of her face. Just from her looks and the funny, prancing way she bobbed to her desk, Shane liked her. Though the more important question was whether she also liked him.

"Please sit down." The intensity of Judge Bilodeaux's voice rasped away some skin from Shane's inner ears, yet it had an endearing sound, almost sultry.

Over the rim of her glasses, Judge Bilodeaux watched the commotion of those in the room taking their seats ebb. "We're here to decide about upholding the warrant of arrest against Shane McAllistair in the matter of aggravated assault on Matt Dermond. The defendant is appearing in person and is represented by his lawyer, Mr. Sanderson." She nodded toward the left table. "The office of the district attorney is represented by Waylon Koch." She turned her head over to the right table, and her forehead creased. "They've sent me a new face. It's your first time, Mr. Koch?"

The blond guy harrumphed. "Yes, Your Honor, it is."

Judge Bilodeaux smirked and looked like a grinning full moon. "We'll be easy on you, won't we, Raymond?" She nodded at Mr. Sanderson, who answered her with one of his lopsided smiles.

The young plaintiff blushed at the reluctant laughter from the audience as he wiped away the sweat from his face with a white handkerchief. Shane pitied him too, while Judge Bilodeaux rose a little more in his esteem. The last one, Judge Zariski, had been so dry that small clouds of dust had come out of his mouth when he opened it. Judge Bilodeaux was sassy, and sassiness always worked for Shane.

Judge Bilodeaux took off her glasses and swirled them between her fingers. "I have to get two things off my chest before this hearing will officially begin." She studied the reporters sitting in the crowd. "First, I learned about this hearing on the radio ten minutes before I got the official call. Whoever tipped off our friends in the press better avoid meeting me in dark alleys." She stopped twisting her glasses. "That the defendant is a nineteen-year-old boy, mentioned by full name as a side note, makes this even worse. Don't you have more important things to report than pushing a teenager, who is in a precarious situation anyway, into the limelight?"

The press guys looked down at their computers, smoothed their clothes, and pretended to be otherwise busy.

Shane didn't like this judge. He loved her. Whatever she may decide later, she had earned his respect for speaking her mind with clear words.

"The second thing is more of an amused remark on a letter I received." Judge Bilodeaux put on her glasses again, fiddled with a file on her desk, and produced a sheet of lavender-colored paper. "It's a handwritten letter that was sent to my office by courier this morning. The author is an eighty-six-year-old woman—" She pursed her lips as she swallowed down a laugh. "—but it contains so many cuss words that I wouldn't have problems believing a foulmouthed dock worker wrote it."

A chuckle floated through the audience.

Estelle! She could've written an e-mail, but she knew how to make a great entrance and thrived on this kind of attention as part of her elixir of eternal youth. At least Judge Bilodeaux didn't seem to be pissed. A shapeless sensation of warmth filled Shane's liquefied intestines. This was a room full of people who right-out hated him or didn't care at all, but the few people who loved him made up for this in full.

"I can't read out all of the letter because there are minors here, but indulge me and let me paraphrase it." She lowered her gaze, and her eyes darted from left to right. "The author tells us in no uncertain words that the defendant is probably the finest guy in the whole city." Judge Bilodeaux looked over at the plaintiff's table. "Whereas she doesn't hold the police in such high regard. Just add a lot of flowery descriptions of human body parts here to get the general mood of the writing."

The audience cackled again, more confident this time.

"She closes with her sincere hopes that this charade ends faster than it began." Judge Bilodeaux folded the letter carefully and laid it back into the file. "Amen to getting this over with as fast as possible, but I beg to differ on calling my hearing a charade."

Shane had to buy a bouquet full of roses for Estelle when he was out of here. The warm feeling collapsed into a ball and went nova, sending out waves that drove away the tingling just in time for the hearing to begin.

Rien ne va plus. Nothing goes any-more.

Estelle would chide him once more for his abysmal French pronunciation if she were here, but laughing out loud now wouldn't help at all, so Shane bit his tongue.

Judge Bilodeaux faced Detective Webb. "I've read your report, Detective, and if such a story happened on my favorite soap opera, I'd sit glued to the screen."

More chuckling from the spectators warbled through the room, but Detective Webb kept his face straight, only slightly knitting his brows.

"Nonetheless, things like this happen all the time, and this theory fits the facts so far."

The waves of cozy warmness stopped dead. Judge Bilodeaux was inclined to follow the hair-raising story of Detective Shit End? Shane looked over to Mr. Sanderson. His lawyer didn't show any signs of anxiousness. Maybe the situation wasn't too bad after all.

"My first question for the detective: Has the weapon used in the attack been identified yet?"

The cop exhaled slowly. "According to the doctors, Mr. Dermond has only been hit once on the back of his head with a blunt object, certainly one of the baseball bats from the storage room where he was found. Unfortunately, Mr. Dermond's blood spread to more than a dozen bats. Our forensic department analyzed them all but wasn't able to identify Mr. McAllistair's fingerprints on any of them. The fingerprints of almost every student of Central High are on those bats, so the results aren't too conclusive."

Judge Bilodeaux clicked her tongue. "I didn't ask you whether you found the defendant's fingerprints on some baseball bats but whether you identified the weapon. We'll decide later who possibly wielded it. Agreed?"

She hit the detective the whole nine yards with her broadside, and another wrinkle emerged on his battered face. Detective Webb grunted and nodded.

"Aggravated assault or murder without a weapon isn't much of a case. You learn that in the first week at law school… but all right." She scribbled something down into the file.

"My second question to Mr. McAllistair. The report contains numerous witness statements about a verbal fight between you and the victim. You put on record that this wasn't an argument. Can you please enlighten me about this?"

Shane's mouth turned dry, and he swallowed. "Matt," he squealed out and cleared his throat. "Matt asked me if I wanted to go to the party, but at that moment, I didn't. He raised his voice during our discussion, but our talk was only animated and emotional. We didn't actually argue." He repeated what Mr. Sanderson had advised him to say. Somehow it felt like blaming Matt. He sighed, loud enough for everyone to hear.

Judge Bilodeaux eyed him while she swayed her mouth left and right. "The difference between an argument and an emotional talk is only a matter of nuances, Mr. McAllistair." She wrote into the file once more. "But this leads to another question that the report doesn't answer to my satisfaction. What exactly is the nature of your relationship with Matt Dermond?"

The blood flowed out of Shane's head, and a cotton-like lightness filled his skull. He swallowed once more, but the dryness stuck to his throat, and a raw pain clawed his neck. That question came up too early, but no time would've been enough to prepare for it.

"Your Honor, may I answer in place of Mr. McAllistair?" Nick got up and straightened his suit.

This was his last chance to make Nick stop. But then what? The question would still hang in the room, and it deserved an honest answer. If Matt were here, he would stand by their relationship and speak about it with his small chest bursting with pride.

"And you are…." Judge Bilodeaux referred to another sheet of paper on her desk. "Dr. Agathangelos Nicolaides, I presume? The defense's character witness?"

Good angel. That was the meaning of Agathangelos, and Nick's mother had chosen the name well. It was a pity that he had stopped using it.

"Yes, Your Honor, that's me." Nick nodded slowly.

"You've got me a little confused here, and I hate being confused. Call it a vocational disease if you like. So why can't Mr. McAllistair answer the question himself?" Judge Bilodeaux tilted her head sideways.

"If this is an unusual request, excuse me, Your Honor, but I gave Mr. McAllistair my word to speak in his place. He feels as if he would be betraying Matt when answering this question."

Judge Bilodeaux furrowed her brows. "Then put me out of my misery and reveal this dark secret to us." She made an opening gesture with her arm toward Nick.

Shane closed his eyes, and he yearned to cover his ears as well. He had said so many times that he had failed Matt, had overused that phrase ad nauseam, but now it was happening for real.

"Shane and Matt are in a serious relationship. They are boyfriends."

Nick's words bored into Shane's skull, and not even the cotton in there dampened their impact. They cannonballed through his body and smote everything in their wake.

I'm sorry, Matt.

"He's a filthy liar!" Mrs. Dermond's voice boomed through the court. "That's not—" The eruption ended as abruptly as it had begun.

Shane opened his eyes. Mrs. Dermond had jumped up from her seat, and her face shone bright red. Mr. Dermond stood by her side, holding her arm and whispering into her ear. She turned pale, her mouth opening and closing, before she slumped onto her chair again with empty eyes. Shane had done this to her. She was right to call him names. This insight laid its fingers around his neck and pressed close. He gasped for air.

Mr. Dermond turned around to address Judge Bilodeaux, letting his hand slide down Mrs. Dermond's arm and intertwining their fingers. "Please excuse my wife's outburst, but she has gone through a lot since yesterday. Nonetheless, I have to concur with Dr. Nicolaides."

A murmur spread through the audience and turned louder by the second.

He and Matt had suspected that Mr. Dermond knew about them, but hearing the words for real stirred Shane anyway. At least he could breathe again.

"Quiet please!" Judge Bilodeaux frowned at the spectators over her glasses. "This hearing can turn nonpublic like this." She snapped her fingers and wiggled her head.

The room fell silent. No one wanted to miss a spectacle as exciting as this.

"First of all, I want to express my compassion for what happened to your son, Mr. and Mrs. Dermond. I have a daughter of fourteen, and I don't know what I'd do if something like this happened to her."

"Thank you, Your Honor." A short-lived smile bent up Mr. Dermond's lips.

Judge Bilodeaux smiled back at him, but like Mr. Dermond's, her smile didn't last long. "You see me confused again. The report states that you and your wife explicitly named Mr. McAllistair as the main suspect."

"My wife might have testified this, though I wasn't with her during her interrogation. I definitely told Detective Webb that Shane isn't responsible for the attack."

Mr. Dermond joined Team Justice. The warm feeling returned to Shane's belly. If Matt's dad was on their side, they just had to win. He'd get to see Matt today.

"Interesting." Judge Bilodeaux puckered her lips and looked over to the plaintiff's table. "Detective Webb obviously forgot to include this little fact in his report."

No emotion showed on the face of the detective. Breathing shallowly, he stared at the desk before him. The plaintiff's forehead glistened with sweat, and he didn't even bother to wipe it away this time.

"Mr. Dermond"—Judge Bilodeaux turned back—"you can confirm that Mr. McAllistair and your son are in a romantic relationship?"

"Matt didn't say it with so many words, but they got together about a month ago, if I had to guess." Mr. Dermond's gaze switched to Shane, who nodded in a silent reply. Another smile flashed on Mr. Dermond's lips. "I haven't seen Matt happier in years. He might not have told us he's… gay, but he told me that he trusts Shane more than any other person in the world and that Shane has given life back to him."

Matt had entrusted him with his life, and Shane hadn't guarded it as much as he should have.

I love you, you know, but could you just shut up? Every word my dad says is true. Without you, there wouldn't be much to guard anyway.

Shane was going mad. Hearing Matt's voice alone was a bad sign, but not even believing in something that sprang from his own unconscious mind made him a first-rate nutjob.

"The witness cannot testify for sure that the supposed relationship is a fact," Mr. Koch said barely audibly.

Judge Bilodeaux tilted her head again and pressed her lips tight. "Mr. Koch, it's your first actual assignment and you don't know better yet, but if a father is convinced that his son and another guy are a couple, then I'm most inclined to believe him. Additionally, Dr. Nicolaides confirms this relationship as well, witness for the defendant or not. So we can safely assume that the victim and the defendant are boyfriends, can't we?"

Another blast to Team Evil and their ship was going down bow-first. This may give Shane some more bad karma points, but he allowed the glee about Detective Shit End's demise to run free. This asshole deserved a nut shot.

Mr. Koch's face froze, and he flipped through the file before him with shivering fingers. "Even if the victim and the defendant are in a relationship, this doesn't exclude the possibility of… domestic violence." His gaze followed a line on a page of the file. "Mr. McAllistair has already been convicted of another assault and has exhibited a tendency toward violence."

Karma struck fast today and landed a good hit on Shane's balls in return. The detective's cock-and-bull story still made sense if he and Matt were a couple. Perhaps even more so. Shane had torn down Matt's closet in vain. His eyes began to burn, and his vision blurred.

"That's not true!"

This couldn't be *his* voice! This couldn't be *him*! Shane wiped his eyes with the back of his hand. The slender guy in the gray hoodie who had hidden behind the man got up from his seat and pushed back his hood.

"Jer!" Shane breathed out.

SHANE WAS melting. His body dripped onto the floor, trickling from the rostrum his chair stood on. The disrupted fragments of his mind leaked out, and his thoughts dissipated into the air around him. Jer didn't belong here. He should've been in court with him last year, but he hadn't been. That trial was in the past, and that was where it should stay.

"The next surprise witness. This hearing is coming awfully close to an episode of the aforementioned soap opera." Judge Bilodeaux pinched the bridge of her nose and closed her eyes. She let out a moan. "Be that as it may, I always wanted to have a soap opera of my own." She opened her eyes again and situated them on Jer. "And who are you, young man?"

"My name's Jer Prescott, excuse me, Jeremiah Prescott. I was involved in the—" He swallowed. "—assault. The first one, I mean."

Shane had already ruined Matt's life by not watching out for him and by exposing their relationship today. He wouldn't let the same thing happen to Jer. By his own volition, Shane had sacrificed himself for the first small guy in his life, and that sacrifice had been too costly to just throw away. "Jer, don't!" He leaped to his feet.

The police officers in the room stirred, reaching for their guns. Detective Webb jumped up and was already halfway around the desk.

"Officers, back up!" Judge Bilodeaux said with a firm voice as she waved her hands.

The cops froze, alternating gazes between Judge Bilodeaux and Detective Webb. The detective nodded but stood rooted in place.

Judge Bilodeaux gave a yelp. "I have five people standing around in my court now. Seats don't go by the minute here, so Dr. Nicolaides, Mr. Dermond, Detective Webb, and Mr. McAllistair, would you mind sitting down again? You—" She pointed at Jer. "—come here!" Her finger switched to the empty space before her desk.

Shane took his seat again, and so did the other people Judge Bilodeaux had called out. In the meantime, Jer scraped by the spectators sitting in the same row, all gazes resting on him. This had to be hell for Jer. He hated attention so much, and he shouldn't have come here in the first place. Shane turned to the desk of Team Justice and found his parents staring at him. Sho-prises didn't only exist between Matt and him. He shrugged them an apology, though he didn't know why. Jer's appearance was one of the few things he didn't have to feel responsible for.

"Mr. Prescott, your name doesn't sound familiar at all. I read the file of Mr. McAllistair's previous trial, but you're not mentioned. Neither as a witness nor as anything else." Judge Bilodeaux glowered down at Jer, who stood with his arms crossed before his belly and a drooping head in front of her desk.

"He wasn't there, and he didn't have anything to do with it." A trace of begging weaved into Shane's voice. Jer had to change his mind, had to say that it was only a misunderstanding, that it was a bad prank.

"No, Shane, it's time to tell the truth." Jer raised his head, and his green gaze drilled into him. "I'm so grateful for what you've done, all the things you've done, and I can't live with this debt anymore."

"It's not your debt. You owe me nothing." Whatever Shane might say, he wouldn't dissuade Jer. Like Estelle, Jer was too bullheaded for this.

"I do, Shane, I do."

That was the smile Shane had fallen for, but it had lost its power. Only one smile made him go crazy these days.

"Young gentlemen, you might be aware of what all this stuff means, but I think I speak for all the people in this court when I ask what the heck are you talking about?" Judge Bilodeaux's arms soared in despair.

This time no one dared to laugh. The fear of missing any of this tragedy was too great.

Jer turned his head and faced Judge Bilodeaux again. "Excuse me, ma'am, Your Honor." He squinted his eyes for a moment. "Shane saved me from Hayden." Jer looked over his shoulder to the plaintiff's desk. "It wasn't a violent outbreak."

Mr. Koch rubbed his hands against each other. "If that were true, why didn't Mr. McAllistair state so in the trial? That would have changed the entire case." He hid his hands beneath the desk.

"Our young plaintiff makes a valid point here." Judge Bilodeaux's features hardened.

This hearing would cost her a wrinkle or two. One more thing Shane felt sorry for.

"Almost no one knows what really happened," Shane said. "Yes, it's true. Hayden attacked Jer, but still, I overreacted and deserved to be punished." Maybe he could get away with leaving out the details and save Jer any further embarrassment.

"Overreacted?" Jer yelled at Shane. "Hayden *attacked* me?" His head spun around toward Judge Bilodeaux, his green eyes aflame with fury. "Hayden didn't attack me, he raped me. In my mouth."

Shane shut his eyes. Absolute silence fell over the room. Nothing but the chop-chop beat of his heart, the whirring rush of blood, and the heavy sound of his breathing droned in his ears. The blackness behind his closed eyes wasn't a safe place either, for it turned into a silver screen for the images. He had tried to erase those scenes from his head, cut them out and cast them away, but they were elusive and persistent. They dwelled in the same place as the memories of the car accident. Like those, the images would live there forever. Shane yanked his eyes open and looked at Jer. Poor, fragile, haunted Jer.

"That's a very severe accusation, Mr. Prescott. I hope you aren't making such an allegation lightly." Judge Bilodeaux's face had got stuck somewhere between skepticism and shock.

"I have proof." Jer's voice sounded so thin and meek.

Stars burst before Shane's eyes, as if someone had punched him in the stomach with full force. Once again he couldn't breathe, and his lungs began to burn. There was proof? He didn't know this. He wouldn't have wanted to know this. Those images also existed outside of his mind. They shouldn't. They mustn't. Their mere existence gave the events of that night more reality than Shane was willing to concede them. They had to remain a nightmare, a gruesome, terrible, dreadful nightmare in his head.

Jer produced a small device from the pocket of his hoodie, slightly larger than a cell. "A friend of mine, a member of the school's AV club, asked me to wear a mini-cam to the prom for some live footage. I didn't switch it off after… the talk with Shane." Jer drew in a deep breath. "It recorded what Hayden did to me." He sniffled, and a tear rolled down his cheek. With a quick swipe of his hand, he wiped it away. "I copied those minutes before deleting them from the cam." He held out the device for Judge Bilodeaux with trembling fingers.

She bent forward over her desk and took the recorder from him. Judge Bilodeaux looked at it as if she were holding something hideous and alive that squirmed in her hand. "Mr. Sanderson, Mr. Koch, would you please join me to watch this piece of evidence."

Jer hadn't told Shane about the cam. Not on that evening or afterward. They hadn't spoken with each other at all. But that movie didn't change a thing. Shane would've made the same decisions if he had known about it. Taking the blame for this incident had been the right thing, and it still was.

Mr. Sanderson and Mr. Koch went up to the desk of Judge Bilodeaux. Standing behind her and peeking over her shoulders, they stared at the screen of the recorder. Some tidbits of sound reached Shane. Hayden's voice, haughty and aggressive. Jer's voice, begging and screaming, then dying down to a whimper. His own voice and the cracking noise of shattering bones.

Judge Bilodeaux pressed a button on the device, and silence ensued. Her face had turned gray, and a muscle in her cheek kept twitching. Mr. Koch covered his mouth with his hand, and his Adam's apple bobbed up and down from gagging. In Mr. Sanderson's eyes, a green lightning storm raged.

"I apologize for voicing any doubts about... this... atrocity." Judge Bilodeaux looked down at Jer, and all hardness was gone from her features.

Jer kept his gaze on the edge of the desk, his eyes unfocused. "Can you understand now why I couldn't speak about this? Why I didn't want anyone to know?" He shook his head and stared at Judge Bilodeaux. "Sad as it is, the guys at school wouldn't have pitied me but would've blamed me for being responsible for destroying their hopes of winning the football championship." Another tear coursed down his cheek.

"Being young today is different than it was when I was that age, but don't underestimate your fellow students, Mr. Prescott. They are human beings, and this—" Judge Bilodeaux gestured at the recorder. "—cannot leave anyone unaffected."

No one had dared to say anything to Shane's face, but he had gotten anonymous letters and e-mails full of swears and curses for taking Hayden out of the championship. The writers of these letters hadn't known about the rape, though. Shane jolted. It was the first time he'd called that crime by its proper name. *Rape*. His mind had come up with countless descriptions to avoid that word, but it was the only word for it, and he'd never use another euphemism again.

"Mr. Prescott, you can sit down again, but I think Mr. Koch wants to talk to you after this hearing." Judge Bilodeaux turned around. "Don't you?"

Mr. Koch nodded, hesitantly at first but with increasing confidence. "Of course, Your Honor. I will personally see to the appeal of Mr. McAllistair's prior case."

A smile came about on Judge Bilodeaux's mouth. "You may have lost your first case, Mr. Koch, but as long as justice wins, who cares? I'm not psychic like my late aunt Adele claimed to be, but I dare to predict that you will win the next one."

"Thanks, Your Honor." Mr. Koch smiled for the first time since the hearing began. For once, he didn't shiver, sweat, or anything.

"Gentlemen, please take your seats again." Judge Bilodeaux turned back to the audience.

Mr. Sanderson and Mr. Koch returned to their desks, and Mr. Sanderson invited Jer to sit with him. Jer heaved a relieved sigh, possibly because this was over but also possibly because he was thankful he didn't have to squeeze his way back through the spectators to return to his seat. Shane could still read Jer, though this ability had miserably failed when declaring his love to him. Another jolt shook Shane. The wicker basket with the things for his perfect moment with Matt probably still stood on his table. His declaration of love to go. He would never postpone saying "I love you" to Matt again. Each time this thought crossed his mind, he'd speak it.

"The letter of the sharp-tongued lady makes more sense to me now," Judge Bilodeaux said. "As a judge, I have to call Mr. McAllistair's reaction excessive defense of others, a deed that deserves punishment. Not as drastic as the one he received, but punishment for sure." She faced Shane, looking over the rim of her glasses. "As a mother, I have to call Mr. McAllistair a hero. Anyone who stands up and helps people who cannot fight for themselves is one."

A person in the audience started to clap. Another one followed, and soon the room boomed with applause. Some of the spectators got up on their feet, including Mr. Koch, Team Justice, and Jer. Detective Webb, however, crossed his arms over his chest, frowned, and stayed seated. While Mr. Dermond stood and applauded with everyone else, Mrs. Dermond sat motionless, her face rigid. She had so much to cope with that it was admirable that she was still here and wasn't bolting away, screaming at the top of her lungs. She deserved the applause, not Shane. He lowered his gaze to the floor. He wasn't a hero. Heroes were confident and knew what they were doing at all times, acting purposefully. When Shane broke Hayden's arms, nothing of that had been true. He had yearned to hurt Hayden. Nothing else.

Judge Bilodeaux waved her arms. The applause died away, and the spectators sat down again. "We're embarrassing the defendant, and he has suffered enough." Amusement vibrated in her voice.

The audience answered her with another chuckle.

"Let me summarize the facts we have heard so far. Firstly, we don't have a weapon yet. Secondly, there was an emotional talk between the defendant and the victim about going to the party. Thirdly, the defendant and the victim are boyfriends. Fourthly, the defendant is a man of character and not a violent person per se." Judge Bilodeaux folded her hands over the file. "This court can only come to one decision. Shane McAllistair is acquitted on the charge of aggravated assault on Matt Dermond."

Shane closed his eyes and exhaled.

Matt, I'm coming. Oh, and I love you.

The imaginary Head-Matt smiled at Shane and nodded, blinking slowly.

Another wave of applause washed over the room, and Shane opened his eyes. Judge Bilodeaux calmed the uproar with a gesture of her hand.

"Quiet, please." A grin settled on her lips. "We're almost done, so just indulge me for my grand finale." She adjusted her glasses. "This court advises the police to cease investigations concerning Mr. McAllistair. There isn't any evidence substantiating the involvement of Mr. McAllistair in this crime. Mr. McAllistair is to be released from investigative custody with immediate effect." She puffed. "To my friends of the press, go and report this! It's one hell of a story." Judge Bilodeaux made a sweeping gesture with her hand. "And now the ovations please."

Laughter spread through the audience before the people followed her judicial order and began clapping their hands again.

It *was* one hell of a story. This hearing had dragged all of Shane's secrets into broad daylight—at least the big ones—but the world was still turning. Of course it was. The universe had enough work on its hands, and the paranoid worries of a teenager didn't matter that much in the overall picture. If the universe would only invest a little of its precious time to look after Matt and give him a gentle prod toward the path of healthiness, Shane wouldn't bother it ever again with any of his otherwise trivial problems.

CHAPTER THIRTY-ONE

SHANE DRANK in one last breath before he stood up from the chair and turned toward Judge Bilodeaux. "Thank you, Your Honor." He extended his hand.

Judge Bilodeaux smiled, wiggling her head. "It doesn't happen all too often that the defendant thanks me after a trial. In your case, it's definitely not necessary. I just set the facts straight. That's my job...." She grasped Shane's hand. "But I wanted to shake the hand of the hero anyway. Just kidding!" Her chuckle, tinted by the sultry tone of her voice, was a force to be reckoned with.

Good that this force had sided with him.

They let go of each other's hands.

"Please stop calling me that." Shane raised one corner of his mouth and tilted his head, making her chuckle again.

The courtroom suddenly swiveled around, and only Shane's toes still touched the floor. "Oh, big boy, I have to lift some more iron to get you off the ground." Nick put him down again and groaned, just to sling his arms around him in the next moment. "I knew everything would work out. Everything."

Shane rested his cheek against Nick's head. "Thank you, buddy." He better refrain from any more praise. Nick probably didn't want to hear it anyway, because even that simple expression of gratitude already made him stiffen up.

"You'd have done the same for me." Nick patted Shane's back so forcefully that less sturdy guys may have simply broken in two.

Small hands tried to push Nick and Shane apart. "It's my turn, you line cutter." His mom squeezed herself between them.

"If you finally did the cardio training I recommended, Heather, you might actually beat me in running."

She rammed her elbow into Nick's stomach, and he huffed with a moan.

"Blah, blah, blah, sports blah, blah, blah." Shane's mom rolled her eyes before she closed her arms around him. "My Little Thumbling, I'm so... I'm so... ahhh!" She tightened her hug and nestled up to him, obviously giving up on finding an appropriate name for what she was feeling.

Warm wetness soaked Shane's shirt. "Thank you too, Mom." He kissed the top of her head. "Stop crying, please, or I'll start weeping along," he whispered. Shane had battled bravely against the tears until now, but seeing her cry boosted the fighting morale of his sappy side.

Another pair of arms joined the hug, embracing him and his mom. "And if you both bawl your eyes out, so will I. You don't want that, do you?" His dad cuddled up against them. "I love the both of you," he said, only for Shane and his mom to hear.

His father close to tears? That meant he was absolutely devastated and on the verge of an emotional breakdown. Shane freed his arms and wrapped them around his parents.

"That's the first trial in which I didn't say a word, yet we've won." Mr. Sanderson laughed out loud.

Shane released his parents from the embrace and extended his hand. "I had to make up for last time." He grinned at Mr. Sanderson.

"You know what? I won't charge for defending you in this hearing if you let me represent you on the appeal." Mr. Sanderson took Shane's hand. "I think, apart from clearing your record, we can get good compensation for the excessive punishment you received."

That hadn't occurred to Shane yet. He hadn't cooperated with the court and had brought the harsh sentence on himself. Moreover, he didn't want any money. What for? Having met Estelle? Having found a job he loved? On the other hand, Mr. Sanderson deserved a chance to prove that he was an awesome lawyer. "Deal." They shook hands once and let go of each other.

"Mr. McAllistair?" a pinched voice asked from behind.

Shane turned around. A small, stubby man with a knob for a nose looked up at him.

"My name is Roger Galinski from the *Daily Herald*." He pulled a business card out of the pocket of his dark blue sport coat. The seam of the pocket had come apart in several places already, and the business card was dog-eared. "My paper would like to make you an offer for the exclusive rights to your and Mr. Dermond's story."

Shane still had scruples about outing Matt in court. What weighed even more gravely was the fact that it had been done in front of Mr. and Mrs. Dermond. Now he was supposed to sell the story to a paper? "Thanks, sir, but no thanks." Shane waved his hands and turned back, but Mr. Galinski grabbed him by his arm.

"My paper is very generous when it comes to exclusive rights. I think you *should* consider our offer."

The *Daily Herald* obviously wasn't that generous with the wages they offered their reporters and not too picky about them either. "It's not about the money, sir." Shane pulled his arm away, but Mr. Galinski held on to it.

"Just consider the offer, Mr. McAllistair. You don't have to answer me right now. Take my business card and phone me anytime." The reporter shoved the card into his face.

"I won't change my mind, sir. Would you please let go of me?" If Shane jolted his hand away, he might hurt the man, and even this petulant jerk didn't deserve that.

One of the police officers approached them. "Would you take your hand off Mr. McAllistair and leave the room please, sir?" The features of the cop hardened, and the firm sound of his voice cut through the awkwardness of the situation.

For the first time in hours, Shane was glad to see a policeman.

"This is a free country with free press, Officer." Mr. Galinski pursed his lips while the nasal tone of his voice became more prominent.

"This is also a country with personal rights, and you are violating Mr. McAllistair's, sir. Would you please leave the court?" The demeanor of the officer didn't change, but he squinted his eyes ever so slightly while his words acquired a sharper edge.

"That's outrageous. A clear case of police arbitrariness. I'll file a complaint, Officer…." Mr. Galinski bowed forward and ogled the cop's name tag.

Judge Bilodeaux, looking up at Mr. Galinski over the rim of her glasses, joined the group. "You won't file anything, Roger. Just get out of my court or I'll instruct the officer to remove you." She tilted her head. "And I so hope you'll resist."

The force had struck again, and thankfully, Shane wasn't sitting at the receiving end of her glare.

Mr. Galinski wheezed and mumbled something under his breath. Finally he opened his fingers and Shane retracted his arm. He swept over the spot where the reporter had grasped him. After glowering at Shane, Judge Bilodeaux, and the officer, Mr. Galinski twirled around on his heels and stomped away with heavy steps.

"The vultures of the press don't wait too long before descending on their prey." Judge Bilodeaux smiled apologetically. "You'll get more of those requests, I fear. My advice, stay adamant about them."

"I will, Your Honor." Even if Shane didn't sell the story to the papers, they would print their own spins on it. There was no way around his fifteen minutes of fame. And better a hero than a thug.

The officer nodded at Shane and Judge Bilodeaux before returning to his post at the exit.

Mr. Koch took the cop's place in their circle. "Congratulations, Mr. McAllistair. I hope that Mr. Dermond will recover soon and that the police will find the real perpetrator."

Iain! Shane had to tell someone about Iain. "Is Detective Webb still here? There's this guy at school who has bullied Matt for years."

"Are you talking about Iain O'Sullivan?" Mr. Koch's forehead wrinkled.

"Yes, that's him." If they knew about Iain, why had they only arrested him? Shane fit the role of the felon better, of course.

"I've read the full transcripts of the witnesses' testimonies. Most of them named you and Mr. O'Sullivan as the most probable offenders." Mr. Koch shrugged with one shoulder only. "The report further states that Mr. O'Sullivan and the entire baseball team got an official dispensation from school for that afternoon to attend a Boy Scout assembly as guests. They left Central High at two o'clock by bus, and Mr. Dermond was last seen around a quarter to three in the school stadium. Mr. O'Sullivan cannot be responsible for this attack."

Iain had offered his goons money before for turning Matt in. But no, he wouldn't let anyone else do the actual dirty work. He enjoyed hurting people too much to pass up a chance to torture Matt himself. Then it must've really been someone who overheard Shane's talk with Matt. There had been so many students that he couldn't remember all of them. It was hopeless.

"Don't give up, Mr. McAllistair." Judge Bilodeaux knocked his arm gently. "We'll pray for Mr. Dermond and you in my church and ask that the police find the one who has done this. That person will need the Lord's mercy for sure if he ends up in my court."

Was it appropriate to hug a judge? It might be better to play it safe, though, and he didn't. "That's very nice of you, Your Honor."

Judge Bilodeaux thumped Shane's arm again. "It's the least I can do." She bent to the side and looked behind him. "I think there's someone waiting for you."

Shane turned around. Jer stood some yards away, a grin flashing across his face. He drew in his shoulders, which made him appear even smaller than he was. Shane took a step forward and stopped again. The last thing Jer had said to him on that prom night had been that he should stay away. That didn't apply anymore after today, did it?

"Thank you so much for telling the truth." He still had to make up his mind whether sharing this truth with the public was ultimately a good or a bad thing, but he had to honor Jer's courage.

"If I had told it one year ago, you could've thanked me, but not now. Not after what you've done for me. Not for the way I treated you after your—confession."

"I had good reasons for what I did." Shane wouldn't name the feelings he had "confessed" on that prom night again. They had freaked Jer out then, and with the careful way he chose his words, they'd freak him out now.

"You loved me." Jer grinned. "I don't know whether this counts as a good reason."

So much for the freaking out. Jer had changed. The Jer from a year ago wouldn't have treated this subject as lightly. It was sad, however, that it had taken something as dreadful as a rape for him to open up.

Shane returned the grin. "For me, yes, it does."

Jer's grin faded down to a smile. "This sounds strange after dumping you like I did, but I also loved you... as a friend. I just didn't have the sort of feelings you had—and I was a homophobic asshole." He laughed a high, ringing laugh, not unlike Matt's. The laughter died away, taking the smile with it. "It's poetic justice that I got raped by the straight alpha jock of our school."

"Don't say that. There is nothing poetic nor just about what Hayden did to you."

Jer filled his lungs to the brim with air. He let it go in a slow sigh. "My shrink keeps telling me not to blame myself, but she also says that it's a typical reaction for rape victims." He wagged his head. "I couldn't love you back the way you loved me, but Matt is so fortunate to have you as his boyfriend." The smile returned to Jer's lips.

"When Matt gets well again, you have to meet him. You two will like each other." It was a weird thing to think right now, even harsh, but all this talk about love thrust it right into Shane's face. His feelings for Jer were gone, a memory of a past he had outgrown. Shane was glad to see him again, but as Jer had put it... only as a friend. Estelle had hit the mark with her one-person-heart theory, and its exclusive inhabitant was Matt. "I hope it won't take a year before we see each other again."

"Definitely not." Jer's smile changed gears and became a grin again.

"I got my freedom and a friend back on the same day. Not bad." And three was a charm, wasn't it? Maybe Matt would wake up too. Shane extended his hand. "We're friends again, right?"

"You goofy giant, of course we are." Jer pushed Shane's hand away and slung his arms around him. "Just forget the things I said that evening, okay?" he whispered into Shane's chest.

"What things, you defiant dwarf?" Shane rubbed Jer's back. The angel's wing hadn't been wasted after all. That angel had just lost its way for some time but had found it again at last.

Jer cracked up. "Like old times, eh?" He backed up from Shane.

"Sure." One year ago and they called it old times. Estelle would chastise them for this with a wink.

A hand touched his shoulder. "Shane?"

He spun around. "Mr. Dermond!" Shane ordered his heart to beat slower. "I want to thank you for the things you said during the hearing about me, and I want to apologize for the way you learned about Matt and me." The words blurted out of him at high speed, and his heart obviously wasn't too responsive to orders. It kept drumming on relentlessly.

Mr. Dermond shook his head, and the corners of his mouth curved up a little. "I only repeated the things Matt said to me. Nothing more. And for your own sake, you had to tell the court about your relationship." His subtle smile changed into a not-so-subtle grin. "I definitely don't want my son's boyfriend to go to jail just because he thinks he has to spare us."

Shane's head felt light and dizzy. His son's boyfriend? "Thanks, Mr. Dermond."

"My name's Ralph. I definitely don't want my son's boyfriend to call me Mr. Dermond either."

How serious Mr. Der… Ralph was about their relationship. "And Mrs. Dermond?" Shane closed his eyes for a moment. What an insensitive question.

Ralph pressed his lips together tightly and drew in air through his teeth. "Just give her time. She's very… let's say firm… in her convictions." A subdued snort of laughter erupted from him. "Her first impression of you was wrong, and it'll take an immense effort on her side to admit this, but all she wants is for Matt to be safe and happy." Ralph squeezed Shane's shoulder. "And you're giving Matt both."

Shane sighed. "I didn't keep him safe."

"What happened wasn't your fault. No one expects you to watch Matt 24/7." Ralph gave his shoulder another squeeze before dropping his hand.

What Ralph had said wasn't correct. Shane expected himself to watch Matt 24/7.

"Mr. Dermond is right," Jer said, coming up on Shane's side. "I don't know whether this helps you, but if you hadn't walked in on Hayden and me, you would've been the last person I blamed. I'm living proof that you're a defender, and even the best defender can't be everywhere."

Coming from Jer, this statement bore gravity. He was the one who could relate most to what Matt was going through. Still, Shane couldn't forgive himself that easily, even if everyone else in the world did.

Do you really think I want you to feel responsible? What has become of the WWMW test?

Shane felt guilty for feeling guilty now. He had to cut himself some slack if he intended to keep a minimum of sanity. But this whole situation was sheer lunacy, flooding over him from all sides.

"We have to look ahead, Shane, not back." Ralph grasped his shoulders with both hands. "Matt isn't awake, but I know he's waiting for you. Monica, my wife's sister, is taking care of her now, so I can drive you to the hospital and bring you home later. I already asked your parents, and they're okay with it."

"I can't keep you away from your wife." Not after all the things that had happened today.

"My wife needs some time for herself now." A subtle smile appeared on Ralph's lips. "And you need to spend time with Matt. Let's go." He squeezed Shane's shoulders once more, released them, and turned around.

At last Shane would see Matt. His boyfriend was the fixed point in this torrent of madness, and Shane had to hold on to him.

"Phone me later and tell me everything about Matt, okay?" Jer pushed with both hands against him. "And now go. What are you waiting for?"

"I will." Shane grabbed Jer and pressed him close. "Thank you," he whispered.

In a weird twist of fate, keeping Jer's secret had set in motion the chain of events that had led to Matt and him becoming boyfriends. One more thing to be grateful for.

CHAPTER THIRTY-TWO

LIKE SCHOOL cafeterias, hospitals always smelled the same. A pungent stench of disinfectant and the rank stink of illness itself turned Shane's stomach around, but he didn't want to be in any other place. Ralph led the way through the winding corridors of the intensive care wing of St. Christopher's Hospital. They passed by many doors, each of them hiding another fate. Finally, Ralph stopped before one of them.

"This is Matt's room." Ralph heaved a sigh. "You'll spend a moment with him alone." His tone didn't brook any dissent. "I'll go and ask the nurses about granting you access at any time. You're family, after all."

None of the things that came to Shane's mind made any sense, and he couldn't say anything in reply. So he slung his arms around Ralph and pulled him close. Showing what he felt when words failed always worked with Matt. Consequently, it was his best shot with Matt's dad too.

"You're welcome, Shane." A subdued groan escaped from Ralph's throat. "And you're really strong."

Shane opened his arms, and blood rushed to his cheeks. "I'm sorry. It's just...."

Ralph waved his hand. "Don't you dare apologize." He shook his head and smiled. "You go in there, and I'll go find the nurses."

Matt shared more traits with his dad than he probably knew himself, at least when it came to accepting apologies. Shane nodded and watched Ralph until he vanished behind a corner, then grabbed the handle of the door. What if he couldn't bear seeing Matt? If it was too much? He had waited for this moment since being arrested, and now he was hesitating. How batshit crazy was that? He turned the knob and pushed open the door.

Heavy black curtains had been drawn, and the room lay in twilight. An eerie blue hue surrounded the life monitor, whose rhythmic beeping disrupted the flow of time by cutting it into equally sized chunks. So that was the sound of life? Shane inhaled before he crossed the threshold, closing the door as quietly as possible.

Matt's skin was always pale, but in the artificial shine of the monitor, it looked solidly white yet transparent. His hair clung to his scalp in matted hanks, drained of the life that usually turned the dark blond mass into an untamed mess. The doctors had attached electrodes to his head, and the wires coming out of them disappeared into the monitor. A white gauze bandage covered the back of his head. IV lines protruded from everywhere on his boyfriend's arm, liquids of all colors dripping through them. Shane clapped his hand over his mouth, keeping his cry inside. It was worse than he had imagined. Still, seeing Matt at last alleviated Shane's pain, toned it down to a dull droning in his mind.

With wobbly steps, he approached and held on to the bed rail, because he couldn't trust his knees anymore. Matt was breathing, but his chest barely moved. Shane extended his hand toward the bloodless face, sunken and hollow, but he froze an inch before it. Matt's body looked so frail, like it might disintegrate at the slightest touch. No, that wouldn't happen, because Matt was stronger and sturdier than everyone else. Shane let the tips of his fingers graze over the soft skin of Matt's cheek. It felt so cold, and the iciness crept into his hand, eliciting a shiver that slithered down his spine.

"I'm here, Matt, and I'm sorry for being late. You hate apologies, I know, but indulge me just this time, okay?" Shane's voice broke. Matt shouldn't see how cast down he was. People in comas were aware of everything that happened around them, even more aware than an awake person. At least, he had read that somewhere. He had to give Matt strength and shouldn't suck it out of him like a vampire. "You didn't let me say it yesterday because you feared I might just parrot you, but you should've let me do it. It was as true yesterday as it is today, and as it will be any other day. I love you, Matt." Shane didn't need the things from the wicker basket to make this their special moment. Every moment with Matt was special, and he would never postpone anything again. Two lessons this tragedy had taught him already. He lowered his lips to Matt's and brushed a kiss onto them. Like his skin, they felt chilly, and Shane pulled up the blanket a little more, tucking Matt in. He caressed the pallid cheek again in the hope that some of his warmth might trickle over. Slowly, he sank down to his knees, still fondling Matt.

"Mr. McAllistair?" A female voice asked so softly that it didn't even startle him.

He turned around and looked up. A brunette woman, dressed in blue scrubs and her hair tied up into a ponytail, smiled down at him. The name on her coat identified her as Dr. Karatovic. Ralph stood beside her.

"Matt is so cold." And he was so impolite. No hello, no answer to her question. But she needed to tell him why Matt was freezing.

"Most coma patients react like this. Their metabolisms are reduced to a minimum. That's nothing to be worried about." Dr. Karatovic's smile deepened. "It may sound strange, but Matt's coma is a good sign. His brain is repairing itself and shut down the rest of his body to fully concentrate on the task."

"Will he recover completely?" Shane's question was selfish. He wanted Matt back, the very Matt who told him that he loved him. Still, Shane would never abandon him, whatever might happen.

Dr. Karatovic tilted her head slightly. "I cannot guarantee anything, of course. But for a young and otherwise healthy boy like Matt, the chances for permanent damage are very, very low."

Shane nodded, and Dr. Karatovic's smile rubbed off on him. "Thank you, Doctor." He felt his lips sag down as he turned back to Matt. "I know it's childish, but I'd hoped he'd wake up when he heard my voice." Or when he kissed him, which was even beyond childish. Shane wasn't the fairy-tale prince whose lips broke the evil spell and saved the sleeping beauty. "He didn't even react."

Dr. Karatovic walked over to the monitor and slid her fingers over its touch screen. She knitted her brows as she scanned the clutter of lines and peaks. The corners of her mouth bent up into a smile again. "Would you please come here, Mr. McAllistair? Mr. Dermond?" She beckoned them over, eyes still on the monitor.

Shane got up from his knees. Ralph and he exchanged a puzzled look before joining Dr. Karatovic.

"Do you see the jagged lines here?" Dr. Karatovic pointed at the screen. "These are delta waves. They usually indicate a state of deep sleep and are the predominant wave pattern for most coma patients." She scrolled the diagram to the left. "About five minutes ago, there was a significant increase in theta wave activity, those peaks here. They hint at subconscious processes." Dr. Karatovic grabbed Shane's hand. "Like an emotional reaction, for example."

Shane's gaze switched from the monitor to Dr. Karatovic and back. "You mean Matt noticed me?"

"Noticed?" Dr. Karatovic tittered. "I haven't seen such amplitudes in conscious persons, let alone in a comatose one."

Ralph patted his back. "I told you Matt was waiting to see you. Is this proof enough for you that the things he said, and which I only repeated in court, are true?"

Shane eyed Ralph, whose face was beaming. "It is." He turned around to look at Matt, and warmness flared up in Shane's chest, spreading through his limbs. He had to share this warmth with Matt, for he needed it more than him. "Can I please stay? Perhaps even overnight? I'll phone my parents, and I'll go home in the morning, but just let me stay tonight."

Dr. Karatovic gave Shane's hand a squeeze. "We have to bend some regulations, but that's what they are there for, aren't they?" She looked at Ralph. "You don't object, I assume?"

"Of course not. Being with his boyfriend is the best therapy for Matt, don't you think?"

"Definitely." Dr. Karatovic chuckled once more. "I'll inform the nurses and my colleagues. Perhaps we can even organize a spare bed for Mr. McAllistair."

"Thank you. I don't want to cause you any inconvenience, and I don't think a bed is necessary." He wouldn't sleep anyway. Occupying as little space as possible, he'd huddle up to Matt, hold him, talk to him, and simply be there for him.

"You're an integral part of Matt's therapy. So by definition, you're not an inconvenience." Dr. Karatovic pressed Shane's hand before she let go of it. "I'll take care of the details, and you just take care of Matt."

Shane nodded.

"See you later, Mr. McAllistair, Mr. Dermond." Dr. Karatovic left the room as silently as she had entered it.

"I'll tell my wife about Matt's reaction to you. Maybe this will speed up the process of her coming around." Ralph gave a one-sided grin. "One or two shots of elder schnapps might do the rest." His face straightened. "I'll make sure she won't come to the hospital today in any case."

Shane hadn't thought about that. "I don't want to keep her from visiting her son." She was his mom, and she had more right to be here than he did. "I can—"

"Bullshit!" Ralph shook his head with forceful jerks. "She spent all of last evening and the whole night here, only leaving for the hearing. It's better for her to have a day of rest." He sighed. "Until she comes to her senses about you, we'll find a way for both of you to see Matt without running into each other."

At all costs, Shane had to avoid further alienating Mrs. Dermond, but Ralph had apparently made up his mind about today. Stubbornness ran strongly in the Dermonds, and Shane wouldn't talk back to his boyfriend's dad. *His boyfriend's dad.* He loved the sound of those words, though it'd take some time to even think them without hesitation. Having Ralph on his side was simply awesome. Mrs. Dermond didn't stand much of a chance against the united front of the men in her life. Enough reason for Shane to pity her again. "Please tell her that I'll leave anytime she wants to come here. Okay?"

"You're such a wonderful guy, Shane. She just has to see this, but I'll pass your offer on to her." Ralph rubbed his back. "I'll leave the both of you alone now. Here." He produced a business card from his wallet. "Call me anytime on my cell. I won't be at work for the next week. But in the future, you can phone me there too."

Shane accepted the card. "I've said this over and over again today, but thank you. Usually I'm better with words. Just now they are playing hide-and-seek with me." Matt's presence always had this effect on him, and this place and the whole situation goaded the words on to find even better hideouts.

"Words are just words. Your actions speak for you, and they do so very eloquently."

The predilection for deeds was obviously another thing the Dermond men had in common.

"See you later, Shane." Ralph patted his back once more before heading for the door.

"See you later." Shane considered the screen of the life monitor again. Some colorful lines, seemingly chaotic and random, were the closest thing to hope he had. He walked around the bed and lay down beside Matt. It didn't matter that one of his legs dangled down and his torso barely fit onto the sheet. Careful not to remove any of the cables and tubes, he laid his arm around Matt and nestled up as closely as possible.

"I'll keep you warm. Just relax and let your brain do the self-repair stuff. Deal?" He rested his cheek against Matt's, and the cold touch caused goose bumps to travel over Shane's skin.

Theta waves. He had to give Matt subconscious, caring, and loving peaks of theta waves. They would mend him. They had to mend him.

CHAPTER THIRTY-THREE

TWO-DOZEN RED roses. Were these too many? Or not enough? It was too late to change that number anyway. Shane knocked at Estelle's door and entered. He found his friend sitting in her bed and listening to music from her cell while swaying her head to the rhythm.

She took out the earbuds. "Lord bless my soul, are you crazy, Shane?" Estelle placed her hands on her cheeks and gave him her best mock exasperation, usually reserved for Sundays and the holiest of holidays.

He only had to look into her eyes to see what she really felt. That gleam hadn't left her eyes in all the time that he'd known her, and it never would. "It's a pleasure to see you too, my lovely lady."

"Oh, bollocks." After spending twenty years of her life in Europe, strange phrases bubbled out of Estelle at times without her even realizing it. She was in her British phase apparently. Still better than the fragments of French, which Shane didn't understand at all.

He opened the cupboard and got out the crystal flower vase, one of the few things from Estelle's past she had brought to the home. "The saleswoman said she already cut the stems and that we can put them directly into the water." Whatever the nice lady had tried to tell him with those mysterious words, Estelle nodded. He hadn't talked complete nonsense, then.

The bouquet, exuding a sweet and beguiling fragrance, looked beautiful in the bellied shape of the vase. Shane placed it on the sideboard where the crystal refracted the rays of the autumn sun and created small rainbows all over the wall.

"These are for the wonderful letter you wrote." Shane chuckled. "You certainly impressed Judge Bilodeaux with your fanciful choice of words."

Estelle raised an eyebrow, doubling the number of wrinkles on that side of her face. "I only put down the truth with the exact words I deemed necessary." She sighed. "But you make a federal case out of the smallest thing, of course."

Shane slumped onto the chair. "That wasn't a small thing." He scratched his nape. "I have to thank you for another thing. You're the first person who isn't treating me like I'm made of china."

"You're my bad-boy-ersatz-grandson who's already been to prison twice. How else should I treat you?" Estelle cackled. "Seriously, it's that bad?"

Shane shrugged. "Mr. Lockson from the home administration said that I don't have to come to work. I've accrued so many extra hours that he granted me a month of paid vacation time. Principal Wagner gave me a special courtesy week off from school. Nick doesn't even let me come close to the gym." He whistled through his teeth. "Good thing is, I can spend all the extra time with Matt, at least if his mom isn't at the hospital."

"She still doesn't talk to you?" Estelle smiled, and for one of her smiles, it was terrifyingly sympathetic.

Even she was affected by the "poor gay guy whose boyfriend is in the hospital and who has been falsely accused of it" effect. Shane had to come up with a handier abbreviation for that because it happened so often these days it deserved to have a proper name.

"We haven't been in the same room since the hearing. It was only three days ago, so I can't blame her. Her son has been attacked, and the guy she hates the most turns out to be her son's boyfriend."

Estelle tsked. "She hates the guy who attacked Matt more, I'd say."

"It's a close call." Shane sighed. "At least Mr. Dermond and I get along just fine. On the days we don't see each other, we talk over the phone, sometimes for hours." He and Ralph had formed a symbiotic pact, keeping each other from sinking too deep into the black hole that was their feelings. They were two guys who worried for the same beloved person, and that turned their bond into something special. "Oh, I have to show you this." Shane got out the pink envelope with the crayon drawings of flowers on it. "We've been getting hundreds of letters and e-mails. Most of them wish Matt and me all the best." There were some homophobic rants among them, but those were only five or six letters out of hundreds. His mom had taken on the full-time job of reading them and sorting out the bad ones upon herself. "This one is from a person we know. You want to read it?" Shane offered Estelle the letter.

"I misplaced my glasses again. Can you read it for me?"

That would've been more convincing if Estelle hadn't batted her eyelashes at him. She was just too vain to wear her glasses in public, but Shane was off duty as a nurse and here as her friend only. A friend should bear his friend's infirmities. Mr. Shakespeare had got this one right.

He cleared his throat.

"Dear giant Shane. I'm Natalie, the girl you met on the train with the evil granny. I can only write the letters *a*, *b*, and *c*, but my mommy knows all the other ones, and she is writing

this for me. I wrote *a*, *b*, and *c* for you at the bottom of this
letter. And I drew a picture of you and your boyfriend. You're
kissing like Uncle Henry and Uncle Barney."

Two stickmen, a large one with colorful thick arms and a small one,
stuck their heads together on the back of the letter.

> "The lady on TV says that your boyfriend is very sick.
> I pray every evening that your boyfriend stops being sick
> and that you can kiss again very soon. Oh, and thank you so
> much for the chocolate. There is nothing left of it. I ate just
> one piece every day, but only because mommy didn't allow
> me to eat more. It was so good. I love you, Natalie."

Shane extended his hands to show Estelle the drawing of Matt and
him. "Isn't that cute?"

"Looks exactly like you." Estelle put on her haughty smile. "And that
clever little lady already knows what the most important things in life are—
kisses and chocolate."

Shane and Estelle laughed. It was the first time since visiting Matt in
the hospital that Shane was laughing out loud. The bad conscience piped up
promptly, asking with a whisper how on earth it was possible that he could
be having fun when Matt was suffering.

*How often do I have to say this? Don't grieve just because of me.
Quite the contrary. As long as I'm knocked out, you're supposed to have fun
for the both of us.*

Head-Matt was adamant about a lot of things. For being a figment of
Shane's mind, Head-Matt was also surprisingly wayward. Just like the real
one. At times Shane considered the possibility of Matt communicating with
him through some mumbo-jumbo telepathy thing. However Head-Matt
came into his head, he kept Shane grounded. Why question something that
worked?

Their laughter ebbed down. He folded the letter and put it back into
the envelope. Those declarations of support together with Head-Matt kept
him from despair.

Estelle puckered her lips, and her features tensed up. "How is Matt?"

"No real change." Shane's gaze sank to the floor. "Dr. Karatovic says
that there are subtle signs in Matt's brain activity, which might indicate the

beginning of recovery, but that those are inconclusive and that we have to be patient. I'm not my dad, who turned patience into a religion."

Estelle put her hand on Shane's knee, her fingers as fragile as Matt's but so much warmer than his. "How are *you*, Shane?"

He raised his head. Estelle peered at him. The lively gleam in her eyes shone a little brighter, as if she were trying to send some of it over to him.

"Everyone handles me with kid gloves, but you're the first to ask that question." That included himself. He hadn't allowed himself to experience anything else but his love for Matt. Before Head-Matt could berate him, he would answer Estelle, and himself, as frankly as possible. "I'm feeling helpless. There's nothing I can do. At least nothing that yields tangible results. Of course it's important to spend time with Matt, to encourage and to take care of him, but all that happens are subtle hints that might indicate something or nothing at all." Shane turned his hands around and let them hover over his knees. "Look at these paws. They've been made for tackling problems and for coming to grips with difficulties. All they do right now is hold Matt and caress him. All wonderful things, of course, but there must be something more they can accomplish."

"Everyone else will tell you there isn't anything more you can do, but I say sod that!" Estelle tightened her grip on his knee to the point that a dull pain throbbed through it. "You know what I think about the cops. And let me guess. They haven't made any progress in finding the bastard who attacked Matt?"

Shane shook his head. "No, they haven't. With Iain and me exonerated, they have no clue where to start." He didn't like where this talk was heading.

"An adult cannot understand how a high school kid thinks, but a high school kid can. It's always easier to find someone from the inside than from the outside." The shine in her eyes changed, tinted by an angry glow, and the skin around her eyes became taut.

"I can't take the law into my own hands." He had just convinced everyone that he wasn't a brute. Now he was supposed to go catch the son of a bitch who assaulted Matt? "If I actually found the guy, I'm afraid of what I'd do." Two broken arms would be peanuts in comparison. Shane's scar pulsated as blood shot into his head, and heat spread from his cheeks, over his scalp to his ears.

"That lousy bugger deserves a good roughing up, but you won't do it." Estelle's grip on his knee slackened, and compassion smoothed down the hard edges of her features. "I've known you for over a year now, and yes, you could rip someone's head off with one hand tied behind your back. But that's not what those paws will do." She let go of Shane's knee and grabbed both of his hands, the slender shapes of her fingers barely reaching around. "They'll find that asshole, and then they'll deliver him to the police without a single scratch."

If only Shane shared Estelle's confidence about keeping that much control. He had lost it once, and the situations were so eerily similar. "Even if I tried to find the scumbag, I'd have the same problem as the cops. I don't know where to start. I can't walk around school, grab any guy I see by the collar, and try to glower a confession out of him."

"You only need a little help." Estelle wiggled Shane's hands. "If you want to catch a devil, you need the help of a devil. Who knows more about assholes than another asshole? You don't have to try to glower a confession out of every student. Just concentrate on the usual suspects handpicked by an expert."

Searing heat and a chilly feeling of cold alternated in Shane's head. They came in waves crashing at the walls of his skull. What Estelle said made sense, yet her words didn't silence the second thoughts clamoring in his mind. He could at least give it a shot. His paws needed something else to do, and finding the attacker was something useful at last. Granted, it didn't help Matt's condition in the slightest, but it would help him. What would Matt want?

As long as it gets you out of the dumps, go for it. Oh, by the way, I love you.

Shane smiled.

I love you too.

"I'll get you another bouquet of roses when I catch the guy." Shane closed his fingers around Estelle's and rubbed her knuckles with his thumb.

"I'd prefer a necklace made of that swine's teeth, but flowers will do." Estelle combined the haughtiness of her smiles with the slyness of her grins, and the result frightened Shane. "I'm just kidding." To his relief she decided on grinning only. "Do you already have an idea which devil you'll ask for help?"

Shane brought his hands, still holding Estelle's, together. "Yes, I do." He couldn't see his own face, but his grin had to rival hers in shiftiness.

Why settle for anyone less than the high king of all assholes?

CHAPTER THIRTY-FOUR

TWO STEPS led up to the veranda, and it'd take him just one more step to stand in front of the door. Shane had walked all the other hundreds of footsteps before with ease, but those last three planted themselves before him, insurmountable and threatening. The plan had been so clear-cut and logical when he had left Estelle's room. Somewhere between there and here, it had turned into a jumbled mess—something a kindergarten kid might have come up with. That comparison wasn't fair, because even Natalie would've created a better plan and written it with crayons on pink paper, using only the first three letters of the alphabet. Despite all his doubts, he had to do something, even if it was sheer madness and doomed to fail. He climbed the first step. That hadn't been that difficult. He ascended the next one. Not giving himself any time to think about it, he took the last step to the door. Lately doors had developed the unnerving habit of scaring him. But in his defense, more often than not, nasty things lurked behind them. He rang the bell, and his guts knotted up. If no one answered, he could get out of this and pretend it had never happened. The pitter-patter of feet hurrying down a staircase snatched away that last straw to clutch at. Shane startled as the door flew open, seemingly all by itself, and he let his gaze wander down. A red-haired boy, perhaps twelve years old, stared up at him. Ginger freckles covered almost all of his slender face, and only a few spots of fair skin showed. The color of his eyes reminded Shane of moss. Those eyes were wide now, but overall this boy looked more curious than shocked.

"Hi, my name's Shane. Is your brother…?"

"Seamus, you dipstick, how often have I told you not to open the door if Mom and Dad aren't… whoa!" Iain came down the stairs and stopped cold at the bottom. He drew in a deep breath, and his face turned a chalky white. "Shane!" He choked and waved his hands around. "It wasn't me. I swear! It wasn't me." He stumbled backward and crashed onto the steps with a dull thud. Even the sound was painful.

Seamus jumped back and extended both arms. "Don't hurt him, please!" He shook his head, sending the red wisps of his hair flying. "I know he's an asshole at school, but Iain didn't touch your friend." Seamus swallowed. "At least, not this time," he added ruefully. "He's not nice at school, but he's a good brother and came to my Boy Scout meeting with all of his teammates on that Thursday. It really wasn't him."

Shane's head was swimming. First of all, he hadn't known that Iain had a brother, but the most disturbing fact was that Seamus called him a *good* brother. Iain was the devil, the villain, pure evil. He was the terror of Central High, not the guy who scratched the back of his baby brother. Shane would sort out this bullshit of contradictions later, but first he had to calm Seamus.

"I know it wasn't Iain." He took a step inside and knelt down before Seamus. This was something to be discussed at face level. "The plaintiff told me that Iain attended the Boy Scout meeting." Shane turned his hands around, showing his open palms. "I'm not here to hurt your brother. I only want to ask him something." He extended his hand. "I've never been a Boy Scout, but I give you my word of honor that I won't lay a finger on Iain." He smiled, enduring the green intensity of Seamus's gaze resting on him.

The younger O'Sullivan's mouth kept moving, almost as if he were chewing on the things Shane had said. He nodded his head once, obviously having made up his mind, and grasped Shane's hand. "You're a sportsman. A sportsman's word counts almost as much as a Boy Scout's." He smiled back at Shane and shook his hand before stepping aside.

"Thank you, Seamus."

Shane turned his head to look at Iain. Pale and panting, he was still half-lying on the stairs. This wasn't the devil. A very bad guy, yes, but still human. Hopefully, he was devil enough to find the one who had hurt Matt. Shane got up and walked forward, Iain's gaze following him. He offered Iain his hand. "I'm here for talking only. You heard the promise I gave your brother, didn't you?"

Iain eyed Shane's hand, then looked up into his face. He nodded, grabbed the hand, and Shane pulled him up to a stand.

"Let's go to my room, and you, dipstick—" Iain pointed at Seamus. "—go to yours, and if the fucking doorbell rings, you'll let *me* answer. Got it?"

If Shane had heard this sentence a minute ago, he would have treated it as a brush-off only, absolutely typical for Iain. Now he took his time to consider Iain's eyes and found worry in them. Worry for his little brother being kidnaped or worse. Of all people, Shane should know best that there was more to a person than what was up-front, though in Iain's case this "more" hid very, very deep inside.

Iain spun around and bolted up the stairs. Shane faced Seamus, rolled his eyes, and shrugged. A dimple formed on Seamus's cheek as he grinned back. Who was the black sheep in this family? Seamus or Iain? Shane chuckled inside and followed Iain upstairs.

IF ONE exchanged the baseball posters for bodybuilding ones, Iain's room would've looked just like his. One difference consisted of a shelf with different-sized trophies, some golden, some silver, but all of them with little batter figurines on top. Another obvious difference, Iain was a clutterer. Lying all over the room were scattered clothes, used dishes, and empty bottles of soda. The smell reminded Shane of a locker room that had been built around the waste dump of a fast-food outlet. Spending time with Iain didn't rank high on his priority list, and the special aroma here didn't entice him to stay any longer either. He would deliver his request and then leave as fast as possible.

"Sit down, dude." Iain glanced at him from the corners of his eyes.

Shane wiped some clothes away from the bed, hoping that they were T-shirts only. "Sure, dude." He had told Iain in the cafeteria fight not to call him dude ever again, but a little friendliness went well with the favor he was about to ask. Shane slumped onto the bed.

Iain furrowed his brows for a moment, but his features relaxed again. Seemingly, he remembered their "dude arrangement" as well.

"This sounds fucking ridiculous coming from me, but I'm so pissed at what happened to Matty." Iain grabbed his lower arms and massaged them. "I don't know how often I've said I'd kill him, but that some douche actually tried sucks big time."

"Thanks, dude." Shane believed him. It contradicted everything he knew about Iain or what he thought he knew about him, but this was the truth and probably the closest thing to an apology Iain would ever offer.

"So, you and Matty are… together?"

Shane didn't want to know which word "together" had replaced. "Yes, we're boyfriends."

"You're the man in that relationship, dude?"

If this was Iain's take on casual small talk, he should stop. Regurgitating decades-old prejudices made Shane's blood boil, and Iain shouldn't want him to get angry. "Last time I checked, Matt was a man too." The tone of Shane's voice sounded like teeth gnawing on iron.

"Okay, man." Iain's grip around his arms tightened, and they turned white. "You want to ask me something."

The breathing crap didn't work that often, but Shane inhaled and exhaled nonetheless. It filled up at least a little of the emptiness in his guts. "The police have no clue who attacked Matt. They can only assume that it was a student." He drew in another breath, but this one had no effect at all. "Would you help me to find the bastard? I'm still the new one at Central High, and you know the school so much better. People respect you, dude." Some flattery would work better than repeating Estelle's colorful wording about devils and assholes.

"You mean people fear me, and I'm the gang leader of the school scum?" Iain pulled up one corner of his mouth into a crooked grin, and a dimple formed on his other cheek. He looked just like Seamus.

Shane shrugged and grinned back. "That's what you said." When it came to manipulation, Iain was the master and outwitted Shane with years of experience. Fortunately he hadn't taken it the wrong way.

The corner of Iain's mouth dropped again, and he lowered his gaze to the ground. "Do you really think Matty wants me to help you? He has to fucking hate me for millions of good reasons."

"Funny thing is, he doesn't. He'd be happy if he didn't see you ever again in his life, but he doesn't hate you." Matt wasn't only the stronger one of them. He also had the bigger heart. Shane despised Iain for the things he had done, but his worry for Matt outweighed everything. "You keep calling him Matty. Do you only do so to make fun of him, or do you actually care for him in an effing, twisted way?" It was a random shot, and Shane couldn't say from where this idea had come.

"I've known Matty...." Iain closed his eyes for a moment. "I've known him since kindergarten. You can't fucking ignore someone you've known for such a long time."

"And you chose torture as your way of letting him know you didn't forget him?" Shane's plan was going down the drain, but he had to know the answer to this question. Iain was an athlete, like him. How could someone strong get a thrill out of picking on someone weak? There was nothing to be gained, no merit whatsoever. Why did a sportsman ignore the foundations of what he loved?

"Matty was always a weirdo. He was a year older than us and still the freaking smallest kid in kindergarten. When we played ball, he just stood there and watched us from the sideline while shuffling his feet. He was fucking six years old and could read like an adult. The kindergartners let him read to us in the chair circle every day. And what did my parents do?" Iain's chest rose and fell in shallow, fast gasps. He pitched up his voice into a squeaky falsetto. "Iain, look at Matt. He can read. Don't you want to try and learn reading too?" His knuckles stood out as he grabbed his lower arms even tighter. "Oh, I tried, but Seamus is the clever O'Sullivan brother. I'm only good for wielding a bat and running around the diamond." Iain shook his head and stared at Shane, pressing his lips shut. "Sorry, dude, for telling you the fucking story of my miserable life."

Simple, banal, childish envy. Matt had suffered all of his life just because he had something that Iain didn't. Shane's hands closed into fists, and the empty feeling in his intestines ignited. If there existed any good reasons for bullying someone, this wasn't one of them. Iain's explanation sounded petty and small-minded. "Have you ever asked Matt? Asked him to join your games? Asked him to teach you how to read? He would've sat down with you all day long, cheering you on, until *you* could read to the other kids." Shane jumped up from the bed and advanced a step toward Iain. "If you had asked Matt nicely to help you with your essays, he would've done so too. He's so fucking amiable that he would've even written them for you, handed them over with a smile on his face and been happy that you got a good grade." He crossed the distance between them, and Iain pressed himself against his desk. "You haven't asked him, of course." They stood so close together that Shane's breath caused Iain's hair to flap.

"I'm sorry, dude." Iain held Shane's gaze, and the panic on his face was mixed with remorse.

The true thing. Not a fake for saving his own skin.

Shane closed his eyes. "Don't tell me! Tell Matt!" He unclenched his fists, opened his eyes, and heaved a sigh. "I won't hurt you. Not only because I promised your brother, but because this won't undo a single damn thing you've ever done to Matt." He walked backward and let himself plonk onto the bed again, burying his head in his hands. "I could say some stale bullshit like 'You owe him,' but I won't. Do you know who you owe? Seamus." Shane raised his head and looked into Iain's eyes. "He loves you. There aren't many guys who'd jump between me and their brother to protect him. And you love him too. Do you really want him to think you're an asshole?"

Iain's face moved as a whole, one twitch chasing another tic. His forehead creased as he looked at the door. "Come in, dipstick. Even a deaf man could hear you breathing."

Seamus appeared in the crack of the door, eyes down, his face beet red at having been caught eavesdropping. His head shot up. "Shane's right.

If you help him find that asshole, I won't call you one again. Ever. Scout's honor." Seamus raised two fingers.

Iain put his head back and snorted out a single laugh. "I've been fucking outvoted." He lowered his head and grinned at Seamus. "Shane already had me when he asked me the first time, but now I have your word not to call me an asshole ever again. How awesome is that?"

Seamus's mouth fell open, and he let his hand drop, but his lips bent up into a grin. "Only if you make a real effort to help Shane."

Iain pushed away from his desk and walked over to Shane. He closed his hand into a fist and offered it. "Asshole's honor that I'll give my best at finding that douche. No one lays a finger on Matty except me."

Shane stiffened up.

"Just kidding, dude." Iain extended his fist a little more, giving him a two-dimpled smile.

"If he ever touches Matt again," Seamus said with a voice of pure innocence, "you have my permission to rough him up."

"Hey, dipstick, you—"

"That's an offer I won't let pass," Shane said.

A fist bump sealed the pact with the devil who wasn't one. Strange situations created strange bedfellows, but a fist bump had also marked the beginning of his friendship with Matt. Perhaps this was a good sign.

Seamus cackled, the bell-like laughing of a boy, and Iain and Shane joined in.

This pact would work, and they would find the attacker. Shane ignored the little voice in his head that talked about how desperate and futile this search was. He wouldn't allow it to rob him of his hope.

CHAPTER THIRTY-FIVE

"HAPPY BIRTHDAY, my love Ma-att, happy birthday to you!"

Shane switched off the LED candle on the piece of cheesecake he had bought in the Lazy Bean. He tittered. "If you weren't in a coma yet, my lousy singing would've knocked you out for sure." He put the plate with the cake on the nightstand. "So once again, happy birthday, Matt." Shane planted a kiss on each of Matt's lips. "Time for your presents."

He opened the first four buttons of his shirt, still holding it closed. "I hope you like it. It was finished only yesterday, so the skin is still rather irritated." He pulled apart the two halves of the shirt, revealing the tattoo of a green hummingbird flapping its wings right over his heart. "One of the first things we talked about when we met was my tats, and I told you that I've got one for every person who's important in my life. You hate it when I get sappy." Shane chuckled. "At least, you pretend to hate it when I get sappy, but there isn't a person more important in my life than you. If anyone deserves an ink, you do." Shane took Matt's hand, the left one that wasn't pricked with needles, and placed it over the tattoo. The coldness eased the burn of his battered skin. "Why a hummingbird, you ask? A really good question. First, hummingbirds are the cutest animals of all and the only one fitting for you." Shane's features sagged, pulled down by the graveness of the other reason. "Second, a hummingbird never gives up. It flies from flower to flower all day just to find enough nectar to survive. A hummingbird looks frail on the outside but is so strong on the inside. Just like you." Shane wiped his eyes. He wouldn't cry on Matt's birthday, for he had sworn to make it as cheerful as possible. Carefully, he lowered his hand down to the bed again.

Shane bowed down and opened his backpack, producing from it the envelope with the silver bands tied around it. "But that's not all." He chuckled again. "Please note that this time I spared you the tackiness of golden bows or boxes. Here." He positioned the envelope under Matt's fingers. "I simply know that you'll like this one. On the second day, you came to the library and told me you'd give our friendship a chance. I recounted the story of the car accident and my aquaphobia. You may not even remember, but you mentioned how much you love the sea." Shane placed his hand on Matt's.

"Since I love you more than I fear anything, I bought a voucher for a holiday on the beaches of Hawaii. You can redeem it anytime within a year, so don't feel rushed to get well soon." Shane rubbed Matt's wrist. "You'll need all of your strength to calm the shivering picture of misery that will be your wimpy giant of a boyfriend." He guffawed.

With his other hand, Shane caressed Matt's pale cheek. "I already told you about the tickets for the party. You wanted them as a gift as well...." He kissed Matt's nose. "But even if you woke up right now, Dr. Karatovic wouldn't let you go tomorrow evening." Shane rubbed his nose against Matt's. "I hope you don't mind that I donated them to students who couldn't afford a ticket on their own. Oh, I haven't told you. The shirt I'm wearing is the one I would've worn to the party. My mom sewed it. You know how difficult it is for me to find clothes that fit and I don't hate, but my mom can do wonders with a sewing machine." If she could only mend Matt's brain with some of her perfect stitches.

No gloomy thoughts today!

He let go of Matt's cheek and rummaged through his backpack. "There is one last present for you." He got out the black box with the Egyptian hieroglyphs. Shane lowered his mouth to Matt's ear and whispered, "I wanted to wrap this up perfectly, so I decided to put it into your masterpiece, but you better keep it hidden and only open it when you're back at home." Another chuckle burst out of him. "The nurse or, even worse, your mom, might be irritated to find an assortment of rubbers and lube." Shane kissed Matt's neck. "I was an idiot for making a fuss about fucking you. You said it first, but it's just as true for me. I want to be with you in every way possible. I promise to never underestimate you again and to fulfill all of your wishes that I can." He placed another kiss on Matt's neck. "Happy birthday, Matt. I love you."

Shane opened the drawer of the nightstand. "I'll hide the box here in the very back. Just keep your fingers crossed that the nurse doesn't get too nosy." He pushed the drawer shut.

"It's your birthday, so what are you up to?" Shane lay down at Matt's side and watched the up and down of his chest. "A comfy day in bed, you say? With cuddling and kissing and chilling out?" He snuggled up closer. "That's a really good idea."

Someone pushed the door handle down, and Shane turned around. It was too early for the nurse, and Dr. Karatovic had already visited half an hour ago.

A smiling Ralph stuck his head inside. "Hi, you two. I brought some more party people, if you don't mind."

Party people? He sat up on the bed and buttoned up his shirt. Ralph pushed open the door, and Shane's fingers froze, the last button gliding out of them. Mrs. Dermond stood behind Ralph, a birthday cake with white frosting in her hand. He'd have to leave now. At least he had spent some moments with Matt alone and had been able to give him all his presents. Perhaps Dr. Karatovic would let him stay here for another night, but the Dermonds took precedence over him, especially on Matt's birthday.

Shane rose up from the bed. Mrs. Dermond wouldn't want to see Matt and him so close together. "I'll go, then…." He knitted his brows. Coming into the room right behind Mrs. Dermond was his mom. She carried two of the folding chairs usually stored in their shed, bought for a camping trip that would never happen. Shane's heart added an extra beat that was completely out of sync with the others, and he felt nauseated. "What the heck are you…." Another one of those misplaced heartbeats drove him back, and he flopped onto the bed. His dad entered, the folding table and one more chair under his arms. One of the oxygen supplies had to be leaking and he was hallucinating from an overdose.

"You were right, Gordon," Ralph said and laughed out loud. "We scared the crap out of him."

"Ralph!" Mrs. Dermond shook her head. "Watch your mouth!" She looked at his mom and shrugged with a tilted smile on her lips.

His mother cackled. "We are both cursed with having to deal with two men in our houses. Cussing is the least of my problems, I can tell you."

The other corner of Mrs. Dermond's mouth joined the smile, and she nodded. "Amen to that."

This was the most vivid and realistic dream—nightmare—Shane ever had. Pure oxygen seemed to be excellent stuff.

"Won't you help your old dad with the furniture, son?"

He jumped up before thinking about it. Was it a good idea to play along in a horror trip? He reached out for the chair and the table, and their plastic surfaces felt cold and hard. This wasn't a hallucination caused by his overexcited brain, but that insight didn't make the nausea in his stomach go away. He'd throw up any moment.

Ralph laid his arm around Shane. At least he tried to, but his hand only barely reached Shane's other shoulder. "You're spending so much time here keeping Matt company. On his birthday, you can at least share him with us." He snickered. "In fact, we're all here for the both of you."

Shane's gaze jolted over to Mrs. Dermond. He had given in to another knee-jerk reaction and shouldn't stare so unabashedly, but he couldn't help it. Mrs. Dermond's facial muscles strained, though traces of her smile still lingered on her lips. She nodded at him and closed her eyes, like a cat showing that it wouldn't scratch his face… at least not straightaway.

"My Little Thumbling, Ralph is right," his dad said. "You're doing so much for Matt. Let us do something for you in return."

Mrs. Dermond puckered her lips, and a single snort came out of them. She covered them with one hand, the other still balancing the cake. Clapping her mouth closed didn't work, though. The laughter burst out of her and shook the slender frame of her body. She stopped, taking a deep breath, but in the next moment, another fit of chortling followed. "I'm sorry." She puffed, and one more giggle slipped out. "You call him"—she pointed at Shane—"your Little Thumbling?"

Some seconds ticked by, and four gazes rested on Mrs. Dermond before the room boomed with laughter once more.

"When he turned fourteen, he was taller than both of us," his mother said, "and his grandma called him Little Thumbling first. It just stuck."

"I hated that nickname with a vengeance, but Mom and Dad didn't stop using it anyway." Shane grinned. "When I didn't stop growing, both in height and width, the name also grew on me. Now I just love the irony of it." That nickname also gave him a sense of normality. The two extremes of being a giant and being called a dwarf canceled each other out. Maybe he burdened that simple term of endearment with too much responsibility, but it bore the task without a murmur.

"I don't know about you, but I'm starving." Ralph eyed the cake in Mrs. Dermond's hand and licked his lips. "I'll go and get some coffee from the cafeteria while you set the table, okay?"

"Sounds like a plan," his mom said. "My Little Thumbling—" She chuckled. "—just put up the table and sit down with Matt. We'll take care of the rest."

Shane still doubted that what was happening here was real, but it wasn't a nightmare either. He'd enjoy it as long as it lasted.

AFTER THREE pieces of Mrs. Dermond's cake and a quarter of the cheesecake, Shane was full. "I'm in hog rigor now." He patted his belly.

Ralph and Mrs. Dermond spun their heads toward him.

"You know that phrase?" Ralph raised an eyebrow.

Shane moved some crumbs on the plate with his fork. "Matt used it the first time he visited me at home." Had it been okay to tell them that? He looked over at Matt. Of course it was. Matt was with them in this room, and not talking about him would've been even weirder than keeping silent.

"It's a Dermond family heirloom. My gramps always used it." Ralph sniggered. "Nice to hear that Matt honors it too."

"What about taking a little walk?" his dad asked. "I'm in hog rigor as well and might fall asleep and off my chair if I don't move these tired limbs." He stretched out his arms.

"That's a wonderful idea," Ralph said.

His mom and Mrs. Dermond nodded, already getting up from their chairs.

"I'll tell Matt and join you in a minute, okay?" He had to talk to Matt about this spontaneous coffee klatch. Surely Matt had listened to it and was wondering what the hell was going on.

"Sure," Ralph said.

Shane rose up from his chair, walked over to Matt's bed, and knelt down beside it. "Matt?" he whispered. "You already heard most of it, but I'm guessing you're as confused as I am. We'll talk about this later, okay? Your parents, my parents, and I are going for a walk. Isn't that awesome?" He kissed Matt on his cheek. "I love you."

"Shane?"

He startled, for he had been sure that everyone had left the room already. Shane peeked up and found Mrs. Dermond looking down at him. She had watched that scene, had seen the kiss, and heat flared up in Shane's cheeks. After a moment of hesitation, he got up, and Mrs. Dermond's gaze followed him. "I'm sorry," he said.

"You really love him, don't you?" Mrs. Dermond turned her head and considered her son. "My husband is right. Matt was never this happy before he met you. He must love you too."

Shane gasped for air. Mrs. Dermond had spent the afternoon with him, but they hadn't talked with each other. She had led a lively discussion with his mom about needlework, and she had spoken with his dad about the drought of last summer, but the two of them had shied away from addressing each other. Unprepared, her words hit him like a sledgehammer. "I do, and I'm lucky enough that he loves me back, though I don't have a clue why he chose me."

Mrs. Dermond nodded, still looking at Matt. "In a certain sense, I envy him. He doesn't have to spend all day and all night with thoughts that no mother should ever have to think." She faced Shane. "And that no friend should ever have to think."

"He'll wake up any time now. That's the only thought I allow myself." On some days, it worked. On others, it didn't, but Shane set out to stick to that credo on each new day.

"That's a good plan." She closed her eyes and drew a deep breath. "I can't call you Matt's boyfriend like Ralph does or apologize to you, not yet"—she opened her eyes and extended her hand—"but I owe you a handshake."

"You don't have to apologize for protecting Matt. I'm not a parent, but that's something I understand." Shane grasped Mrs. Dermond's hand, her fingers as slender as Matt's. The two resembled each other so much, and he swallowed down the lump in his throat. "I have to show you that I won't harm Matt, and I have to earn the right of you calling me his boyfriend."

"You're on a good path for both." The subtle smile returned to her lips, and she pulled her hand away slowly. "Let's go. The others are already waiting for us, and Matt needs a little quiet after all that noisy chattering."

"Of course." Shane smiled back at her.

Perhaps this talk with Mrs. Dermond was another one of Matt's birthday wishes coming true. If the universe was in the mood to dish out gifts like this, it might care for two teenagers in love after all.

CHAPTER THIRTY-SIX

EVEN THE first day at Central High hadn't felt as strange as returning now did. Apart from the fact that it was a pity Shane couldn't spend all day with Matt anymore, a tingly itching had settled in his stomach. Everyone in the city knew about Matt and him, and the same would hold true at school. Would the other students still keep their distance? They wouldn't do him that favor. He knew how to cope with being avoided, but all the people commiserating with him over the last week—strangers he met in the streets or in the hospital—gave him the creeps. He finally needed to make up his mind whether he wanted attention or not. Right now, he just wanted to get his courses over with and return to Matt. He walked around the corner of the school gate, and each and every student in the yard fell silent.

The stoners stared at him through half-vacant eyes. The cheerleaders dropped their discussions about the health of nail beds, and the latest rumors about some teenage superstar didn't matter anymore. The jocks stopped pounding their chests and boasting about their latest conquest at the party. Everyone had frozen, as if time itself had taken a break to gape at Shane.

Why shouldn't he just turn on his heels and flee? If he begged Principal Wagner, she might grant him another week off and spare him from running this gauntlet. He'd bear anything, but not the concentrated compassion of all his fellow students at once. Shane would rather let the doctors transplant parts of his own brain into Matt—without sedation and with a rusty kitchen knife.

A blur of movement stirred the otherwise stationary scene. Elaine separated from the cluster of cheerleaders and hurried straight toward him, her pigtails swishing to and fro in her brisk walk. She stopped only one step away from him, too far into Shane's comfort zone for his taste. After a moment of gazing at the ground, she put her head back and smiled up at him. This was one of those apologetic smiles filled with sympathy the strangers had given him all week long.

"We're all so upset about what happened to Matt. In the name of the whole student body, I wish him the best and that he will soon return to us."

"Thank you, Elaine. Matt—appreciates the concern of his fellow students." What fucked-up and stilted crap was he stammering? Matt would probably scratch his head in confusion because Elaine knew his name. He'd squish his eyebrows at anyone in this school pretending to care about him, but Shane couldn't say that. He had to smile, bow his head in thankfulness, and hope that the awkward moment would pass soon.

"I have to add something personal." Elaine lowered her gaze once more. "I'm sorry for the things I've said about you." She scraped her fingernails against each other, creating a noise that made his toes curl. "You saved that boy, and no bad guy would do that." Her body gave a start, and she thrust herself at Shane, slinging her arms around his waist. "I'm sorry."

The awkwardness didn't pass but doubled its efforts to embarrass him. Shane stretched his arms out sideways. He was the hug monster, embracing anyone who couldn't get out of reach by the count of three, but this was too much, even for him. "Thank you again, Elaine. Actually, your rumors helped Matt and me come together, so no hard feelings on my side." Just by saying this, Shane brought a little flock of fairy tales into the world and provided a full week's worth of gossip. He mentally bitch slapped himself.

Elaine backed up, and she bared her pearl white teeth in a grin. "Oh, really?"

At least, she had let go of him. "Yes, you're quite the matchmaker." He grinned back but took a step away to prevent another hug attack.

"That's so cool." Elaine giggled before pursing her lips. "Umm, talking about matchmaking." She fiddled with her hands again. "This Jer guy is straight, isn't he?"

What came after awkward? There had to be a word for that. "Yes, he is." Jer and the head cheerleader. Shane had called reality the best scriptwriter, and either it was creating an unprecedented masterpiece crossing all genres from drama, over to love story, and then to comedy—or reality had simply gone bonkers.

Elaine's face lit up. "Perhaps he would pay a visit to Central High and talk about the things he's been through. Prevention by information, you know."

One thing Shane had to say for her, she was shrewder than her clichéd cheerleader demeanor implied. "I'll ask Jer the next time I see him." Was he doing the little one a favor by setting him up with Elaine? Jer would definitely lose it when he learned a cheerleader was interested in him.

"He needs someone he can talk to about this dreadful experience in private, and everyone keeps telling me that I'm such a good listener." Elaine batted her eyelashes, reverting to her manga-spoof behavior.

Shane had to get away from her before she spurted any details about how she'd seduce Jer. What was the most decent way to scram from her?

"Hey, Elaine, sugar darling." Iain clapped Shane's shoulder. "Are you already desperate enough to hit on gay guys?" He pouted, but the dimples on his cheeks gave him away. "I so hoped that you'd come back to me, honey." Iain turned his head. "Listen to the warning of your dude. Don't let yourself in with that bitch, Shaney."

"I'd rather eat my pom-poms before crawling back to a lying, filthy asshole like you." Elaine put her arms akimbo. "I'm not hitting on people in a happy relationship, something that you're evidentially not above." She faced Shane, smiled, and got a pink business card out of the pocket of her skirt. "Could you please give Jer my card? He can phone me anytime."

Shane took the pink slip of cardboard and nodded. "Of course." There even existed something that came after the feeling that came after awkward.

Elaine's smile dissolved as she swiveled her head toward Iain. She snorted in contempt, twirled around, and took off back to her cheerleader friends while shaking her butt more than remotely necessary.

"Thank you, dude," Shane whispered, "but if you ever call me Shaney again, I'll get special permission from Seamus to rearrange your face."

Iain chuckled. "You're welcome, dude. I appreciate your fighting spirit, but you better save it for the top ten of Central High's dirtbags."

Shane's head shot around. "Top ten? You narrowed the field down to ten people?"

"There are only nine, to be precise. In the last week, I asked around a little." A grin came about on Iain's lips. "And before you say something, yes, I only asked. No student was harmed in the making of that list." His features turned earnest. "The baseball team wasn't here, and they wouldn't touch Matt without getting my permission either. The football guys are on probation for a party that got out of hand, and they are treading more than carefully at the moment... those sissies." Iain hissed. "No offense, dude."

Shane pressed his teeth together and opted to ignore that comment. Iain was at least trying to be nice. He just lacked practice. Shane nodded, if only to make Iain continue.

"The lacrosse and basketball players are the goody two-shoes of Central High. So we can strike the athletes off the list. There are some other shady guys here, but most of them have watertight alibis, like detention or some students they sold weed to and such."

What was worse, that guys like those attended this school or the nonchalant way Iain talked about them? How fucking naive Shane was when it came to assessing people. Matt had been absolutely right in suspecting every single person here of being a bully.

"Then there are those nine guys with mysterious whereabouts on that Thursday. My idea is to confront them with the combined powers of asshole and drug lord." Iain cackled.

The dirty sound of that laugh made Shane shudder. "And you think this will work? The"—he gestured up and down at himself—"drug lord has been rehabilitated—mostly."

Iain smacked both of Shane's biceps. "You're a six-foot-seven, muscle-bound hulk with tats all over. You could wear a fucking lace dress and you'd still be more frightening than any other guy here."

"Six feet eight, and thanks, I guess." Shane eyed Iain's hands on his arms. Only a week ago, this would've been the last place where he wanted them, but it was okay. He didn't love it, but it was okay.

A one-dimpled grin formed on Iain's face. "And don't forget about my asshole senses. I'm like Spider-Man, only I can't detect danger but know when someone is talking bullshit to me." Iain peered past him. "Our first candidate, Oliver Bergstein."

Shane turned around. A lanky guy with shaggy brown hair and baggy clothes slunk across the schoolyard. He hunched his shoulders forward and barely lifted his feet off the ground. This pitiful creature could be capable of hurting Matt? Shane needed Iain's help in this search, for his insight into human nature clearly sucked.

"Bergstein!" Iain yelled and pointed at the boy.

Oliver startled, stopped dead in his tracks, and looked around frantically. He spotted Iain and took a step back, almost stumbling over his own feet.

"If you know what's good for you, you won't even think of running away."

He obviously didn't know and backed up some more steps before spinning around and dashing away like the devil himself was after him. Then the devil *was* after him. Iain darted past Shane and sprinted toward the school gate. Oliver made some sidesteps like a panicked rabbit, but Iain closed in on him. At the pillar of the entrance, Iain tackled Oliver face-first into the rough sandstone, pinning him with his body.

Shane would never doubt Iain's asshole senses again. Iain had foreseen Oliver's flight and had reacted so quickly that Shane still stood rooted in place, gawking at the scene with an open mouth. He blinked several times and hurried over to the two to prevent Iain from doing something rash.

"If I say, 'Don't run away,' you don't run away, douche. Got it?" Iain rammed Oliver into the pillar with full force.

The scrawny guy groaned, and pain distorted his face. "Sure, dude. Sorry, dude."

Shane should say something to stop Iain, but Iain had gained the upper hand with Oliver, and he wouldn't jeopardize this. It was true, then. If he dealt with the devil, the devil changed him, and not the other way around. He put his hand on Iain's shoulder, and Iain looked back. Shane shook his head.

Iain shrugged, grabbed both of Oliver's shoulders, and swiveled him around, smashing him against the stones once more. "My friend Shane and I only want to talk to you." He tilted his head. "I'll take my hands away now, and you won't do anything stupid, right?" Iain moved his face closer to Oliver's until their noses almost touched. "Because if you did something stupid, I would have to tell my friend Shane how much money you've leeched from Matt over the past years." Iain pouted and switched to his falsetto voice. "Oopsie! My mistake!"

A tremor shook Shane's chest, working itself down through his guts into his legs and crawling along his arms. His hands clenched into fists. This whiner was one of the assholes who had fleeced Matt. Shane took a step forward, but Iain's arm stopped him, and he grabbed it to push it away. He didn't, for this had to be part of the plan. Oliver should be close to wetting his pants by now and would think twice before lying to them. Pearls of sweat glistened on his forehead, and Matt's comatose complexion looked rosy in comparison. His lips trembled, opening and closing like a carp's gasping for air. This guy was done for.

"Sorry for that, Oli-boy." Iain smiled so falsely the hair on Shane's arms rose up. "So if you don't want me to leave you alone to discuss that topic with Shane, you better be a good boy and answer all of our questions honestly. Deal?"

Oliver glanced at Shane from the corner of his eye, and Shane grunted. He was already knee-deep into this crime, and he would just play along.

"Please don't go!" Shivering, Oliver jerked his head around and stared at Iain. Panic widened his eyes. "I'll tell you everything."

Iain patted Oliver's cheek, too noisily for a friendly clap. "I knew you were a reasonable guy." He lowered his arms. "Only one simple question. Where were you last Thursday?"

"I didn't mob Matt." Oliver yanked his head left and right until Iain grabbed him by his hair, making him hiss out through his teeth.

"That wasn't my question, dude, but we might actually believe you if you backed up your answer with some facts."

"I wasn't even at school, dude. The police collared me for fencing, and I got fifty community service hours for that. On Thursday, I worked at the youth center in downtown from one to seven. You can ask the peeps there."

Another watertight alibi. Shane faced Iain, who was still glaring at Oliver.

Iain's features relaxed, so his asshole senses hadn't detected any bullshit. "Okay, dude, we believe you. You won't tell anyone about this nice little talk, will you? If your birdbrain forgets about this, you might need a private session with Shane after all. Look at him. When he's done with you, you'll be lucky if you only end up in a coma like poor Matty."

Oliver faced Shane again. "No, please, no." The jolts of his head toned down to mere wisps of movement.

Shane pulled up a shoulder and one corner of his mouth. "Just be a nice boy, and nobody gets hurt."

Iain had gone too far. Frightening someone was one thing. Threatening someone with hospital or even death was completely out of the question. Shane's breathing cranked up, and he couldn't stop it.

"I won't tell anyone. I swear." The pleading tone in Oliver's voice tore into Shane's heart. Not even a small-time felon like him deserved this kind of torture.

"Fuck off, dude, and don't come across me again today. Got it?" Iain shot forward, and Oliver flinched. "I said, fuck off!" he yelled into his face.

Without another peep, Oliver dashed onto the schoolyard, running into a group of juniors and dragging two of them to the ground with him. He scrambled back onto his feet and made a run for it, not even apologizing.

Shane grabbed Iain by his shoulders and smashed him against the pillar, just as Iain had done with Oliver. "Don't you ever dare proclaim me a damn hired muscle or hangman again. And what was that whole crap about? Maybe a word of warning in advance would've been nice."

The muscles in Iain's cheeks tensed up. "I'm sorry about the thug thing. Ideas come to my mind and I just blurt them out. I'm sorry, dude." His forehead creased. "Let's face it, Shane, you're too nice for this. Any guy who doesn't beat the shit out of me after what I've done to his boyfriend is too nice for this world. Just three words why I didn't tell you about Oliver leeching Matt—absolutely authentic rage." Iain smiled, but for once, his smile lacked any malice. "I want to find the bastard who beat Matt to a pulp, and you want me to do those awful things because you can't."

Shane's grip slackened. Iain thought so rationally about their search, and he was right. Shane needed him for the dirty parts. "Just skip the thrashing talk, okay? I'll grunt and glare and give you absolutely authentic rage, but don't turn me into a monster." He wasn't like Matt's attacker. He may have doubted everything about himself, but that was a fact.

Four Days Later

SHANE LOOKED after Bernard Klansky bobbing down the school hall, not in a hurry at all to get away from him and Iain. "Do you really think it wasn't him? He was the last one, and he doesn't have any proof for his story. I mean, going for a walk in the forest. How fucked-up is that?"

Iain huffed. "No proof, sure, but my asshole senses tell me he's clean. Bernard's more like barking than actually biting." He placed his hand on Shane's shoulder. "Sorry, dude. We checked the usual suspects. Whoever attacked Matt is an unusual one." He let his arm sink. "I'll keep asking around, but this is poking into the stack of hay, hoping that the fucking needle drops out all by itself."

Shane closed his eyes. "You're right." He opened his eyes and extended his hand. "Thank you, dude. I'd still have no clue where to start without your help." Their search had ended. Shouldn't he feel disappointed about not finding the guy who had hurt Matt? At least he didn't have to test his resolve to keep from mangling the scumbag.

Iain grasped Shane's hand. "Don't go all wussy on me, dude." His trademark one-dimpled grin emerged on his face. "I will miss sowing fear and terror into the hearts of the Central High students just by wandering around with you. The asshole and the drug lord. If you ever wanted to make it big in the bullying business, we'd be a dream team." Iain bellowed a dirty laugh.

"If you ever wanted to quit the bullying business, we could eventually become friends." Shane definitely was a wuss, because he already considered Iain a buddy. He couldn't forget the things Iain had done to Matt, but everyone deserved a second chance, and Iain had proven that he could depend on him.

Iain squinted his eyes and drew in air through his teeth. "Ouch, dude, that hurt. I thought we *were* friends." He laughed again. "I think Matt'd go ballistic if we became bros."

"It'd take him some time to get used to it, for sure." Shane chuckled and let go of Iain's hand.

"I just wanted you to know that I'll leave Matt alone from now on." Iain moaned. "How freaking awkward was that? Your pussiness is already rubbing off on me." He made a face, as if biting into a lemon.

"That's not the worst of things, dude." Shane chuckled once more. Yes, he'd miss hanging around with Iain.

"Nah." Iain waved his hands before he pursed his lips. "Any good news about Matty?"

Shane shook his head. "Unfortunately, no. The doctor says that his brain wave patterns have further stabilized, but she can't say when he'll finally wake up." Dr. Karatovic had actually said "if," but Shane had *x*-ed this word from his vocabulary when talking about Matt.

"Matty is one of the toughest little fellas I know. He'll open his eyes anytime now, and then he'll kick my butt for not finding the douche who did this to him."

Shane slung his arms around Iain and pressed him close. The hug monster struck again, as it always did when he was out of words.

"Hey, dude, I've got a reputation to lose."

If that were true, why was Iain patting his back? Shane fought down the laugh that cooked up in his belly. He stopped short. "Who's that girl over there? I've seen her several times during the last few days, and I think she's watching us." Shane released Iain from the embrace.

"Who?" Iain turned around.

The girl immersed herself into the stream of students filing down the hall, and Shane lost her. "She's gone." He scratched his temple. "Perhaps a head taller than Matt. Brown hair. A Latina most likely."

"Could be Florenca Goncalvez. Matt and she were sorta friends. He tutored her. At least that's what Elaine told me when we were still together, but you know how reliable a source that bitch is."

Matt had never mentioned her. Maybe Iain was right and it was just another one of Elaine's fanciful facts. If Matt had a friend at school, Shane would know. He and Iain together aroused enough attention to make *anyone* curious. "Thank you again, dude. I'll text you at once if I have any news about Matt." Shane offered Iain his fist, and he bumped it back.

"That'd be cool, dude."

The hunt was over for good, then. At least Shane's paws had found something to busy themselves with. They would be more content now with simply holding and caressing Matt, something they excelled at and that really made a difference.

CHAPTER THIRTY-SEVEN

VOICES. MATT heard his mom and Shane talking to each other. Calmly and softly at first, then their tone changed and turned excited, even agitated. Another sound hummed in his ears, a rhythmic noise that drilled into his head, each of those beats a needle driven into his skull. Someone had to make it stop. Matt opened his mouth, but his throat was glued tight by coarse dryness, and nothing came out. He couldn't open his eyes either. His lids felt clotty, like his throat. A wave of panic rushed through him, originating somewhere in his belly and tearing away all rational thought with it.

Shane! Mom! Help me!

He had to help himself. First of all, he had to fight the fear and whip his body into obedience. Shane had told him about the breathing technique his shrink had taught him, inhale through the nose and exhale through the mouth while letting go of everything. In and out. The cold stream of air chafed his sore throat, but he had to breathe on and mustn't give up. In and out. Saliva gathered in his mouth, and he swallowed it down. Matt felt the liquid trickle down each single inch of his gullet, yet the moisture eased the burning pain. In and out. He tried to open his eyes once more and pried his lids apart by sheer force. A blue light blared to his right. A faint hue only, but it stung his eyes and made him squint. In and out once more. Ever so slowly, he opened his eyes, giving them time to adapt. It worked. The twinge in them subsided, and his surroundings came into focus. Half darkness absorbed most of the details, but he apparently lay in a hospital room. The skull-crushing noise droned out of a life monitor, which was also the source of the blue light. Matt turned his head to the right. Something stuck out from his scalp, hampering the agility of his head. And goodness gracious, a good dozen tubes and IV lines cluttered up his arm. He swallowed again and soaked his lungs with air. The panic mustn't come back. It was okay. Someone had put all those needles into his veins to help him.

Matt let go of the air again, slowly yet controlled. He would ignore his arm for the time being. He raised his upper body from the bed, but a pang shot down his spine, making stars burst before his eyes, so he sank down again. Lesson learned. He better not try to come up again anytime soon. Carefully, Matt turned to the left. He had heard the voices of Shane and his mom, yet he was alone. Had the clichés returned and he had only dreamed it? The door, however, was standing ajar, and a beam of light cut into the twilight of the room, the brightness illuminating the foot of the bed. He opened his mouth once more, but only a croaky groan came out. Whoever had left the room had to return, no need for panicking again. He should use that time to answer the most pressing questions—why was he here, and why did he feel as if a minefield had exploded in his head?

"The both of us cannot have imagined the same things, Doctor, can we?" That was his mom.

"His eyes fluttered, and his right hand twitched. The beeps got more urgent too." Shane! Shane was here too!

The staccato of the monitor kicked up a notch.

"I believe you, but please don't build up false hopes." Another female voice that sounded strangely familiar, though Matt couldn't remember having talked to anyone lately. "Events like this happen with coma patients. Some neurons fire wrong, and the body does all kinds of things."

The door opened, and the light hit Matt like a blast, but he had to keep his eyes open, had to get the attention of those three.

"Shane." The sound of his voice resembled a gear that got stuck and ground against some other part of the machine. "Shane." Nothing more than a whisper, yet the first time he uttered an intelligible word. "Shane." Matt's voice broke, and he squealed. Nonetheless, that noise rang loud enough to echo back from the walls.

He could only see the silhouettes of the three people backlit in the doorway, but he'd always recognize the giant shape standing to the right.

"Oh my God." Shane breathed out.

"He's awake!" His mom's yell made him cringe.

Quick footsteps clattered through the room, and the black shadows dissolved into his boyfriend and his mother. Shane dropped down at the left side of the bed and pressed his forehead against Matt's cheek. The warmth of Shane's skin and breath seared his face. Shane's scent billowed around him, and it was as if his nose smelled this aroma for the first time, the intensity fogging his mind. His mom plastered his other cheek with wet kisses and mumbled the words "You're awake!" time and again.

His body felt cold, but the warm place inside of him caught fire and drove out the chill. Whatever had brought him to the hospital, at this moment, he was safe and sound.

"Mrs. Dermond, Mr. McAllistair, I know it's a hard thing to ask of you, but you have to leave the room. At least for now." The woman who spoke advanced into the room, out of the blinding light, and she wore a white lab coat over blue scrubs. "I've informed my colleagues, and they'll be here any minute. We have to examine Matt and make sure that he stays conscious."

"I love you, Matt. I love you," Shane whispered into his ear and pecked his neck, his cheek, his eyelid. "I love you!"

Those were words Matt had only blurted to Gordon and Heather so far. Or hadn't he? The smoke of the minefield in his head made it so difficult to focus. He had to wait for it to settle. Still, Shane's words changed the feeling of warmth. It encompassed Matt now, pulling him in all directions. His body swam on its waves, and his mind was adrift in its tide. He had to answer Shane, let him know he loved him too, but only a weak stream of air flowed out of his mouth. Matt snuggled up against Shane's face. This had to do until his voice returned.

"Just one more minute, Doctor. Please!" his mom said.

Matt had almost forgotten about her, and his blood shot up, making him blush from the neck upward. He turned his head to face her and smiled. It was only the trace of a wisp of a smile, but she must have noticed it anyway, for she returned it.

"Yes, Dr. Karatovic, only one more minute." Shane sounded so desperate.

If only Matt could tell the doctor that he needed some more moments with his family. They gave him strength, and a doctor should know such things.

"You can stay until my colleagues arrive," she said with a choked-up voice. "It's paramount, however, not to expose Matt to too much stress. Waking up is only the first step. He has to catch up with the things that have happened, but only one at a time."

Hello, Doctor? I can hear you!

Matt thought sassy thoughts. Plenty of proof that he was recovered already. Moreover, the doctor should listen to her own advice. Talking about things that he didn't know stressed out a nerd like him. A lot of questions buzzed around in his head, the two whys from earlier only the tip of the iceberg. How long had he been unconscious, for example? If he had a lot to catch up on, though, it might be better not to know. Another interesting question was how Shane and Matt's mom could stay in the same room without tearing each other apart.

Three more white coats emerged from the light coming from the door, and Matt couldn't understand what they were talking about with their subdued voices.

"I'll come back as soon as the doctor lets us. I love you!" Shane placed one more kiss on his lips.

Matt smiled again, giving his all to make it stronger this time. He blinked slowly with both eyes. Shane's face lit up, and he caressed Matt's cheek with the back of his hand, providing more fuel for the warm place.

"I'll call Dad and the rest of the family." His mom patted his other cheek. "Everything will be all right. In no time, you'll be up as if nothing ever happened. I love you too." She planted another kiss on his mouth.

The two of them walked backward through the room, never once turning around and missing a single second to look at him. The door closed, and Matt faced the four doctors.

Whatever they had to do, they had to get it over with as fast as possible. No one should come between him and Shane or his family. Furthermore, no one should ever come between a nerd and his answers either.

CHAPTER THIRTY-EIGHT

THE DOCTORS had left Matt alone over an hour ago, and still no one was admitted into his room. Nothing would keep Shane away if the doctors had given their green light. Matt sighed. At least Dr. Karatovic had allowed him a juice box, though she had refused him the coffee and pizza he had asked for. He understood her caution now. The liquid in the cardboard box was more water than anything else, and it was questionable whether it contained real apples at all, but his stomach grumbled and moaned as if he had gobbled up an entire boar roast. Matt rubbed his complaining belly and felt his ribs poking out. He must have lost four pounds or more. Being even skinnier than before sucked. Shane would probably make him eat entire boar roasts for real to get him back to his former pathetic shape. He chuckled and took another sip from his juice, his tummy groaning in reply.

Dr. Karatovic hadn't told him how long he had been in the hospital. He could recall going home from the gym on Wednesday, and he could recall what Shane and he had done in the treatment room. This memory elicited a goofy grin anyhow. If Matt concentrated really hard, he could summon some pictures from Thursday morning—his dad reading the papers at the breakfast table and his mom wearing her garden apron. After that, only mental static followed. It felt more like a dark and dense fog that didn't disperse upon touching it but solidified instead, like he'd stuck his hands into heavy dough. Without further reference, thoughts like these were moot anyway. It could be Friday today, or a month could have passed for all he knew. He shivered at the idea of having lost a full month—or even more. The doctors had scribbled down a simple side note about his lack of memories before proceeding to their next question.

"Test, test, one, two, three." His voice had returned, but Matt didn't trust it to stay, so he checked on it every quarter of an hour. The last three tests had been positive, so he might eventually overcome his vocal paranoia and drop the self-examinations for good.

He could sit upright again without the sensation of his spine jumping out of his nape. Even the headache had toned down to a subliminal droning, a feeling not unlike spending a whole night with a book and being dead beat in the morning. The doctors had removed all but one of the IV lines, yet they had decided to keep the EEG electrodes strapped to his head for another two days. For half an hour, it had been fun watching the waves traveling over the monitor. Matt could even make them change by relaxing or riling himself up with thoughts about Iain, but this game had turned dull rather quickly. On top of the abysmal entertainment program here, his skin under the bandage itched terribly, but he mustn't scratch. He sighed once more. If he had been comatose—that much he had puzzled together from the medical babble of the doctors—why the heck was he still tired? Shane and his family had to be allowed to come to him sometime soon, or he might lapse back into the coma from sheer boredom. Or he might turn crazy from all the questions cluttering up his head.

The door opened, and Matt's heart made a leap, the life monitor actually showing the extra bounce. All that fuss wasn't necessary, because only another stranger entered his room. This one didn't wear scrubs or a lab coat for a change. The man was in his midthirties, and despite his clothes being clean and without holes, he made a shabby impression. Matt's room didn't have a mirror, but he could only hope he looked more awake than this guy. His senses had become hypersensitive, as if they had supercharged during his coma. Though the visitor was still standing at the door, a sickening smell of tobacco filled the air, and Matt's wary belly went on strike. Any further sip of the juice box would make him heave, so he put it onto the nightstand.

"You're Matt Dermond?" The guy fished a leather wallet out of his coat and flipped it open, showing a police shield. "I'm Detective Webb."

A detective? It didn't take rocket science to conclude that his stay in this hospital wasn't due to an accident, which had been his favorite theory so far. If the police sent a detective, it must've been a serious crime. He would still have preferred an accident. The very thing old Matt had feared for years had happened to new Matt. These two eras didn't belong together, and they shouldn't mix up. A realization stabbed him through the chest and made him gasp. Shane must have suffered even more than he had. Matt slammed his mouth closed with his hand. Shane blamed himself for every small detail that went wrong in Matt's life. How much self-recrimination had he lived through for something as grave as an assault?

"Mr. Dermond?" Detective Webb's forehead creased.

Matt let his hand drop. "Sorry, Detective. Yes, I'm Matt Dermond."

A smile flashed on Detective Webb's lips, baring nicotine-stained teeth. "Do you have a minute for me?"

The doctors sent Detective Webb first. Maybe law required them to. If he talked to Detective Webb now, Shane and his family would be allowed next. Matt nodded. "Of course, Detective."

Another flash of a gruesome smile disfigured Detective Webb's face before he shuffled over to the side of the bed. The stench of cigarettes wrinkled Matt's nose, and he switched to breathing through his mouth to keep the nausea at bay. Detective Webb put away his shield and produced a rumpled notebook from the same pocket.

"Has anyone else spoken to you about the attack?"

"You're the first one to actually tell me I've been attacked."

"That's good." The sagging corners of Detective Webb's mouth rose but dropped the next moment, and he furrowed his brows. "Wait, you didn't even know about the assault? You mean you can't remember?"

Matt's gaze sank down to his hands, and he shook his head. "No, I can't remember anything after Thursday morning." He raised his head. "The doctors didn't even tell me what today's date is."

Detective Webb sniffed. "It's Wednesday today. Tomorrow, it'll be three weeks since the attack."

Not quite a month, but Matt had lost three weeks. Shane had suffered for three weeks. His mom and dad had worried for three weeks.

"Is everything okay with you, Mr. Dermond?" Detective Webb tilted his head slightly.

"Yes, Detective. Almost twenty days is a lot of time." Matt shook his head, trying to fling the gloominess out of his mind. It didn't work. "Did you catch the ass… attacker?" He shouldn't swear in front of a policeman.

Detective Webb drew his lips in. "Unfortunately not. I came here hoping that you could identify the asshole."

Okay, the detective didn't seem to mind cuss words.

"I can barely remember Thursday morning and nothing after that, but there's only one person capable of this. Iain O'Sullivan." Though Matt had no memories to prove his allegation, the police had to know about him. This time, Iain wouldn't get away.

Detective Webb smiled, his lips still pressed together. "We already checked Mr. O'Sullivan. He and the entire baseball team weren't even close to Central High when the attack happened."

Matt sank backward into the pillow until he was almost lying down. There were plenty of bullies at school, but no one as ruthless as Iain. Who else hated him so much that they'd want to see him dead? The rhythm of the life monitor struck up a faster pace, and he began to loathe the machine that served his emotions on a silver platter for everyone to hear and see.

"There was another suspect who we had to release after a ridiculous charade of a hearing." Detective Webb grunted and pulled up one corner of his mouth in derision. "Shane McAllistair."

Matt laughed out loud. He hadn't intended to, but what Detective Webb said was outlandish and grotesque. "Shane's my boyfriend and the most caring guy in the world." The detective's words sank in, and Matt's laughing got stuck in his throat. Shane had been arrested, and there had even been a trial. It wasn't enough that Shane had had to deal with the attack itself, but his past had caught up with him, and he had been suspected of another crime he hadn't committed. "No, no, no. It wasn't Shane. Whatever you think about him, it isn't true." He had promised Shane to not reveal the truth about Jer, but this was an exceptional situation, wasn't it? On the other hand, he didn't know any details and could only tell Detective Webb that Shane had defended Jer from Hayden, but not why or what Hayden had done.

"I know. Shane is the good guy." Detective Webb drew quotation marks in the air. "He stopped that jock from raping that Jeremiah boy. Yadda, yadda, yadda. The young man put on quite a show in court."

Matt's body turned slack, and he sank down into his pillow. Shane had saved Jer from rape? That was why he wouldn't talk about that night. A pang of shame shot through Matt because he had despised Jer for turning his back on Shane. Now he could only feel compassion for him, and he shuddered in disgust for Hayden. There existed guys even worse than Iain. It was a pity, though, that he had learned about the events from Detective Webb and not from Shane himself. Even more so because of Detective Webb's awful attitude. "Shane loves me and would never attack me. Never."

Detective Webb chuckled through his closed mouth. "How cute and naive is that? Love never kept anyone from hurting another person. My ex-wife loved me, she still does, but did this keep her from eloping with my brother? Fuck to the no."

I believe you, but the more important a person is, the simpler it is to hurt that person.

Gordon's words resurfaced in Matt's mind, or better, obtruded themselves upon him. He hadn't wanted them to be true then, and he didn't want them to be true now. What reason should Shane have to hurt him? He was a defender, a protector. He had only hurt Hayden because it had been the only way to save Jer. What if Shane had tried to protect him? Protecting him by hurting him? That was absurd. The only thing he and Shane didn't agree on was his coming-out.

A chill crawled down Matt's spine and crept along his nerves. He already felt cold, but this sensation approached absolute zero. If he had been about to come out, Shane might have panicked and stopped him. Perhaps Shane hadn't even wanted to injure him that badly, but strong as he was, it had just happened. It may have been an accident after all.

"Gave you something to think about, didn't I?" Detective Webb grinned, and Matt felt the urge to punch those yellow ruins out of his ugly mug.

"No." Matt shook his head. "No!" he yelled and jerked his head left and right on the pillow.

A shrill sequence of triple shrieks replaced the constant murmur of the life monitor. Matt groped his head and found three of the electrodes missing, ripped out of their plugs by his jolting head.

The door flew open, and Dr. Karatovic darted into the room, followed by a nurse. They stopped cold.

"You're all right, Matt?" Dr. Karatovic's brows soared.

"Yes, Doctor. Only some of the electrodes came apart. I'm sorry."

Dr. Karatovic's features relaxed, and a subtle smile bent up her lips. "No problem, Matt. Don't worry." Her gaze switched to Detective Webb, and her smile died away. "Who are you?"

The detective reached for his pocket and produced his shield again. "Detective Webb, Precinct Four City Police."

"I don't remember giving you permission to visit my patient." Dr. Karatovic folded her arms over her chest.

"Hospital administration phoned me and told me that the witness regained consciousness."

It felt strange being referred to as "patient" and "witness," though Matt was sitting right next to them.

"Hospital administration didn't tell you that you need approval from the leading medical officer before molesting a patient?" Dr. Karatovic's eyes darkened as she narrowed them.

Matt had only known her for some hours, at least consciously, but he had never thought that this friendly gaze could shoot daggers so fierce.

"This is an official interrogation of a witness. I'm entitled by Municipal Regulation 342 to instigate all steps necessary for gathering evidence relevant to solving a crime." Detective Webb sneered, wrinkles trenching all over his face.

"You can shove that regulation up the dark place we physicians call your rectum." Dr. Karatovic took a step toward Detective Webb. "In this room, I am the only law, and if the president himself walked in here, I'd tell him the same thing I'm telling you now. Get the heck out of here!" She faced the nurse. "Maria, would you please inform security to guide Detective Webb out of the building?"

The nurse nodded and scurried out of the room.

Detective Webb pinched his index finger and thumb together. "You're so close to being arrested for obstruction of justice." He squinted his eyes.

Dr. Karatovic imitated Detective Webb's hand gesture. "And you are so close to being arrested for denial of assistance. You're keeping me away from my patient in a medical emergency."

"You're kidding me." Detective Webb huffed from the corner of his mouth.

"Try me." Dr. Karatovic advanced another step.

Two powerful forces dashed toward each other, and Matt was caught between them. What could an eighteen—oh fuck, he was nineteen already— he had slept through his birthday. But a nineteen-year-old boy couldn't do much to stop them either.

Nurse Maria returned, accompanied by two men in black uniforms.

"Detective Webb wants to leave the hospital, and he doesn't want to enter the building again anytime soon." Dr. Karatovic mimicked Detective Webb's sneer. "Shoot him if he resists." She turned toward Matt and beamed at him. "I've always wanted to say that."

"This will have consequences, Doctor," Detective Webb pressed out through gritted teeth.

"I don't think so." Dr. Karatovic didn't even look at Detective Webb but walked over to the other side of Matt's bed. "Let me reattach the electrodes, please. Could you bow your head down a little? That's enough, thanks."

From the corner of his eye, Matt watched the security men closing in on Detective Webb. They whispered something to him, and one of the men grabbed him by his wrist. The detective jerked his arm away and mumbled something in reply before creeping back to the door.

Detective Webb spun around. "Call me if you remember anything. Just phone Precinct Four and ask for me."

Matt would never call him. He'd tell someone else if he remembered anything, but not this dork.

The security men prodded Detective Webb out of the room. Nurse Maria followed them.

"I'm so sorry about this, Matt." Dr. Karatovic pulled slightly at the electrodes she had just replugged. "I'll make sure that this pest of a cop won't harass you again."

"Thanks." Matt rubbed his hands against each other. "Detective Webb told me about the attack, but I can't remember anything." He looked up and focused on Dr. Karatovic. "Will my memories ever return?" If those memories really showed Shane striking him down, he didn't want them to come back.

Dr. Karatovic sighed and leaned her head to the side. "That's a very difficult question. Blunt brain trauma as you've suffered can disrupt the transfer of short-term memories to long-term engrams. That's the physical aspect of your amnesia, but victims of violent crimes also tend to displace the terrible experiences they've been through. Those psychological effects are even more serious and less easy to quantify." She caressed Matt's cheek. "You have to face the possibility of that day being lost forever."

His brain would definitely choose to displace the memory of being attacked by Shane. He had been wrong. Remembering wasn't the worst option, but never knowing for sure what had happened was.

"Thanks again." Matt smiled at her, though he didn't feel like it at all.

"You're welcome." Dr. Karatovic whirled around and swiped over the touch screen of the monitor. "I have to initiate the recalibration sequence. This will deactivate the alarm in the nurses' room for about ten minutes. If anything doesn't feel right during this time—dizziness, pain, or anything—push the alarm button, however minor the problem seems to be. Okay?"

Matt's real problem was anything but minor. He had to know the truth, and only Shane could tell him. "Okay. Is Shane here in the hospital?"

Smiling again, Dr. Karatovic faced him. "He's in the lobby, asking any person in scrubs he sees whether he can visit you now." She tittered. "I'll do all of us a big favor if I finally let him."

Shane loved him. If he had hurt him, it had been an accident. Matt could ask him and the truth wouldn't change anything between them, for he loved Shane too. Love could bear the truth. "Can you please let him now?" He put on the most amiable grin in his arsenal.

"It's good for my patient, and by all means, it's good for my colleagues." Dr. Karatovic laughed. "That's a win-win situation. I'll send him over as soon as I'm done here."

He would see Shane, and everything would turn out all right the moment he knew the truth.

CHAPTER THIRTY-NINE

DR. KARATOVIC had left the room a minute ago. She was probably talking to Shane right now, and it would take him about—the door crashed against the wall, and the hinges moaned in despair. A blur crossed the room before two strong arms closed around Matt, pulling him tightly against a firm chest. Shane's warm breath rumpled his hair, at least the few strands that peeped out from under the electrodes.

"I missed you so much." Shane tensed up. "Sorry. I saw you every day, but you weren't awake, and it wasn't the same." He chuckled, and his body rumbled, rocking Matt with him. "I'm talking bullshit." Shane planted a kiss on his head.

"Doesn't sound like bullshit to me." It had to feel terrible, sitting helplessly next to a loved one. If Shane had been the one lying here, Matt would've screamed and wailed all day, cursing everyone and everything for letting it happen.

The hug tightened up. Though Matt's body groaned and he had difficulty breathing, he didn't want Shane to let go of him. He had to pose the question, but he could endure some more seconds of uncertainty, even enjoy them in these powerful arms.

"I'm choking you." Shane yanked his hands away. "Sorry again." He shrugged and tilted his head.

"Our no-apologies pact got repealed sometime during the last three weeks?" Matt could get away with anything if he wrapped it up in sassiness. He grinned, and so did Shane, who could look so boyish when he bared his teeth in this over-the-top manner.

Do I want an apology from him for hurting me?

This question shredded Matt's grin, and his features sagged down.

Shane squinted his eyes. "What is it? You're not that upset because of some apologies, are you?" He placed his hands on Matt's cheeks and caressed them with his thumbs. "You're out of the woods. Each day will get a little better. Oh, and your mom will be here any minute. She's phoning your dad, who's about to jump aboard a plane."

Matt had to pull his plan through before Shane's kindness washed away his determination and before his mom joined them. It had been an accident. Shane *was* kind and had just made a mistake. "One Detective Webb questioned me and told me about the attack."

"Detective Shit End was here?" Shane put his head back and growled before lowering it again. "I'm sorry that you learned about the attack from him." He chewed on his lower lip. "Dr. Karatovic said you can't remember anything about that Thursday, so you don't know which sucker did this to you, do you?"

Sucker? He denied that he had hurt him?

"Did you attack me? You can tell me. You have to tell me." It didn't matter to him. He loved Shane, and Shane's lapse wouldn't change that.

"What did you say?" Shane's hands dropped off Matt's face, and deep lines furrowed his forehead. The color of his cheeks dissolved into a grayish white. "You didn't ask me whether I attacked you, did you? You're still confused and mixed some words up, but you didn't just ask me whether I attacked you?" He shook his head, and his lips turned pale.

"The detective said that there were only two suspects and that Iain couldn't have done it." Matt reached out for Shane's face. "You can tell me. It's okay." He smiled.

Shane backed away from his hand. "There's nothing I can tell you." All the strength poured out of his voice, and his words sounded hollow. "What makes you think it was me?"

"I know that you did it to protect me. It was a slip. I can't remember, but I know that you didn't hurt me on purpose."

"You can't remember, and you're still convinced that I attacked you?" The power returned to Shane's words as rage drove them out of him. "You're missing a single day and decide to forget about all the others we had before?" His anger condensed into a tangible force that drove reality apart and tore Matt with it.

"You don't have a clue how that feels." Matt's hands cramped into fists. "Where there should be the memories of a day, there is a hole in my head, a black nothingness. Anything could have happened on that day. Anything!" Matt was yelling. This could've been so simple and over already if Shane had just admitted what he had done.

"No, not anything." Shane's voice lowered down to a whisper again. "If you really think that I'm capable of that, you don't know me at all." He took another step away from Matt. "You told me you love me." Shane covered his mouth with both hands. "I can't stay here." He walked backward, shaking his head. "I can't stay in the same room with you if you think I'm a monster." Shane crashed into the doorframe with his back but didn't even flinch. He rolled around and dashed out of the room, the sound of hurried steps quickly dying away.

"I do love you," Matt muttered, his voice failing him again.

When had he told Shane he loved him?

Anything could have happened on that day.

He had declared his love to Shane and couldn't even remember. His breathing accelerated, and the rat-a-tat of the life monitor hammered into his skull. He felt as if he were sinking, a constant tugging that pulled him toward the center of the earth, down into its molten core.

"Why is Shane running like a madman?" His mom appeared in the still open door, looking down the corridor. "Did you send him to get you ice cream from the top of Mount Everest?" She cackled, but her laughing stopped suddenly as she turned her head to face Matt. "Oh my God, what has happened?" She flew through the room and grabbed his hand.

Matt wiped away the tears that pooled in his eyes with his other hand. "I only asked him one question." How much did she know? What else did "anything" include? Only three weeks, but everything had changed, and not a stone of his world still rested in the same place.

His mom squeezed his hand. "Honey, wars have been fought over asking one wrong question." She stroked away another of his tears with her thumb. "What did you ask him?"

"Whether he attacked me." Those words clutched Matt's throat tightly. Speaking them the first time had been easier. Too easy.

"Oh, honey." She seized his other hand. "How did you come up with this idea? Shane loves you. He'd never do anything to harm you."

She didn't only know about Shane and him, but she even took Shane's side and defended him? His coma had miraculously transported him into a parallel universe. Or he was still unconscious and his mind fabricated disjointed tidbits of flimflam. No, this was the real world, and he had just hurt Shane. Matt's own wounds couldn't sting as much. The feeling of sinking built up to an overwhelming maelstrom. "Detective Webb insinuated it might have been him." Matt's voice broke, and he sniffled.

"That detective is a miserable wretch with an agenda. He interrogated your dad and me for Shane's hearing, and he only considered what I said because it served him." She hesitated. "You already know about the hearing?"

Matt nodded. "But what if Detective Webb's right?" His mom hated Shane… or had hated Shane. If anyone understood his suspicions, she would.

"He isn't, honey." She wiggled his hands. "You haven't seen Shane during the past three weeks." A single laugh blurted out of her. "It puts shame on your dad and me, but Shane spent more time here than both of us together. He talked to you, lay at your side, and on some days, he even washed you when the nurses had too many other things on their hands. And he suffered. He tried to hide it, smiled at everyone and encouraged us to hold on, but he suffered."

"He could've hurt me by accident." Those words sounded outrageous now, and Matt didn't believe them himself anymore. The Shane he knew and loved would do the exact things his mom had listed.

"If Shane had attacked you, he would've told the court. He would've begged the judge to punish him."

"Still, I may never know for sure." What his mom said made sense and rang true, but how was the doubt supposed to go away if his memory didn't return?

She smiled with her lips taut. "Since you've been a toddler, you always had to grasp things with your head alone. Everything has to lead nicely from *A*, over to *B*, and then to *C*." She released his hands and fondled his cheeks. "Now *B* is missing, and your head won't be able to fill this gap. You need faith of heart, at least a little bit."

"You're telling me to listen to my heart?" As usual, his mother resorted to the most awful and stereotypical kitchen psychology.

She chuckled. "I can see you rolling your inner eyes at me." She patted his cheeks. "You know I was Shane's worst critic, so listen to a convert. Do it for him. What do you have to lose anyway? Close your eyes and just listen. Perhaps your heart *has* something to say." His mom took her hands off his face.

He sighed. She made a valid point. He couldn't feel more like shit than right now, and he closed his eyes. How was a lump of flesh and muscles supposed to know more than him? And how did one listen to an organ? The sounds of the life monitor came closest to being the voice of his heart. Those beeps wouldn't tell him anything about Shane, though. The pace of the blips cranked up. Matt only thought Shane's name and got a prompt reply?

Shane.

The rhythm became a tad more urgent.

I love Shane.

A thundering series of beeps answered him. It was amazing, but he had already known that he loved Shane.

Has Shane hurt me?

The pulses thinned out. His heart didn't deem this question worth a reaction.

Because it's ridiculous.

He had found *B*. The missing piece in the chain of logic didn't have anything to do with logic. He believed that Shane hadn't attacked him, and it didn't take more than that. Matt had experienced this sensation of feeling the truth before when Shane had sat shirtless in his room and had worried for him. Like then, a burst of heat erupted from the warm place and rushed through him, stopping his fall at last as it made him light inside. That place, that furnace, it had always been his heart. He just had been too much of a science nerd to admit this sappy fact.

"You're smiling, honey." Amusement and affection mingled in his mom's voice.

Matt opened his eyes, and his mother beamed at him.

"Your mom's crazy ideas sometimes work after all."

"Sometimes they do." Matt grinned back at her, but the gravity of the situation caught up with him and wiped the grin off his lips. "Do you think Shane will come back?"

"Of course he will." She pressed down on his shoulders, pushing him onto his pillow. "You know what, you'll sleep an hour or two, and when you wake up, you'll find Shane, your dad, and me waiting for you."

"But I'm—"

She placed her hand over his mouth. "Dr. Karatovic says that you can't rest enough for a fast recovery. And you want to get well soon, don't you?"

He nodded, for she still clapped his mouth shut.

"I'm in the lobby, honey. Don't worry, and sleep well. I love you." She pecked him on the forehead before taking her hand away.

"I love you too, Mom." Despite all the things he had thought about her, he meant it. Maybe that missing day wasn't just a curse but also a blessing. That gap allowed Matt a clean start, skipping from *A* to *C* with everything and everyone. No, not everyone. He had fucked up the clean start with Shane. He fought to not let his gloomy mood show on his face and held on to the smile with all his might.

His mom waved at him a last time before she closed the door silently. He couldn't lie down and sleep for two hours with only a vague hope of Shane being here when he woke up. What he said to Shane was so terrible that his apology admitted no delay, and no no-apologies pact covered tearing his boyfriend's heart out. He couldn't call Shane. Apart from not having a phone here, this matter had to be dealt with face-to-face. Matt would have to go to him. But where should he start? Shane wouldn't run home. He'd seek the advice of his friends, and he'd go to a place where he could vent his frustration. Matt would find him at the gym, but how could he get out of this room unnoticed? The moment he took off the electrodes, all hell would break loose in the nurses' room.

The recalibration cycle!

Matt had seen Dr. Karatovic do it—not all the details, but he had glimpsed some of the menus and dialogs she had gone through. He grabbed the IV line ending in the winged butterfly on the back of his hand and ripped the needle out. That didn't even hurt. He crawled closer to the monitor and wiped over the screen. A pop-up menu appeared, and he scrolled through the entries. Recalibration cycle! Matt pushed the virtual button. Of course he was sure, had never been surer of anything in his life, so he confirmed his choice with a firm press on the screen. A warning sign blinked on the screen, and a red progress meter filled up. He had ten minutes.

Matt closed his eyes, grabbed one of the electrodes, and pulled it off his head. Silence. He opened his eyes again. With quick flicks of his hands, he removed all the other plugs and unstrapped the heart rate transponder from his chest. He hauled his legs out of the bed before slipping onto his feet. He got up, and his vision turned black. A pressure built up in his ears, damping the noises around him to a faint hum. He grabbed the end of the bed to not drop to the floor. It took some seconds for the darkness to fade away and his hearing to return. He felt dizzy, but his head had also whirled when he'd lain in bed, so he let go of the bed rail. He was standing, swaying a little, yet more stable than expected.

Matt set reaching the cupboard at the other end of the room as his first goal. He couldn't leave the hospital in the thin greenish blue gown that revealed his backside. He took a step, and his legs wobbled. If he didn't speed up, the ten minutes would be over before he had changed clothes. He advanced another step, and the trembling in his legs already subsided. When he arrived at the gray wooden door of the cabinet, his stride had almost normalized, only a slight drag of his feet remaining. He opened the cupboard, and his spirits sank. There were half-a-dozen pajamas and lots of underwear, but no other clothes. In the lowest shelf lay a brown paper bag with the police seal on it. He knelt down and unfolded the top.

A bloodstained hoodie rested on a pair of jeans, and a shudder ran down Matt's back. He had worn these clothes on that Thursday. The police had probably examined them for traces of evidence and returned them to the hospital, while his mom had refused to take them back home. That was absolutely her. Matt swallowed and reached into the bag for the hoodie. His high-charged sense of smell picked up the reek of the clotted blood, brown and cakey blots meandering down the backside of the shirt. He threw up some of the juice, spat it on the floor, and wiped his mouth. Since these were the only clothes available, he had to pull himself together. Shane mattered more than his sensitivities. Additionally, the hood would hide the bandage. He had to maintain a reputation as master of inconspicuousness after all.

Something bulged out the pocket of his pants. His wallet! He opened it and let the napkin glide through his fingers. Waterproof blue on white that Shane would never hurt him. How could he ever forget about that? He rubbed the napkin over his cheek before folding it carefully and putting it back into the wallet.

It took him twice as long to dress as usual, but the progress meter on the monitor only showed half done, so he still had enough time. Matt opened the door and peeked out. The hall was deserted. He had to avoid the lobby because his mom waited there, but he could use the staircase right across from his room. After taking another look left and right, he tiptoed over the tiled floor.

Just like old times.

Matt chuckled. He had known that his skulking skills might save him one day. Today these skills had to save his relationship with Shane. He reached for the knob.

I'm coming, Shane.

CHAPTER FORTY

THE SWEAT stung Shane's eyes, still irritated and overly sensitive from the tears. He had stopped crying halfway between the hospital and the gym when remorse had replaced rage. Feeling like crap had taken over from remorse then. He shouldn't have run from Matt, but Matt's question had ripped off his skin and burned like acid on his bare flesh. Matt had gone through so much, yet this didn't give him the right to lash out at random.

Shane pulled at the handles, and the iron plates of the training machine rose with a creak. All of the plates. He had fidgeted with the small bar that was used to set the weight, but when he hadn't got it into the hole on the third try, he had chucked the fucking thing across the training floor. His muscles protested, and his tendons cursed at the unaccustomed resistance, but he couldn't care less. He deserved to suffer for being a dick, and the suffering made the memory of Matt being a dick go away. However miserable he felt, the anger-remorse-crap mix goosed him up. Panting and trembling, Shane let the weight down again.

"Sorry for the wait, buddy, but I had a nutrition group session. That means I'm in dire need of drugs, booze, or primal scream therapy. Preferably all three of them." Nick chuckled but stopped abruptly with a wheeze. "Whoa! Our Betsy here is the oldest training machine we've got. You're—" He eyed the weight setting. "—thirty pounds over the gym record. This grande dame must be handled with care."

"I need it," Shane pressed out through his teeth and hauled at the handles again.

Old Betsy moaned in indignation.

"What's happened?" Nick's face appeared before him. He raised one corner of his mouth, but for once, he wasn't smiling.

"Matt has happened." Shane lowered the weight. His chest pulsated from all the blood his heart desperately tried to pump into his muscles. He shook out his arms. One more time. He could pull off that exercise at least one more time to keep his rampant emotions from tearing him apart.

Nick placed his hands on Shane's biceps. "What has he done?" He increased the pressure on his arms. "And please stop training, big boy. You'll hurt yourself if you train in this frame of mind."

"That's the idea." Shane braced himself against the combined force of Betsy and Nick. Inch by inch, the steel ropes moved. "When my body aches as much as my heart, then I'll stop." He leaned into the handles, shoving Nick away.

A strange noise sounded, almost like a breaking guitar string. The resistance on Shane's left arm vanished, and he tumbled forward. With an ear-piercing bang, the weights crashed down, and the floor approached fast. His fall ended some two inches over the ground, where he hovered in midair. Nick knelt before him, and the strain contorted his face.

"Are you okay?" Nick squeezed out.

Shane nodded.

"Then get the hell off me, big boy."

After exhaling with a huff, Shane lowered his arms and pushed against the floor to carry his own weight. Nick let himself drop back onto his butt.

"I'm so sorry. I'll pay for a new machine. Just keep my wages until—"

"Shut the fuck up!" Nick wagged his index finger. His features relaxed, and a subtle smile bent his lips up. "That's what insurance is for." He reached out to Shane's shoulder and massaged it. "I don't give a crap about that machine." Nick bent to the right. "Sorry, Betsy old girl—" He faced him again. "—but I care a lot about my buddy, especially if he's set on hurting himself and getting me killed in the process." Nick patted his cheek. "Now, you'll get up from the floor, follow me to the kitchen, drink a gallon of calming tea mix number four, and tell me what Matt has done."

Shane's skull would burst if he didn't get those words out of his head right now. He'd do all the things Nick asked him to, but not in that order. "Matt thinks I attacked him, thinks I beat him into the coma."

"He doesn't." Nick's hand sank down, and he hunched forward. "That's a misunderstanding. A damn misunderstanding."

Shane's gaze dropped to the ground. "Detective Shit End stirred him up. Matt believes it was an accident, that I did it to protect him." In a weird, fucked-up way, this even made sense. He had injured Hayden to protect Jer. It wasn't such a big step from there to assaulting someone he loved. How far would he go? That was the very thing he had asked himself each day after that prom night.

"And he dumped you?" Nick's voice toned down to a feeble whisper.

"No. He even said it was okay." That part didn't make sense at all, not even in the weirdest and most fucked-up way. "I ran off because it hurt so much."

Nick pressed his eyes closed and sighed. "Of course that hurt, big boy, but do you really think Matt would say it was okay if he were convinced you beat the living daylights out of him?" He opened his eyes. "Matt isn't the type who clings to a brute. I mean, you're not a brute… oh fuck, I'm stammering nonsense."

What Nick said was far from being nonsense. After Matt's confrontation with Iain, he'd never yield to someone who gave him shit again. Deep inside he had to know that Shane hadn't decked him, or he would have chased him out of his life for good. Shane, however, had chickened out and taken to his heels. Matt's love endured every agony while his couldn't even stand a small scratch. "You've called me a douche before, and damn, have you been right."

"Don't listen to me. I'm the king of all douches." Nick grinned and bopped him on the shoulder. "You're only a douche if you keep sulking and mourning here on the floor. Go back to the hospital and talk to Matt." His grin morphed into a smirk. "But not before drinking that gallon of tea."

Shane lunged forward and grabbed Nick in a firm embrace. He was and would always be a hug monster. "I love you, Nick."

"You're telling the wrong person, but I love you too." Nick laughed and bumped Shane's back. "The customers are already staring." A choking noise killed off his laughter, and his body went rigid. "Oh, my God!" He breathed into Shane's shoulder.

"Everything all right?" Shane opened his arms and moved back. Maybe Nick had harmed himself when he'd caught him. Regardless of being a brute or not, Shane caused people pain more often than not.

Nick shook his head and stretched out his index finger, and pointed at the center of the room. His tanned Greek complexion bleached out, ending somewhere close to the color of curd. Whatever could shock a cheerful person like Nick into catatonia would certainly kill someone as wimpy as him. Nick grasped Shane's head with both hands and swiveled it around.

"Oh, my God!" Shane said, his voice devoid of any power.

Matt stood in the middle of the room on wobbly legs, swaying to and fro and everywhere else. His skin glared in a pale white, even fainter than during his coma, and a gossamer film of sweat covered his face like a cobweb. He looked so frail and ethereal, a sickly fairy prince.

Shane sprang to his feet, charged across the room, and dropped down on his knees, skidding the last few feet over the ground. "What are you doing here?" The person he loved came for him, and this was the first fucking question he blurted out?

"Don't kneel before me!" Matt's head tipped to the side, but he forced it upright again. He smiled, and his lids fluttered. "You have knelt so often before me without reason, and I'm the one who has to beg on his knees now." Matt descended to the floor in slow motion, the jitters of his legs intensifying with each inch.

Shane reached out for Matt, but his arms didn't dare go the full way and ended up somewhere between them. "You don't have to beg for anything."

Matt shook his head in tardy sweeps, and the muscles in his neck trembled. "I hurt you so much, while you love me without reservation and without compromise. Nothing but groveling before you and asking for your forgiveness will do."

"Don't worry about it." Shane placed his hands on Matt's cheeks, finally allowing himself the touch. Matt risked everything by coming here. What more apology did he need?

"No, you're not taking my guilt away from me this time." Matt rested his head on Shane's hands, and the shaking stopped. "I don't need memories of that Thursday to know it wasn't you. Fuck those memories!" Matt's eyes fell closed, and his lips curved up the tiniest fraction. "There's only one memory I regret losing." Wrinkles creased his forehead, though his smile persisted. "But I can get it back." His eyes opened, and they focused on Shane. "I love you." Matt chuckled, a croaking and coughing sound crawling up from his throat. "Not many people are lucky enough to have two shots at saying 'I love you' for the first time."

"Each time you repeat those words, they feel a little better." Shane propped his forehead against Matt's, and it was searing hot. "I love you, Matt. And now I'll bring you back to the hospital. You're glowing."

Matt sighed, and a rattling wove into his breathing. "Is everything okay between us?" His lids fluttered again, and the lashes tickled Shane.

"Not only okay. Everything's just perfect. Like you." He pecked Matt on his lips. They felt so dry and rough.

"It must be if you're back to your sugary sweet blah." Matt snickered, but it turned into a subdued gasp. His body slackened, and he slowly bent backward.

Shane slung his arms around him to stop his fall. "Stay with me, Matt. You mustn't lose consciousness. Do you hear me?"

No answer.

"Wake up! You have to wake up! I love you. Just listen to my voice, but stay with me." Tears coursed down his cheeks again. This was all his fault. If he hadn't run away, Matt would still be lying safely in his bed.

"He'll be all right." Nick knelt down beside Shane. "Just bring him to my car. Okay, buddy?"

Matt had just awakened from his coma. He couldn't be gone again. What if he didn't wake up this time? What if Shane's cowardice had killed him?

Nick grabbed Shane's head and jerked it around. "Snap out of it!" he yelled. "Matt will be okay. Now get your sorry ass off that floor and into my car."

Shane nodded and gently tilted Matt to the side. He placed his arms beneath Matt's back, lifting him off the ground. His body felt even lighter than before, yet his chest was still rising and falling. Nick had to be right about him getting well. Shane had promised not to bother the universe ever again, but he was only repeating a request he had already solicited. The universe had to understand this and save Matt once more.

"Jared. Dillon." Nick pointed at the two boys standing in the crowd that had gathered around them.

Shane hadn't even noticed all those people before.

"It's your lucky day, guys. I hereby appoint you deputy gym overseers. If this place is still standing when I return, I'll waive your member fees for a full year. Deal?"

Jared and Dillon high-fived each other with loud slapping. "Sure, dude," Dillon said.

"Good." Nick looked at Shane. "What are you waiting for, buddy? Car. Now!"

"Thank you." Shane wiped away his tears on his shoulder.

"Matt and you can thank me later." Nick pushed him in the back with both hands. "Move!"

Shane pressed Matt close. The universe had to answer his plea. Just one more time.

SHANE WALKED the lobby of the second hospital floor in circles. He looked at the clock again. Dr. Karatovic and her colleagues had been tending to Matt for over half an hour now. Was that a good or a bad sign? He resumed chewing on his nails—or what was left of them. It was a bad time to start a nasty habit.

"I love you as Matt's boyfriend, Shane, but if you don't stop running around, I'll kick your butt down the stairs and out of the hospital." Ralph, sitting in one of the black plastic chairs next to his wife, kneaded the bridge of his nose.

"Sit down, please." Mrs. Dermond patted the free seat next to her. "Or I'll help Ralph with his ambitious plan, and the both of us together could actually kick your giant heinie."

"I'm sorry," Shane mumbled around the fingers in his mouth and slumped onto the chair.

Mrs. Dermond grabbed his arms and pushed them onto his lap. "And stop eating yourself. That doesn't help Matt at all." She lifted her hands and let them hover over his for some seconds. When he made no move, she finally pulled them away. "I want my son's boyfriend to have presentable nails."

Shane sighed. "I'm really sor—" His head lurched around all by itself, and he stared at her.

"Don't look at me with your brown teddy bear eyes like that." Mrs. Dermond chortled and covered her mouth with her hand until her cackling stopped. "Before you ask, yes, I called you Matt's boyfriend, and no, I don't know why for goodness' sake I did that." She didn't even try to stop the next fit of laughter. "I always imagined Matt would find a beautiful girl, small and tender like him." Her gaze turned empty. "And I wanted a dream wedding with a bride in a breathtaking white dress. Wouldn't Matt look great in a black tuxedo?" She shook her head. "What did I get instead? A two-hundred-fifty-pound giant with muscles for three and more ink than bare skin." She put her hand on Shane's, her small yet rangy fingers tapping him. "But that behemoth of a man is probably the most loving and caring guy far and wide, and my Matt could have fared worse. Much, much worse. I'll have to settle for two black tuxedos, then."

"It's two-hundred-sixty pounds, if you please." Shane grinned. Matt had made the very same mistake on his first visit to the McAllistairs' house. "Thank you, Mrs. Dermond." For all he knew, he had just witnessed a major miracle. She never admitted making a mistake. Yet right here, she had called him Matt's boyfriend, loving, caring, and not too bad a choice. All this despite the fact that Shane might have sent him back into a coma.

"Mrs. Dermond? That doesn't sound right for someone so close to my son, does it? Call me Audrey, and if you keep up the good work, you might even call me Mom one day." Audrey exploded with laughter again.

Mom? Maybe having her as an enemy hadn't been that bad after all. Still, Shane only barely kept his inner hug monster from crushing her in a tight embrace. He buried her tiny hand beneath his other paw. "I won't say thank you again, but that's how I feel."

"Just keep loving Matt like you do. That's all a mom wants for her son." Audrey crossed her eyes. "Usually, I'm not this corny. Sorry for that."

Matt and his mother did have more in common than their looks, though they would've rejected this vehemently with waving hands and shaking heads.

Ralph jumped up from his seat. Shane and Audrey turned their heads. Dr. Karatovic came around the corner, and they leaped to their feet as well, still holding each other's hands.

Both corners of the doctor's mouth rose in a relieved smile. "Matt is only unconscious from the exertion of his little trip." She scowled at Shane, but her smile persisted and softened the impact of her glower. "It was a close shave, but no further brain damage has occurred. He's sleeping now, and you can see him, but please don't wake him up."

Audrey pressed his hand, and he squeezed back before they let go of each other.

Thank you, universe. That really was the last time you'll hear me asking for anything. I swear.

"Go and visit your son, you two. I'll call Nick, my parents, and Estelle first." Shane took a step toward Dr. Karatovic, who put her head back to keep glaring into his face. "Please, Doctor, can I spend one more night in the hospital? When Matt wakes up, I want to be with him."

The anger in Dr. Karatovic's features melted away, and the small wrinkles that had formed around her eyes smoothed out. "You're like my Great Dane, Prince, cajoling me for something from the table." She tittered. "Though it may not have sounded like one, that was a compliment. For all I care, spend the night half-crouched on a bed with cramps in your back. That's just punishment for making my patient abscond from his bed."

"I accept that punishment." Shane grinned at her and reined back the hug monster one more time.

"Good boy!" Dr. Karatovic shook her head and turned around on her heels. Chuckling, she walked down the hall.

Three calls and he would see Matt all evening and all night long. No aching back could spoil this for him.

SHANE LINGERED in the place between being awake and sleeping. He hadn't even dared to take a nap because he might miss Matt opening his eyes. Yet he drifted off time and again, just to startle himself out of dozing the next moment. Pictures of Matt laughing, being coy, being sassy, drifted to the surface of his mind as he edged along the line between dreams and reality. Those images fueled the thrill of anticipation, conjured a smile on his face, and helped him to bear the pain. Dr. Karatovic had been right about his back, after all.

He rested his head on the bedsheet, close to Matt's chest. The sound of his breathing soothed him, but it also anchored Shane on this side of consciousness. His smile deepened. Everything, at least between Matt and him, had worked out perfectly, just as he had said yesterday. The two of them would face the world as an openly gay couple now, and they had even mutated into some kind of local celebrities. Their story still hit the news with every change and turn in Matt's recovery as well as Shane's wait for it. Had the press already got wind of Matt's visit to the gym? There had been enough bystanders to snitch on them. He would simply keep Matt away from this mayhem as long as possible.

You wanted a coming-out, and you only received what you asked for.

He bit his tongue to not laugh. Matt was a tough little fella. He'd cope better than Shane would with all this attention.

Slender fingers tousled his hair. "You're here already?" Matt's voice was soft but far from sounding as thin as it had in the gym yesterday.

Shane squinted his eyes and let the sensation of Matt's touch spread from his scalp to the rest of his body. A trail of goose bumps followed this wave of bliss. "I never left."

"I love you." Matt's lips joined his hands on Shane's head, and a giggle breezed over his hair. "It's true. It does feel even better when repeated."

"Mmmh… I love you." Shane chuckled into the bedsheet. "Definitely better." He raised his head.

The light blueness of Matt's eyes brimmed with emotions, virtually any emotion, at least the good ones. He still looked pallid, but there was a touch of rosiness, visible even in the cold hue of the life monitor. "I'm really sorry for suspecting you. It's not an excuse, I know. But my amnesia scared the shit out of me. It still does."

Shane pecked Matt on the nose. "We'll just forget about you ever telling me and blame Detective Shit End for everything, okay?" He followed the outline of Matt's lips with his finger. "That's a good type of amnesia, isn't it?" This form of displacement might actually work. Matt had never suspected him for real, so why harp on about a momentary glitch caused by an asshole of a detective? Shane had carried enough guilt—his own and others'. Matt had hit the nail on the head with this insight.

"Yes, it is." Matt giggled once more. His gaze sank down, and he opened his mouth. "You've gotten a new tattoo?" He pointed at Shane's chest.

Shane looked down at himself. A little bit of the bird's head peeped out from under his neckline. He pulled his shirt up with one hand to reveal all of it.

Matt stretched out his fingers but stopped half an inch before the green hummingbird. "May I?"

"Our unlimited touching agreement is still valid. All our agreements are. At least I hope so." Shane grinned. "No holds barred."

Matt's hand crossed the distance to Shane's chest, its touch so much warmer already.

"It's right over your heart. I can feel its beat in my fingertips." Only a trace of a smile came about on his lips, but it was hauntingly beautiful and Shane swallowed. "And this tattoo stands for…?" Matt pressed his mouth into a thin line.

"You, of course. Who else would get that special place?" Shane closed his hand over Matt's on his chest. "I hope you like it. It's one of your birthday presents."

"I love it," Matt whispered, and his gaze stayed on the ink, even though his fingers covered most of it. His brows shot up. "There are other presents? The tattoo's more than enough. I don't need anything else."

"Too late. No refunds possible, I fear." Shane glanced at the nightstand. "Go for it."

Matt turned around, letting his fingers rest on the ink. With the other hand, he opened the drawer and produced the envelope with the silver bow. His gaze wandered to Shane's face and back to the envelope.

"Don't keep me on tenterhooks." Shane lowered his arm. "Look inside."

Reluctantly, Matt took his fingers off Shane's chest and unfolded the flap of the envelope. He pulled out the heavy cardboard voucher, printed with palm trees, a smiling sun, and the ocean. Once more, Matt looked up at him and down to the gift. His hand trembled as he flipped open the certificate. Creases turned Matt's forehead into a canyon.

"A holiday at a beach hotel on Hawaii? But the sea." Matt jerked his head up. "There'll be water all around us."

Shane chuckled. "Hey, even *I* know that Hawaii is an island." He clasped Matt's arms to stop their shivering. "You love the sea, and I love you. Case closed. Whatever happens with me, I don't care, and I'm rather stubborn about going with you on this vacation." It was so sweet how much Matt worried for him. They both protected each other, and for once, Shane had no problems accepting it.

Matt pulled up the corners of his mouth in a tempo that even snails would've frowned upon. He ogled the voucher again, and his smile fizzled out. The rosy tone of his cheeks drained away, and he opened his mouth ever so slowly.

"I don't care, but she's rather stubborn about this." Matt's eyes turned hazy.

Obviously he wasn't talking to Shane. The words had simply flown from Matt's brain to his mouth without him even noticing. Fear welled up in Shane.

"Everything okay with you?" Shane squeezed Matt's arms.

Matt jerked his head left and right. He inhaled deeply with a wheezing noise, as if he were suffocating. "No." He pressed his eyes shut and put his hands on his temples. Shane still held his arms. "It's not possible." Behind the closed lids, Matt's eyes darted around. Suddenly, he froze.

"Please, Matt!" Shane didn't dare move or take his hands away.

Matt yanked his eyes open and turned his head in slow motion. He focused on Shane. "I know who attacked me."

Chapter Forty-One

MATT WATCHED Shane's fingers gliding over his cell. He just needed to look at something. Something that wasn't the pictures in his head. Now that he remembered, he would've given anything to forget again.

"Iain's relayed your message… to the culprit." Shane's features had been stuck in a frown ever since he had told him who his attacker was.

Interestingly, they both had tacitly agreed on not mentioning that person by name again.

"He also swears not to tell anyone." Shane put his phone down while the tension in his face persisted. "Show up within an hour or I'll call the police." He shook his head. "Do you really think this will work?"

"I hope so." Matt folded his hands and nibbled on his knuckles. Giving in to Shane's idea of sending Iain to deliver his ultimatum was plain unreal. "I have to ask again. Iain helped you search for the… wrongdoer?" He had a hard time accepting his mom had come to terms with Shane, but Iain being friendly and cooperative? Rather pigs had grown wings during his coma and glided majestically through the sky now.

Shane smiled, but it looked strange due to the tenseness in his face. "He checked all the usual suspects with me. We had no clue about how unusual a suspect we should've looked for. You may not want to hear this, but deep down, Iain's a good guy. Do you know his brother, Seamus?"

More O'Sullivans meant more problems. "I didn't even know he had one." Maybe he should cut this other O'Sullivan some slack. If Seamus survived with Iain around all day, he had to be one tough boy, deserving his admiration and compassion alike.

"You'd like Seamus, and you might even like Iain."

Only if the flying pigs froze hell by pooping sundaes down on it. Matt shrugged. "Doubtful." The disturbing effect Iain had on him had served as his secret weapon to oust all other thoughts and feelings, but it didn't help in the least against the amalgam of disappointment and rage that boiled in his stomach. Waiting for an hour was ridiculous. He should have set an ultimatum of half an hour. Or no time at all. His hands clenched into fists. The count of his heart rate hadn't stopped blinking orange on the life monitor since the memory had infested his mind. He couldn't call remembering those events anything less dramatic. If he really had to wait an hour, he'd probably rip out the monitor's speaker, silencing those annoying blips once and for all.

Shane sat down beside him on the bed and pulled him close. "Do you know what you'll say?"

"I'll just speak my mind." Matt snuggled up against Shane and his firmness. He concentrated on the beat of Shane's heart. Far from the machine-gun rhythm of his own, but agitated too. "What else can I say?" Matt had discovered the dark side of having friends. He had been betrayed, just like Shane had been betrayed by Jer. Even if Jer hadn't assaulted Shane, at least not physically, Shane must have lived through the same feeling that some part of himself was being torn out. "I hate myself even more now for ever suspecting you."

"Stop it." The gentleness of Shane's voice set off the hardness of his words. "You mustn't hate yourself for this. The idea of hating you never crossed my mind. You made a mistake, realized it was one, and that was it." He buried his nose into Matt's hair around the electrodes.

Shane was a better person than he was, obviously, for Matt couldn't forgive himself or…. He wouldn't even think the name. Not until that person stood before him and he could wield the name like a weapon. "Can you please keep talking? Anything? I've been out for three weeks. There has to be a lot I've missed." Matt slung his arms around Shane as far as he could and cuddled up into his chest.

"Sure." Shane sniffed at his hair and kissed it. "There's a third present, hidden in the back of the nightstand drawer, but only check that out when we're alone, okay?" His laughter resonated through his body. "I'd even prefer it if I wasn't there, because I don't want to see your first reaction." More of Shane's laughing rocked Matt, the sound amplified by listening to it through his chest.

Shane still hadn't understood the power curiosity held over a nerd, or he was using it expertly to get Matt's thoughts off the time ticking by too slowly. Matt closed his eyes and let the deep vibes of Shane's voice carry him away. The words didn't matter as long as Shane just went on.

MATT'S MIND hovered in the bubble of Shane's tales. Nothing could intrude into this space where peace surrounded him, and he had lost track of what Shane was telling him. Shane loved him enough to simply relate story after story, knowing perfectly well that he didn't pay attention. His lips bent up all by themselves. If this wasn't true love, what was?

The bubble burst at a gentle rapping at the door. All the thoughts, images, and emotions it had kept away from him surged back into his head. He moaned. This was too much of everything. Shane had stopped talking, and the silence weighed down on Matt. Even the whining of the life monitor had faded down to a faraway murmur in the background of his mind.

Another knock on the door cut into the silence.

"Matt?" Shane rubbed his back with tender fingers. "Someone's at the door."

Not someone. The one person Matt didn't want to see right now, but he had to. He opened his arms and sat up. "I love you." Strength flowed from those words, coming in waves from the warm place. Oh right, he had a name for that place now—his heart.

"I love you too, my hummingbird." Shane gave his back another rub, smiled his angelic smile, and stood up from the bed.

Matt closed his eyes and filled his lungs with air. "Come in!" He startled at the firmness of his own voice. It didn't match the shivering little boy he had reverted to inside. He opened his eyes.

The door opened just enough for Florenca to squeeze herself through. She held her head low, so that the dark mass of her hair hid her olive-colored features. With a click, the door snapped back into the lock. She flinched.

Inside Matt, the fearful little boy was gone, and the voices had taken over again. For once, they agreed with one another, venting their anger and frustration about the girl who had outdone all the other bullies, including Iain.

"You wanted to talk to me?" That whisper had nothing in common with Florenca's snarly and obtrusive alto rasp, which usually spat venom at everyone and everything.

"I don't want to talk to you, but I haven't got much of a choice." Matt was the one breathing poison now.

Florenca's neck tensed as she swallowed and nodded.

"There are pictures in my head"—Matt tapped his temple—"of you holding a baseball bat, of you striking out with it, but there's nothing about the why." Matt bit his lower lip. "Why?" he screamed out.

"Bigfoot has to go first," Florenca said under her breath as she bent her head sideways.

Shane stirred, and Matt grasped his arm without taking his gaze off Florenca.

"He won't be going anywhere." Matt eased his grip. "Shane's my boyfriend, and what I know, he knows."

Florenca raised her head with a jerk, and fire flared up in her eyes. She opened her mouth but didn't say anything.

"You can tell us or the police. It's up to you." Matt should inform the cops anyway. On the other hand, his ultimatum bound him, and somehow, it contained a promise to not turn her in.

"Do I actually have to spell it out for you? You're the clever guy." Florenca's nose creased in derision, and she folded her arms across her chest.

"Snarking at me won't help you this time." His tone was matter-of-fact and even. "You might have browbeaten old Matt with that, but you won't boss new Matt around with a little barking. I've given you a lot of Matt-magic, so it's time to repay me with some Florenca-magic, because I don't understand what happened in that storeroom. We were friends!"

"Friends?" Florenca huffed out and advanced a step. "You aren't that fucking clever if you didn't realize that I wanted…." She averted her eyes to the floor again. "That I really liked you."

"And how was I supposed to realize this? By you ordering me around? By snubbing me for reading my favorite books and poems? Or by not backing me against Iain and his dumbos?" If she had liked him, it would've been her damn duty to help him. Matt pressed Shane's arm. Shane had done everything for him—and more.

"You liked me too, didn't you?" Florenca took another step forward, ending up directly beside the bed.

"Of course I liked you. As a friend." Matt had switched off his emotions, but she had never been anything other than a friend. Now he couldn't even see her as that.

Florenca's hands clenched so tightly that her arms began to shake, the tremor creeping all over her body. She squinted her eyes. "That's exactly what you said in the storeroom. Just after telling me…." She pitched up her voice. "Oh, but I'm together with Shane, and oh, I love him so much."

"You lashed out at me for telling you the truth?" He had obviously hurt her with his words of three weeks ago, but not intentionally. "You claim you like me, and just because I don't feel the same way, you try to kill me?"

"That's not what I wanted!" Florenca's shouting boomed through the room. "I just wanted to shut you up. Stop you from trampling on my feelings." Each word lowered the volume of her voice until it reduced to a mere breath.

"I hurt you, and you hurt me. We're even." Matt bent forward, grabbing the edge of the bed with his free hand. He was panting. "But I can't forgive you for what you've done to Shane."

Florenca opened her mouth, but Matt hushed her with a wave of his hand.

"I can understand that you were afraid of turning yourself in. But when Shane was arrested and had his hearing, how could you fucking sleep and walk around in school as if nothing had happened? Then you watched him look for the attacker and let him sic Iain on some innocent guys. How cruel and cold are you?" Calling the guys Iain and Shane had grilled innocent was bizarre, but in this case, their slates had been clean.

Florenca raised her fist. "Shut up, you motherfucking fag!"

Shane tensed up. He would lurch over the bed and strangle Florenca, but Matt had to protect his boyfriend, so he tightened his grip around Shane's arm and turned his head to face him.

"Don't!" Matt smiled at him. "She won't hurt me again." He looked at Florenca. "You will never hurt me again." No one would. That was his promise to himself.

The trembling in Florenca's hands reduced to some sporadic tics. She let her fist drop down and opened it. Her eyes dilated, and her face turned a queasy white-green. "What now?"

"You'll go, and we'll never see each other again. I won't talk to you. I won't even turn my head to look at you. You're dead to me." Matt sank back into the bed. "I won't tell the police, because what's the use in beating a corpse?" He rolled his head around, gazing up at Shane. "Tell me more about the things I've missed... please."

Shane looked at Florenca, then at him again. His scar was aflame on a pale cheek, his skin still taut. He knelt down and fondled Matt's face. "What do you want to know? Anything in particular?"

The tap-tap of quick steps resounded through the room, and the door smashed closed with a smack that rocked the bed.

A tear coursed down Matt's cheek, but he forced his lips up into a smile. "Something more about that third present, perhaps?"

Shane wiped away Matt's tear. "You wanna guess?" He mimicked Matt's smile.

De mortuis nil nisi bonum. Say nothing but good of the dead. Matt wouldn't speak about Florenca ever again. Given enough time, he might even forget about her completely.

CHAPTER FORTY-TWO

MATT LOOKED out the car window and watched the houses of the city fly by. He was finally going home after six weeks in the hospital. It already took him some effort to remember what his room looked like, so it was high time to return there.

On this Friday, Shane had gotten another special courtesy day from Principal Wagner, and he held Matt's hand in the backseat of Nick's car. Nick had volunteered to pick him up from the hospital because he was the only one who could make his own hours at work. Even more so since he had hired his two new deputies.

"Jared and Dillon are really good at keeping an eye on the gym. A little too good." Nick chuckled. "Some customers have complained about the two of them being too harsh about the house rules. No one dares to use a machine without a towel during their shift."

The three of them laughed.

"Can I ask you something I always wanted to know, Nick?" Matt smirked at Shane, who returned a silly smile.

"Shoot! You've got one question for free on your release day." Nick, grinning of course, looked at Matt through the rearview mirror.

"Why do you call yourself Nick?"

"You told him to ask me, didn't you?" Nick's gaze fastened on Shane in the mirror, and he waved his index finger.

Shane raised both arms, palms facing forward but still holding Matt's hand. "I swear I didn't. He asked me, and I only said that's something you should ask him yourself."

Nick poked his tongue out at Shane through the mirror. "But this stays in this car, right?"

"I promise!" Matt raised two fingers.

"You know my first name is Agathangelos, which means 'good angel' in Greek. As if that isn't embarrassing enough, all the other kids in high school called me Agatha."

Matt stepped on his own foot to not crack up. He coerced his features into a serious expression and nodded.

"When I went to college, I decided to get rid of the name once and for all and called myself Nick, short for Nicolaides."

"Okay, I can see why you did that, but Agathangelos is such a nice name, and it suits you perfectly."

"I'd thank you if I didn't know for sure that you're pulling my leg." Nick poked his tongue out again.

Matt pouted his best fake pout. "You doubt the words of a sick man? Pah!"

"You're neither a man nor ill, so what? There we are!" Nick steered the car to the curbside opposite the Dermond house.

"Thank you for taking me home—and chipping away at my self-esteem." So many things had changed. At the beginning of the school year, Matt wouldn't have talked like this to anyone, especially not an athletic man in his thirties.

"My pleasure. For taking you home *and* belittling you, of course." Nick bared his teeth.

Matt let go of Shane and reached for the door handle, but Shane stopped him by putting his hand on his shoulder.

"Just a sec!" Shane yanked open the door and jumped out of the car. He hurried to the trunk, got Matt's duffel bag out, and draped it over his shoulder. With two more long strides, he completed the half circle around the car and opened the door. "As a sick man, Matt—" Shane turned his head, and now he poked his tongue out at Nick before continuing. "—you have to take it easy." He shoved his arms behind Matt's back and under his knees, lifting him out of the backseat like a toddler.

There came some benefits with having a muscle-bound giant as his boyfriend.

"See you tomorrow morning, Nick," Shane said.

"See ya, buddy, and you, Matt, enjoy the last three days before the school hassle has you back."

Like Matt's room, the memories of school were already fading, but he'd prefer anything to lying in bed all day. "Thank you again, and see ya."

Shane closed the door with his foot. They watched Nick drive away as he waved at them one last time.

"You can let me down now." This sentence would've sounded more convincing if he hadn't snuggled up against Shane. The warm shape of his body was just too enticing not to cuddle with.

"No way!" Shane looked left and right before walking across the street. "I wasn't kidding when I said that you have to spare yourself."

"The very point of getting out of the hospital is that you don't have to spare yourself anymore." Why exactly was he protesting being carried around?

"Just indulge your overprotective-and-fond-of-sentimental-moves boyfriend." Shane smiled as he ascended the steps to the veranda. "Watch out!" He shifted Matt up, placing him across his shoulder, and fished the key out of his pocket.

"There is a thin line between sentimental move and humiliation, and you're dangerously close to the latter." Matt propped his elbows onto Shane's back and rested his head on his hands. "I'm not a sack of potatoes."

"A sack of potatoes would be more grateful for being carried around."

Matt could hear the amusement in Shane's voice. He had to be grinning like a Cheshire cat, and Matt couldn't help smiling himself. Hopefully, no one was filming this like the scene in the gym, because the video would probably go just as viral. Matt had begged for a coming-out, but becoming one of those "aww" stories at the end of a national news broadcast was the hard-core version, and he could do without the added publicity.

Shane carefully kicked the door shut. "I just carried you over the threshold. Guess who's namby-pamby enough to like that?" He tittered. "Next stop, Matt's room."

"You won't let me go up there by myself, will you?"

"Not for all the fucking tea in China." Shane ducked down so he wouldn't bang his head on the low ceiling of the staircase. This house hadn't been built with titans in mind.

"This is only the second time that you're here with me," Matt said. Most of their relationship had taken place at the McAllistairs' house, the gym, and the school. Even the hospital room had seen more affection between the two of them than his home.

"Your parents have invited me to stay the whole weekend. We can do a lot of catching up in two and a half days." Shane chuckled, the muscles in his back tightening and relaxing.

Being carried around wasn't that bad after all, and the backside view was fantastic. Matt let his head slump down on Shane's shoulder blade. "We'll do a lot of catching up," he whispered.

Shane put Matt down in the middle of the room. "Ding! Second floor. Beautiful wood art and cute boyfriends." Chuckling again, he let the duffel bag slide from his shoulder.

"You forgot the mawkish but adorable giants." Matt pulled up one corner of his mouth and looked around. Everything seemed to be so much more colorful in comparison to the white tiles of the hospital. He trudged over to his woodworking desk and drew back the white sheet that covered the tools and his latest project. The oaken disk with the half-finished Celtic triskelion lay as he had left it six weeks ago. Matt followed the whirling grooves with his fingers. He would finish this, but not this weekend. They had better things, more important things, to do.

Matt lifted his fingers off the unfinished triskelion. What would his next project be?

Shane buried his shoulders with both of his hands, and Matt caressed his fingers in return.

"Beautiful!" Shane breathed a kiss on Matt's nape. "Oh, the disk too, of course." One more peck made Matt shut his eyes for a moment.

"It's supposed to be a present for you." He pulled up his shoulder and pressed his cheek against Shane's hand. "Oh, the disk too, of course." A single snort of laughter bubbled out of him.

Shane moaned, and his breath tickled Matt's neck, raising the fine hairs on it. "I hope you'll soon be fit enough for your third present." His lips brushed Matt's skin again.

"I... I actually asked Dr. Karatovic, and she said it was okay."

With a huff, Shane exhaled and gave Matt another flock of goose bumps that flew down south. "You asked her whether or not we could have sex?"

"I'm not *that* brazen." Sassy Matt could pull off a lot of stuff that plain and simple Matt couldn't, but even he didn't dare everything. Not yet. "I camouflaged it as a question about physical exertion." He swallowed down the cackle that hiked up in his throat. "Since I asked her for a full blood test, including STIs, before that question, she'll have put one and one together, however." The face and the grin she had given Matt had spoken volumes. "According to the test, we can forget about one half of the things in the box." He only whispered the last part. In his mind, the idea of not needing the rubbers still rang wonderful, but now that he had said it aloud, it sounded kind of filthy.

Shane's warm breath kept sweeping over his neck, and for some long seconds, he didn't answer. A tickling feeling of nervousness cramped Matt's stomach.

"Ever since I turned sixteen, Nick has made me get tested every month. That's mainly for training purposes, but he checks the STI boxes on the lab form each time. All of them have come back clean. The results of the last one were returned only the day before yesterday."

The tickling in Matt's intestines ramped up, but for completely different reasons than the ones that got it started. "We're alone in the house, and my parents won't return before seven this evening. Moreover, I've got doctor's approval." He swallowed. "But perhaps you're not in the mood right now."

"Not in the mood?" Shane nestled up against him.

The twitching hardness of his erection poked into the small of Matt's back, and his own cock stirred in his briefs.

"Nick was lucky that I didn't dry hump you right in his car." Shane kissed his nape again and let his tongue circle around it. "That's how much I'm in the mood for your third present, but there's one string attached."

The waves of pleasure originating in Matt's spine crashed against his mind, and a moan came out of his mouth. "Which one?" He'd do anything.

"Before I fuck you, you'll fuck me."

Matt flinched, for Shane couldn't have said what he thought he had. He swiveled around, sending Shane's hands flying off his shoulders. "What?" Matt strained his neck to look up into the brown embers of Shane's eyes. He had to be kidding him.

"I want you to fuck me first." Shane smiled his horny angel smile. "It would be a little unfair if you were the only one having all the fun, wouldn't it?" He pressed close to Matt again. "And your down low seems to like that idea too." His smile waned, and his features turned serious. "I want you inside of me as much as you want me inside of you."

Shane meant it, and what he said sounded absolutely logical, but one of Matt's latest lessons had been that logic didn't answer everything. He had never considered fucking Shane. Why not? Shane's butt was definitely hot enough to stick his cock in. And he hadn't just thought this, had he?

"Or are *you* not in the mood for this?" Shane knitted his brows, but a tad of a grin sneaked onto his face.

"Get out of your shirt before I have too much time to think this over." Matt grabbed Shane by his buttocks and ground himself against his crotch. Not enough blood remained in his brain for thinking anyway.

Shane groaned. "As you wish." He pulled up the hem of his T-shirt with both hands and flung it onto the floor.

Matt's cock almost busted his briefs at the sight of Shane's bare chest alone. He lowered his mouth to one of Shane's nipples, nibbling on it and pulling it with his teeth. His hand closed over the other pec, massaging it in eights and circles.

For fifteen years, he had lived like a monk. Now he couldn't even tolerate six sexless weeks without eating Shane alive.

He sucked in more of Shane's nipple, working it with his tongue and eliciting a roar more feral than anything this room had witnessed so far. Shane reached out for Matt's shirt, and it was gone as fast as his own. The sensation of skin on skin met with the tickling in Matt's stomach, and they united into a powerful surge that pulled him with it.

Shane slung his arms around him, tugging him backward. Still holding Matt with one arm, he bent his knees and rummaged through the duffel bag without looking at it. After some seconds, he produced the black box with the golden writing. He tightened his grip around Matt and lifted him off the ground. Their mouths locked, and their tongues danced around each other.

They had kissed often during those six weeks, yet this kiss wasn't tender and gentle like those had been, but raw and fueled by passion.

Matt's naked back touched the crumpled surface of his bedcover as Shane lowered him down. The black box dropped onto the sheet beside his head. Shane broke their kiss and fumbled with the button fly of Matt's pants. A grunt of despair and Shane's wrinkled forehead commented on the lack of progress he made. Matt chuckled and opened the remaining three buttons himself.

With a grin on his face and his scar pulsating in a deep shade of crimson, Shane freed Matt from his pants and briefs in one go. Matt's cock jolted around, almost as if his member felt as nervous as he did himself. It paid that Shane wore sweatpants in his free time because, unlike their cumbersomely buttoned-up counterparts, he got out of them with lightning speed. Another quick flick and Shane's boxers flew across the room before they landed on the woodworking desk. The giant shape of his cock glowed bright red, and Matt would never have enough of that sight. Shane lowered his lips to Matt's navel and slipped his tongue in, exploring it.

Matt's body arched up, and he squeezed out a yelp. That body part was called a belly button for a reason, for Shane just had to press it to switch off his brain for good. Some more of those switches rested underneath Matt's skin from his navel to his crotch, and Shane's tongue hit each and every one of them as he worked his way down. Shane pecked the base of Matt's cock, and the lower part of his body went up in flames. If Shane wanted to be fucked, he should slow down, or they would never get that far. More of Shane's kisses left a trail of wet spots on his dick. As Shane tilted his head, his breath flowed over this moist archipelago. The contradiction of searing heat and ice cold fried Matt's nerves, and he roared, the ferocity of his howl in no way inferior to Shane's.

"Not so fast!" The begging tone of Matt's voice contrasted with the wildness of his roar just seconds ago, but Shane churned up his emotions until they merged into one all-encompassing, primal feeling.

"Time for a changeover anyway." Shane lay down sideways on the bed and crawled up until their crotches were level. He slung his arms around Matt and rolled over, ending up on his back with Matt lying on top of him. The heads of their cocks bumped into each other, and they moaned in unison. Shane took one hand off Matt's back, opened the box, and got out the clear pump bottle of lube.

"Put some on your cock and some in my hole." Shane spoke in short gasps. "I don't need more preparation." He snorted and laughed. "I couldn't bear more preparation."

Matt knew the one-finger-two-fingers-three-fingers technique from the instructional videos he had watched, but given the size of his cock, they could skip that. One of Shane's fingers was barely thinner than Matt's member. Would Shane feel him at all?

Shane dropped the bottle, put a hand on either side of Matt's head, and made him look into his eyes. "I want you inside of me. Whatever doubts are whisking around in here"—he tapped on Matt's temples with his index fingers—"they are baseless." Shane tensed his abs and raised his torso from the bed. "I love you." He placed a soft kiss on Matt's lips. "That's all you have to keep in mind."

Matt swiped another kiss from Shane. "In fact, there are two things on my mind. My love keeps your love company."

"My sappiness is rubbing off on you." Shane crossed his hands behind his neck and grinned.

Whether sappy or not, it was the truth.

"Awesome." Shane lowered his upper body back to the bed. "Grease us up and show me your love." He somehow succeeded in adding slyness and desperation to his grin in equal parts. He picked up the bottle and held it out for Matt.

Matt's fingers trembled as he took the lube out of Shane's hand. He pressed the pump, and the clear gel felt cold on his skin. Perhaps he should warm it up a little? He rubbed it in his palm. Much better. He sat back on his bed while Shane lifted his legs, holding them in place with both hands. Even Shane's butt teemed with muscles, and they formed two sexy dents on either cheek. Shane shaved down here as well. Only a slight shadow of his dark hair showed in the crack. Matt had never looked at a butt hole for real. The web videos had shown them, of course, but seeing Shane's up close made his cock twitch again. Though his member had forgotten about its nervousness and couldn't wait to begin its adventure tour, the nerves of its owner still lay in shambles. Matt swept up the lube with two fingers and closed in on Shane's hole. The crinkly skin felt soft and warm. Shane gurgled, a noise of horniness and contentment alike. With circling motions, he spread the gel around the hole first before poking into it with the tip of his finger. Shane's gurgling turned deeper and more savage as the muscle clenched around Matt's finger. The very same thing would happen to his cock. He inhaled and exhaled to breathe away the rush of excitement caused by that insight.

"More. Hurry. Please." Shane wove those words into one long, stretched-out moan.

Matt pushed his finger in up to his knuckle, the hot and tight sensation engulfing it completely. The intensity of this experience entranced him and threatened to haul him away. He pulled his finger out again, squirted two more dashes of lube into his palm, and gave himself some time to recuperate. After warming the cold liquid, he covered Shane's insides with it.

"Your cock and go." Pure desperation resonated in Shane's voice.

Matt nodded and shrieked out a squeaky "Uh-huh." He smeared his cock with two more squirts of lube until it looked all shiny and slick.

Shane tipped his hips backward, lifting his ass up from the bed a little higher. "I love you." The desperation in Shane's voice had vanished, and his face was aglow.

"I love you too." Matt could only whisper. Skidding over the bed on his knees, he brought his dick close to Shane's hole. Just one more inch and he would be inside his boyfriend. He closed his eyes and tilted his lower body forward. His cock head touched the warm skin, and the chute opened up. Stars burst before Matt's eyes, caused by the heat and tightness around his member. He breathed in, but the air refused to flow out again.

Shane screamed, a deep, jarring rumble, and a searing blast of panic ignited Matt's insides. He pulled out.

"I'm hurting you!" He had underestimated his size and caused Shane pain.

"No, please, no, stay inside!" Shane grasped him by his shoulders. "Please!" His eyes begged Matt. "You're not hurting me!" He massaged Matt with both hands. "Your cock head ends up directly over my prostate. This is perfect! This is....." The rest of the sentence got lost in a whimper, and he yanked on Matt's shoulders, just trying to get him inside again.

Matt stopped thinking and thrust his hips forward. His cock sank into the hole until his balls slapped against Shane's buttcheeks. The giant body beneath him bent upward, and Shane's bellow mixed with a guttural purr, his voice fading slowly until it died away.

All those sensations burned out Matt's brain. This was too much, yet not nearly enough. He pulled out a little, just to shove his dick back in. His vision turned black. Then a white flash blinded him. Shane's groaning reverberated through his body, and his bones resonated with it. The next thrust made Matt's ears ring. All of his senses overloaded, and he wouldn't last much longer.

"Kiss me!" Shane lowered his thighs and pulled Matt down while rising up from the bed.

Shane's face was burning, and drops of sweat meandered down his cheeks. Matt slammed his mouth onto Shane's. Their tongues lashed out at each other. The power of their kiss washed over him and tore with it the last remnants of his self-control.

His crotch contracted, and that first squirt of cum would've shot right across to the other side of his room if his cock hadn't been buried deep inside of Shane. Matt cried out into Shane's mouth while Shane's hands wandered up to his head, pulling him even tighter into their kiss. The next squirt sent a tremor up Matt's body. He breathed in, and the mere smell of Shane's sweat made him shoot another load. One more tremble rocked him, and he slumped down on Shane, rising and falling with the movement of his mighty chest.

The trunks of Shane's arms closed around his back, their kiss still unbroken. Shane rolled over, his powerful frame hovering above, and Matt's cock winced one last time. Matt felt spent, energized, and safe in Shane's arms. His brain had shut off and wouldn't enter thinking mode anytime soon. What would he think about anyway, when his emotions already filled him completely?

"Don't move, or I won't be able to return that favor." Shane rested his forehead on Matt's, and his cock throbbed between their bellies. The warm wafts of his breath swept over Matt's face. "That was absolutely fucking amazing," Shane whispered.

Matt laughed. "Yes, that wraps it up quite nicely."

"You pounded all the good words out of me." Shane joined in laughing before he placed a peck on Matt's nose.

"I want you to feel the same. I want to give you those exact sensations." Matt's sentences didn't make any more sense than Shane's. Sometimes those empty hulls called words just didn't cut it. He kissed Shane, letting his lips do the talking for him.

CHAPTER FORTY-THREE

SHANE LET Matt's taste spread across his tongue. He wouldn't back out of fucking Matt, because doing so would underestimate him, and he would never make that mistake again. Still, a tad of bitterness dampened his excitement. He moved his head back and encountered the clear blueness of Matt's eyes.

"If it hurts too much, tell me. I know you don't want to hear this, but I'd rather never fuck you than cause you pain." He let his fingers glide over Matt's face, the soft cheeks and the tender lips. "I already made you promise this before, but stop me if you can't bear it. Swear it!" He braced for Matt's outbreak that would chide him for his lack of trust, but Shane needed that promise, needed at least the illusion of safety. He closed his eyes and rubbed his forehead against Matt's.

"I swear." Matt's voice came even and calm.

Shane jolted away, opening his eyes, and Matt's lips curved up.

"You expected a different answer, didn't you?" Matt placed a hand on his scar.

Shane nodded and nestled up against the fingers on his cheek.

"It's important to you, so it's important to me. Easy as that." Matt bent up, and he brushed a kiss on Shane's other cheek. "I want you to promise me something in return. If I say 'Go on!', you'll go on."

The aftereffect of the kiss still echoed through Shane, a rippling not unlike the one he had felt when Matt had fallen asleep on him in his room. He skidded down a little and rested his head on Matt's shoulder. "I swear." So Matt didn't blame him for lacking trust but allowed him to show it with this promise instead.

The man snuggled up against him was a different person from the trembling boy who had cowered before him in the locker room. Shane loved both of them. He loved the very kernel of Matt, the essence that never changed. Being nineteen, Shane was still a boy himself, but true love didn't give a fuck about age or a damn about time. He kissed Matt on his neck and sat back on his knees.

Matt felt for the bottle of lube, grabbed it, and held it out for him. "I'll need a little more preparation than you, but we'll do it. You'll fuck me, and it will be as wonderful for me as fucking you was."

That little pep talk was solely meant to calm Shane's nerves because Matt definitely didn't entertain any doubts about getting the beast inside of him.

"Can you lend me a hand, please?" Shane raised one corner of his mouth. "I mean literally." He extended his index finger. "Beginning your preparation with this would be like doing an archeological excavation with a stick of dynamite." His huge digits could only be stage three or four in their preparation.

"Very vivid description." Matt chuckled. "But you're right. Shall I lift my legs like you did?"

"Good idea."

Matt raised his legs and grabbed them with his hands. Shane should hurry, for this posture could become rather painful. He had an idea for the perfect position in which to fuck Matt later. *If* they got that far.

We will get that far!

Matt had shown enough confidence for both of them, and he trusted Shane. It would work. Shane slid down to the end of the bed on his knees. The bitter feeling that marred his horniness didn't stand the slightest chance against the sight of Matt's flawless butt. Everything about Matt was so delicate, but this all came down to patience. And Shane could be patient. If it took hours to get Matt ready, he would put in that time while suffering from a painful, continuous erection.

Tempting prospects!

Shane chuckled and tried to cover it up with coughing. The impish look in Matt's eyes gave him away. He had noticed but had the courtesy to not inquire. Shane pumped a dash of lube into his palm, stirred it with his finger until it had body heat, and spread it over Matt's hole. The chute opened and closed as he circled around it. Matt really was eager to have Shane inside of him, and he bit down another chuckle to not raise further suspicions.

"Gimme your hand, please." Shane propped his shoulder up against Matt's leg so that he could take away the hand holding it. The soft pressure caused more of those skin ripples, and as predicted, keeping his boner was the last thing he had to worry about.

"Here." Matt squeezed his hand between them.

The touch made Shane's cock bob up and down, and he sighed. A grin appeared on Matt's face, but that was okay. Shane deserved a little mockery for his all too obvious excitement. With two more squirts of lube, he greased Matt's finger and guided it to his hole. "Try to get it in, but slowly and deliberately."

Matt nodded, and the tip of his finger disappeared into the rosebud. He sighed. "Feels good."

He would change his mind if something the size of a signpost was shoved up his ass, but Shane had to encourage him.

"That's awesome! A little deeper?"

"Sure." The tip of Matt's tongue poked out as his finger sank into his hole up to the knuckle. "Still good." He exhaled the breath he had held.

"Turn it around. Wiggle it a little. If it stops feeling good, we'll use more lube."

Matt closed his eyes as he moved his finger in his chute. "Whoa!" His eyes shot open. "What was that? There's a little knob, and when I"—he groaned and flinched—"touch it, a jolt runs up my spine, and it feels like I have to pee." He snickered.

"Congratulations, sir. You've found your prostate." Shane chortled. "Can you now imagine what your cock did to me as it rubbed over my *knob* time and again?"

"Will your cock feel the same inside me?" Matt's mouth dropped open.

"Frankly, I don't know. My cock head will be past your prostate." Very far. "You'll have to find out yourself."

Matt nodded, and a smile flashed on his lips. "I wanna try a second finger." He pulled his finger out with a plop and held two of them out for him.

Shane lubed them and guided them back to Matt's entrance. With a deep breath, Matt closed his eyes and pushed in.

"Already a little more crowded down there." Matt chuckled again. "But still good. Even very good. A third one?"

"Don't get too cocky!" Shane squished his brows and sucked in air through his teeth. "Pun not intended."

Matt's body convulsed with his laughter. "I want to get fingery first. Cocky comes later." He pulled out the two fingers. "I can take three of mine. Really!"

Shane had promised to go on if Matt said so. "Okay." He covered three fingers with the transparent gel. "Give it a try."

"There is a sensation of tension now. A stretch in my sphincter. Does that make sense?" Creases formed on Matt's forehead as he rotated his fingers left and right.

"Of course it does. Relax. You're doing it right. Play around until the tension goes away." Shane could only hope that the tension would go away. Compared to the real thing, three of Matt's fingers were piece of cake. Was he a sicko for enjoying the show of Matt fingering himself?

"Better already." Matt adjusted his position, and the pressure on Shane's shoulder increased.

They should hurry before Matt's legs cramped up, but rushing this process would do neither of them a favor.

Matt bit his lower lip. "The tension is gone." His cheeks turned a dash rosier. "Your finger now?"

It was cute that the idea of Shane touching his ass embarrassed him. Matt spoke with confidence when it came to sex, but obviously there existed a part of him that still had to adjust, even after gobbling up two-thirds of Shane's cock and drinking his cum like soda. Clearly, Matt loved him so deeply that he overcame his inhibitions and even goaded Shane on while expanding his own limits. Using *expanding* here was another unintended pun, but thank goodness he hadn't blurted this one out. "I'll be careful, and you know to pipe up if anything feels wrong, right?"

Matt nodded and pulled his fingers out while Shane lubricated his own. "Ready?"

"Go for it." Matt's rosebud opened and closed.

Eager for sure.

Shane placed his finger on Matt's hole and pushed ever so slightly. His finger slid in up to the first joint. "Okay?"

"It's even a little less than my three fingers. Try more."

Shane increased the pressure, and his finger vanished in the chute. Matt did so well. He was relaxed and easy. If he had chosen a boyfriend who wasn't a giant freak of nature, he would already be having sex now. Shane closed his eyes and banished this thought to the dark backside of his mind, for it was fucking bullshit. Matt would give him hell if he ever learned about it.

He opened his eyes again and looked up at Matt's face. Matt had closed his eyes too, and a touch of a smile played around his lips.

Never underestimate Matt!

This matter of course would need a lot of repetitions before his knee-jerk resistance disappeared. Until then, Shane had to keep reminding himself. "Ready for a second one?"

Matt sighed contentedly. "Yes, please."

Shane repeated the procedure with a second and, not much later, with a third finger. How brave Matt was. His smile never wavered and even deepened, though having three of Shane's monster digits inside couldn't give him much reason for smiling. He had to trust Matt and stop the patronizing, even if it only took place in his own mind.

"Shane?" Matt's voice sounded gentle and composed.

He looked up again, and a bright glow lit Matt's features.

"I can see the tension in your face. Don't worry. I'm ready." Matt crooked his finger. "Come up here."

After pulling out, Shane bent forward. He hadn't even realized how taut the skin of his face had become. Matt put his hands on the back of Shane's head and pulled him in for a kiss. This kiss was gentle and caring, melting away all of his strain. Matt breathed his confidence into him, and he shouldn't think about the how, because it would only break the magic.

"I'm ready," Matt whispered into his mouth.

Shane rose up and stroked Matt's other leg as he rested it against his shoulder. His cock had been rock hard ever since Matt had talked about fucking the first time. It felt searing hot and pulsated under his fingers when he covered it with a generous amount of lube. He skidded forward until the head rested on Matt's hole. "I love you." Love would make this possible. It was part of that magic, the most important ingredient of the spell.

"I love you." Matt closed his eyes, and a beatific smile perfected his beauty.

Shane pushed forward, and the much too large shape of his cock pried open the much too small opening of Matt's butt. Half of the head was inside already, the point where most of Shane's fucking experiences had ended, but Matt kept smiling, a vibrant groan rolling up his throat. This was a damn miracle as the spell unfolded before Shane's eyes. When the rim of the head slid through the hole, Matt furrowed his brows and hissed. The circular muscle clamped his cock.

"I'll pull out!"

"No!" Matt's upper body soared off the bed. He grabbed Shane by both shoulders. "No! Give me a little time. Distract me. Kiss me."

Trust Matt!

Shane bowed forward, careful to not move his crotch, and placed his lips on Matt's. He spread them, and Matt sucked Shane's tongue into his mouth. With it, he soaked in part of his soul as well, but not without surrendering some of his own in return. Shane flowed into the kiss, and so did the room around them. Everything existed within the both of them, yet they were separate from the world, a universe unto themselves.

"You're inside of me. All of you." Matt's voice turned into a blanket, wrapping around them.

It took some moments for his words to sink in. Shane hadn't moved, but his balls rested against the soft skin of Matt's buttcheeks. The beat of his heart stumbled, and he felt dizzy. His cock twitched, and he almost came as the realization hit him with a blast. He giggled, an unashamed, childish babble. The spell was complete. Shane nibbled on Matt's lips one last time before he sat back. He placed a kiss on each of Matt's shins, lowered the legs down, and wrapped them around his waist.

Gently, he placed his hands underneath Matt's shoulder blades, lifting him from the bed until he held him in an embrace that connected every square inch of their skin. He closed his arms so tight that he could grab his own shoulders. From the outside, he had to look like a possessive man clutching the object of his desire. But in reality, it was Matt who permitted Shane to hold him like this and who surrounded him with a feeling of security. Matt controlled this situation, and Shane didn't want it any other way. "Ride me!" he breathed into Matt's hair, imbibing the sweet fragrance of it.

Matt bobbed up and down, a soft stirring at first but ramping up to a frenzied rhythm that electrified Shane's crotch. Both of their bodies glowed with heat, and their sweat mingled between them, dropping down on Shane's thighs. His ass contracted as Matt's humping carried Shane beyond the point of no return. The first shot of his cum erupted inside of Matt. It was nothing short of a miracle that his jizz didn't bubble out of Matt's mouth. Ripples of ecstasy bounced off Shane's insides and rocked his body. The next wad of semen burst out of his cock. This orgasm would never end. He unloaded five more blasts of cum into Matt, and only the last one shot out a little less forcefully than the others had. Panting, he slumped down and sat on his feet.

"Stay in me. Please, just stay in me, okay?" Matt's words came out choppy, and he was gasping for air himself. He rubbed up and down Shane's back with both hands, creating a pattern of shivers and shudders.

Shane only nodded. He pecked Matt's neck, the skin smoldering under his lips.

For a minute, they just sat like that, fondling and kissing each other. This was bliss. Pure, unadulterated bliss. The magic hadn't ended yet, and a little of it would stay with them forever.

"Calling this wonderful doesn't do it justice. So let's not call it anything, okay?" Matt heaved a sigh and cuddled up against him even closer.

"I second that." Another giggle bubbled out of Shane.

Matt joined in with a titter. "You haven't turned soft yet."

"No, and I could go at it right now again." Shane's giggle turned into full-out laughter.

"I wouldn't say anything against a round two." Matt stopped chuckling and gave Shane's pec a lick. "It took us so much effort to get me ready. Anything else would be a waste, wouldn't it? And before you say anything, I hereby claim a second round of fucking you as well. There's still so much time left before my parents return." Matt's voice was pure innocence, and without waiting for Shane's answer, he pumped his hips forward and backward in a slow pace.

"Deal," Shane moaned, rising up and nibbling Matt's shoulder.

Matt could be cute, coy, and embarrassed in one moment, and insatiable, seductive, and smutty in the next. What more did Shane need in the love of his life?

CHAPTER FORTY-FOUR

EVERYONE IN Central High considered Matt a nerd, a know-it-all overachiever, but he had never been to school on a late Saturday afternoon before. The place looked so peaceful without any students there. It felt like coming to school for the first time, and in a certain sense, he was. The fear that had permeated these halls and rooms, seeming an integral part of them, had bid him farewell, and he hadn't even noticed it leaving for good until now.

"And you really don't mind coming here with me to get the book I forgot?" Shane walked by his side as they ascended the stairs to the school's back entrance. "I'm screwing up your last school-free weekend with my daffiness."

"As long as you'll screw *me* for compensation, no, I don't mind."

Shane chuckled, a deep, guttural purring that echoed off the buildings around them and wandered up Matt's spine. "Have you seen your mom's looks? I don't want to know what pictures are playing in her head when she stares at us like that."

Most likely the right reel rattled through her inner projector, but in between those sizing-them-up looks, she sported that gleam in her eyes Matt had only noticed in Heather and Gordon before. It was the happy-parent glow. He grinned. "I don't think she'll ever walk in on us again like that first time when you sat shirtless in my room." His mom would probably drop dead to the floor if she did.

"Hopefully." Shane opened the door and held it for him.

"I thought they'd lock the school up on weekends." Matt entered the building.

"I need that book for an essay, so I won't question my good luck." Shane scooped him up from behind, sticking his arms through Matt's just under the armpits and crossing them over his chest. He nuzzled Matt's hair and kissed him on the back of his head. "Speaking of good luck." Shane laughed as he carried Matt down the school hall.

"You're set on not letting me walk too much this weekend, aren't you?" His legs dangled around with each of Shane's steps.

"Our, umm, other activities are wearing you out enough, so I have to take care of my only recently recovered boyfriend." Shane planted another kiss on top of Matt's head.

Sassy Matt had a zillion snarky remarks bustling around in his head, but plain Matt just enjoyed this too much to let any of them out. Shane's chest tightening against his back and those abs rubbing over his ass were too hot an experience to give up for a little thrill of spite.

They arrived at Shane's locker, and he put him down. "Don't get used to standing on your feet too much. I only have to get the book out." Shane tousled Matt's hair before fiddling around with the lock.

"You'll have to screw me a lot to make up for all these insolences." Matt bopped Shane in the side with his elbow. "And be prepared to get screwed a lot too."

"If those are supposed to be threats, you have to take some private lessons with Iain, I fear." Shane cackled as his head vanished in the locker, his laughter resonating through the metal.

Even mentioning Iain right here in school didn't affect Matt anymore. Another sentiment that had waved him an unnoticed good-bye.

The faint hue of a cell display illuminated Shane's locker.

"My phone has an integrated flashlight. Shall I help you?" Matt leaned his head against Shane's biceps, trying to peep past it.

"Thank you, but I'm done in here."

Shane had just finished talking when the hammering but subdued beat of a techno song filled the hall, coming from somewhere outside the building.

"Do you hear that?" Matt turned his head left and right to locate the source. "Someone's playing music in the schoolyard."

"Sure." Shane reappeared from the locker. He raised an ear. "Sounds like a party." He shut the door. "Let's have a look."

"We can't crash someone else's party, can we… whoa!"

Shane picked him up as he was still talking and placed him over his shoulder. "This is our school. If someone is having fun here, it's our fun too." He strolled down the hall toward the main exit that led to the yard, the music getting louder as they approached.

"Do you really think this is such a good idea?" Matt's stomach turned a tad ticklish. Walking in on someone having an illegal event on a school campus didn't sound like a good idea at all. Matt sniffed. Was something burning?

"We'll see." Shane pushed open the door and walked outside.

Matt clearly smelled a fire now, but Shane's massive frame blocked his sight.

Shane grabbed him by his waist, lifted him off his shoulder, and brought their faces level. "I love you." He pecked him on his lips. "And…." He put Matt back on the ground and spun him around.

"Surprise!" The schoolyard was brimming with people, students of Central High, yelling out in unison.

What was going on here?

In the middle of the schoolyard, a huge fire burned brightly. At one end, a platform with DJ equipment had been erected. Speakers blasted the techno song over the crowd, and the beat of the music made Matt's pants flap.

Snuggling up to his back, Shane placed his hands on Matt's upper arms. "You missed the party in October, and the students of Central High wanted to make up for it. So welcome to the 'More Acceptance and Tolerance Tribute' bonfire party." He squeezed Matt's arms gently.

Matt looked around. The people cheered at him, and the idea of having been transported to an alternative universe popped back into his mind. His head whirled, and his heartbeat even surpassed the techno rhythm.

"Wait." An embarrassing insight caused nausea and vertigo in equal parts. "More, acceptance, tolerance, tribute. That's me. That's the Matt party." Blood shot into his cheeks while his temples throbbed with his breakneck pulse.

Shane guffawed and rocked Matt with him. "This was Elaine's idea. We couldn't talk her out of it, and for the love of God, we tried. She organized all this, and she can be quite the slave driver." Another snort of Shane's laughter shook them both. "You wouldn't think that, seeing her wear that cheerleader uniform."

Principal Wagner stepped out of the crowd and scurried up the steps leading to the entrance. "Welcome back, Mr. Dermond." She extended her hand.

"Thank you, ma'am." Matt shook it. He should say something, anything, but his head was empty. His brain needed all its capacity to process what was going on here, and he could almost hear the sound of gears grating against one another in his skull. They didn't expect him to make a speech, did they? He nestled closer to Shane. How was he supposed to talk to a crowd of people when minutes ago he still had thought they didn't even know his name?

"It's so bold and inspiring to come out in high school. I'm so proud that you two decided to do so in our Central High."

Bold? He had been unconscious, lying in a hospital bed. It didn't take much courage to oversleep his own coming-out, especially if it had been necessary to save Shane from another trial, or even prison. Maybe it would require some guts to visit school from now on, but with Shane by his side, what could happen anyway? Not much remained that Matt hadn't gone through already in this school, and he was probably the only person in the whole wide world whose social life had actually improved by admitting that he was gay. "Thank you, ma'am." He was also the only person who gave thanks for virtually everything—okay, with Shane as a close second.

"Have fun, you two. I'm going back to Nick." She harrumphed. "Dr. Nicolaides, I mean. He has lots of fascinating ideas for improving phys ed." Dusk was already falling, and the bonfire cast a fiery glow on everything, but Principal Wagner blushed right before his eyes.

Matt nodded and smiled, fighting hard to not let it transform into a smirk that would rank rather high on the slyness scale. Principal Wagner returned the nod, flushed a little more, and hurried down the stairs, vanishing into the crowd.

"Nick and Principal Wagner?" Matt lost the fight against the smirk at last. "I'm not sure whether this is a good or a bad thing."

"Me neither." Shane rubbed over Matt's arms. "Nick is like a brother to me, so Principal Wagner would be my sister-in-law, and that feels just plain weird. On the other hand, they'd be quite the power couple, don't ya think?" Shane made him walk forward, pushing him on from behind. "Now let's meet our inspired fellow students."

Even though Matt wasn't looking at Shane, there had to be a smirk on his face too.

"Hey, Matt. Hey, Shane." A guy, tall and lanky with long blond hair, touched him on his shoulder, and Matt didn't have a clue who he was.

"Hey." Matt raised his hand and smiled.

The guy smiled back before continuing his talk with a girl.

Matt turned his head. "Do you know him?" he whispered to Shane.

"Nope."

A girl waved at him. They attended the same history class, but they had never exchanged a word. She giggled and bent to the side, saying something in the ear of another girl, who tittered in reply. Matt waved back. Given the strange behavior of his fellow students, he already missed being the invisible outcast.

"Matty?" an all too familiar voice said from behind him.

He inhaled and let the air flow out in a thin stream through his pursed lips. Matt swiveled around. "Hey, Iain." Thinking that name might not have affected him anymore, but standing before him did. His heart remembered the

DEFCON routine all too well, and so did his adrenal glands. Matt searched for Shane's hand and found it behind his back. Shane's fingers closed around his, giving them a gentle squeeze.

Dimples formed on Iain's cheek as he smiled. Matt had never seen him smiling—smirks, sneers, venomous grins, yes, but not a single smile.

"I'm glad you're back, dude." Insecurely, Iain ruffled his strawberry-blond hair.

Calling him "dude"? Another thing Iain had never done before. Neither Matt's heart nor his glands knew what to make of this and simply stuck to the approved plans of hammering against his ribs and flooding his veins with nervousness.

The dimples on Iain's cheeks faded, and his lips straightened. "This isn't the right place or time, but I want you to know I'm sorry." Iain huffed. "It's a fucking lame excuse, I know, dude, but perhaps we could meet at my place, drink a beer or something, and talk about all this shit." His gaze sank down to the ground. "I'd understand if you couldn't bear being in a room with me alone." He jerked his head up. "You can bring Shaney, umm, Shane if you like."

What would he talk with Iain about? They should just keep their past six feet under. Matt chewed his lower lip.

The corners of Iain's mouth drooped down. "You don't want to stir that crap up. That's okay, dude. At least I want to thank you for not finking on me for the essays." He laughed a short and bitter laugh. "My grades will take a plunge without your genius bolstering them up."

"I won't write an essay for you ever again, but I could help you with them, tutor you. I've got some free time lately." Matt's mouth worked faster than his brain. He hadn't just offered to help Iain, had he? On the other hand, he enjoyed casting his Matt-magic. Florenca had never truly needed it, but Iain did. Moreover, it gave them some context for talking with each other. Sitting down to discuss years of bullying was just awkward, but dropping a remark or two during a tutoring lesson could work.

"You'd fucking tutor me, dude?" Iain furrowed his brows, and he wiggled his lips left and right.

"Shane told me about how much you helped him search for my attacker. That's my way of thanking you for that… dude?" Had he used it correctly? One simply had to end every other sentence with "dude," but perhaps there existed some kind of "dudiquette" that Matt just wasn't aware of. "Moreover, you… conveyed my message without telling anyone else." Iain had proven himself reliable in his own assholeish kind of way, just as Shane had said.

"Awesome, dude." Iain raised his arm but stopped halfway and let it sink down again. He shrugged, and his smile turned one-dimpled.

Matt offered Iain his fist. "That's okay. Anything smaller than a baseball bat doesn't even make me flinch anymore."

All conversations within ten yards ended abruptly, and the gazes of a dozen people burned on Matt's skin.

"Umm… that was a joke." Matt looked around with a cocked eyebrow.

A stocky guy with a baseball cap laughed first, a girl chimed in, and soon the whole group around them joined their laughter.

Iain finally bumped his fist.

Ouch!

A pang shot up Matt's knuckles down to his wrist, and he wrestled with his facial muscles to keep smiling. Iain needed some tutoring on moderating his strength as well. Perhaps Shane could volunteer to teach him this subject.

Iain's dimples disappeared. "Regarding the message, I haven't seen her here tonight." In a whisper, he continued, "I can still take care of her on Monday."

Matt closed his eyes and exhaled. Of course he would have to see Florenca at school again, but his mind had chosen to bury this thought in the darkest and most secluded part of his brain. He opened his eyes again. "Thanks, but no thanks." Even the dead didn't deserve to be handed over to Iain. Still, the offer was nice… in a thuggish kind of way. Matt's life had been simpler when he only had to be the victim, but those days had ended. He'd never go back to his old habits. He moved a little closer to Shane, feeling the warmth and firmness of his boyfriend. Shane was worth every minor and major complication.

"Oh, I better piss off." Iain pointed at a gap opening in the dancing crowd. "Elaine's coming over, and I'm not in a fucked-up-bitch mood. See ya on Monday, Matt." A two-dimpled grin reemerged on his face. "See ya, *Shaney*."

Shane's body gave a start, and he grunted. "See ya, and greetings to Seamus," he pressed through his teeth.

Iain shrugged once more, and the grin took up some degrees of slyness before he dove into the mass of people.

"Matt! Shane! Woo-hoo!" Elaine's voice even pierced through the deep bass of the music, and she probably could cut diamonds with it. She waved at them.

For the first time ever, Matt saw Elaine without a cheerleader's uniform. He had already theorized about the possibility that the uniform was part of her body and that she simply grew a new one each day. This evening, however, she wore a long black dress with a coat over it and her curly hair down for a change. Without the pigtails, she looked at least five years older, not a girl but a woman. Holding her hand, a blond guy of Matt's size with bright green eyes trotted along behind her.

Jer!

Elaine grasped Matt's hand and shook it in sweeping bows. "I'm so glad you're back. We've missed you so much. I so hope you like this party, because it was such a pity you and Shane couldn't attend the one in October. You're such a cute couple, you two. Has anyone told you yet? Absolutely sweet. Don't you think so, honey?" She tugged at Jer's hand, and he almost stumbled.

"Sure, honey." Jer smiled, exactly as he had in the photo over the McAllistairs' staircase.

Shane coughed, an unsuccessful attempt at covering up his chuckle. Jer looked up at Shane and jerked his head in Elaine's direction.

What had Elaine said? Matt had already forgotten. It had been so many different things crammed into a torrent of words plus the additional distraction of the silent exchange between Shane and Jer. His memory had just given up. "Thank you, Elaine." Since his answer would've been "thank you" anyway, it didn't really matter whether or not he knew what he was grateful for.

"You're welcome!" Elaine reeled Matt's hand around and giggled.

Matt liked Shane's giggles better. They sounded much cuter and not so shrill. Eventually she let go of his hand. He held it out for Jer.

"Nice to finally meet you, and thanks for your get-well card." Except for one or two details, Jer and Matt could be twins, as Gordon had said. They even shared the experience of being bullying victims, though what Jer had lived through had been so much more gruesome.

"Nice to meet you, and my pleasure."

They shook hands.

Before the voices in his head could make a din again, he better admit that he had been jealous of Jer. His almost twin had been Shane's first love, and a first love counted more than any other love. Matt knew what he was talking about. He pressed Shane's hand, getting a gentle squeeze in return. No, he had no reason to be jealous.

Matt's cell vibrated in his pocket. He got it out, and an unknown caller ID flashed on the display.

"Excuse me for a moment, please."

The others nodded, and Matt turned around, ambling to the back of the schoolyard, away from the music.

Surely, Shane and Jer wouldn't mind a private moment anyway, though Elaine was concentrated antiprivacy. Matt would probably learn every word of the conversation, plus some totally fabricated ones, by school gossip. He tittered to himself and snapped open the lid of his phone. "Matt Dermond."

"Good evening, Mr. Dermond. My name's Waylon Koch, district attorney. I beg your pardon for this untimely call on a Saturday evening, but I've got some news regarding your case that you need to know right away. Your attacker has handed herself over to the police this afternoon. It's one of your fellow students. Florenca Goncalvez."

A FEELING of cold settled in Matt's stomach. Sweat rolled down his back in thick drops, and a rattle accompanied his breathing. Why had Florenca done this? She had committed the perfect crime. No one had even come up with the idea of the attacker being a girl. Moreover, he was either a pansy or just plain dumb, because he would never turn her in.

"Mr. Dermond? Is everything okay?"

"Of course, Mr. Koch. I'm just—shocked." He had to play along and shouldn't admit that his memories of that Thursday had returned, at least the horrible parts. Maybe he was committing a crime himself by holding back that info.

"Absolutely understandable. Ms. Goncalvez has been arrested at Precinct Four. My colleagues and I are aiming for a trial within a month, and you'll be summoned as a witness, even if you don't have any recollection of the events. Dr. Karatovic has certified that the loss of your memory is most probably irreversible. I'm sorry, Mr. Dermond."

"At least I know who did it. This certainty is a kind of solace for me." It hadn't been and still wasn't. Lying to an attorney had to be a felony as well.

"I'm glad to hear this, Mr. Dermond. Oh, before I forget, can you please tell Mr. McAllistair that we'll soon inform him about the date of his appeal?"

"Of course, Mr. Koch." That was a piece of good news at last.

"Have a nice evening. I'm looking forward to meeting you in person. You've become quite a celebrity." Mr. Koch chuckled.

Matt's cheeks pulsed again, and the heat in them almost scorched him. "I'm looking forward to meeting you too. Have a nice weekend. Bye."

"Bye." The light tone of Mr. Koch's voice hinted at a smile, perhaps even a grin.

The cell beeped once as the call ended, but Matt kept holding the phone to his ear. Whatever reasons had moved Florenca to go to the police, she had done the right thing. Even obnoxious Detective Webb had to give up on putting Shane in jail now. Matt would have loved to hear the input of the voices in his head, but they chose this moment to remain silent for once. They were just as clueless as he was, though they usually had an opinion on everything, even more than one at most times. He had to work this out on his own. Florenca had returned from the dead, and he mustn't ignore it. Matt couldn't forgive her, not yet, maybe never, but he had to react, let her know how much he appreciated her decision. And he had to tell her before he talked himself out of it. Finally he let his hand sink down and put the cell back into his pocket. He couldn't do it without Shane.

Matt turned around and took a step, but someone called out to him. He stopped and looked around.

"Wait a moment, Matt." Oliver Bergstein elbowed his way through the crowd, which bounced to the sound of the techno song.

Not another bully apologizing to him. If every person who had ever mistreated him approached him, this would be a long evening with an awful lot of handshakes. Couldn't they just let it rest like he did?

Oliver hastened across the last few yards free of dancers. This was obviously the evening of first times. Matt couldn't remember having seen him move that fast before.

"Thanks for waiting." Oliver looked pale, and his eyes flitted around constantly. He chewed on his thumb, already battered and scabbed. With his other hand, he reached into his pocket and fished out a crinkled brown envelope. "Please take this. It's not as much as it should be, but I don't have more right now." He extended his hand. "I'll give you the rest. Promise! Just don't send Shane after me. Please accept it." His voice broke, and he squealed.

Send Shane after him? Matt would never set Shane on anyone. Apart from that, Shane was as dangerous as a kitten riding on a puppy. What exactly had Iain and Shane done to him?

Oliver pressed the envelope against Matt's chest. "Please take it!" Tears welled up in his eyes.

In a knee-jerk reaction, Matt clutched it.

"Thank you! Thank you! Thank you!" Oliver repeated over and over again. "You'll get the rest. I promise. Thank you!" He peeked left and right again.

Matt raised the hand with the envelope and opened his mouth, but Oliver only smiled nervously, nodded, and ran off, vanishing into the crowd again. That had been weird. Absolutely fucking weird. He looked down at the envelope, opened its flap, and his breath caught in his lungs. This had to be more than two hundred dollars, perhaps even three hundred, in rumpled bills of all denominations. Even some nickels and dimes rattled in the brown paper. It was better not to know where this money came from, and Matt folded the envelope closed. He wouldn't keep it. Perhaps donating these bucks would offset the bad karma that stuck to them. He stuffed the envelope into his pocket and hurried through the crowd.

Shane still stood with Jer and Elaine where Matt had left them. They laughed out loud, holding their bellies. It was a pity Matt had to ruin the party for them, but some things didn't allow for a delay. He tapped Shane on his shoulder.

Chuckling, Shane turned around, but he stopped snickering, and wrinkles formed on his forehead. "Is everything all right? You look tired." He reached out for Matt's cheek and caressed it. "You aren't feverish, are you?" He heaved a deep sigh. "This is still too much for you. Shall we—"

"Can you please take me to Precinct Four?" The words bubbled out of Matt, but they were out at last. "Please," he added in a whisper and leaned into the hand on his cheek.

The wrinkles on Shane's face deepened. He opened his mouth and closed it again. His features relaxed, and even a faint smile appeared on his lips. "Sure."

Shane would do anything for him. That was an incontrovertible fact. When Matt had seen him for the first time, he had imagined him holding a beating heart in his hand. He hadn't envisioned, though, that it would be his own heart and that he would've surrendered it to Shane voluntarily. It was in good hands. The best.

SITTING IN the chair of the interrogation room felt uncomfortable even if Matt occupied the one reserved for the cop. Hopefully he would never have to visit such a room again. Only Shane standing at his side, his warm hand on Matt's shoulder, kept him from freaking out.

"This is the very room Detective Shit End grilled me in." Shane's deep yet mellow voice cut into the silence. He chuckled under his breath. "Something always brings me back here."

Shane just tried to relieve the tension, but being reminded how much he had gone through because of Matt didn't help his churning stomach either. "If one person doesn't belong here, it's you." He intertwined his fingers with Shane's on his shoulder.

"Neither do you." Shane kissed him on the top of his head.

It didn't matter whether Matt belonged here or not. Some necessities he couldn't dodge.

The door opened. Matt startled, and his heart raced. He spun around, yanking his hand out of Shane's. Why did he react so strongly? This confrontation with Florenca wasn't nearly as bad as the first in the hospital. He had already gone through the hard part. No, he hadn't.

Detective Webb led Florenca into the room. She wore handcuffs, and the detective held her by them. When Detective Webb passed by Shane, contempt flashed up in the cop's eyes. In addition to being a miserable wretch, the detective also seemed to be a sore loser. At the very least, he owed Shane an apology, but that would never happen. Florenca kept her gaze to the ground, concealing what was going on in her face.

With a rude thrust, Detective Webb pushed Florenca onto her chair. She glared at the detective but didn't say a word. If she didn't fly off the handle, Matt had good reason to worry for her. Webb crossed his hands over his chest and grunted.

"Could you please leave us alone for a minute, Detective?" Matt forced a smile onto his face.

"Security regulations require me to witness this laughable face-off." Detective Webb waved his hands around, and a smell of old nicotine and rancid frying fat wafted into Matt's nose.

"I think I am perfectly safe." Matt nodded sideward at Shane. Apart from having a bodyguard who would sacrifice his life for him, Florenca meant no danger. She wouldn't hurt him ever again. Another incontrovertible fact.

The detective's gaze switched between Matt, Florenca, and Shane. He shrugged. "Fine. Let the youngest drug lord ever watch over you." Not losing a second, he whirled around and headed for the exit. Webb glowered at Shane one last time before he smashed the door closed, and the crash echoed back from the naked concrete walls.

Matt took his time to inhale and exhale once more before he faced Florenca.

"I didn't expect you to come here." She sounded so matter-of-fact and calm, not the slightest trace of a sneer in her voice.

"You have done the right thing." Matt didn't have to force this smile. "I thought you should know."

Florenca picked up the smile. "I'm just a coward. Better arrested than dealing with my parents." She laughed mirthlessly. "If I had told them first, I'd lie shackled in the trunk of our car now, heading for Mexico." The smile faded, and she chewed on her lower lip. "I'm sorry," she whispered.

From anyone else, this would've been a miserable joke of an apology, but she had probably never uttered those words before in her life. From her, it counted more than an elaborate plea filling thousands of pages.

"I know." Like hers, Matt's voice was devoid of emotions, yet his mind brimmed with them. Too many of them to feel at all. "We can never go back to where we were." He laid his hands flat on the table. "I can't trust you anymore, and maybe I won't be able to forget you." He heaved a sigh. "Yet I can forgive. I will treat you like any fellow student, but not more." Matt folded his hands. "And *that* is what I'm sorry for." It still felt like losing a friend, though she had given up on them when Shane had entered his life. She had almost killed him on a whim of jealousy. She had tried to let Shane take the rap for her deeds.

"Don't be!" Florenca shook her head and sent her brown hair flying. "That's more forgiveness than I deserve." She stretched out her handcuffed arms.

Shane stirred, and Matt sought for him with his left hand. He found his thigh, giving it a slight squeeze. With his other hand, he grabbed Florenca's and shook it. Her fingers were cold to the touch, and she held him too tightly, yet this gesture was sincere. His heart told him so, and it had never lied to him.

"You better leave." Florenca let go of him. "My parents will come back soon, and you shouldn't be here then." She smiled faintly. "And you don't want to miss your very own party, do you?"

Matt smiled back at her. "Probably not." The party was the last place he wanted to be right now, but he had to return and honor the efforts of his fellow students.

Closure.

With this visit, he had taken the first step on the trail leading there. He would take all the other ones together with Shane, and he couldn't wish for a better traveling companion.

Epilogue

SHANE WOULD be glad to get out of the suit as soon as possible, but Matt and he had promised to visit Estelle when the appeal had ended. He loosened his tie a little. Estelle wouldn't notice without her glasses anyway.

"I'm more nervous than I was during your trial." Matt also fingered his tie, but he tightened it instead. He strained his features, and cute wrinkles adorned his forehead.

"Estelle will love you. I promise. And you have roses as an offering to appease her. Here we are."

Matt shrugged and made a grimace as he looked at the bouquet of red roses in his hands. "It's like meeting your grandma, only worse."

Shane knocked at the door and stroked Matt's back with his other hand. "You survived Iain, my parents, and Florenca. I'd say you're prepared for anything." He grinned down at Matt.

"That doesn't make it better." Matt pouted, but that twinkle shone in his eyes.

Still grinning, Shane opened the door. "Be greeted, beautiful young lady." He made a bow. "I come with illustrious company today. May I introduce to you the sublime Matt Dermond?"

Estelle sat in her bed as always, but today she had dressed up, wearing a fancy-schmancy lace nightgown. So much pomp for Matt? Shane kept his head down so that she wouldn't see his grin grow.

"You're a whacko, Shane." Estelle threw back her head and shook it. She lowered it again and looked at Matt. "How can you stand being together with this nutcase?"

"He can be kinda cute, like an oversized baby animal. Moreover, he reaches up to the high shelves in the supermarkets. That's quite useful at times," Matt said with a deadpan face.

"And you know those jars with pickles where the lid won't budge?" Estelle made a screwing motion with her hands. "He's rather talented in getting those open too."

"So, I'm a replacement ladder and a can opener?" Shane crossed his arms over his chest and glowered down at the two.

Estelle tilted her head and brought her brows together. "Yes, that sums it up perfectly."

"I have never been insulted like that before." Shane turned around, struggling to keep the grin off his lips. Maybe he should reconsider his opinion on sassiness, but the grin won out, so changing his attitude was probably a lost cause anyway.

"Oh, poor little Shane." Matt caressed his upper arm.

That touch created a current that flowed over Shane's skin. He shuddered, his eyes dropped shut for a moment, and he sighed. "That's not fair. You know very well what effect your fingers have on me." He spun around and grabbed Matt, twirling him around before pulling him close so that he was looking at Estelle. "Once more and a little less nutty. Estelle Vespucci, this is Matt Dermond. Matt Dermond, this is Estelle Vespucci."

"Nice to finally meet you, Mrs. Vespucci. I'm sorry for not being able to come here earlier." Matt offered her the bouquet.

"Just call me Estelle, cutie, and don't worry, you've got *big* trouble on your hands. I understand." She clapped her hand over her mouth and tee-heed. "Thanks for the roses, cutie. Shane, would you please get a vase for them?"

"Sure." Cutie? Tee-heeing? He better watch out, for Estelle might try to snatch Matt from him for herself. It had to be a serious crush if she didn't insult him within the first three sentences.

Matt handed Shane the roses and smiled.

Of course Matt liked Estelle and vice versa. They had already become the dynamic duo of banter, and he would stand helplessly at the sideline, watching them with his mouth open. Another grin sneaked across Shane's face as he got the crystal vase out of the cupboard.

"Don't keep me on the rack, boys, how did the trial go?"

"Judge Bilodeaux presided, and the whole appeal was over in less than an hour." Shane chuckled. "I'm a free man with an almost clean slate." Saving Jer had been the right thing, and if this had meant that the world considered him a brute, then he would've endured it. Yet it was nice to have it in black and white that he was a nice guy. Shane poured water into the vase. "I'm a rich man too." He tittered. At least it was enough money to invite all the people involved in his case to a first-class restaurant. "They reduced my sentence to twenty community service hours, and I'll be reimbursed for the other eighty." Finally Mr. Sanderson had gotten his chance at showing his talents as a lawyer. That counted even more to Shane than the bucks.

"Congratulations." Estelle raised an eyebrow. "Even though I'm slightly disappointed. You aren't my bad-boy trump any longer. How am I supposed to silence Mrs. Kellerman and Mr. Tottenham now and avoid their awful grandchildren stories?" She clicked her tongue and made a sour face.

"Play the hero card instead." Matt turned his head and gave Shane a one-sided smile. "Judge Bilodeaux called Shane a hero for saving Jer from Hayden."

"Please no!" he howled. He put the vase down on the sideboard, rearranging some of the roses. "I'm *not* a hero." It had embarrassed him when Judge Bilodeaux had called him that the first time, and it embarrassed him now.

"You two are a famous gay couple. Perhaps I can harness this?" Estelle tapped her lips with her index finger.

He and Matt sighed in unison. The press had attended the trial again, and the both of them had gotten more offers like the one from yucky Mr. Galinski over the last few weeks. They had turned them all down and were looking forward to the next scandal or miracle to take over the headlines.

"Okay. Okay. I'll find something else." Estelle chuckled once more. "What about this Latina girl? Would she be interested in another grandma?"

"Probably not. It's already difficult to keep track of Florenca's relatives without adding some more." Bursting out laughing, Matt shook his head. Shane and Estelle joined in.

Florenca's trial would be next week, but Mr. Sanderson said that her chances were good. She was remorseful, and Matt refused to press charges. When asked for the reasons behind his leniency with her, Matt just mumbled the word "closure." Maybe she'd also get away with community service hours only. Estelle could actually meet her if she did them here. Hayden wouldn't get off so easily, however, and rightly so.

"You'll have to settle for two normal guys in love, I fear." Shane put his hands on Matt's shoulders and massaged them. All the knots in them had disappeared. When Matt was relaxed, so was he.

Matt leaned back against him. "I'm not a bad boy or a badass Latina, but perhaps I can contribute a sweet little story to silence the Kellermans and Tottenhams here." He moved away from Shane and turned around, a radiant smile on his face. "Your victory in court deserves a celebration and even a small gift," Matt said, then chortled, "but since you're a rich man now, it was difficult to come up with the right present." He opened three buttons of his shirt, revealing a white bandage over his heart. "It's still rather swollen and burns like hell, but please see for yourself."

Shane trembled and panted in short gasps. Matt hadn't done this. No, this would be too awesome to be true. He shook his head and raised his hand, but his fingers sank down again before touching the cloth.

"I'd hoped for a little more enthusiasm." Matt chuckled again and grasped Shane's hand, guiding it to the bandage. "For you."

Shane swallowed, nodded, and with unsteady fingers, he pulled the white gauze to the side. A yelp escaped from his mouth, followed by a single snort of laughter.

A roaring lion with a gorgeous mane and a scar running down across its right cheek graced the place directly over Matt's heart.

"The first day we met, I thought you were the lion and I was the antelope." Matt closed his fingers around Shane's hand. "I still think you're a lion because you're strong and your heart beats fiercely for the ones you love." He lowered his voice down to a whisper. "I hope you like it."

Shane slung his arms around Matt and pulled him close. Words couldn't express how he felt, so he wouldn't even try and resorted to the language of the hug monster instead. The warmth had come back to Matt's body, a small furnace burning hot. He tightened his arms a little more to encase this heat. His heart was beating fiercely indeed. He looked over to Estelle. Shane had seen her cry only once before, on the day his community service had ended and before he'd told her that he would continue to work here. She wiped away her tears and smiled at him, a heartfelt, true smile. Another thing that she didn't do all too often. He returned it.

"I love it, and I love you." Shane nuzzled Matt's hair and kissed the top of his head.

The hummingbird and the lion.

Nothing in this world was powerful enough to get between them.

MARIO KAI LIPINSKI lives in Herne, Germany.

He is a spare-time author, and his evil day job, teaching mathematics at university level, isn't that evil after all. Granted, on some days he wants to strangle his students, but it only takes a coffee or two and he remembers how much he loves them. He loves nerdy science stuff too. Does it show in his books? Of course it does.

English is not his native language, and he frequently gets asked why he writes in English. The answer has two parts. Firstly, he has slightly masochistic tendencies. Secondly, most books he reads are in English. So it feels only natural to write in this language too. English is beautiful—until it isn't. Never, absolutely never, get him started on comma rules.

One reader described his books as "sexually explicit Disney movies." That hits the nail on the head. Mario is into romance with a capital R and loves his cheesy. He is so good at channeling his inner teenager that sometimes he doubts he even has an inner adult.

Facebook: www.facebook.com/M.K.Lipinski

after the romance novel

Susan Laine

www.dreamspinnerpress.com

Also from Dreamspinner Press

DAVID CONNOR • E.F. MULDER

TRUTH
PRIDE
VICTORY
LOVE

www.ingramcontent.com/pod-product-compliance
Lightning Source LLC
Chambersburg PA
CBHW050033030726
47506CB00001B/251